ADAM W. SCHMITZ

ALISTER

THE ARCHIVES OF EDGAR BRAVE

Alister: The Archives of Edgar Brave, Book 1 by Adam W Schmitz

Published by Wit & Ramble Publishing

witandramble.com

Cover Art by Dissect Designs

Editing by Allister Thompson

Developmental Editing by Ellen Walters

ISBN: 979-8-9870491-0-5 (paperback) | 979-8-9870491-1-2 (ebook)

Printed in the United States of America

First Edition

To those old eyes
Budding in spirit
And tattered souls
Too young to hear it

May they feel cool water
Upon cracked skin
And never want
For home again

ALISTER

THE ARCHIVES OF EDGAR BRAVE

ADAM W SCHMITZ

WIT & RAMBLE PUBLISHING

PROLOGUE

B LACK MIST CREPT ALONG the cracked desert plain, meandering with the subtle wind until it arrived at the prone man who refused to die.

Regaldo looked up at his older brother towering over him and pushed a smile past his pain to retain the last bit of satisfaction Aiken could take from him. The two Cassinians had age lines tracing their faces, their skin a rougher leather than it once was.

He saw Aiken transform his skin blue, with wisps of teal, giving the impression of calm in such horrid times. While Regaldo could conceal his pain, the reds and yellows that traced his skin gave him away.

"Shall we do this wretched dance again?" asked the tall and boney Aiken, scratching his long fingers along his bald chin. "I grow weary of this cadence."

Regaldo tucked in his chest, reacting to the surge of agony radiating along his torso. Not only was he feeling the weight of his defeat, but sadness also filled his gut as he looked across the once beautiful garden, now blackened with billows of smoke ascending from the flat desert. Or perhaps the sadness wasn't from the ruined world, but in the betrayal from the ones he called kin.

"Where's our younger brother?" Regaldo asked. "Surely, he must be part of this. We both know you'd never be so capable."

The black mist along the ground collected and took shape, but not enough to resemble the Cassinian Regaldo once knew. His vague form floated as a dark cloud, reacting to sudden shifts in the wind.

"Ah, little brother, is that you?" Regaldo asked. "You do not look yourself. Though perhaps this is more true to form. The darkness looks good on you."

A sudden jolt seized Regaldo's teeth, traveling through his skull and down along his spine. He cried out, causing the rats and winged beasts to scatter.

"No, no, brother," said Aiken. "Let Regaldo have his last words. He can do little with them now."

The suffering stopped, and the three could hear only the sounds of the distant gases fleeing from the ground.

Regaldo chose not to speak. Instead, his eyes followed a small silver bird as it fluttered between the three brothers. Regaldo knew this bird. They all did. It knew neither good nor ill, only what was before and what was to come. A single feather fell to the cracked ground, and with it came a smile and a wink through Regaldo's knowing eyes.

Aiken's skin shifted to red from the realization. A granite spire ignited from the earth, sending Regaldo's brothers into the air.

Water gurgled from every crevice, and massive trees vined out from the desert floor. Before he could gasp for air, Regaldo could see the garden renewed once more. It was as glorious as it ever was, teeming with life, spelling out a promise that would one day come to pass.

As the ground shook, a deep cavern formed below him, just as he knew it would. This time it was Regaldo that shifted his skin to blue as he willingly rolled into the diminishing abyss, the earth closing back around him as he fell.

And in the darkness, he smiled and waited for their next wretched dance.

ONE

PRESENT DAY EARTH

A T THE LESS-THAN-WONDERFUL AGE of fifteen, Edgar Brave had spent far too many years at the Friars' foster home. It was not the Friars that concerned Edgar, but his situation.

Edgar was a homebody. At an age where he ought to sneak out and make life-altering errors, he preferred to stay home. Every step away from his front door was a step against the tether that pulled him back.

And it was in this foster home, where he spent most of his idle time, that he lived surrounded by children much younger than him. Children that wanted to play and scream and hit. Children that didn't know his past. Many that had pasts of their own they had yet to wrap their grimy hands around.

In such a home, Edgar could only truly relate to his older brother Simon, who was most certainly not a homebody.

Edgar had friends and enjoyed their company, genuinely so, but to leave the house as frequently as his brother did would alter who he was (he was quite happy with who he was, thank you).

Edgar read books and wrote in journals. He invented board games only he could play, with creatures that only he could describe, but to leave and socialize would be to ignore the tether pulling him back to his bed.

Simon was a different story. Two years his senior, Simon spent most of his days out on adventures in the nearby woods, socializing with friends and doing odd jobs for cabin owners. If Edgar had a tether pulling him home, Simon's pulled him away.

It was Simon's tether that likely bothered Edgar the most. He had been at the Friar home for many years but still longed for his old life. If there was one connection to that old life that Edgar still had, it was Simon. For that reason, he held a deep love for his brother, to which few others could compare.

Still, the two Brave boys were complete opposites. Edgar combed his dark hair neatly every day. In jeans and a flannel shirt, he looked just normal enough to get lost in a crowd. Simon, with his shaggy hair and torn shirts, would stand out in that crowd, but only because he should have bathed. He also walked with a limp, one that he had earned the night they entered the foster care system, which made him all the easier to spot when lost.

Despite their opposing natures, the two were genuine friends. Edgar watched over his older brother as though Simon was the younger of the two. Simon allowed it, mostly because he wasn't paying attention long enough to be annoyed.

Edgar woke up at six thirty every morning to trek to school, leaving Simon behind to oversleep. When he returned home in the evening, the house buzzed with children from every age group.

The first thing Edgar Brave noticed from his time at the Friar household was how effective Susan Friar was at directing a mob of children. Over the years, her tactics had evolved to funneling the flock into an area where they could let out energy without destroying property or hurting themselves.

With the Brave boys as the longest tenured foster children, he came to observe Susan from angles the other children hadn't bothered to notice.

Susan was moderately thin, with dyed brown hair pushed out by gray roots. Since she was on the far end of her fifties, Edgar suspected she took in young foster children not out of a hole in her heart but because she recognized she was one of the essential cogs that rotated the world.

As Edgar watched her work with these children, he noticed she never directed the individual. That was her husband's forte. Ben could inspire an individual to do better in school or find the spirit within themselves to play the piano with more passion than they could have hoped for. But if Ben needed to get a gaggle of children to school on time, he would deliver them four hours later than intended, if at all. Susan knew the forest and Ben knew the trees.

Edgar suspected it was Susan's talent with a crowd that enabled her to command a string of chaotic children to gallop, in unison, inside for dinner. With this herd of beasts, Edgar speculated a few followed her call out of obligation, and the rest followed solely because that was where the flock was migrating.

On that evening, each child dashed inside from a muddy lawn with little care for what they tracked in. Many of them, boys and girls alike, shoved, pushed, and punched each other, disregarding who was bigger than whom.

There were scatterings of several age groups, though Edgar and Simon were noticeably the oldest. Most of the children the Friar family took in were very young. They started at just a few months old and ranged to twelve years of age. The Brave brothers were no exception. They had come into the Friar home when they were ten and twelve years old and were now fifteen and seventeen.

Most of the energy in the household came from the children in the middle age group. Children below seven had enough energy to threaten a bull before its dinner. Edgar was never sure how Susan could accomplish taming them. He suspected she learned to use the fear of the pack against itself.

"Out, out," said Susan. "Wash up outside. It's time for dinner. In fact, it's already cold. And you've tracked in too much mud. I'm going to be here all night, if you don't kill me before then."

The children scampered to the outdoor shower. While still dressed, each child took their turn scurrying under the stream of water, washing off all the mud and leaves they had collected on their faces and clothes. They then marched to one community towel, awaiting them next to a swamp fan turned to full speed. The routine was to use the two in conjunction to reach some level of dryness. Some dried off violently, as though their faces themselves were stains. Others barely visited the towel, picking it up and dropping it again just long enough that they could answer Susan affirmatively when she asked if they had tried at all. If a child did not properly dry enough to avoid tracking in water, they would need to change into oversized generic sweatshirts and pants.

They could only enter the house with clean, bare feet. This inevitably resulted in a heap of mixed shoes constructed just outside the door.

After five years of living with the Friars, Edgar had seen this process evolve through many iterations. This was by far the most effective method. Effective in the sense that it required the least amount of work from Susan Friar.

Edgar had wondered how Susan and Ben could avoid ruining their nice furniture. The answer came quicker than he thought. They didn't own nice furniture. The Friars carefully designed the home for the quickest cleanup and the least costly repairs, often at the cost of aesthetics. Any furniture with fabric was dark microfiber with covers they regularly removed and washed. They recently replaced the couch, but only after the frame itself gave way.

If a guest were to walk between rooms while staring at the ground, it would seem like they were traversing between squares on a patchwork quilt. Each floor was vinyl or tile and styled with little regard for the bordering room.

After the children came in, they each grabbed a bowl, plastic and reused over decades, and made a line to the chili pot that sat simmering on the stove. The pot was as big as Edgar's torso and was too full to carry without spilling.

After slopping the chili into their bowl, each child reached their hand into a bag of generic white bread and pulled out a slice, some grabbing several, and laid it over the chili as a side dish that wasn't literally on the side. It was just easier to use the chili bowl to hold the entirety of their meal than to manage multiple plates across so many children.

"Only one slice," Susan said. "There's barely enough to go around, and I'm not buying any more. For every extra slice you take, I want you to look at the last kid in line: Steven. Steven's the last. If anyone grabs two slices, it will be Steven that goes without. I hope you all know that."

The children assembled along a table that stretched longer than the dining room, encroaching into the family room. The children that were late (that night it was Steven) didn't get to sit. They stood while they ate, holding the bowl up to their chin as they rapidly scooped the food into their mouths.

The kids yelled, hit, threw bread, and hit again. In the end, Susan only caught the truly horrible offenses and dealt with everything else using various methods of crowd control.

After dinner, the swarm washed up and prepared themselves for bed. Many children shared toothbrushes and swapped t-shirts. They slept in their clothes for the next day, of course. Pajamas were for families that had time to change again when they awoke. It was routine for each child to dress themselves in the jeans they were going to wear to school the next day. If anyone wore pajamas, they would need to be responsible enough to wake up ten minutes early to change into their day clothes or get left behind when Susan left for school drop-off. If they overslept *and* didn't wear their day clothes, they'd get a stern look from Susan implying they shouldn't have worn pajamas.

Certainly, every child was a unique and precious snowflake. But after years of living with the Friars, Edgar noticed Susan did not take to admiring each snowflake. She dealt with large mounds of snow. Her job was to make sure those mounds were not blocking traffic. It was the job of the idle mind to admire the snowflake. She left that job to Ben, who was good at being idle.

Ben Friar, the jovial head of the household, entered the living room after Susan had completed all the bedtime preparations.

He called the room to attention, assuming they'd all snap into place but also not checking to see that they had. It was not so much the sort of call that a military sergeant would make, commanding the focus of those beneath him. Rather, he made calls to those he assumed were already listening, poised and ready, and forgot the rest.

Ben was ten years older than Susan by Edgar's recollection. He wore a smile permanently painted across his face as though tattooed on. It would appear as though he had wrinkles along the corners of his mouth and eyes, although his smile never rested long enough to be sure. If he ever grew cross, he'd forget the reason before he had time to build on his anger. One man might call him intelligent and another would call him absent-minded. Both men would be correct.

"Come gather around, young children," Ben said. "I will sing you a short song before bed."

"Oh please do, I love your songs," is what he expected them to say. It was also likely what he heard. What actually happened was something entirely different. The children stayed where they were, in the family room, not the living room where Ben sat. Ben did not seem bothered by that. Surely they were too excited to move, so Ben came to them.

"I will sing to you my favorite song as a child, 'Adarian Circus.'"

Susan retreated to her wine, which was intended for after the children went to bed, though she was happy for the early break.

Ben began his song.

The big top is rising
Despite for the few
We lost in the journey
To bring this to you

The specters are hiding
The shadows they keep
They don't mean to harm you
Unless you're asleep

The gazes varied across the room, though all expressions were negative, as Ben sung on with little concern or recognition for his audience. Children either held fast to fearful expressions of hauntings in their imaginations or remained discomforted by the old man singing in a room full of uninterested children, unassisted by instruments or accompanied voices.

The path that you walk now
The past of the true
The beaten, forgotten
The meek and the few

The twin tides, they're locked
The footsteps, the lore
All that's forgotten
Forgotten no more

The song continued, describing scenes of the dead rising from the grave and haunting a circus. Considering all the years Edgar had been in the Friar household, he and his brother had heard that song many times. This part of the song was frightening to young minds, particularly before sending them off to bed.

Edgar looked over at Susan to intervene. She saw Edgar's look, let out a deep sigh, and set down her glass. She looked back and forth between the group and observed a completely quiet room. She nodded in approval and picked up her glass once more.

"Susan," Edgar said, nudging.

She scowled over the edge of her glass as though someone had interrupted a delightful book. Edgar motioned toward the smaller children. Susan grumbled something below her breath and then spoke aloud.

"Ben, perhaps you shouldn't sing that part of the song."

"Well, why not?" asked Ben.

"The children are getting ready for bed, and a song about a haunted circus is probably not the best idea. Also, you've sung me that song before in its entirety, and you've chosen the worst section of the entire song. When people want to hear a song, they want to hear the chorus. You've chosen an obscure part of an endless ballad and left out its chorus."

"Right. I like it. It makes you think."

"Makes you think of what?" asked a small child sitting on the couch.

"It makes you wonder what happened before. It tells a new story while hinting at the one that preceded it. The best part is actually that they never tell you about the original story. They leave that part for you to wonder about, to dream about. It gives you the gift of filling in the gaps."

"Right," said Susan. "Well, everyone, Ben is in charge. If you're scared tonight, do not call me. I will have locked my bedroom door. Talk to Ben."

"Oh, I would love to talk about it," said Ben. "Please come to me."

"Let's head off to bed," Edgar said to the kids who hadn't already snuck away.

The children promptly ran off. One small child, trampled in the stampede, had a look of panic as Ben acknowledged him.

"Steven, you've stayed," Ben said. "Oh, how lovely? Let's discuss the song."

Steven cried and scurried off to join his friends. Ben did not seem offended. He simply redirected his attention to Edgar.

"Have you heard that song, Edgar?"

"I have," said Edgar, smiling. "We've listened to it together several times, remember?" Edgar saw the soul behind Ben's eyes, and it comforted him. "Would you like to chat about it?"

"No, no, that's all right. But I think there will be lessons to draw from it as you grow. Instead, for now I'd like for you to think about it. Keep it in the back of your mind."

Edgar nodded.

"I thought we might discuss something else," continued Ben.

Edgar had an idea about what Ben spoke of. He was interested and wanted to know but did not expect the best of news.

"I heard from your mother today. Well, to be more precise, I heard *about* your mother. I didn't actually speak with her. Her court date was today."

Edgar sank deeper into the couch and stared ahead at nothing in particular.

Ben continued. "It seems you and Simon will stay with us a while longer."

This was exactly the sort of disappointment that Edgar had been expecting. He wouldn't describe what he was feeling as sadness. Sadness was when he first came to the Friar House. Over time, with every bit of bad news he had heard about his mother, his mattress had felt more permanent.

"I would share your disappointment, dear Edgar, but Susan and I are growing rather fond of you. Perhaps it's selfish of me. Actually, I know for a fact it is. Still, you've had a good number of happy years here, and a bit of an extension isn't so bad, is it?"

Edgar smiled at the old man. "I'm growing fond of you too, Ben."

"Susan too," his foster mother said from the next room.

"You too, Susan," Edgar called back. It was the truth. The fact was that she was the broken back to which many children owed their childhood. When she wasn't there to add a smile to the owner of a full belly, Ben was there instead.

"We love having you two here, wherever Simon is off to," said Ben. "Still, if you feel mad about what I just told you, that's normal and certainly you're allowed to be."

"I know."

"Do you? I mean it. It's normal to be upset. The fantastic thing is that there are loads of things we can do to let it out. Want to go for a jog? I think we should go for a jog." Ben stood from the couch and fetched his shoes from the shoe rack. The suit he wore was not ideal for jogging, but Edgar was certain Ben would run in it, regardless.

"No, no, sit down," Edgar said, allowing a laugh to trickle out.

"Well, how about a punching bag? I saw one for sale on my way home today."

Edgar thought a moment, a smile creeping onto his face. "How about a drum kit?"

"A drum kit? You're going to bleed me dry, boy."

"No drum kit," said Susan, still in the next room. "The small ones will bang it day after day. I don't have the wine for it."

"Okay, fine," said Edgar. "No drum kit. I'll take you up on that punching bag, though. Can I take boxing lessons?"

"I can afford an Internet search on *how to punch*. How's that for boxing lessons?"

"Take the deal, Edgar," said Susan. "He'll be offering to teach you himself. Take the deal before things escalate."

"Sure, Ben. Thank you."

"Then there we have it," said Ben. "We'll pick a bag up tomorrow after school, and we can install it together."

"Deal," said Edgar.

"Oh, and I'd like to give you something that has helped through many emotional binds in the past."

Ben walked over to the bookshelf and removed a black hardcover. Frequent readings had tattered the pages over the years, and Edgar could make out water stains along the side. As Ben handed it down, Edgar saw it was a collection of poems and musings.

"These are my favorite poems," Ben said. "Not all will appeal to you, but you may just find that a few say precisely what you need to hear."

Edgar looked up and smiled at the man. He did not have a particular fondness for literature, especially poems, but he appreciated it all the same.

Ben gestured to the book. "Skim to page 95, if you could."

Edgar did so and found a Robert Frost poem with notes scribbled along the margins in Ben's handwriting.

"'A Servant to Servants,'" Edgar said, reading the title of the poem aloud.

"Yes, that's perhaps my favorite and is of particular importance on a day such as this. If you could read the underlined part, I think you'd find it helpful."

Edgar did just as he asked.

He says the best way out is always through.
And I agree to that, or in so far
As that I can see no way out but through.

"That must be my favorite poem in all of poetry," Ben said. "You might prefer the phrasing that most people use when quoting it—'The only way out is through.'"

Edgar smiled at Ben. He had such an innocent soul. "I like it."

"It is through the tribulations of life that we grow, Edgar. There is no strong character that a man can build from having only treasure and nothing else. When you have these hard times, remember that. You say 'the only way out is through' and you keep going."

Edgar appreciated this side of Ben, but for now he only needed sleep. "Thank you, Ben. This is great. If you don't mind, I'll read this in my room."

The old man nodded with his permanent grin a little more relaxed.

"Goodnight, Edgar."

"Goodnight, Ben."

"And Susan," called Susan.

"Goodnight, Susan," Edgar called back.

Edgar walked down the hallway to his room, closed the door, and lay down in bed, thumbing the pages of the worn book.

"The only way out is through," he said to himself. "I kind of like that."

He closed his eyes and laid the book along his chest, repeating the quote over again to himself as he drifted to sleep. "The only way out is through."

TWO

A JOLT OF PAIN along his teeth woke Edgar. He had felt it several times that week, and each time he told himself he'd ask Susan to make a dentist appointment.

As he stared through the window in his unlit room, he saw the shadows wave in the wind as the branches danced with the coming storm. While Edgar expected all this with the looming dark clouds, this time a chill glided down his spine as the shadows collected into a single silhouette of a man peering through the glass.

The window burst open and revealed the peach-fuzz face of his brother.

"Simon?" Edgar asked. "What are you doing?"

Edgar scurried to the light switch and turned it on. As he looked back at the window, Simon had already begun climbing in.

Edgar exhaled his frustration as he observed the rainwater dripping over their clean floor. With the expected storm and the likelihood that it wouldn't slow down his brother, Edgar made a mental note to keep a towel by the window.

"Go through the front door, like a normal person," Edgar said.

Simon looked at Edgar, unaware of his disruption to the clean room and genuinely confused by Edgar's command. "I don't want to wake anyone."

"You weren't worried about waking me?"

"Well, you're different. You're not Susan. Oh, which reminds me, do you think she'll make me a sandwich?"

"After all that, you're going to wake her up to ask her for food?"

"No," he said, cracking the door to the unlit hallway and peeking out. "But wouldn't a sandwich be great?"

"She's not gonna make you a sandwich, Simon."

Simon continued his stare out their bedroom door, but Edgar could see his mind busy with invading thoughts. "Hmmm, I wonder if anyone else would want to make me one."

"Simon, honestly, just make yourself one."

"You're right, it's a lost cause." Simon turned and pulled Edgar in for a hug, smearing his brother's clean nightshirt with wet leaves and dirt. Edgar pushed him back and stared down at his damp clothes. Simon seemed unaware of the offense. "Brother, how've you been today? Can you believe this weather? I could handle a full storm, but we've had a bit of rain, and then none, and then rain again. It's confusing. I don't know whether to make plans."

"Eh, you never make plans anyway," Edgar said with a smirk. "You're always busy, but I've never known you to plan."

"Ha! Was that a joke? I mean, it's not a good one, but for you, that's incredible. Well done, Edgar. Now you just need a driver's permit and you'll be a real boy."

Edgar smiled at Simon as he changed out of his soiled shirt.

"But seriously, Edgar," Simon said. "How have you been?"

Edgar's face drooped as he recalled their mother's court hearing. "Ah, well, Ben heard news about Mom today."

Simon's expression fell to match Edgar's, who shook his head to communicate the bad news. Simon walked over to his bed, which sat next to Edgar's, and rested upon it.

Edgar could never train himself to get used to this. They were fine—not perfect, but fine—at the Friar house, and they knew they could live there as long as they needed. If it were a long vacation or a summer camp, his only complaints would be surface-level. He'd yell at the younger children for using the toilet paper as streamers to decorate their rooms or scold Steven for stealing his pillow to use as a sled when tobogganing down the stairs. But after their parents left, they stopped complaining about most things.

He believed there wasn't anything he could do but proceed. He recalled the poem from earlier that night: *The only way out is through.*

They could talk to each other about such things, but it didn't get too far. Edgar read books as a distraction and worked with Ben to release his energy. Simon, though, closed himself off. Edgar came to recognize the difference between Simon's depression and his own. Edgar was a deep well and Simon was a door voluntarily locked.

Edgar walked over and joined his brother on the bed. He searched his brain for how to comfort Simon, but everything he found was only a solution for Edgar, not his brother.

Finally, he glanced back at the open window, and the solution came to him.

"I'd bet even at this hour there are people we can meet up with to get your mind off things."

Simon perked his ears and smiled in acknowledgment.

"It's a quiet town," Edgar said. "But you know people, right?"

"Indeed I do."

This time, when they left the room, they used the door and not the window.

Mist haunted the streetlamps as dark clouds covered the moonlight. Though they tried to avoid the litter of puddles along the sidewalk, they couldn't help but splash droplets onto their pant legs as they strolled to Simon's usual meetup spot with a gaggle of friends.

With the looming storm, their walk took longer than Edgar would have liked, with Simon's limp slowing them down. Over the years since his brother hurt his leg, Edgar had gotten used to slowing his pace so that his brother didn't end up too far behind. Edgar was also a slow walker in his own right, so he normally didn't mind it when Simon trailed. It meant that Edgar wasn't the slowest one. Though on a dreary night such as this one, Edgar would have appreciated getting to their destination sooner.

Many weeks before, someone had cut a hole along the fence to the baseball field, which they could easily cover with brush. If the groundskeeper knew anything about the hole, it was a task far enough down the to-do list that he never got to it.

Edgar rarely came with Simon on his late-night outings, but with the looming storm, this night felt more ominous than others. As he snuck through the opening in the fence, an awkward feeling of invading privacy hung along the back of his head. It seemed like someone was watching them, though he was too self-conscious to bring it up.

Elena and Jude, each seventeen, waited within the dugout, though neither was actively talking. The two looked too oddly paired to be a proper couple. Elena had the face of a pixie with the confident eyes of someone who had lived to be four times her age. Her hair was black, with the tips dyed pink just past her shoulders. Her style of dress was to mismatch, selecting the runt of the litter when she shopped for clothes.

Jude was Elena's opposite. If God made Elena in His image, He made Jude in the image of a tired ogre. Jude combed his hair but left a pronounced cowlick in the back and lived most of his life with a scowled resting face. Despite this, he was rarely ever angry enough to lose his temper. Rather, he had too little energy to be angry. His moods seemed to oscillate between indifference and slight annoyance. He grumbled often but never yelled.

The pairing of these two always perplexed Edgar. They were a couple, but Edgar couldn't determine why. Elena never seemed to enjoy being around Jude, and Jude didn't seem to enjoy anything at all.

Jude sat deep along the back wall of the dugout, fiddling with something unrecognizable in his hands, as Elena delivered a welcoming smile at the front.

"The Brave boys," Elena said, her face lighting up as she waved. "Simple Simon, and… I'm just now realizing I don't have a nickname for you, Edgar. I'll think of one."

"It's all right," Edgar said with a playful smirk.

"Nah, come on. You gotta have a nickname. With my luck, it'll come to me while I'm falling asleep, and then I'll be up all night. Gah! No way. We can't go with Ed, that's too obvious. Give me some time. It'll come to me. Now, Simon, it's only been an hour, and you're back already. Talk."

"Couldn't sleep," Simon said.

"You're a cruddy liar."

"Ha! I'm an incredible liar. Trust me, when I lie, you'll know."

Elena paused and exchanged an awkward glance with Edgar. "I'm not sure any of that made sense, but welcome all the same." She turned to Edgar. "Glad to see you left your cave."

Edgar only responded with a shrug. He wasn't great with words, even in the simplest social situations. If someone he didn't frequently interact with complimented his shirt, Edgar would respond with an instinctive "I'm fine, thanks," leaving the other person unsure on how to proceed. Not that the person he spoke to made him nervous. It was more that the driver in charge of his brain when he left the house was always experiencing his first day on the job.

Edgar was glad to see that Elena didn't press him into conversation. Or if she intended to, Simon cut her short.

"I want to teach you a card trick," said Simon, plucking a deck from his pocket and setting out five cards on the ground in front of Elena.

"Random, but I like where you're taking this. Let's do it," said Elena.

Jude perked up and moved closer to the gang, peeking over Elena's shoulder. Edgar noticed she recoiled slightly at his approach but did not move away.

"Let's see if you can guess the trick," said Simon.

"Ah, don't tempt her," Jude said. "She'll be trying it all night. It'll be all we hear about."

Elena ignored her boyfriend and looked directly at Simon. "I want to see it. Please, show me."

"Pick a card and flip it over so that everyone can see it."

Elena chose the card right of center and flipped it to reveal the Jack of Clubs.

"Okay, now mix up all five and hand them to me."

She did just as he told her, focusing closely as Simon accepted each card and integrated them into the deck. He shuffled three times and held out the deck.

"Now, please take the top five cards and lay them back down, just as I did before."

Again, she followed his directions precisely as instructed, her eyes intent on finding his sleight of hand.

"Now flip over the center card."

As she did so, a smile spread across her face as she revealed the Jack of Clubs.

"That's amazing," she said and then eagerly grabbed for the cards. "Now give it over."

"What? Okay, sure, here you go. It's not a trick deck, I promise."

"She doesn't think it's a trick deck," said Jude, rolling his eyes. "But she still wants to figure it out."

"Edgar," Elena said, patting the ground and sitting down. "Try this with me."

Edgar sat down opposite Elena as she laid the cards down, just as they were with Simon. "Now, go, pick one."

Edgar did as instructed, and she continued the trick just as she observed from Simon.

"That's not going to—" said Simon before Elena held up a hand to stop him.

She continued on with the trick. As Edgar flipped the card that should have been his, Elena growled, revealing an incorrect card.

"See, I told you," said Simon.

"Stop," Elena said, focused on the deck. Edgar could see the thrill of solving a puzzle in her eyes. "That's not helping."

"She'll be at this for hours," said Jude.

She continued with two more failed attempts before asking Simon to perform the trick again. Another failed attempt from Elena left her almost throwing the deck across the dugout. Though just as she was about to let the cards go, she breathed in deep and closed her eyes. When she opened them again, there was a new fire ignited within them. She gripped the deck and laid out another five cards.

Simon watched carefully, smiling when he saw her figure out the sleight of hand.

Edgar lifted the card and infected the group with grins and cheers as they each saw the desired Queen of Hearts.

"Ha! I got it," she said. "Now you take the deck back, but I'm keeping the Queen."

Simon shrugged. "That's fine; it's Susan's."

"Okay, okay," said Jude. "Good trick, I'll give you that. You have something new for a few parties."

Elena's smile waned as she stared off across the baseball field, and Edgar felt a mild pain along his teeth.

"Who's Mr. Friendly back here?" Elena asked.

They all looked and saw a lean man with stubble along his pronounced jaw walking just beyond the fence. He looked to be in his fifties, with a dark raincoat and his hood draped over his head. Black hair speckled with gray peeked through his hood. The group would have shrugged him off, assuming he was on a leisurely stroll. But there was no walking path for several miles, and for this small, woodsy town, with most of its inhabitants old and early risers, it was rare to see any activity at this hour beyond their own.

The man made eye contact with them all and continued his slow saunter along the grass beyond the fence. He did not pretend to look away as the group stared back. Instead, he smiled at them and whistled a ghostly tune.

His lack of fear was the most unsettling to Edgar. The dark clouds and a mysterious man along a school baseball field would have unnerved him. But this man did not fear the teens calling the police. He didn't seem to fear anything. The whistling man was perfectly comfortable inducing anxiety amongst the teens and perhaps preferred it that way.

"Let's go," said Simon under his breath.

"Yeah, I think we should too," said Jude.

It was Elena who surprised them all as she leaned forward, trying to gain more detail about the whistling stranger. To the boys' surprise, she walked toward the man. She squinted as she crept, as though trying to read the details on the strange man's face.

"Elena," said Jude, grabbing her arm. She recoiled, but from Jude, not the whistling stranger. It was as though he offended her. She rushed past the group, walking away from the whistling man.

Edgar and Jude exchanged glances.

Why would Elena act so strangely?

Perhaps she was curious about the whistling stranger. From what Edgar knew about her, that didn't surprise him. Her curiosity about the most thrilling pieces of life had come up before tonight. It was the way she looked at Jude that took Edgar aback.

Why would she fear her boyfriend and not this strange man?

THREE

They took the long way home that night, traveling through the best lit parts of town in case the whistling man returned.

Jude glared back at Simon as his limp held the group back from what would have been a rushed walk home.

"Don't worry about him," Edgar said to Simon. "He's just nervous."

"You mean you're not?" Simon said. "You saw him too. I wouldn't want to meet him again on a night like this."

"No, I agree. Just don't let him blame his nerves on your limp."

"Trust me, I want to get home, too."

As they walked from streetlamp to streetlamp, Edgar noticed Elena peering off in between houses. Edgar and Simon did the same throughout the walk, but Elena was the only one that looked eager to find the man—a white rabbit for Alice to chase.

Elena was as odd a girl as Jude a boy, each in their own distinct way. As Edgar observed Jude walking, he saw he was the only one not looking out for the whistling man. If Edgar were to discover that someone he knew was a serial killer, his first bet would be on Jude. Not for any hunger to inflict pain or ignite chaos. Rather, Jude didn't seem to feel much at all beyond the occasional annoyance. When he was happy, it was from something that only mildly affected his life. When he was sad...well, Jude didn't get sad.

A series of light droplets landed on Edgar's face, and they all looked up at the sky with the same sigh.

They increased their pace just as a flash of lightning illuminated the space between two houses ahead of them, revealing the silhouette of the whistling man, waiting.

The group gasped in unison but did not move. Through the light of the streetlamps, the whistling man smirked and calmly walked toward them.

"We need to leave," said Elena, abandoning her curiosity. They all followed her down a side street. Continuously, they looked back but saw only an empty street where the whistling man ought to have been.

They had traveled a block before they heard the whistling again. They all looked around for the source but found none.

The whistling abruptly stopped, and the only remaining sound was the patter of light rain against the sidewalk.

Edgar felt his heartbeat through his chest and the color draining from his face. He looked around and saw the same fear in his friends. Who was this man, and why was he chasing them? What could an adult man gain from tormenting teenagers?

The pain in his teeth jolted once more, and they heard the whistling man's voice, soft and questioning, with giddy laughter. "Simple Simon?"

He stood across the street, gazing at them from a neighbor's front yard, and Edgar felt a fight-or-flight panic spread from his chest to his toes.

They scattered, Jude and Elena each separating off on their own, and Edgar with Simon running down a side street.

Edgar ran ahead at first but then looked back at Simon, dragging his leg. The limp from Simon's first day in foster care had slowed him to little more than a hurried walk. Edgar stayed back, his arms around Simon, ushering him along. A demon deep within Edgar's mind told him that the man would kill them both, but he couldn't leave his brother. He pushed the demon down and pulled his brother forward.

Edgar looked around but could no longer see the whistling man. Where was he now? He had to be toying with them.

They came to a steep hill leading to an adjacent neighborhood, and gravity carried them faster down the slope until they approached a slow run, with Edgar supporting his brother with his arm.

Edgar could feel the rain striking his face more heavily now. The droplets collected along his eyes, blurring his vision.

And then Simon released his arm. Edgar's heart dropped when he felt his brother fall and roll. Edgar reacted as quickly as he could, reaching out to grab hold of his brother's jacket, but he caught only air.

Edgar's momentum caused him to slip, and he too fell and rolled down the slope.

The streetlamps spun as he tucked his arms in, building speed as he tumbled down the hill. With a jolt, Edgar's head hit concrete, and a rainbow of colors blurred his vision. He came to a halt at the bottom of the hill, feeling only the sidewalk beneath him and little else. The spiral of distorted colors obscured his vision.

He tried to stand but was still too dizzy to regain balance.

It couldn't end here. Not like this. He pushed through it, willing his legs to stand and forcing his eyes to search for anything that could reorient him. Eventually, he could make out vague details of the neighborhood, and he focused on them. He saw no one along the empty streets. There was no Simon, nor the whistling man. There was no Elena or Jude, or even a soul awake to ask for help.

His pulsating heart distorted the dizzying colors in his eyes with every beat.

Edgar rested his hands on his knees. What could he do now? Where had Simon gone, and how could he find him?

Simon couldn't have gone far. They were together only seconds ago.

Edgar leapt between houses, still drunk from dizziness, invading backyards, desperate for a sign of his brother.

After twenty minutes of searching in a panic, he realized what he needed to do. He needed Ben and Susan's help. It was a five-minute run, but he needed more eyes and an adult's judgment.

He ran, disregarding the rain, the chill along his chest and his heart pleading for rest. Wherever Simon was, Edgar needed to save his brother.

Mist droplets collected on Simon's face as he slowed to a hobbled trot. He glanced behind. No one was there. At least he didn't think anyone had followed him.

Where did Edgar get to? Did he even make it? Who is that guy chasing us?

Simon stopped and surveyed the neighborhood. He was now several blocks from the hill they had rolled down, facing the forest on the edge of town.

He collapsed on the sidewalk in front of a series of houses and looked out at the trees.

Simon felt a combination of many emotions. Regret that he left his brother, but glad he was still alive. Nervousness crept in too. Was his brother okay? He had to be. Edgar was smarter than him. If Simon was safe, then Edgar needed to be.

A crack echoed against the trees from the forest just ahead, outside of town.

An eerie, ball-shaped glow hung silently between two distant trees. It floated before him, a crackling blue fireball.

Was this the source of the sound?

He doubted his senses, but he wasn't sure why. It was as though someone had captured lightning in a fishbowl. As his eyes focused, his mind became more skeptical. He had heard of ball lightning before from Ben but was sure it was rare enough for him never to see in person, if it was real at all. The ancient will-o'-the-wisp from folklore. Could that object before him be it?

I bet that's what this is.

As he focused longer on it, he felt it pull him in. It invited him. He lost awareness of where he was, and the world disappeared around him, gradually fading to nothing. It wanted him to come closer. It wanted *him*.

"See something odd?" The voice was male and disembodied, somewhere amongst the trees.

And then there he was: the whistling man. Simon did not remember ever looking away from the light, but he must have. He gazed at the tall man, now wearing a slim fitted suit and a clever smile. He looked different, but Simon couldn't tell how. Unlike before, Simon did not want to run.

Simon spoke, but he didn't remember willing it. "Oh, um. I saw...well, I thought I saw...I mean—"

"A light?" the man asked, head tilted slightly.

"Well, yes. How did you—"

"It was over there, right? I saw it too." The man didn't look nearly as surprised as he should have. He didn't appear to be shaken by the orb at all. He reminded Simon of an old game show host that knew what the writers had scheduled next.

"I need to go home," said Simon, feeling a strong sense of unease but still not wanting to leave.

"But we need to go see that light," the man said in hushed excitement, as though he were containing a coiled spring. "You are interested, aren't you?"

"Well, sure, but I'm supposed to meet up with my brother."

"He'll be fine." The man leaned in closer. Simon hadn't realized how close he had gotten until that moment, when the man lowered his tone to a whisper. "Let's go check it out."

The man once again stepped gracefully to the side to reveal the ball of light. It was miraculous. Simon was certain there was nothing more delightful in this world. If there was, he wouldn't want to see it lest he betray this alluring glow.

I ought to run. Why am I not running?

"You know why, Simon." The man responded to something Simon hadn't thought he said aloud.

Somewhere, deep in Simon's mind, he realized he had never woken up from the trance of the blue orb. This part of him wanted to scream or run or do absolutely anything at all but comply. Still, this part of Simon's mind was not in control. Desire was in control now. Happy desire.

"What's going to happen to me?"

"You don't need to worry about that. You don't need to worry about anything anymore."

Edgar gave little thought to the puddles, soaking his shoes through to his socks as he ran. He needed to make it back to the Friar house to wake Ben and Susan. They'd know what to do. They needed to. This was far beyond his scope.

Simon was the last piece of this world that Edgar loved. Too much of his past had died. He felt the life from before drain away with each step along the sidewalk. If Simon was gone...

He was nearing the corner of his neighborhood when the streetlamps went dark.

Edgar stopped and looked around. It must have been a power outage, but why now? Why tonight?

This is all too strange.

He slowed his pace as his eyes adjusted to the darkness. Each flash of lightning gave him a glimpse of the road ahead before stealing it away.

The Friar house was within view. He'd wake them up, and Susan would call the police while Ben used the car to look for Simon. This plan had to work.

He was at the steps to his house when he felt the familiar feeling that someone was watching him. Slowly, he turned and saw the whistling man creep carefully toward him with his hands up, as though bracing himself. Why the defensive stance?

Edgar froze. The man looked different this time. In place of the sly grin, he had a look of panic and worry. Edgar no longer felt the pain in his teeth at the sight of the man. Something had changed, but he wasn't sure what.

Why the shift? What happened to Simon?

He felt a void in the world around him. There was some-thing wrong with Simon.

It came to him like thunder rattling his world. Simon was gone, abducted by this man. That was the feeling of the void, the abrupt change in the man's behavior.

Rage filled Edgar as he lunged at the whistling man, not sure what he'd do but no longer concerned for his own safety.

Behind him, Edgar heard Ben walking down the stairs. "Hold on, Susan, hold on," Ben said through the muffled walls. "I'm sure the circuit breaker just needs a quick flip of the switch. Simply amazing that you caught the outage in the dead of darkness. You ought to be studied."

The man turned and ran, but Edgar refused to let him go. Not now that Simon was gone. He didn't think. There was no time. He went after his brother's captor in a full sprint.

They dodged between houses and over fences. With the darkened street, all sight dimmed around him. It magnified the sounds of rain and heavy breathing, the feeling of sloshing mud that caked onto his shoes as he ran.

After he cleared another house, he found himself along a new road. He looked left and saw nothing. A rapid glance to the right revealed the man taking a hard turn down a narrow alleyway.

He chased after him once more. As he took the corner, a painful throb struck the back of his head.

Edgar's balance gave way, and the world spun around him. His hands flailed to brace his fall as he landed in a puddle of murky rainwater.

He had to push forward. He owed it to Simon, the last piece of his former life.

The man towered above him, but he no longer looked as menacing. Though he had the same characteristics, he carried himself like an entirely different man. His face was more frantic than menacing. He pleaded for Edgar to calm down with palms up.

He turned one hand to his chest and said, "Alister."

He said more words, all in a language that Edgar couldn't place. It wasn't Italian, but Edgar couldn't speak Italian. If he had to place it, he'd combine Arabic and Hawaiian.

The man reached out his hand, eager for Edgar to take it, as though placing his trust in this horrible stranger was the only viable option.

The moment stood still as the rain drenched both of their faces, becoming the only movement in this otherwise void space of inactivity. They stared at each other through the drops of rain.

The crash of tin trash cans and the voices of Elena and Jude fumbling through the darkness broke the void. Jude made a mumbled comment, and Elena responded. Neither of them seemed to see what was happening.

Seizing his only opportunity, or perhaps making a mistake of desperation, Alister sprinted ahead down the alleyway. Ahead of him, an enormous ball of light burst into existence. For a moment, all Edgar could see was the radiance given off by this miraculous orb. It was not blinding. Instead, it beckoned him like a gravitational pull. It would have hypnotized him had Alister not broken his line of sight and jumped into it.

And then Alister vanished, his body absorbed by the orb as though he belonged to another world.

For a single moment, nothing happened. The three teens, Edgar, Elena, and Jude, stared at the orb before them, trying to comprehend what they just saw. They each stood staring at the orb, disbelieving their senses.

"That man has Simon," Edgar said to the other two.

Jude froze in place, facing the orb before them. Elena, however, had a fire in her eyes. She shoved Jude aside and, through the sudden outbursts of Edgar and Jude, made the same dash at the orb as Alister.

It happened too quickly to react. Both boys screamed. Their voices echoed down the alleyway, but it was too late. Elena had disappeared into the portal.

The two boys sat wide-eyed and stunned with the orb still before them, both unsure what to do next.

Waves of emotion picked him up in their wake. First was the realization that Elena was no longer there, followed by the disbelief that any of it had happened at all. Last was the astonishment that the portal still lay before them. The rational side of Edgar was at war with his senses. The orb was still glowing. Still shrinking. If it had happened any quicker, Edgar would have denied that any of it happened. A twist of the senses must have caused his mind to play tricks. Yet there it was, the portal before him, begging him to question everything.

Jude turned to plead with Edgar. "You need to go in there, Edgar. That man...he has Simon."

Edgar looked at Jude in disbelief.

"He has Simon. You just said so. And now he has Elena."

Edgar froze, unsure and unwilling to move. With every bone in his body screaming to save his brother, his muscles froze with fear.

The portal continued to shrink.

"You need to go through. That's where your brother is. You won't get this opportunity back."

Edgar looked at Jude with fear radiating from his eyes. Jude was right. The last piece of this world that Edgar loved was through that portal, and this was the last moment that he could do anything about it.

The portal continued to reduce in size. It was now half the size of a door.

Jude scoffed, looking at the trembling Edgar, and launched at the portal.

"No!" said Edgar.

It swallowed him whole, just as it had Elena and Alister.

Edgar was now alone, with only the rain and the glowing orb.

Edgar tried to convince himself that none of this was real, but each second that passed proved him wrong.

Edgar muttered curses as the portal shrank to a size just larger than an oven.

Edgar screamed as he ran forward and dove in with arms outstretched.

He passed through and into another world.

Lights flashed by him as though he was racing along a freeway of white streaks. His mind had no capacity to comprehend much of anything but the streams that soared past. It was impossible to tell if each passing light lay inches from his fingertips or a galaxy away. He reached out but touched nothing.

Though he seemed to move with tremendous momentum, he also experienced no drag or wind. It was as though he were in a still room with stale air, despite the certainty of his own self hurling through space. The river of lights made no sound, yet they had the intensity of a silent scream. The scream of a child in utter horror.

His flight abruptly stopped.

Still in the darkness, a cluster of orbs replaced the streams. Each glowing ball revolved around him with wisps of blue and white, as though created by a divine artist. Some were enormous, likely to swallow him whole if he drifted near them. Others were not much larger than a pinprick.

The massive collection of these orbs together formed a sphere around him, placing him in the center. Each sphere had a faint tail of light behind it, as though they were the heads of celestial tadpoles and moved along a common tidal path.

Then, as quickly as he had arrived, a mystical force propelled him forward. The light before him grew larger with every breath until it engulfed him.

He felt himself break through a thin veil. A fabric. A barrier. On the other end was the familiar feeling of air brushing against his face as he splashed down into salt water.

FOUR

EDGAR BRAVE HAD LANDED in water, of that much he was certain. Whether his brother was nearby was another matter entirely.

The fall guided his body past one current and into another, tossing him about like a leaf in the wind. Water rushed past his nose and in along his tongue, the unwelcome taste of salt tempting him to spit, if only there were air to draw back in.

But of course, there was no air.

Darkness cast a blanket around him beneath the surface swells as he hunted, disoriented, for a point of reference.

Far off, a vague blue light ebbed and flowed as he swayed in the sea's rushing waters, revealing itself to be a cave deep along the ocean floor. The light within shone as though left on by an absentminded occupant.

Before it came to focus, buoyancy pulled his body to the surface, and he gratefully found air.

He gasped, greedy for life and relieved that he had a moment more of it.

He scanned the horizon for a clue, anything at all, that would tell him where to swim.

The moon bathed the coastal cliffs with light as an eerie blue glow traced the waves that washed up along the shore.

He swam, grateful when his shoes, still attached to his feet, met the continental shelf. He trudged through the current, his legs heavy as though dragging sandbags. With each step, more of his body emerged from the water, his clothes clinging to his skin with every inch. Any energy he had leaked down through his torso and out through the tips of his toes. As he reached the shore, his muscles gave in as his strength failed and he collapsed on the sand.

Where am I? Am I even on Earth?

He pleaded with the night sky, hunting for a constellation he recognized. A web of stars clustered above him, as thick as clouds, more than he could comprehend, more than his mind could let in. To spot a constellation amongst this rich sky was to find a pattern along the sand at his feet.

He took in a deep breath and tasted clean air, baptizing his dull, suburban-made lungs. This was fresh, more so than back home. He ballooned his lungs and held the breath a moment longer before he expelled it back out into this world, now poisoned by his breath. It was all too much to take in—the salt along the wind; the sand powdering between his fingers and the pulsing vibrato of the waves rushing at his feet and then retreating.

Finally, he beheld a sight that filled him with both awe and horror. A second moon raced across the night sky, the speed like a plane in flight. Yet this was no plane. He could see the pockmarks of ancient asteroids on its dark gray skin as it dashed past its larger sister. He remained transfixed, refusing to budge until it had left his field of view.

This was not Earth. He didn't know where he was or how to get home. He could be in the center of the galaxy or at the other end of the universe. It almost didn't matter. It was an alien world and likely the place he would die.

Is my brother here, too? At least give me that.

Edgar Brave, the boy who prided himself on being the stronger of the two Braves, pulled his knees to his chest and wept. He expelled tears like vomit from a poisoned stomach.

"What do I do?" The words spilled from his mouth quietly several times and waited as if for a response. Instead, this world gave only silence save the gentle wash of the waves. "What do I do?"

He sat a moment longer, rocking while hugging his knees. Soon, the sound of the waves became the only presence in his mind. Then came thoughts of the cave beneath the sea. He remembered it being the only source of light when he was underwater. Why was it glowing? Perhaps that was normal here. The coastline glowed. Why wouldn't an underwater cave also glow? On Earth, sure, that would be intriguing. Here, he didn't know what was worth exploring and what was normal.

How strange and horrifying this entire experience was. Several moments ago, he was at home. A single moment ago, he was spiraling across the universe. Now, he was trying to explain a light at the bottom of an alien ocean. If there were words to explain it, he didn't know them. He wondered why anything would seem unordinary in a world where he couldn't define what ordinary was.

He set aside the thought of the underwater cave and directed his attention to the cliffs behind him. They seemed to touch the sky from his perspective along the sand. They were difficult to see in the pale light of the moon. Still, he could observe a granite-like stone with speckles of trees growing in shelved areas up the cliff's face. Simply looking at them made him an ant among giants.

Looking up the coast, he discovered it was an elongated cove. The cliff walls framed the sand of the beach opposite the glowing blue waves. As he inspected the glow, he saw scatterings of small, animated lights just below the surface of the water. If they had been above water, floating within the surrounding air, he might confuse them with fireflies back home. These lights scurried about in much the same way. While each individual light moved chaotically on its own, the aggregate motion was itself pulsating in a beautiful and puzzling way.

Curious, Edgar walked up to the busy display and reached below the surface. Though it was dim compared to the glow, he could make out small fish radiating the light at their body's center. As they reacted to his hand, he could feel dozens of tails flapping against his palm and scurrying away.

The amount of discoveries he had made within such a short time amazed him. The smaller moon racing across the sky was the first. Second was this array of glowing fish.

He stood and reexamined the coastline. There was no point within the washing waves of the cove that the fish were not abundant. He guessed there were millions of these creatures riding the gentle waves to the shore.

Embedded in this was another discovery. These fish either preferred the waves to the deep sea or were only visible in their frolicking along the coastline. As he looked beyond the waves and out to the wide ocean, he saw no similar glow. There were small schools of fish randomly moving about, but none beyond the tracing of the coast. The dashes were short bursts of light, similar to a shooting star, as a fish joined its family on the shore, like a schoolchild racing to meet her friends at the playground. He wondered why these fish hurried so quickly to meet up with their companions. Was it an impulse built into their making, or a desire to fit in, or were both the same?

Abruptly, the ground shook. The headless rumbling left him uncertain which direction to look and where to run. As the water thrashed, he noticed the dark shadow of an island off the coast. The island was several miles in girth and made up entirely of cliffs that jutted into the sky.

As though the island itself were alive, it crept below the surface of the water. The displaced ocean expanded onto Edgar's new beachfront home, pushing him to retreat. His legs seemed to run on their own, detached from his instruction. Edgar leapt onto a bolder at the base of the cliff behind him and climbed several feet upward until he found a ledge he could hoist himself up on.

Within a moment, the island descended completely into the water as the sea sloshed beneath him. He looked on into the dark horizon where the web of stars met the glistening water around the spot where the mysterious island had been.

Only a moment passed before he heard the rumbling again. This time, another island a mile up the coast launched upward from the water and settled into place. The tide receded to its original position, a complete reversal of the pervious event. The new island looked remarkably similar to the first, so much so that he wondered if the two were the same and had simply moved to a new, more suitable location.

Along the sand, he saw the glowing fish, now beached, wiggling toward the water like baby snakes learning how to slither.

They eventually joined their friends in and amongst the waves and resumed their dance along the coastline. They were not frantic. Quite the opposite. They knew it all too well. Everything he had just witnessed was new only to him.

The entire experience alienated Edgar. In fact, he was the alien from most points of view. The events he had just experienced, however mysterious and awe-striking they may be, were likely not at all special in this world. The assembly of oddities around him was only odd to him, and he was odd to them. He was the outlier.

Where am I?

As he sat there on the beach, contemplating everything, the now distant memory of Ben Friar and his book of poems entered his mind.

What was that poem? Was it Robert Frost?

He remembered now a particular phrase and spoke it aloud. "The only way out is through." He realized he might need that mantra for many days to come. He'd need it to push forward, for his brother and for survival.

On the right, something caught his attention. The vague silhouette of a young girl strolled along the shore. She was no older than nine years of age, with a long summer dress that swayed with the chaotic pattern of the wind. Her light brown hair fell past her shoulders and danced to the same tune as her dress.

He leapt from his ledge, taking a tumble as he gained his footing along the sand.

He cried out to her, but she did not respond. Was she just like him, lost and desperate to survive? Perhaps they could be a team, solving their problems together.

The young girl turned her head and gave him a knowing smile. As he cried out again, she drifted away like the wind carrying the fog out to sea. It was over as quickly as it came. Once more, he was alone on the beach.

The only way out is through.

He said this to calm his panicked mind. Nothing would be normal again.

The only way out is through.

Elena awoke to vague darkness, grains of sand trickling between her fingers. She heard calm waves sweep up just below her feet and pull back.

Her eyes adjusted, and she saw the seaweed left behind in the wake of the washing waves.

Elena could not tell how late it was or how long she had been unconscious. She could only tell time by how dry and cracked her lips had become.

Her back ached dully, though she couldn't tell if it was from falling or resting on it for too long in a contorted pose.

The next sight dismissed all that she felt. The sight of an alien sky blanketed the world above her.

As she lay on her back, looking up at the night sky, she saw a display incomparable to anything she had seen on Earth. Elena had studied astronomy in school and had found the night sky fascinating as she stared up at the stars on camping trips or in the grassy field behind her home. She certainly had never memorized all the constellations, but there were at least several that she could spot after a moment of orienting herself.

Still, she could tell right away that this was a different sky than her own.

First, it had two moons. One was immense, bright, and bold, and hung prominently like the night belonged to it. Nothing could move unless this moon willed it.

Below the large moon was a second, smaller one. This one, Elena guessed, must be closer to this planet than the larger sibling as it sailed across the sky as quick as clouds on a windy day. It was also dark. Even though this moon was full, it was a dark gray, as though sitting and waiting in the shadows of a dim alley.

The starry sky beyond the moons presented a sheet on which the moon lay. Stars were always certainly chaotic and random in their placement as they scattered across the sky, yet these stars were different.

There were more speckles of light above her now than she'd ever seen. They congregated into immense clusters, each edge thinning out just to join another as though they all had joined hands. This, along with the various colors illuminating the night sky, brought character and personality. The sky was alive and smiling back. Elena could live another thousand years and see nothing as stunning as the light show in front of her.

She pulled herself up into a sitting position and examined the surrounding area.

The ocean near the shore, and the radiant fish that swam within it, had a pulsating quality, as though the fish together were a life on its own with a beating heart.

It was too much. The scene around her was more than she could take in, more than her mind could comprehend. She felt like she had stumbled into a secret world made for people more privileged than herself. An outdoor palace. An area that anyone else would have paid their entire life's savings to experience.

It was then that the wonderful sense of freedom filled her chest, pushing out an uncontrollable laugh. She was free of Jude. No longer did she need to give in to his blackmail and the hold he had on her life.

She should feel panic, trapped within a world where she knew little, if anything at all. Instead, she felt the liberties he had removed from her take root once more.

That was why she had leapt through the rabbit hole. Not to find Simon, but to find anything else.

Fear and anxiety would come soon enough, but for that time, she would focus on the positive. She'd have plenty of time for regret and despair. Elena was free of Jude and everything that had plagued her back home.

But soon idle thought brought torment, and anxiety poked through.

No. She decided she would not panic. Maybe sometime soon, but she'd stave it off as long as she could.

She pulled back from the water but immediately realized she was up against a cave wall. If she were to hug the wall and go far enough back, she would disappear into a shadow that held more mystery than moonlight. She pulled away from the cave, still several yards back from the sweeping waves, and curled up in a tight ball in the light of the brilliant moon.

The despair she had just pushed away came back, pulsating like the glow of the waves. It was there, in the space of the least unknown, that she dismissed her restraint and wept.

She wanted to go back to the positive thoughts that filled her with such glee, though the world around her was very real and she would likely die here.

Where am I? I can't be on Earth. This sky is not my sky. Will I ever get home?

She knew she wouldn't sleep. If she closed her eyes out of exhaustion, one moment later she would jump awake at the sound of an unknown creature in the cave. Perhaps it would just be a crab. Perhaps it could be something else. Something worse.

Maybe this was hell. Hell, to Elena, would be something as uncontrollable as this. A dark room with levers just out of grasp. How could she build a sense of control there? There was nothing to hold on to, nothing she could predict. The sky itself had changed.

As if reading her thoughts and fears, a low rumble shook the water. The waves that had just been so gentle rushed up against her and hurled her back against the cave wall. Her head thudded against the stone, and searing pain painted colorful light in her head.

Engulfed in water, she searched desperately for air. She found it and gasped in panic. She felt the cave arc just above her head. She was grateful the stone hadn't knocked her unconscious and fearful that another gust of water would leave little room for survival.

As swiftly as the water had rushed in, it receded. The current pulled at her, threatening to take her out to sea. When she felt the ground beneath her, she thrust her feet into the sand, a desperate plea for resistance against opposing forces. As if coming to her aid, the current pulled her past a large rock buried securely in the ground.

She grabbed on desperately. The water raced past her and out to sea. Dancing along with the receding water, she saw a familiar red playing card, the Queen of Hearts.

"No," she said, a plea to the world around her. "That's mine."

She didn't know why the card meant so much to her. It was a reminder of the other world, the one she had left. The one she had tossed away. Why did she care so much?

She let go of the rock that kept her anchored and swam with all her might.

The water calmed, and she realized it wasn't deep at all. She stood in the shallow water and ran in the direction where she saw the card float. Though it had disappeared. The night sky had hidden it from her. She hunted, unsure why she cared so much for something so simple.

It was gone.

She staggered back to the beach, fell to the sand, and cried.

The glowing fish scurried back into their regular rhythm, and as she sat with the breeze against her cheeks, her fears escalated to panic.

Suddenly, every sound she heard left her fearful for her life. She didn't know this world, and she was wrong to think this would be better than staying with Jude.

Movement came from the water. At first she leapt up, thinking the water would turn to a flood once more. Then she saw it was a large gurgle from a single source.

Elena hoped it was a docile animal, like a dolphin, although she knew that wouldn't be the case. Whatever it was, she hoped it wouldn't harm her. She told herself that not every bump in the night was evil. Not everything wanted to hurt her. There was life here, though. That much was clear already from the fish she saw earlier, but she was confident it didn't stop there. She felt life surround her, and it was unsettling. She heard the clicking of animals against the cave stones behind her and more gurgling from the water in front of her.

Elena sat sandwiched between two unknown threats, the cave and the ocean. To maintain sanity, she thought of all the animals back at home that would make noises but also not hurt her. Rabbits. Squirrels. Deer. Even coyotes weren't a threat to her. It was probably the same here. That howl she just heard could easily belong to a creature that would run skittishly from her if they met face to face.

As though detecting her fears, a shadow the size of a rat scurried past her feet, and she pulled herself back in a shriek.

She curled up and wept whispered tears, struggling for her cries to go unheard by the bumps in the night. She shivered, though she was not cold.

FIVE

S TELLAMARIS HOVERED JUST ABOVE the ground, crouching in the tall grass. A tall and skilled Cassinian hunter, she willed her skin to shift its hue to its familiar greenish blue form, camouflaged within the surrounding vegetation. At twenty-five years of age, her jet-black hair had not yet received its gray streaks. She bundled it up in a warrior braid, too tight to loosen during her hunt.

Wind from the valley below raced up the face of the steep hill, skimming the summit where she waited. Part of a repeated cadence. The trees rustled above her and then grew silent as the gust of wind settled to a calm.

She loved the hunt. Even as she progressed into her leadership role as the King-Daughter, she insisted on continuing it. It felt appropriate to her that a leader should provide her people with food, instead of commanding others to do so. Certainly, no one would fault her for delegating the job to others, since there were many tasks to be done in the Laniakea Warrior Tribe. Still, there was symbolism in feeding her people, and no one could hold her back from the thrill of chasing something designed to be faster than her.

All was visible from her location, staring down at the valley, including the vernagrande. Since they traveled in packs, they were easy to spot and therefore perfect for hunting. The only challenge was to get as close to them as possible, close enough to make an effective kill without being noticed.

They were a particular challenge to catch, which only added to the excitement. The position of their eyes and ears paired with the circular form in which they congregated made an effortless task of finding predators and alerting the rest of the pack to flee. Still, if she only caught a few, she could provide several meals for her village. The challenge wasn't to catch them off guard, but to get close enough to pick off the slower ones while the others ran away. This was just as it should be, since the slower ones were often the oldest, naturally sparing the youngest to grow old themselves.

When she was only a nah'air, not yet twelve years of age, the older Laniakea warriors trained her to fight using the game of the hunt. It was a thrill she had waited years for, often not getting over two hours of sleep the night before each hunt.

Often, the students would see how close they could get to the vernagrande before they ran off. Some did not to return for an entire day.

A nah'air student would get one point if they touched a vernagrande and two points for mounting. Only those who graduated to hunter in their later years would make the kill, separating the skill and respect of the hunt from childish fun.

While the point system was static, nah'airs would make it dynamic by racing against one another. The young nah'airs who couldn't even reach a vernagrande could only hope to place bets on who would get the closest. Students that finally touched a vernagrande would challenge their peers to see how many more they could touch before the entire pack had fled. This would at least factor into the point system, since touching multiple vernagrande would accumulate multiple points.

The older nah'airs could eventually mount the vernagrande. The challenge amongst peers was to see how long they could stay on as the beasts bucked wildly.

This was where the point system broke free from the personal challenges. If a student only cared about points, then the simpler feat would be to touch as many as they could. A teenage nah'air could easily gather five points using this method, whereas mounting a vernagrande was much more difficult a task but would only result in two points.

If a nah'air were to mount a vernagrande and stay mounted for longer than ten seconds, the other nah'airs would hold them in high regard, despite taking home fewer points.

The issues with the point system had been a subject of debate amongst Stellamaris's people, but the Laniakea ultimately kept it in place because of the various lessons a student could learn by thinking it through and making a distinct choice between reward and respect.

One summer many years ago, Lane had mounted a vernagrande and continued to ride it into the crevice between the cliffs. The other children hoisted him on their shoulders and shouted his name to celebrate the new Laniakea record. King Semian awarded him first pick of the meat at the nightly dinner, sitting him at the table of honor at the grand feast.

Perhaps that day should have been a foretelling of the man he would become. That day, Lane chose honor over reward, and ironically, or perhaps appropriately, received his reward.

That day was about the hunt. It was about food and providing for her people.

Stellamaris lay crouched amongst the grass, the familiar pattern of the wind flying through her hair. As she waited, she took careful note of the way the trees at the base of the cliff moved. The wind had a pattern to it, changing slowly enough to be counted on like the swaying of a pendulum. As the trees finished their dance several spans along the incline, the brush swayed next. The pattern continued up the mountain until finally it again reached the trees above her head. It was the repeated verse to a song that made the summit its refrain.

She took her position, gripping her spear in her right hand, placing one foot behind her, waiting, ready for the pattern to repeat.

At the moment the trees rustled at the base of the hill, she whispered "go" and began her light-footed dash downward. Gravity took over, and she allowed it. It was the same routine that her father had taught her in her youth.

"Like a sharp knife into bread," he would say, "it is better to let the weight and sharpness of the blade carry you through the cut than to push out of impatience and deform the bread."

Silent and swift, she closed the distance down the hill. The moment the vernagrande noticed her, it was too late for them. There were at least one hundred animals, and though they fled, she could readily pick off three in the stampede that trampled away.

Without losing the momentum of her descent, she hurled the spear at the largest of the pack, hitting her target directly in the meat of its side. It fell to the ground, where it remained. She allowed her legs to carry her into the pack itself, joining them as though she were one of their own as they trampled away. A hidden assassin amongst the crowd. With her right hand now free, she pulled the sword from its home against her back. With a swift rotation of her body, she swung the sword at a second vernagrande and watched it fall. Still running in and amongst the pack, she grabbed hold of a third by the neck and took to mounting it. Stable atop the third vernagrande, she pulled the dagger from her belt and finished the job with swift and humane accuracy.

As the beast fell, she hopped off and watched the other animals flee. With her remaining time, she could gather an additional two as they ran by. Although she only needed three, and that was all she took. It was not right to take more, since it would reduce the numbers and the meat would spoil. If she was greedy and thoughtless, it would hurt both the vernagrande and her people. No one would benefit.

She slowed her run to a jog and then to a walk as she panted, trying to catch her breath. Returning her blades to their home, she collected her spear and pulled all three fallen animals to one pile, where she could prepare to take them home.

In a small, hidden area between the cliffs, she brought out the carriage she had planted there ahead of her hunt. She gently grabbed hold of the althorse's rein. The massive creature towered above her but was submissive by nature. As she extended her hand, it complied by lowering its head so that she could take hold of the rein and lead both it and the carriage over to the fallen animals.

When they had reached the vernagrande, she unclipped the carriage and allowed the back end to lower to the ground, making it easier to load the meat.

As she pulled the second animal onto the carriage, she heard the clumsy footsteps of a man struggling to find his breath as he entered the valley from the steep hill.

"We really need to schedule who has the mountain on which days," said the runner, hands resting above his head to open his lungs.

"Ilgene?" Stellamaris said. It was a pleasant surprise as a smile painted her face from cheek to cheek.

"I'll let you take these, but in three days' time, I'll need the mountain," Ilgene said, smirking. His breath had escaped him as he bent over and sat down on a log.

She laughed at the poor display of jest. "Are you sure you can take three? You scare them off."

Ilgene pointed a finger at her as he spoke. "That was a bad day. Your trick with the wind. I tried it, and the wind wasn't right. I don't even think Semian could pull that off."

She shook her head, loading the animals into the cart. "You said that the time before last as well."

Ilgene shrugged. "It's been a terrible month for wind."

Stellamaris stopped and set aside the animal to examine her friend more carefully. "Is that a war blade?" The familiar smile of a friend ready to volley teases at her companion graced her mouth.

"It's my backup. I, um, I lost my hunting blade."

"You lost it?" She pretended to look shocked.

"It's up there." Ilgene gestured up the mountain. "Somewhere up there, at least. I just need to look for it."

"How long has it been missing?"

"About a week," he said. Stellamaris didn't think he meant to, but his skin tone shifted from its calm blue and green hue to a fiery red and orange. For Ilgene, this was a tell that he was lying. The people of Cassini shifted their skin tone often. Sometimes it was intentional, but it commonly happened out of reflex, like a facial contortion after a rude comment or an amusing joke. Though some individuals could change into multiple color combinations, most people on this end of the continent shifted between the red and orange combination and the blue and green.

"A week?" As though to synchronize with Ilgene, Stellamaris also turned red and orange. Her change was also unintentional, but for her it was out of anger.

"I'll find it today. Now that I'm out here and unable to hunt, I might as well." Her anger subsided slightly, though her color remained. This seemed like the least he could do. "Oh, and by the way, King Semian is looking for you."

"And why is that?" she asked, returning to her task of preparing the fallen animals for travel.

"We found a small boy. He doesn't look like he's from a tribe we're familiar with. He doesn't look like any of us, but he has the unchanging skin of your father. The boy calls himself Jude. The king has tasked you with handling him."

She casually acknowledged Ilgene's statement as she hoisted the vernagrande onto the cart. "Tell me more about this boy."

"Well, like I said, it doesn't seem like he's from any of the neighboring tribes. To add to that, he's in hysterics. He just keeps ranting on about his home. It was the most work we've done in two weeks getting him into some clean clothes and fed. The clothes he was wearing were tight and restrictive. With his stumpy build, I'd be curious what title or duty he held back home. I'd venture to guess it was that of an intellectual or other form of thought worker. Yet he didn't appear outwardly intelligent. Perhaps his tribe is dull-witted. I'm also not sure if anyone's tried bathing him. It's surely something everyone wants done, given his stench, but goodness knows who is brave enough to do it. What do you plan to do?"

She wasn't sure. She'd likely spend the entire trip home coming up with a plan. None of this was apparent from her demeanor.

"We've already given him his necessities, but it sounds like he needs one more," she said.

"And what is that?"

"Time."

Elena spent the night without sleep. Her muscles ached as though activated the entire night, holding tense.

The sun slowly rose and exposed the cave wall, shedding light on the mystery that had teased her in the darkness. She could see everything that was hidden the night before. Small crustaceans scurried about, finding food and hiding it.

She scanned the cave in the new light that day had brought. Or rather, she had assumed it was a cave, but, in fact, it was not a cave at all. Her beach was a small inset cove, and a charming one at that. She could sprint the entire distance without stopping to catch her breath. She might need to do just that to keep up on exercise, assuming this would be her home for the foreseeable future.

The wall curved up above her new beach home to create a half dome made up of ashen stone. She scanned the dome, trying to locate the spot where the flood had carried her the night before. The dome rose so high above her head that the flood couldn't possibly have carried her up to the top. Instead, she saw a litter of shelves, which she had likely confused for such a ceiling in the dim light of the moon.

The wall was fairly smooth and framed the entire cove until it disappeared into a dark passageway cluttered with a scattered collection of rocks. The assembly of the stones suggested that a cave-in had happened here, although it was not apparent if it were recent or long ago. She could explore that area more, but that would need to happen at a different time. There was much more to this beach, and most of it was much better lit and with fewer hazards than the passageway. She made a mental note to come back to it later. Maybe there was a way out down that passageway, but without the beach explored, any direction was equal parts promising and perilous.

Out in the sunlight, she found her spirits higher than she would have expected. There was surely a demon in her mind wrestling to get free and drive her to insanity if she let it, but for now the light of the new day left her hopeful.

The breeze cooled her cheeks and presented a welcome contrast to the warm sand. As she walked out from the shade of the half dome, the sunlight was not nearly as warm as she would have predicted. Elena would have expected a steady heat that would toast her skin, but the sun in this world was less obnoxious. It warmed the air to a comfortable temperature, and though she would undoubtedly get a burn at some point, she didn't expect this sun would toast her soon.

Now equipped with newfound energy, she felt it was time to saunter into the water. She kicked off her shoes and rolled her loose-fit pants up above her knees. As she entered the water, she shuffled her feet to let the local creatures that made their home in the sand know that she was coming.

The glowing fish had left. Apparently, they were night creatures, or they flocked to a new home during the day. She saw a few small fish that could have been the same ones, but they gave off no glow. The number of fish was also far less, though she saw the occasional crab emerge from the sand to dart ahead and hide beneath a rock. The night before had millions of fish, and this morning presented only a random friend each minute.

Several small fish jutted out through the sand and danced about, splashing before her as though begging her to play. They swirled around each other as though in busy laughter, leaves caught in the wind.

Elena laughed as a rollercoaster of emotions flooded her. She had survived the night and was now in active play with her own pets. The tug of war between fright and joy was like a drug, stretching her psyche to newfound lengths.

Elena turned and looked back at the half dome. While it was still the same shape from her original perspective underneath it, she could now see that it was the base of a very tall cliff. The stone wall ventured to such high altitudes, they seemed to kiss the clouds. It was both awe-inspiring and dizzying to look at. It made her new home seem like an insignificant part of a greater world. Birds flew and made homes just halfway up the wall's face. She could see that there was a top but could not make out details.

Her half dome appeared to be close to the end of a land formation, as though marking the end of a continent before the endless ocean took over. There was an area on the right of her beach where the cliff wall ascended just briefly over the half dome. Its height paled compared to the giant on the left. The opposite end curved out into the water, forming a small inlet just for her.

She paused, absorbing the surrounding scene. A foot deep in water and in no hurry, she allowed the moment to stretch out. She had worried about this new situation the entire night. Her brain hadn't yet thoroughly rested. Elena let her mental walls fall lazily to her side, taking several deep breaths and allowing her mind to fall into restfulness as she stared at the cove and the cliff wall. The wind brushed against her cheeks, with the water lapping against her legs as it danced in the breeze. The tide ebbed and flowed against the shore, depositing new sand and pulling back the old.

The moment didn't last long, but she enjoyed it and made a mental note to do it regularly. If she could survive long enough to find a way home, she'd need to have a strategy for staying calm. She wasn't yet sure what that strategy would be, but taking those breaks would certainly be part of it. They needn't be long, but they could be. Knowing her own mind allowed her the confidence that she wouldn't fall into laziness. She pursued survival in whatever way that might entail. Her weapon of will would need to be sharpened regularly, and she decided moments like this would be how she would do it.

She turned back and continued to wander farther out to sea. If there was a decline, she didn't notice it. The water itself was clear enough to see every small stone by her toes. The sand was pure white, with a scattering of dark black rocks the size of a coin and just as smooth.

She had traveled far enough out that details of her home along the beach shrank to resemble city streets below a skyscraper. If the water were any deeper, this would cause for concern. As it stood, she felt no pull of current and no risk to venturing out farther.

Suddenly, the sand gave way beneath her feet and she plunged into the water.

The surrounding water was abruptly darker than before. This was the shelf to her inlet, and it apparently had weak edges. The water flooded through her nose and mouth as she gasped for air, bobbing up and down along the surface.

She suppressed panic. The frantic struggle of her arms allowed her to stay afloat as she pulled herself together and scanned her brain to develop a semblance of a strategy.

What could she do? How could she get back onto the sand shelf?

From here, the beach looked so much farther away. The current wasn't strong enough to be a threat, since she did not seem to move much from her focal point along the beach, though there was *some* undercurrent causing a slight drift out to sea.

She recalled the sense of calm she had reached earlier and took in several deep breaths. There was no ground beneath her. At least not that she could feel. The depth could be ten feet or a thousand. By the sudden contrasting darkness of the water, she assumed it was closer to the latter.

As the cloud of sand around her subsided, she noticed small fish were swimming busily around her. Fish on their own didn't bother her, but it reminded her of the life that existed here. If she were swimming in a familiar beach on Earth, she could assume with some probability that there wasn't a shark beneath her feet. This world was strange to her, and she was strange to it, and so she could not calculate any such safety.

She swam toward the beach and found the shallow sand again. This time it was at the level of her chest. It resembled the side of a pool, which she would normally hoist herself up on. The difference here was that the sand was much less secure, as she had earlier experienced.

Elena attempted to secure herself on the crest of the sand. It gave way, and a rush of sand clouded the water once more. More panic flooded in.

She focused on the cliff and tried not to submit to what was brewing inside her. After a few deep breaths, she swam parallel with the crest until she found another area that was firmer to hold on to.

Immediately, another current picked her up with such speed that she did not need to swim, nor would swimming do any good. To her surprise, it pulled her closer to the beach, but to the right corner. Soon she could feel the ground beneath her. Instead of the white sand she had felt before, this was stronger, like a riverbed.

The current led her closer to the edge of the half dome near the end of the land formation itself. She stretched to grab hold of a rock and repositioned herself as the current led her closer to the security of her beach.

She corrected herself as she came closer. Ahead of her, she could see that the current did not lead to the beach itself, but instead around the half dome and into a dark cave. If she missed the rock, the water would rush her into the darkness of that cave.

She pushed her legs on the floor to propel herself closer to the rocks as she situated her arms to grab hold. In a few breaths, the current guided her near the stone as she lunged forward, attempting to find purchase. To her dismay, she felt her hands slip. The rocks left her grasp as the water led her toward the cave with too much force to resist.

She turned and saw the darkness of the cave approach. She dug her feet into the ground to gain traction, but the current was too strong to counter. Entering the darkness, she could see nothing as the water forced her around corners as she ping-ponged between cave walls. The only sound was the rushing of the water against the enclosed canal she was now in.

The panic she had pushed away for so long now flooded her mind. Elena sobbed uncontrollably, using the little air she had access to as water lapped across her face, mocking her. Images of her family raced through her mind, dancing from frame to frame.

Never in her wildest fantasies would she ever have thought this was how she would die. Her family would live the rest of their days without closure, hoping for the best but assuming the worst. Only Elena would truly know how she died. Her death would orphan these last moments along the cove.

As she turned the last corner, she finally saw a light emerge, though the water only rushed past it and not into it. The light meant hope, or something resembling it. From what she could tell, it was another beach. The opening before her was only six feet wide.

She had only an instant to act. With the additional source of light, she quickly found the opposite end of the canal and positioned her legs against the wall, ready to hurl herself at the sandbank. As it approached, she pushed off with her legs with all the strength available.

Half her body landed on the sand and the rest dangled in the water. She hoisted the rest of her body onto the dry sand, using the edge of the entrance to secure herself.

She lay there with no thought but pure joy. An uncontrollable howl that aggregated every emotion she had built up burrowed through her chest and out through her mouth. It was a giddy mixture of excitement and relief that married laughter with tears as she rolled through the sand. In that moment, she had won. Death was a faceless beast that would fear her and let her be.

SIX

Unsure of what she would do when she saw the boy, Stellamaris slowed her pace as she entered the village. The Laniakea received visitors from the neighboring villages often. They were partners in trade with almost everyone, save the Drominion. Though there was diversity in language, there wasn't much in outward appearance. Her father was the only one she knew of that looked the way Ilgene described this boy, and King Semian was originally from the other end of the sea. Her father said little about the village that raised him, save for tales of fabricated cliffs and birds ridden by men, masters of flight.

Still, her father never elaborated on how he got here. As a young girl, she had always assumed his boat had a giant sail. She was confident people capable of constructing a mountain must also be capable of building a sail massive enough to carry them across the sea. But if they made one, why not make ten more? And if ten more existed, why weren't there more people that looked like him that had made a similar journey?

Yes, this was quite an opportunity indeed. The tales her father kept private could finally be verified through the tale of someone else.

She pulled back the door to the round hut where the boy was resting and entered. She looked him over, examining him as he lay asleep. He assuredly warranted the commotion he had caused, and Ilgene's description was accurate. The boy's body type was indeed stumpy, like her father. Similarly, his skin tone was the shade of dry sand along the coastline and appeared to be just as rough. Her father had pushed past the limitations of his body to become one of the most threatening forces of the Laniakea, with wits worthy of his title as king.

She saw the boy still had some weight along his sides, suggesting that he had not kept up his physical form as well as King Semian. If his intelligence truly was lacking, Ilgene's assessment that he was neither thought worker nor physical worker was likely accurate. Like Ilgene, she wasn't sure where to place him. Perhaps he was a street vendor or made ale.

He wore the light, draping fabric of her people, which, she recalled, they had dressed him in shortly after he arrived.

She idly felt the thickness of the cloth, wondering if the clothes belonged to her father.

At that moment, she caught herself gazing at him for too long and standing too close. She found herself close enough to sense his nervousness, though he slept. It radiated from him as though his dreams released a stench.

She examined the hut to make sure it was suitable for a foreign guest under their care. It had two beds with a washbasin in the center. Its standard circular architecture and wooden frame gave it strength to hold up against harsh wind and rain. It was on the smaller side, but a single visitor needed little. That there were two beds meant that there were no single-bedded huts, like Ilgene's, available.

The boy woke with a jolt and backed away suddenly. This was her fault. He must have thought she was a threat.

"My apologies, child," she said. "I am Stellamaris, King-Daughter of the Laniakea, which is the village you are currently in. I represent King Semian, who wishes he could be here himself."

He shook. Stellamaris's words did not calm him. Rather, he sat terrified as though the specters of the Rambling Forest were present in this hut.

He trembled as though someone had thrown him into a winter storm. "I don't know where I am. They found me after I went through a blue light, or whatever that was. How do I get home?"

The boy's confused words rattled Stellamaris, but she immediately shrugged them off. "Yes, that is something I was hoping to talk to you about. Perhaps if we found out more about where you were from and how you got here, then we can help you return."

She had an ulterior motive. If she could find out more about where he was from, then perhaps she could find out more about her father's birthplace as well. Though, with every passing moment, he seemed to sink deeper into despair. "I don't know where I am. I went through a blue light and—"

The boy stopped, and she thought he might cry. Instead of tears, he bit his lip and shook his head, annoyed at something, though she did not know what.

She shouldn't have pushed him. She should have assessed him further and helped him calm down before diving into such troubling topics.

"Why don't we start over? You are our guest, and you will want for nothing. We will hold a welcome dinner. Would you like that?"

"I've already eaten." The odor of his nerves lightened, and his body shook just a little less.

"Certainly you've eaten, but I have not properly hosted you. We have our harvest festival in a month's time. I'm sure we have enough food, drink, and games stored up to present a proper celebration for our new guest. Through such a celebration you'll find that you have nothing to fear here."

He relaxed his shoulders and approached her at the side of the bed.

"How do you people understand me?" He asked. "You're a...I mean, you're from far away. Or *I'm* from far away. We shouldn't be able to understand each other."

Stellamaris let the question settle into place. It wasn't a rude question, but it surprised her to hear it. She had known that her little corner of Cassini was unique, but she didn't know the extent.

"We understand you because of our history, and we can speak back to you in your tongue for that same reason. We've learned to adapt because we've needed to."

She stopped there, unsure about how much more to say to someone in his state. Taking a moment to observe his reaction, she assessed whether he was curious for more or if this would be enough of an answer. She was more interested in understanding him as a being. As an entity. Would he demand a better answer? She could never hope to give him what he needed unless she understood him for what he was.

It seemed enough for now, since he said nothing in response. Rather, he seemed to dismiss the topic entirely, lying back down in his bed.

"What is your name?" she asked, though she already knew from Ilgene. She wanted him to give it freely.

"Jude."

"Well, Jude, it makes sense that you're scared. I need you to understand that you are safe and that I will get you back home."

He stirred once more. "How will you? It's not possible. It's not even possible that I'm here."

This amused her. Rare as it was for her people to travel across the sea, it was unquestionably possible. The king certainly had. She'd get him home.

She stood and dusted off her legs. "Well, you are my guest here, and you are under my care." She leaned forward and looked him in the eyes. "I will get you to where you need to be."

She smiled at him, sensing that was what he needed. The odor of his nerves lessened further but was still present. It was a small step, but it worked and would have to do for now. That's how she would handle this. Small steps.

The largest round hut in the village belonged to King Semian, and Stellamaris did not need to slow her stride as she entered.

The guards at the door knew the King-Daughter well, having broken bread with her many times.

Semian looked up, grinning at her from the small tablet the councilman presented to him. The king wore casual robes and not his formal attire, which he normally wore when meeting with the council. However, he had a small design inked below his left eye, displaying a small bird, a type she didn't recognize.

Many of the townspeople would mark themselves with temporary drawings depending on their style and mood. Often the markings would illustrate animals, but it was also common to display fire, landmarks, and weaponry on various parts of the body. For reasons she didn't know, the king chose strange animals and objects she had never seen.

"My beauty," her father said with bright eyes. "What brings you here today?"

"The boy, actually. He's called Jude. Have you met with him?"

"Oh, briefly," Semian said, dismissing the councilman. "He is, in fact, our guest. But I must admit other matters claimed my attention, and I have had little time to give to the poor soul. I am pleased that you, it seems, have met with him. I was actually hoping you could take to figuring out what he's about and how we can help him."

"Yes, actually—"

"I know you are busy as well, and please accept my apology for passing him off on you. With our new guest, I'd prefer that we send the message not only that we welcome him, but also that the village leadership is personally taking on the responsibility of assuring his comfort."

Stellamaris smiled with her eyes. She loved the warm side of her father, showing such consideration for his guests. There was no such custom that he needed to keep. Rather, his consideration for his people and guests was his own. He was a kind soul. She enjoyed it when he taught it as a conscious and earnest effort, as he did to Stellamaris.

"Of course, Pietro." Pietro was a term of endearment she used for him occasionally. This time, it was intentional and not out of habit. He loved her using that term instead of Father, since it was something often used by young children. As an adult, her use of this caused this great king to lower any barrier as he imagined her as the small girl he raised. To him it meant *I will grow beyond, but I will never grow past. I will never part from you.*

"What am I thinking?" her father continued. "It is in your nature to care for these guests, as it is in your soul to care for your people. You will be a great queen one day, with that heart of yours. Still, if you sow your compassion and motherly love too broadly, it will destroy you."

She smirked. "It's a reflex, I guess."

"And reflexes can kill you without the proper training. You must delegate your love and allow others to tend to these guests. Do that, or the anxiety of being a queen one day will kill you." He took her hand and sat with her along the padded chairs that surrounded the table centered in the hut. "So, what have you learned from him?"

"He seems confused and worried. Which, I must admit, isn't much of a mystery. I'm sure anyone at his age unintentionally far from home would have the same worry."

"You believe he's far from home?"

Stellamaris was more than taken aback by this. It was plain to see that the boy was from far away.

"He must be, not looking like any of us. He only really looks like you, if I may be so blunt."

Her father tilted his head and smiled to himself. He looked at his daughter with strangely welcoming eyes, as though she had finally arrived to meet him at a place he had reached long before, patiently waiting. He was always a mysterious man, but this look was unusually difficult to interpret.

"Yes," he said. "I noticed that as well."

"It seems to me he must be from far over the Poor Man's Sea. Farther than any town we've visited. If I were the type to gamble, I'd venture that he came from an area not that dissimilar from your hometown."

Stellamaris examined Semian, studying any slight movements in his face to pull the information out of him. His past was something she was always curious about. He shared everything he owned, and perhaps that was why this one exception left her so mystified.

"If he is from beyond the sea, then there is little we can do. At least, not now. We cannot send him back in our boats, since they are too small and we cannot afford to lose the guide that we would need to send with him. This will be an excellent test for you, I think. It has all the markings of a good problem for you to solve, not having previously been accomplished by an elder and requiring resources we do not have. Yes, I think this problem is perfect for our future leader."

"My King," said the councilman, reentering.

"Yes, yes," Semian said, signaling for the man to come in. "I'm sorry, my beauty, but I must get back to work. Please keep me informed, though. And tell the boy that it pains my soul not to be more present with him."

"Yes, Pietro."

SEVEN

A DISTANT MEMORY, FOGGY but still present, disrupted Edgar's sleep.

His parents were happy and beautiful, and his brother belly-laughed at them overcooking their cake for the fourth time.

His mother examined the cake, which could hardly deserve that title. "I think the problem is it's not rising."

A quick glance from his father, back and forth between his lovely bride and the blackened disk that he could have confused for a pancake, confirmed her suspicions with a grin.

They started over from scratch, this time adding more eggs. He took the whisk and began once more.

She took it back from him. "Here, like this." But she never meant it as instruction. It was flirtation, both raw and familiar.

He held her hand as they both rocked side to side to music that wasn't playing.

Simon sat locked in, transfixed as he relished every moment as though it were cool lemonade on a summer day.

Edgar recognized all this. He was dreaming and somehow knew it.

If he wanted, he could will himself to fly or perform acrobatics across the room, which he could easily transform into a circus tent. After all, it was a dream and he could control it.

He didn't, though. He didn't want to. Instead, he stared at his brother as his brother stared at his parents.

The busy-minded Simon was calm. He didn't have a plan that he needed to act on, as he normally did, nor did he fidget with his fingers as an outlet during idle time.

These certainly weren't negative traits. Simon was Simon, and that was all there was to it.

Still, the serene face before him interested Edgar. There was no bottled-up energy needling its way out. Where did it go?

Edgar knew, though. He also knew back then, when this event actually happened.

Something had calmed the thrashing waters of the busy sea. The energy didn't disappear, but it was more directed as he stared with a wide smile at his parents' happiness. They were happy *with* each other, as though it were a mutual gift.

There were many forms of love. Euphoria was the beginning, though it laced itself throughout, ever present, though not always constant. It didn't owe anyone consistency.

Then there was the unsettled feeling of walking on a rickety bridge, unsure of what was going to happen.

There was the uncomfortable growth, creating new skin to shed the old.

And last, the worn and comfortable shoes that fit so well, you'd keep them on forever. Though they may wear thin with age, torn along the seams, you'd plead with gods and demons for another year. Please.

Perhaps what they witnessed now was euphoria. Edgar knew it wasn't all there was.

But it was all there was for them.

Edgar awoke upon his ledge, although he couldn't remember falling asleep. He welcomed the warmth of the sun, though he could do without its brightness. Sunglasses would be nice, but he'd take normalcy any way he could find it. At that moment, with the fog of sleep wearing off, he desired the aroma of a brewing pot and the sound of Ben Friar humming one of his many tunes from the kitchen.

The beach was how he had left it the night before, though he could see more in the light of day. Calm waves brushed along the sand and then receded. Out along the horizon, he saw more detail of the mystic cliffs off the coast. Grassy vegetation capped the summit, leaving only steep walls of stone with distinct sections and shelves scattered about the face. The sections were like granite towers that must have clashed together thousands of years ago. Each was tall enough to extend beyond the height birds would fly. He was sure there was someone alive who could climb it, but he hadn't met that person. If he ever did, they'd be an athlete that would put their life on the line to attain their goal.

He turned around and examined the cliffs behind him. In the light, they looked different than the island cliffs off the coast, though they still resembled granite, as he had thought the night before. These were darker and more compact than their island cousin. When he looked closer, he could see occasional streaks of copper race up the face of the cliffs, as though an artist painted them in.

The sound of movement in the water, distinct from the washing waves, broke into his admiration. The head of a sea creature bobbed briefly above the surface and then sank back down before he had time to make out its shape. A moment later, the same movement occurred with the same vague shape several yards away from the first.

Edgar carefully climbed down from his resting spot to examine closer. The creature bobbed once more, and Edgar saw it did not resemble any sea creature he had seen before. It had the head of a bird. A crane, perhaps. It also became apparent that there were multiple birds. More of its brethren leapt out of the water until a flock of at least three dozen were present and in motion, bobbing along the coast, in and out of the water.

As the flock grew, the distance between them and Edgar lessened. As they proceeded to shallower waters, their heads broke from the surface completely, displaying long, black necks with gills below their beaks.

The color drained from Edgar's face as he realized they weren't swimming. Swimming would have confined them to the water. Rather, the flock migrated out of the water and onto the dry land of the beach toward Edgar.

He ran in a sweat-filled panic. As he looked back, he saw the birds were fully on dry land, their bodies rapidly expanding as they shook off the water, puffing out their feathers. As they gained on him, their bodies were like large, bulbous pillows held up by long twigs for legs.

It did not take long at all for the birds to gain speed, their webbed feet padding in a sprint along the sand. Soon they were inches behind Edgar. He couldn't bank, slow his pace, or leap out of the way for fear of being trampled. The flock had swallowed him in full sprint.

To his surprise, these birds did not attack him. The first one passed him by as though he were not even there. Another did the same. Only a moment passed before he found himself amongst the flock, running as though they were all part of the same race.

His panic drained into a fit of laughter as he glided across the sand with the alien birds. This was historic. Edgar Brave was the first human to discover alien life, initially with the fish the night before and now with enormous birds as they danced along the coast. He let the adrenaline rush through his mind as he threw his head back and yelled with glee.

As he lowered his head, he saw a new creature rise out of the water farther up the coast in the direction they were running. This time, the creature was slow and subtle. He looked human in form, his skin a dark shade of blue, and he draped a blanket of seaweed over his shoulders and head to blend in with the plant life along the coast.

He extended a long spear above himself and swiftly launched it at the bird directly in front of him.

The bird fell lifeless to the ground, and in shock, Edgar fell with it. The flock dispersed in various modes of transport. Some took to the air, their tremendous wings violently flapping. Others dashed back to the water from where they came. Edgar lay next to his new friend, now a victim.

Edgar waited quietly, unsure if he should move. As the man in the water slowly marched out to the dry sand, Edgar slid back into the shadows of the cliff wall. He hid out of instinct, though he did not think he had eluded the hunter.

"*Mah'cal leh mudinai,*" said the hunter, his voice echoing off the cliffs. Edgar was pleased to see that the man was acting friendly to him, but the situation was still confusing. The hunter extended his arms outward as though he were ready to embrace an old friend. "*Shahlah, mal tuce?*"

Still shaking from his nerves, Edgar did not respond.

"*Tuco?*" The man had stopped several feet from Edgar, hands on his hips. His eyes looked as though he were trying to solve a puzzle. He stood tall enough to block the sun with broad shoulders, massive enough to hold two Edgars on either side. "*Tuco*, now me follow?"

Edgar recognized a few of those words, and apparently the man saw it in his face, because he threw up his hands in cele-bration.

"*Closer tahl gather.*" He turned back for another try. "This going?"

Edgar nodded in approval. The man was clearly delighted but tried to hold down his enthusiasm as he attempted once more.

"How about this?"

Edgar gave a timid nod and let the word slip out in a whisper. "Yes."

The man exploded in a cheer, his laughter loud enough to bottle and sell as fireworks. He was far less reserved than Edgar and not at all worried about scaring him off.

"Yes, yes, the boy says." He threw his hands up in the air as though he were praising the sun. "I think I got the hang of it now, if I say so myself."

The clarity in the man's speech gave Edgar a visible shock. "How did you do that?"

The man, still excited, crouched down to speak to Edgar at eye level. "Boy. May I call you Boy?"

Edgar nodded in the man's shadow, finding it difficult to insist on anything else.

"My people have a long history with language. It's actually not really a gift with *language* as much as it is a gift with the senses. You give off your language like an odor. And that's actually a good comparison, because you stink. You stink very much."

Edgar smirked in mock offense. "Well, you're certainly polite."

"Thank you." The man accepted the apparent compliment, missing the sarcasm. "My name is Mahla, of the Laniakea. It is wonderful to meet you. Come, stand with me."

Mahla helped him to his feet, and Edgar shook the sand from his pants. Edgar could now more clearly see the man that held up the seaweed cloak. He was still large, but a different large than he would see on Earth. His deep blue skin looked as though he had caked on pastel chalk powder. The various shades of blue drifted off to teal and green in the edges along his hands, feet, and cheekbones. Occasionally, when Mahla got excited, his skin would shift to red, fading to yellow. The frame of his body was also larger than a standard human's. It was difficult to tell if he was from a large race of people or if Mahla was large for his kind. His black mop of hair lay tangled as he discarded his seaweed cap. It was not long, but it was also not well kept, since he shook sand and water from his scalp.

"Now, boy," Mahla said, putting his hands on Edgar's shoulders.

"My name is Edgar, by the way." Edgar felt his voice squeak as though he were a mouse held in the grip of Mahla's palm.

"Ah, yes, thank you, Edgar. That is your name. You're certainly polite." He wasn't sure if Mahla returned his apparent compliment or if Mahla had adapted to his sarcasm.

"Edgar, how long has it been since you ate?"

Edgar let out a depressed chuckle like a week-old balloon. "A very long time."

"We need to get you fed and, unquestionably, washed. Have I mentioned you stink?"

"Well, yes, just five seconds ago."

"Edgar boy, I spent an hour crouched down in the water covered in seaweed."

"Well yes, I mean..."

"And you're the one giving off a stench."

"Okay, I understand."

"There's a reason the birds thought you were one of them."

"Mahla, yes, I'd love a bath. And food. Thank you."

"Wonderful." The man threw up his arms and let out a laugh rooted deep within his barrel-sized belly. "But I have one rule."

"Yes?"

"You carry the bird."

EIGHT

E LENA DIDN'T KNOW SHE had fallen asleep until she awoke. Now, as the sunlight tugged her eyelids open, a cocktail of emotions flooded in.

She was thankful that she had survived the near drowning, but she was now in a completely new place that needed exploring.

Elena looked around and saw she was now in a cave, not another beach, as she had assumed. In fact, the only body of water was the narrow entrance she had come in through. This would be ideal for protection from the elements, but she now lacked all the necessities that the beach provided. There was no apparent food or drinkable water, and she had no way out aside from the violent waters that had carried her here. Her new cave had all the safety of a prison cell.

Elena's heart raced as pinpricks raced up her arms and panic settled into her hurried breathing. She'd hardly survive on the cove, and now her chances waned with every passing moment.

She remembered her spot along the water, which had calmed her earlier. She closed her eyes and slowed her breath, imagining the birds in flight and the domed cliffs of her beach. With every breath, her heartbeat slowed, and she regained control.

There was no time for this demon. The puzzle before her was her very own survival, and panic would do only harm.

She gathered her wits and opened her eyes once more.

Down at her feet, water rushed past her heels. She stood and stretched. This place was a new mystery, a hidden palace she was unexpectedly eager to rummage through. In fact, it was in the rummaging, she decided, that she would solve the puzzle of her escape.

The cave itself was cylindrical and wide. White sand blanketed the ground. The wall climbed at an inward slant, the height of a two-story home, with a wide opening at the top. There was no roof. Instead, the sun illuminated the cave through a circular opening, slightly smaller than the diameter of the ground, the wall narrowing evenly as it approached the natural skylight.

She looked down at the water near her feet. No observable life was present, neither fish nor plants. She gave credit to the ocean fish. They either powered through the current that had caught her or avoided it altogether.

Something else caught her attention about the water. As she poked her head out through the opening, the hurried water was quieter to the right than it was to the left. But the sound on her left was almost deafening. Perhaps it was a waterfall. If that were true, she'd do best to find another way out.

As she stepped away, she heard a rattle from across her colosseum-shaped home. A small set of stones moved and then resettled back into place as though they were uncomfortable.

She squinted and gently approached. As she did so, a modest creature emerged.

At first Elena was frightened. She wasn't the type to trust animals, even back home. Here, she did not know what would eat her and what would leave her be. Hoping that a domestic cat would emerge to purr by her feet was out of the question. But where on the spectrum would this land? Still, sandwiched between the rushing river and the animal before her, she was cautiously optimistic, an improvement from the night before.

A large frog emerged, or so it seemed. It stood on hind legs and stalked around with purpose. Its green torso was lean with tight skin, rather than the loose-fitting slime-leather worn by the frogs she knew. The frog's height was modest, stopping only barely above her knees. Its arms and legs were thin, like that of a human, but with no discernable biceps or calves. It was a puppet made real.

As it moved, reshuffling the rocks, it acted as though a dominant force had tasked it to do it. Neither snow nor gloom of night would prevent this creature from completing its job.

Given its focus, she felt comfortable approaching. She borrowed each inch of space she took, not sure when the frog would want it back.

This did not bother the frog or even distract it. It continued on with his accounting, diligent as ever.

After some time, Elena closed enough distance to touch it if she felt so compelled, which she did not. Still, the animal seemed disinterested.

Instead, the frog decided that the stone behind Elena was the one it wanted. Without pause, the determined accountant reached between her ankles and plucked the stone from the ground. Elena let out a scream as though a spring in her heart had coiled and then sprung. She scrambled to the opposite end of her colosseum home.

Unflappably, the frog continued.

Calming her nerves and noting that the frog did not actually do anything harmful, Elena approached once again. A foot away, the creature stopped, let out a sigh of frustration, and looked up at Elena.

She suppressed a gasp. This was the first sign of awareness from the animal. Stalemated between curiosity and fear, she did nothing.

With several elongated breaths, neither animal nor girl made any sort of movement. The frog sighed again. This time it submitted to its frustration as though it were a tax it would grudgingly pay and continued to rearrange the rocks.

Elena watched.

A pattern emerged. It targeted particular rocks stuck in the cave wall, only ones that it deemed worthy. It plucked them out and assembled a pile of loose stones and then repeated it. The pile grew with each repetition.

It did this for twenty more minutes. Then, without breaking stride, it trotted to a small, rabbit-sized hole and released a high-pitched, crackling howl, startling Elena into covering her ears.

A long line of smaller frogs funneled out of the hole.

If Elena's scream earlier had been loud, this new scream was hysterical. She dashed to the opposite end near the water.

The creatures each picked up a rock from the pile and scurried toward her. She screamed a third time and darted out of the way as the frogs ran past. There were hundreds of them.

She gathered her wits.

The frogs were not jumping into the water as they went through the cave mouth. Instead, they promptly climbed the wall of the corridor and funneled out. Elena poked her head through the cave opening and saw each creature trotting along a small ledge.

She hadn't noticed it earlier. The ledge was five inches deep and positioned near the height of her waist. It appeared rough enough for her to grip with her fingers if she needed to.

As the last frogling, as she now called them, escaped from her colosseum, the original animal approached her, holding the remaining stone. It placed the last stone in front of her as though in payment for the burden.

The frog waited, as though expecting a receipt. If it had tapped its foot in impatience, it wouldn't surprise her in the slightest. Finally, it sighed to itself, and climbed out along the ledge, following the others.

She picked up the rock, confused yet mildly entertained.

As she examined it, she saw a shimmering hue. It was like gold back home. No, closer to amber. She kept it, though she didn't know what for. If these creatures found value in it, then she would too. At least she would give them the benefit of the doubt that it might hold some value. If there was nothing beyond the sentimental, it would serve as a reminder of this event. She wasn't sure if she considered *the event* to be the incident with the froglings or her traveling across the universe, but she left that thought alone for now and placed the stone in her pocket.

She turned back to the corridor with new focus and examined the ledge once again. It appeared to have all the strength and grip she needed to help her climb back to the beach.

This discovery meant a great deal to her. It was a way back to her home along the cove. The beach had fish, which she could catch. Her colosseum cave provided protection from the elements. With a bridge between the two, she could survive until the seasons changed. She didn't know what would happen after that, but this ledge gave her something to hold on to in more ways than one.

Now that she knew a way to get back to her beach, she temporarily focused her attention on the sand trapped between her skin and clothes. Try as she might, she could not seem to brush the granules free from her wet skin. Over the last two days, her skin had become sore from the abrasion, and she worried about how much of a role cleanliness would play in the long term.

The problem of hunger was more pressing, but she shelved it for the time being, seeing as she now had a ledge to use. The problem of hunger would be a puzzle worth solving once she reached her beach and those glowing fish. At least while the sun shone through the skylight, presenting a heat source, she could solve the problem of cleanliness.

She couldn't submerge herself for fear of being swept down the dark corridor, though the rushing water proved itself useful for washing debris loose from her skin and clothes.

She eventually developed a system for staying clean. She moved several medium-sized rocks from their settlement along the perimeter to the center of the colosseum. With the sun in the two o'clock position, she had enough heat gathered along the rocks to act as a drying spot for her clothes. She placed each article of clothing in the rushing water and let the current do the work of loosening the sand from the fabric. Once satisfied, she wrung out the excess water and carried each piece to the rocks, laying it flat in the sunlight.

She dangled her limbs and head in the water, refreshed. As for the rest of her body, a sponge bath would have to do. She didn't have a sponge, but she could cup her hands to gather enough water to splash away the excess dirt. She was as close as she could ever hope to being clean.

Elena pulled her clothes back on, though they weren't completely dry. If her plan worked, she'd soon be back on her beach. With the current position of the sun, her half-dome along the beach would be bathed in sunlight once she arrived. Damp clothes upon her back would be pleasant against the heat of the sun.

She peered down the corridor toward the beach and examined the ridge that the froglings had filed out on. She tested it, proving to herself that it would give her enough grip and strength to climb out. It needed to. Thankfully, there wasn't any moss to make it slippery, or at least none that she could see from within the cave.

She just needed a spot for her feet. The distance was far, too far to take it on without support. She saw no options above the water, but six inches below the surface, she found a rock embedded in the wall.

A wave of determination flooded in.

"I'm just going to do it."

What did she have to lose? It wasn't confidence, necessarily. Confidence was something that came later, after she had proved it to herself. This was more of a decided ignorance. The fear of the waterfall crept in from time to time, but she always swept it aside. The thought of death was a prisoner in her psyche, guarded by her strength of will. If she did this successfully, she would release death and name it. But she wasn't there yet.

She placed both hands on the ridge and extended her first foot out onto the stone. Carefully, her remaining foot left the safety of the colosseum and joined its twin on the rock.

"Okay, I've done it."

She shook away the realization that she was now in much more danger than she was seconds ago. Danger, she decided, was waiting to die in her colosseum shelter.

Cautiously, she repositioned her right foot, taking over the burden of support, and extended her left foot, hoping to find another similar stone. There was an inset in place of the expected stone. That would have to do.

She shifted her weight once more to her left foot and shimmied to the inset.

She slipped.

The momentum caused her hands to lose grip, and she plunged into the water.

Without thinking, she pushed with her legs off the wall as the current pulled her back toward her cave. Desperately, she bent her knees and placed her feet behind her, lunging forward and into the colosseum entrance.

Though this should have frustrated her, she settled on a laugh.

She had failed her first attempt, but this was still good news. She had survived the current twice and now had a routine for survival. The risk of the waterfall was less now than before.

She continued with more determination. As time went by, her muscles and hands grew increasingly sore. Blood and bruises covered her arms and legs. Still, she did not yield.

The light in the colosseum weakened, and nightfall was imminent.

Each attempt brought her closer to her beach. She had memorized the foot placements and the areas along the ridge that required special maneuvers to keep from falling.

As the sun slipping beneath the water and the beach in view, she pushed forward through shaking limbs. Her fingers and toes were numb and no longer obeyed. They worked, though, enough to take one more step, followed by another.

Finally, she could see, in the dim light of the beach, a giant stone, massive and flat enough for seals to lie upon. It was just out of reach. With her final ounce of energy, she leapt for it but once she landed slid inelegantly back. She refused, kicking and grasping to hold on to anything. Her hand grabbed something, but she didn't see what. She pulled on it, her muscles screaming, pleading for rest.

And then she felt it, the lack of movement. The lack of slipping. She was on flat stone.

A smile leapt to her face, and she gazed at the most gratifying sunset she had ever witnessed. It was a view that would have been wondrous to experience as a gift. Here, however, she had earned it. It was hers.

NINE

IT WAS A GOOD day for Ilgene, as rare an occurrence as that was. Not only was the old man happy with him for finding the strange boy, a thrill too embarrassing to admit, but he had also located his favorite cloak for the celebratory dinner that night.

The dinner alone was a reason to call this day good. The feeling of merriment and ale filling his belly made him look forward to nights like these. They hadn't removed the Harvest Festival in favor of this night, either. The dinner was a bonus. With his luck, he'd end up seated either at the head table or directly next to the food. He would have welcomed either.

The new boy was odd. He went by Jude. Ilgene had to admit that he hadn't expected him. He was used to picking up travelers, but Jude was an unexpected and delightful surprise.

The old man had told him to keep most travelers a secret. Jude was an exciting change. He could tell everyone about the young lad, and he proudly did just that. Moments like these gave him a thrill, and his only outlet was to tell everyone he saw. Though as regretful as it made him, he had already told everyone. He even told the Lady Stellamaris, and she wasn't even in town when he found the boy.

A familiar bellowing voice shook his front door. There were many deep and loud voices in the warrior tribe of the Laniakea, but this one was distinct.

Mahla.

Ilgene flung open his door and ran to go see his close friend. Well, frankly, they weren't close. He wasn't particularly a friend, either. More accurately, he was the only person in town that hadn't heard this gossip about the boy. For this, Ilgene was gleeful.

If Mahla's unabashed singsong howls didn't reveal his direction, the cloud of dirt he kicked up when he walked would. The immense cloud surrounded the titan, who seemed not to care. Instead, he belted out Laniakean drinking songs as if he were already around the table with his fellow warriors and hunters.

"Mahla, you'll never believe—"

The sight of another small boy cut Ilgene short as the dust settled. The child stood by Mahla's side. He felt discontent, akin to finding a soiled cloak balled up in the corner after delivering all the dirty clothes to the washing crew.

"Oh," Ilgene said. "You found one, too."

The two men exchanged looks, Mahla in blissful ignorance and Ilgene with the expression of someone who had dropped his food in the dirt.

"Well, he'll need to get ready for the dinner."

"Dinner," said Mahla to Edgar, his voice reverberating through the trees, shaking the flaps of the huts that lined the road. "I was just telling you about dinner. It's fantastic here, you'll see, boy, you'll see. You'll get to have some sooner than expected, it seems. The sun is shining bright today, my boy, in more ways than one."

The statement came with an eager pat on the back, nearly causing Edgar to fall over. Edgar favored his balance at the cost of dropping the bird hoisted over his shoulders. Though it was all for naught, since the momentum of the falling bird pulled Edgar down with it.

As he stood, the familiar jolt of pain struck his teeth. Could Alister be near? He scanned the surrounding trees for signs of the whistling man but saw none. Bushes rustled and shadows danced, but none distinct enough to stand out from the others.

"Ah, don't worry, boy," said Mahla as he looked down at the bird in the dirt with troubled eyes. His voice took on a consoling tone that Edgar could tell he wasn't used to. "This bird has gotten into a lot worse things than it can find rolling in the dirt. I can tell you stories that will make you want to release your insides, but seeing as you'll be eating that thing for dinner, I'll save you the tale."

"That would explain the stench," said Ilgene.

"No, no, that's the boy," said Mahla with no intention of hiding his statement from Edgar. "This boy is a man that smells greater than the dung of a thousand vernagrande." Mahla redirected his attention back to Edgar, who couldn't help but lower his head sheepishly. "In the middle of the summer, mind you. When the heat of the sun makes the dung smell most disgusting."

"Oh yes, that must be his people's way," said Ilgene. "We found another of his kind and could not remedy him after several baths."

"There's another one?" Edgar asked. "Someone like me?"

"Oh, yes. He's back there in that corner hut."

Edgar left little time for the man to finish. His legs, still weak from travel, carried him up the center of town along the dirt road to the hut, leaving Ilgene and Mahla behind. He threw open the door without knocking and saw Jude splashing water on his face from a large bowl. Jude's shock was like Edgar's but in certain ways much different. While the sight of his long-lost traveling companion animated Edgar, Jude stood perplexed as though he needed to solve the problem of *how* before he could enjoy the old friend in front of him. Still, the two boys had one thing in common. They were both eager for answers after days of only questions.

"Edgar," Jude said. "You're alive? How did you get here?"

"Long story. I can't believe you're alive."

"Where are we?" Jude oscillated between happiness and panic. "How did we get here? What is this place?"

"I know as much as you. I spent the night on the beach. Wait, I arrived just now. I should ask you all the questions. Who are these people?"

"They're actually okay. They've been nice to me so far, but we'll see. It takes a while to get past how weird they look. I've been wanting to talk to someone about it. I needed to catch myself getting startled when one of them changes color after using the toilet-thing they have here. They turn such weird colors and boy are they tall!"

"Yeah, I know what you mean. I met one. Well, I guess I met two."

The door opened, cutting their reunion short. Edgar watched a woman enter, towering a foot above him. She wore a kind, soft smile, carrying her shoulders high with confidence. If it weren't for her inviting eyes, she'd intimidate him. Despite her being an entirely new race that he was only recently familiar with, he noticed both her elegance and beauty. Without her saying a word, he felt at home immediately after she entered. It had been a long time since he saw his mother and even longer since he saw her as the wonderful person she once was. Perhaps the woman before him was who a mother ought to be. A mother from storybooks that would mend your wounds, feeding you graham crackers and milk when you came home crying from a hurt knee.

"My name is Stellamaris," said the woman. "I am the King-Daughter of the Laniakea. This village is my home."

Edgar felt he should bow, and so he started to, though Jude nudged him back up. After an awkward exchange with Jude, he said, "My name is Edgar."

"That is a good name, Edgar. Your friend Jude has been our guest since last night, and like him, you are welcome to stay with us as long as you'd like."

He couldn't help the smile that nudged its way out. "I can't thank you enough."

"There is no need. You may share this hut with your friend. We can draw you a bath, and you can use this area to prepare for the welcoming dinner tonight."

"A welcoming dinner?" Edgar looked at Jude in disbelief.

She raised her hand to calm his excitement, a brief grin flickering. "It's fine, really. You came at a good time, in fact. We have been preparing for the Harvest Festival, and we gathered too much food and drink for only one event. It would go to waste otherwise. I should thank you for the excuse you gave us."

An overwhelming flood of warmth covered him. This morning he had thought he would die on the beach, baking in the sun, plagued by thirst and hunger. Now he was to prepare for a feast. "This is incredible. When that man picked me up...do you know Mahla?"

Her face changed from inviting to casual laughter. "Yes, yes, I know Mahla. Everyone knows Mahla. How could you not?"

"I got to hear him speak your language. Or at least I think it was. He seemed to run through a few different languages."

"Well, I'm sure that was exciting if you had never witnessed it before. What did he say? Do you remember?"

"Actually, I do. He said...something...it was *Mah'cal leh mudinai*."

This caused her to her break her strong, formal stance and instead laugh instinctively into her palm.

"He..." she said, shaking her head in disapproval as she collected herself. "He shouldn't have said that to a young boy."

"Oh."

"I'm afraid I'll need to apologize for several things you'll likely hear come out of his mouth for the entirety of your stay here. Particularly now that he knows your language."

"I'm hard to offend. I'm sure it will be fine."

"Well, Edgar. It was nice to meet you. I'll leave you two to continue catching up. I'll see you tonight."

She left the room, shutting the door quietly behind her.

Edgar approached Jude, looking for someone to share his excitement. "Can you believe this? I'm just happy to be alive, and here we are, taken in by a town gracious enough to host a feast in our honor."

Jude looked significantly more bothered than Edgar. "I wouldn't call any of this luck. Luck would be if we were still at home. Your brother wouldn't be missing if you were lucky. As it stands, we're on an alien planet with no way home, and now we're forced to socialize like polite robots."

"They don't need to feed us, but they are. They could have left us out there to die, fending for ourselves. And what do you mean by polite robots?"

"Have you heard how they talk? It's so formal. I'm sure if I don't talk like them, they'll find something rude in what I say. Honestly, if I could, I'd just take the food and come back to the hut. People back on Earth were always getting mad when I spoke my mind. What happens here if I speak honestly about what I'm thinking? They're so primitive, they'll probably chop my hands off."

"You're crazy."

Jude shot to his feet, delivering an icy stare. "Don't call me crazy."

Jude's statement and scowl brought a thickness to the air around them and made Edgar want to leave the room just moments after being reunited with his companion.

Edgar didn't want to start a fight after all that he had to be grateful for. He just wanted to enjoy that moment. "Fine. Fine, you're not crazy. I don't think we have anything to worry about, though. I'm serious. It'll just be a really pleasant dinner."

Jude relaxed his shoulders, and silence hung between them for a moment before Jude broke it, turning quizzically to Edgar. "Who's Mahla?"

TEN

THE SETTING SUN INVITED a dim veil over the town as the festivities began. The townspeople treated Edgar and Jude like royalty. Small bars of soap sat along their bathtubs like an arrangement of pastries at a French bakery. Buckets of water rotated, one at a time, through a fire pit in the room's corner, filling the bathhouse with a consistent cloud of steam, creating droplets along Edgar's cheeks.

For a fleeting moment, he forgot entirely about his brother and their predicament. The worry of the whistling man, Alister, and his trip across the universe floated away as easily as clouds on a windy day.

Jude was another matter. He enjoyed the same rewards as Edgar, but through stony eyes, neither eager to return home nor frantic at the unknown world surrounding him. When their hosts brought him more water to heat his bath, he glanced at them as though it were an act of nature rather than a kindness. An included benefit of his stay, which they promised him and he must have already paid for. He was never rude to them, like a spoiled prince scolding the staff when the water wasn't the perfect temperature, but there was no smile in his eyes at their generosity. It would be easier to compare him to a rock than any living thing. A deer would be skittish and a dog would be loving. Jude simply existed and nothing more.

As they changed into their robes, music and laughter seeped through the vents separating the walls from the ceiling. They laced their sandals and pulled back the door, releasing the cloud behind them and accepting cool air into their lungs.

Jugglers, magicians, and showmen entertained patrons as they walked along the dirt path that led all the village to this festival.

Edgar still longed for the normalcy of his home, but the inviting liveliness of the town and its people made him wish parts of his own home were like this place.

The town was littered with people meandering along dirt paths that cut the place into rounded sections of grass. Huts of wood bound with rope lined the perimeter, with their roofs ascending to a point. The locals themselves gathered into small groups as they walked toward the festivities, but a quick wave from a friend would cause the younger ones to run ahead and join another flock.

As they strolled along the central road, following the wandering crowd, the musicians came into view. There were stringed oval drums played like guitars, immense blocks of metal that vibrated with every strike of a hammer, and long wooden flutes ranging in size and shape. Edgar eyed a performer who held an instrument resembling a teardrop expanded to the size of his body and made of polished wood. The musician secured the base of the tear between his knees as he sat and blew into an opening. He made a show of madly striking various parts of the teardrop with one hand while the other changed notes by depressing buttons along the side.

A tall and slender woman sang in the center of the band with no need for amplification. Her words flew from her toes up and out through her lips as though she were a conduit for a trapped banshee that would pull you in if you stared too long.

Kyel and his Wondress
Alive they may be
Well, life is what life is
But that's no life for me

Twin stars in mist
Green oceans glow clear
They whisper in secret
Expecting you'll hear

The path that you walk now
The past of the true
The beaten, forgotten
The meek and the few

The twin tides, they're locked
The footsteps, the lore
All that's forgotten
Forgotten no more

"That song," Edgar said, nudging Jude. "I've heard that song before. Or at least that last bit. My foster father used to sing it back home."

Jude shrugged, not nearly as interested as Edgar was. "Ah well. Must be a popular song." He maintained his disinterest as he pushed his way through the crowd.

"How do they know it out here?"

The town itself lay in a valley by a lake framed by the same granite that he observed on the moving island. However, these large cliff walls tilted at slight angles, forming a bowl with their valley at its base. The dizzying height of the cliffs became more pronounced as they stretched to the sky. These rocks could touch the moon if they wanted. He stood where he was for a long time, neck sore from his frozen upward gaze. He wished he could stay trapped in this moment.

Filling the space between the rocks were families of grand redwoods. At least that's the name he assigned to them. As far as he could tell, these were a different species than the redwoods that he knew. Why would they be any similar this far from home? Still, they appeared so, and they finally made him feel like he was back home in that one sliver of time.

At the center of the valley was a modest lake. The water was serene, seemingly unconnected to any larger source such as a waterfall or the great ocean from which he had come. If he looked close enough, he could make out small ripples washing up against dark sand, small enough to be caused by the scurrying of tiny fish.

Tall grass separated the lake from their eating area, though it did not grow unruly. At roughly the height of his knee, the blades of grass faded from olive to silver. The grass swayed in the same calm motion as the rippling water near the sand as it brushed the wind that kissed his cheeks.

Fire danced along torches on tall pikes surrounding the eating area. Young children ran past them to play in the center of a series of tables. Each table seemed fairly well constructed, considering their lack of machinery or advanced tools. No two tables were completely alike, but they all looked as though the same builder had made them. Each was a long slab of rust-colored wood, sanded neatly and covered in a glaze that made them elegantly smooth.

There was no order to the seating, so Edgar took the first table he could find, and Jude followed.

"You look funny!" A young girl whose voice was more pronounced than her size, roughly his own age, cut into the melodic tune of the band as she plunked down across from him. She was short, with a round, blue face and black hair that extended just past her shoulders. She squinted at him curiously, like a toddler exploring the world. "Are you funny?"

Edgar didn't know what to say and looked to Jude for help. Jude had none to give.

"Not funny-*looking*, I mean," she said, to clear up any confusion. "Although you are. But in this case, I mean funny as in different. Possibly hilarious, but not necessarily. Did you know we've only seen one person with your build and complexion? He's our king, actually. It's actually a peculiar story, if you want to hear it."

"You're wondering if I'm funny or you're noting that I'm different?"

"Yes to both. You look like you could tell a good joke. You could tell by the way you wear your eyes."

"My eyes?"

She nodded. "You know how if you look at your eyes, it looks like you're incredibly nervous?" She looked at Jude for confirmation. "Do you see that too?"

"Yes," said Jude. The two of them nodded at each other.

"Your eyes look like you're constantly trying to get comfortable and doing a really horrible job of it. Anyway, I've met people like you, and they're usually hilarious. The best jokes, those guys."

She slapped her hands on the table, laughing at a joke that must have been replaying in her head. Jude laughed along with her, but he directed his laughter at Edgar, acknowledging the awkwardness of the situation as it finally broke his stony face.

"What's going on?" Edgar said. "Why am I funny? What about Jude?"

"Hi, Jude," the girl said, shaking his hand. "I'm Ahletta, but people call me Letty."

"Hi, Letty," said Jude.

"Anyway," said Letty. "Back to those eyes."

Her eyes widened in excitement at something behind them. She threw her hand up in a wave.

"Mr. Crisp. Hello, Mr. Crisp. Over here. Why did you look at me and then look away? Mr. Crisp, I found a table for us. I know you can hear me. Over here."

She pulled her arm back down with a satisfied grin. "Great, he heard me. He's coming. Good old Mr. Crisp. Always up for a laugh."

"Hello, Ahletta," said Mr. Crisp. As Edgar turned, he saw an old, stern man of Edgar's height. In a world where the local people were slightly taller than humans, matching Edgar's height made him short. He was overweight, but not by much. He might consider Mr. Crisp to have a normal build if not for the warriors that populated this town. A small creature stood on all fours beside the old man. It resembled a medium-sized dog, except its fur, which was mostly black, swayed lazily through the air, refracting light like it had fireflies for fleas. The dog-creature panted and wore a permanent smile.

Ahletta extended her index finger at the old man. "Call me Letty, remember?"

"You don't like Ahletta?" asked Mr. Crisp.

Her eyes narrowed in mild frustration. "No, Mr. Crisp. I prefer Letty."

"Oh." Mr. Crisp paused, unsure how to proceed, until he looked up at the two boys. "Can you introduce me to your friends here?"

"Ah yes, this is Jude and this is..." Letty stopped, her inward dialog creeping onto her face again as she scrambled to remember his name. "I, well, I don't think we've introduced ourselves yet."

"I'm Edgar."

"Hello there, Edgar. My name is Letty, and this is Mr. Crisp." She paused for a moment and then glared down at the creature at Mr. Crisp's legs. "And this is Dog Thing."

"Her name is Becca," snapped Mr. Crisp.

"She doesn't look like a Becca," said Letty.

"She certainly doesn't look like a *Dog Thing*."

"Actually, she does."

Jude nodded again, repeating the only gesture he seemed comfortable with that night.

"I'm done here. Come on, Becca." Crisp marched away with his dog in tow.

Letty, seemingly unaffected by all of this, turned back to the two boys. "Would you like some ale?"

The two boys exchanged approving smiles. They couldn't drink back home, though it was common for a teenager to sneak stolen alcohol out into the neighboring forest. Here, there appeared to be no issue with teenagers drinking.

"Allow me," said a man standing next to Mahla as the two flanked the table. With the town filled with warriors and vendors, both Mahla and the stranger were obviously the former. Though that commonality was where it stopped. While Mahla was a giant of his own breed, with tousled hair, the stranger kept his appearance neat and wore a brightly colored cloak, free from the wrinkles that littered Mahla's clothing. With his formal attire, Edgar would have placed him as Stellamaris's husband, if it hadn't been for the next thing he saw. A woman, the same age as the stranger and just as attractive, approached with a goblet in one hand, extending the other to hold the stranger by the biceps. A small boy tagged closely along the draped dress of the woman. The child possessed the face of the woman but the deep, dark hair of the man.

"My name is Lane. This is my wife, Karian, and Laneson is my boy. Don't worry, you won't need to remember any of that."

"Ha! I'll try to remember, but yeah, I'll probably forget," said Edgar.

"What is this?" Jude asked.

Edgar sipped the amber drink before him and pulled back at the bitterness. At his age, he only had a couple of experiences with alcohol and so had little to compare with. The quality was likely high, judging by the quality of everything else at the party, and he was certain that an educated drinker would detect an ocean breeze and the nectar from local fruits sown into the beverage. But to Edgar it was simply bitter and that was all.

"That's just ale," Lane asked. "Do you not have ale across the sea?"

"Oh no, we do," said Jude. "Ours is just different."

"This is super generous," said Edgar. "Thank you. Really."

"Well, there will be plenty tonight," said Mahla. He sat down next to the boys, causing the table to lift at the opposite end. "Lane's the leader of King Semian's army." He looked up at Lane and pointed at Edgar. "I found the funny one along the beach."

Ahletta cut in. "See?"

Mahla gestured at Jude. "Ilgene found this one out amongst the trees, hiding from a small woodland creature."

Edgar's ears perked up. "He did? I never heard this story."

Jude receded back in his seat with a scowl. "It's really not that interesting."

"No, don't sell yourself short," said Mahla. "It's very interesting. If I were you, I'd be telling the entire town how incredibly powerful such a small animal could be."

Lane seemed to be the only one sensing the awkward tension and cut in. "Mahla, leave the boys be. They're obviously uncomfortable."

Mahla looked at the two boys as though he were trying to make out the answer to a puzzle. "Awkward?" he said below his breath.

"Boys," Lane continued, "if you need anything at all during your stay, let us know. We're in the third hut over as you enter the village. Karian makes a crescent oakalberry pie that has made her famous."

"It would be more famous if you didn't always eat it before I could share it," Karian said, releasing a flirtatious smile toward her husband. "But he's giving you excellent advice. If you want for anything, you come to my hut. I'll not have guests go hungry in my lady's village."

"Lady?" asked Edgar. "I thought it was the king's village."

"She's speaking of the King-Daughter, Stellamaris," Mahla said. "It's our king's village, and we would die for him. But we would live for our lady."

"Come, friends," said Lane. "Let's leave these kids to their ways. We'll have plenty of time for lively discussion."

The adults and the small boy walked off, mingling with the congregating guests. The two boys took deep gulps of their ale, reacting harshly at first and then with a smile at the bite.

"If you like that," Ahletta said, "you need to see what I have for you."

The entire night was like free entry into a county fair. The jugglers, magicians, and band members took turns entertaining the guests while the others joined the party on their breaks.

King Semian entered, eventually. Although his presence commanded attention, there was no formal announcement. Still, every head turned as he strolled in.

There were two characteristics of the king that distinguished him from the rest of the Laniakea. The first was his unmistakable confidence as he greeted each person and stared into their eyes with a warm grin, reciting their name.

The second characteristic made the two boys share a silence amongst the roaring crowd. He was like them. Edgar had heard this muttered amongst the locals, but it was indisputable. This man looked more like a large, well-built human than he looked like the Laniakea. Was he human? Did they have humans on this planet?

The king made his way slowly to the center of the festivities. Someone gave him a glass of wine, and Semian accepted it with an affectionate nod and a thank-you. He lifted his arms, and the crowd immediately quieted.

"I'll be brief. We all know you'd all prefer to continue your conversations and merrymaking." The crowd laughed as though being cued to do so. "But I'd be remiss if I didn't say how happy I am to invite, not one, but two new guests to our town. The Laniakea and its allies are very familiar with one another. It's rare that we get such travelers. Surely we must talk soon about what partnerships we can put into place with your people. We have a rich and fruitful land. Each kingdom in our trade agreement has their goods and talents. In fact, the rich treats and ale you enjoy are from our neighbors in Kalagora. I am overjoyed at the possibilities that a partnership could bring." He spoke more in their native tongue, and several townspeople who had been struggling to understand him earlier nodded.

Frequently throughout his speech, the king directed his attention toward the two boys, placing them as the acknowledged guests of honor. Occasionally he would look amongst his people, either soliciting for their agreement at what he had just said or looking for laughter after a joke.

"And that's enough of me," King Semian said, closing the floor. "I'll give you back your party." The crowd erupted into applause, a little too eagerly. Some had clearly progressed too swiftly through their drinks. Most were guilty of the same but concealed it better.

King Semian quietly vanished into the crowd like a rogue in the night. Edgar got the strong suspicion that he would not stay to eat.

The two boys had several plates of dinner. They tasted meats with sugary marinade seeping to the bone, beads of doughy treats glazed with sour custard, and flowery fruits that he swore were smiling back at him. There was enough to go around for many more celebrations, and the boys took full advantage.

It wasn't long before Edgar's stomach turned. He looked over at Jude, who had a lost and vague expression.

There was dancing occurring in the center space between the tables, but the boys did not partake. They'd had plenty of social time earlier in the night, but as their stomachs turned, so too did their eagerness to move about. Suddenly, their best course of action was to sit perfectly still. As he looked along the tables at the empty glasses of ale, he doubted his pains were solely from his full belly.

Stellamaris approached and sat down next to them, leaving Edgar with flushed cheeks and shamed eyes. He'd had this feeling once before in front of Susan Friar when he and Simon had found her wine bottles.

"How are you two boys coming along?" Stellamaris asked.

"This is amazing," Edgar said, intending to be cautious but failing. "This whole thing. I just can't believe I spent last night asleep on the beach. Actually, a rock. Actually, both."

She laughed, which to Edgar either meant she didn't disapprove or didn't recognize what he was trying to conceal.

"Yes," said Jude, a little too excited. "This party. Well, it's a party. We need to stop. Well, Edgar does. I could have more. To eat, I mean. But I'll choose not to. For reasons."

Stellamaris turned from laughter to concern. "What are you drinking?"

"It's ale," said Jude. "And it's delicious."

"That's dark. Our ale is amber."

"I had thought it was a stout."

"Are stouts considered ales?" Edgar asked Jude.

Jude looked twice at Edgar and then exaggerated his words. "You're on an alien planet."

"Someone has been having fun with you," said Stellamaris.

"We've been having fun, too." Jude's voice was a loud whisper.

"Come with me, sweet pea," said Stellamaris, collecting the boys. "We'll get you rested. I can't promise you'll feel very good tomorrow."

Stellamaris led them back to their hut and tucked them into their beds. Edgar was confident that the room would soon spin, but for now the only thing that was spinning was his stomach.

"What did we have? The dark ale. You looked like we shouldn't be drinking it."

"Well, you two are children. No one would have given you anything strong tonight. By the looks of things, it appears someone has slipped you a glass of Revenge Ale in jest."

"What's Revenge Ale?" Asked Jude.

"It's a short-term poison. No, don't worry. By the look of things, you've likely only had a glass or two toward the end. Nothing serious. Otherwise, it wouldn't be that funny of a prank, now would it?"

As the two boys settled into their beds, Stellamaris found a spot to sit at the edge of Edgar's bed.

"Revenge Ale has an interesting story behind it. Perhaps it will help distract your bellies to hear the tale. It's about a kingdom plagued by war. One night, they were preparing for what would be their last stand after losing most of their warriors. They knew their foes to be brutal and that they would face fates worse than death if they were to be pulled into servitude. Rather than surrender, the remaining survivors gathered together and marched off to a fight they knew they'd lose. Mind you, this group included the elderly, the sick, the young, and everyone else that the fallen warriors before them swore to protect until they died."

Stellamaris finished tucking them in and sat in a chair in the middle of the room. It felt remarkably reminiscent of a bedtime story.

"But before marching off to their last stand, they poisoned all the ale in their barrels. They knew they'd die, but they also knew the enemy soldiers would loot their town and drink them dry in celebration."

"The poison would kill all the soldiers," Edgar said.

"Yes, exactly. The tribe would die, but so would the invading army."

Fear struck Jude's face. "Are we going to die?"

Stellamaris laughed, but mostly to herself. "Of course not. The story helped name Revenge Ale, but what you just drank won't kill you. You'll be up all night, and I'll recommend now that *when* you throw up, you do it outside. This entire hut will stink worse than an oro fish stew."

"Thank you, King-Daughter." Edgar's voice was just above a whisper.

"You can call me Stellamaris. And it's no trouble."

"For everything, I mean. I don't know how we're going to get home, but..." Edgar drifted off to a half slumber as Stellamaris left the room. Never completely asleep or awake, he listened to the sounds around the hut and the chatter of people walking home. The lullaby of the Laniakea would need to be his only distraction in the night ahead.

ELEVEN

T HE BOYS SURPRISED STELLAMARIS by falling asleep so abruptly, though she would take the win where she could get it. While still convinced that they would not do well that night, she settled on the good news that they were at least asleep for now.

A silhouette emerged from along the trail. "Oh, hello there, King-Daughter," said a familiar voice. "You startled me." The friendly face of Ilgene materialized in the light of the tiki lamps. "I came to check on the boys. Rumor told that they had fallen ill."

Her eyes rolled hard enough to be confused for somersaults, yet she allowed a grin to poke through. "You and your rumors. Yes, that is correct. I'm afraid they've been the target of a practical joke. Someone slipped them a bit of our Revenge Ale."

"Isn't that odd? I haven't seen that concoction used in ages."

"Neither had I. Most of it goes sour after a month, making it far too obvious to be a real joke. I couldn't imagine anyone brewing it for an event such as this. Though with your ear permanently affixed to the ground, I'm surprised you're just now hearing about it."

His skin flashed a red shade as a smirk slipped out. "I may have heard a thing or two. Word gets around. Such is the nature of things."

Stellamaris gave him a nudge, gentle and knowing. "Oh, I'm sure." Her sarcasm was clear. "Anyway, it was nice of you to check on them, even if you are just filling the gossip trough."

He laughed it off. "It's no trouble, really. I had little chance to talk with the new boy, Edgar. I spoke with the other one, but with such commotion I would have liked to speak with the one Mahla found."

"And I'd wager meeting both would complete the set. Too talented, you are. The collector of information. No wonder you're my father's best scout."

"You know me too well, my lady."

"I'm sure they're not good company at the moment. Tomorrow will be better regardless."

He deflated but didn't press. "I suppose you're right. I'm off then. Are you staying up, Lady Stellamaris?"

"Just for a while longer. I want to make sure the boys need for nothing. Besides, my mind is still swimming from the party."

"That's a sign of a remarkable party. I'll be looking forward to the Harvest Festival after this one. Have a pleasant night, King-Daughter."

"Goodnight, Ilgene."

Stellamaris surveyed the grounds as Ilgene wandered off to his hut. The party gradually drifted off to a trickle of citizenry stumbling off to their huts, arms intertwined. This was the case for most. Their exhaustion had lured them to their beds, met with the temptation of a soft pillow and warm blankets. Those who had not retired were the usual folk.

The mind was a curious puzzle. For many, a night of interacting with people would leave them weary and worn down. For others, the social interaction was like spinning a top on its edge. Once their mind raced from social inputs, there would be no stopping it until it suddenly lost its balance and collapsed, hopefully near a bed.

Those spinning tops were the typical few, now settled around the campfire to the east of the dining area. There was Mr. Crisp, awake but quiet, racing in his own mind. Ahletta, Lane, and Mahla joined him, doing all the talking.

There too was the bard, a guest of the town, though she frequented it often. She had come to lead the band with her elegant voice. Now she sat idly around the fire, strumming the strings of her lute.

"It ran thrice the speed of the vernagrande," said Mahla, extending his arms, mimicking a colossal beast. "I never saw it coming until it hovered over me."

"What are you going on about now?" Stellamaris asked, taking a seat on one of the large rocks around the fire.

As she asked this, Edgar startled her, calmly appearing next to her, taking a similar rock at her left. The area around his eyes sagged. He had wrapped his blanket around his shoulders, with his head sunk low.

"That didn't take long," she said.

The words limped out of his mouth. "The room was spinning. It still is, but I'm hoping the fire will help."

Mahla's story did not miss a beat, though he shifted to Edgar's language to be polite. "The Demon in the Water takes many forms. Here, it was a hairless creature that ran on all four legs until it was right up on me. As it stood, it blocked out the light of the moons."

"Both?" Ahletta asked.

"Yes, of course. Its jowls expanding from a small hole in its face until it was an enormous, toothy grin that was ready to eat—"

"It's just that...how would it block out both moons?" Ahletta asked. "It would block out one moon, and then the other would be somewhere else. He could only block out one at a time."

"That's beside the point. It was big enough to block out all the light from the—" Mahla stopped and thought. "Hearing myself, I understand what you're saying. I recall I could see its ferocious grin, which means there was light. Yes, it blocked out one moon. The other must have been somewhere else." He looked over to Ahletta for approval, and she nodded. He smiled back proudly.

"What is this creature?" Edgar asked. His voice was just above a whisper.

Lane turned toward Edgar. "It's a ghost story. It's normally told by small children. I'd bet we're the oldest people even to bring it up."

"The Demon in the Water is more than simple lore, General," said Mahla. "The Wondress herself created it."

The bard leapt to her feet and extended a hand to Edgar. "So sorry, young one, so sorry. I would have introduced myself, except I was deep in music, you see. My name is Elix, as in 'The Elixir of the Khoms.' A great tune, but one for another time."

Edgar slowly extended his hand. She juddered it up and down, delivering a pale color to Edgar's lips.

Ahletta joined in on Mahla's tale, ignoring Elix. "I've seen him as well. He lives off the coast in a glowing underwater cave.

He only comes up on land to feed. Perhaps he hates the taste of fish, the demon he is."

Lane shook his head. "Letty, I'd love to join you on this, but in all the hunting I've done and the battles I've seen, I've discovered nothing like what you two are describing. We've had plenty of opportunity. The war with Aiken and the Drominion has featured many battles at night along the cost line. I've never seen the Demon or the Wondress, despite many opportunities."

"I've seen it," said Mr. Crisp. The group all directed their attention to the old man, who had remained withdrawn until that point. He continued his dead stare into the fire. "The Demon in the Water. I've felt its cool breath against my face. Becca had as well. It leaves a mark, and I don't mean the physical kind. I have an exorbitant amount of respect for you, Lane, leading our forces into battle as often as you have, forfeiting your own well-being so that we may sleep peacefully in our huts. It takes courage and confidence. I've lived to be an old man solely because you have kept this village safe, and for that I owe you a great deal. But I'm sorry, you're wrong on this one."

The silence hung for a moment. Mr. Crisp stood and began walking back to his hut, Becca following close behind without needing to be called.

"I've seen it too," said Edgar. Mr. Crisp paused. "Or the cave, I mean. When I first arrived, I splashed down in the ocean just off the shore. For a moment, I saw a glowing cave under the water. You said he lives in a glowing underwater cave, right? That must have been him." He said this to Mr. Crisp's back. The old man continued to stand there, motionless.

"You've *got* to show this to me," Ahletta said. Mahla nodded in excitement as Lane rolled his eyes at his fellow warrior. When the group looked back at Mr. Crisp, he had left.

"What do you believe, Stellamaris?" asked Edgar.

She looked over at the boy sitting beside her. Surely he was old enough to hear such ghost stories without being frightened. Still, she worried about the impression these tales gave her young guest regarding the safety he'd enjoy here.

"I think it's a delightful story. Mr. Crisp is a very well respected man in this village. He has served us longer than many on the council. However, the mind can play tricks on you. You shouldn't always trust what you see in the dim light of the moons. As for what you saw underwater, there are many such things under the sea. Have you seen our oro fish? They radiate a blue light. I'm sure if you huddled enough together underneath a large rock, it would appear to be a glowing cave belonging to a legendary demon."

"Ah, you don't believe in the Demon, my lady, but surely you believe in the Wondress," Mahla said. "I'm certain I recall you telling tales of the woman."

The bard sprang up with lute in hand. "Ah, I have just the tune for the Wondress." She peered down at Edgar, realizing she had startled him. "So sorry, young one, so sorry. Didn't mean to rattle the bars. Though, as they're clearly already in full vibrato, let us enjoy a tune. This is the Tale of the Wondress. Don't mind the missed notes, since my voice is perfect. It's your ears that are wrong."

There thy Wondress
There thy Wondress agleam
May she grace the coast over
In blue colors, a dream

The woman stilled the crowd with her voice, singing along with each pluck of her lute as though the instrument extended from her voice. The slow and misty ballad seeped into their ears, rocking them in a lullaby as their gaze on the flame hardened.

The specter, she glides
Her radiant theme
A woman, no age
Or a child, may seem

I've bathed in moonlight

Waiting, though rare
For my Wondress to waltz by
Moonbeams in her hair

There thy Wondress
There thy Wondress agleam
May she grace the coast over
In blue colors, a dream

When she stopped, those sitting by the fire were too deep in thought to clap. Smiles and transfixed eyes were her prize. As she settled back into her seat, she delivered a single wink to Edgar.

Mahla, the least lulled, leapt up, causing the crowd to jolt. "Ah, boy, it's good luck to receive a wink from a bard. Ain't you ever heard that?"

"That's rubbish," said Elix. "I've winked at plenty of folk."

"I wouldn't be bragging about handing out luck so readily," said Mahla. "You risk tales being spun that you'd best not sing about."

Elix laughed at the oaf and threw a hand full of pebbles his way, causing his hands to fly up in defense. His face behind the hands smiled and did not flinch.

Stellamaris leaned over to Edgar. "Most of these stories are only interesting because they are far-fetched. This one, though, I remember my father telling the story of the Wondress. If I were to search my heart, I'm sure the practical part of me would not believe it. Although my father has a history of only telling me truths. A lie, even a fun one such as this, would show an inconsistency in my father that I couldn't believe. I also choose to believe this one because I love the idea of it, though that is foolish."

Elix overheard Stellamaris's whisper and joined in. "I've heard many tales of that lovely woman, and can tell you what I know to be true. The story of the Wondress is that she appears as a beautiful woman radiating a blue light, just as you heard in my song. She is calm but often impatient. It is said that all of time and space are chaotic, but she brings order to that chaos. She puts paths in motion, not for good or ill, but simply because that is the way of things."

Edgar turned to Stellamaris. "And what did she do for your father?"

"He just said that she brought him to where he needed to be."

The stories continued. The tickling tips of the fire pulled in Edgar's gaze. He didn't welcome movement in his current state, and his concentration seemed to reinforce that. His mind rested while his eyes remained wakeful.

He continued like that for what felt like an hour. The group continued their tales of glory and the unknown, occasionally telling jokes he did not understand.

The ghost stories were the most intriguing, but then they moved on to local politics. Most he didn't care to understand, just that Lane and Mahla disagreed over obscure laws and customs. As peculiar as it was, they felt comfortable in their disagreement. It was a dance they rehearsed, finding pleasure in the other's misstep. Back home, Edgar would avoid such conversations, although he knew many who did not. Unlike back home, these disagreements were comfortable, with neither person awkward or upset. He envied them in that way; a friendly disagreement that was actually friendly.

If only he and Simon had such a relationship. Simon constantly annoyed Edgar, despite Simon having no ill will toward him. A thread of regret wormed its way into Edgar's mind, but just for a moment. To acknowledge that regret would mean that he had lost Simon forever, and Edgar would not let that be the case.

The only way out is through.

Stellamaris broke his trance as she abruptly stood. The sound of arguing broke through the crackle of the fire. There was a commotion near the village entrance. That must not have been normal, for Stellamaris dashed toward the source in a sprint that would have bested Olympians. When Edgar's eyes focused, he could see why.

Smoke rose in billows against the night sky. When Edgar stood, he could see the tips of flames as they covered a far-off structure.

The others followed their King-Daughter, and Edgar, forced into sobriety, followed. As he got closer, he noticed he saw the others, but not Stellamaris. Amongst the chaos, townspeople left their huts, dressed in draping loungewear. A gang of men in studded leather and littered with tattoos on their exposed skin volleyed arrows into the crowd, causing many unarmed villagers to fall limp.

This was an attack. Bodies fell to the dirt, and the fire spread. Edgar, fearing for his life, dived for cover behind a nearby hut.

He looked beyond the town border and saw a thick forest. The woods could provide shelter, a place to hide until the raid was complete. He could come back in the morning and scout for survivors.

What use would he be if he stayed? This wasn't his town, and the warriors here proved far more capable than him. It was reason enough that he had just met these people, but more so, he knew that if he tried to help with no weapons and no training, he'd undoubtedly die along with any fleeting hope of saving his brother. Any help he could give would be a sacrifice of his own life just so that any survivors might know, maybe, that he hadn't run like a coward.

Another thought occurred to him. When Edgar had left the hut, Jude was asleep. Would he sleep through this attack?

That was his compromise. He wouldn't attack the enemy, but he would wake his friend and then seek refuge in the woods until morning. He would be neither a coward nor a sacrifice.

The best way to reach Jude would be to run through the woods, hiding in the shadows of the trees, and emerge behind his hut. That would keep attackers from seeing him.

He darted toward the first tree. No one saw him. He ran for the next.

It was then that a dark silhouette emerged from the trees before him. Edgar experienced the entire series of events from outside his body. The man standing before him was Alister, no longer in the clothes he wore on Earth, but draped in armor varying between brown, red, and black.

Had this man returned for Edgar?

His pupils expanded, and his frigid breath left his lungs in a gust of white smoke. Somehow, the expression on Alister's face was not hatred or anger, as Edgar would have predicted. There was something that caused this man to panic, similar to how he looked standing outside of the Friar house.

He reached for Edgar, but Edgar could not retreat. He froze, standing dead in his skin.

"Come," said Alister. "*Gah'la gusar.*"

Edgar wanted to run from this man, but his legs refused his will.

Stellamaris leapt from the trees above them both. Her sword reflected the light of the moons as she swung. With a small blade in his hand, the man deflected the attack as Stellamaris reached for his neck with her left hand. Missing, she grabbed hold of his necklace, ripping it from him as he stumbled back. Stellamaris pushed forward in an aggressive pursuit, her skin in deep shades of red and yellow.

Alister stumbled to the ground as Stellamaris raised her sword. As she guided a downward thrust, the familiar blue portal Edgar recalled from Earth ignited the air around Alister and swallowed him whole. Stellamaris's sword hit naked dirt as a streak of confusion spread across her face.

The King-Daughter ordered Edgar to follow as she darted into town. Edgar tried to keep up, but as she danced between shadows, it was difficult for him to see. Before long, he had lost her.

As he surveyed the land, he saw a man in the center of town dressed in the same studded leather as the gang. The man held one of the local Laniakea by the hair.

This local was dressed as though he was actively working in midday. Behind him lay a stack of discarded weapons, too many to belong only to him. The gang member guided his movement by clenching tightly to the local's scalp, with the victim's hands bound behind his back. The oppressor forced the local to his knees as the Laniakea sneered through clenched teeth.

A third man stepped forward, though this one did so of his own accord. Edgar could barely make out the outline of the third man but saw enough from the light of the roaring flame to make out the form of King Semian.

They spoke in a strange language, but Edgar could tell by their body movements that they were conducting a negotiation over the captured man.

Semian knelt down and placed his hands atop his head. Edgar could see Laniakean townspeople clenching fists and grabbing hold of their loved ones. Gang members surrounded Semian and tied his hands.

A high-pitched war cry cut through the air. Edgar felt his heart rattle and mind ring in pain.

From the tops of a nearby hut, Stellamaris leapt down, landing behind the gang. In one fluid movement, she severed the head of the gang leader and freed her father.

Lane and Mahla, their king now safe, moved in unison through the gang members. Though without weapons, these two elite soldiers of the Laniakea disarmed and dropped each enemy combatant into the dirt without contest.

Laniakean warriors sprang for the pile of discarded weapons. The gang, with their leader fallen and the townspeople fully armed, retreated into the woods.

And it was over. The fires still continued to burn, but the Laniakea had quickly taken their town back.

Edgar noticed Ahletta watching the entire scene with a wooden staff in her left hand. He walked over to join her, though her focus remained on the scene before them.

"Aiken's henchmen from Drominion." She tightened her grip on the wooden staff as she uttered his name. "He wants to take this town so that he is better suited to invade the north. The coward knows he cannot defeat us fairly, so he tries attacks like this, targeting innocent people while they lay in their beds." She nodded toward the retreating men. The disgust radiated from her body, trembling in anger. "We're not used to this type of enemy. We've bested many, which earned us the title of Warrior Tribe amongst the Coastal Cliffs. That's what we trade. Protection. But we've never seen such an enemy, one as calculated as the Drominion. It's unsettling to lie in your beds knowing that cowards can sneak in while we rest and slit our throats."

Edgar did not understand her next whisper, but he did not need to. "*Mah'ta la crossia.*"

TWELVE

"We're safe, Becca," Mr. Crisp said. His dog whimpered in concern as they took shelter from the riot beyond the barricaded doors, safe within their home.

An idea occurred to him. He knew of a way they could be safer still. In his younger years, much younger in fact, he had dug a tremendous hole beneath his home. He had taken clay from the lakebed to reinforce the walls and ceiling to fashion an underground cellar for his wine and brandy. The door was flush with the floor of the hut.

He led Becca to the cellar, grabbing several large blankets. Two he intended for him and Becca, while the third he placed over the cellar door as he closed it behind him. He positioned it just so, hoping any intruders would see a bunched-up blanket rather than a door.

"We're safe, Becca," he said. "Yes, I'm sure we're quite safe here."

As he lit a small candle, he saw his friend tilt her head as the light illuminated the room.

"I said we're safe. Don't look at me that way. That's not what I meant. You know that's not what I meant, Becca."

He looked around with growing concern apparent in the way he fidgeted and fumbled. He looked up at the door. Would it hold if there was a fire? He had seen a fire across town. Surely these madmen intended to burn the entire village.

"I'm sure they won't set each of these huts on fire. Don't look at me that way. You know you were thinking it too. Anyway, the clay walls will hold. I'm sure of it."

He was no religious man, but he'd pray to the gods directly if it meant that they'd get him out of this.

"Do you suppose I'd upset the gods if I only starting praying to them now that I want something? Yes, I thought so too."

He cursed himself for the life he'd led. What sort of man was he that he came to the gods on his deathbed as a beggar? Faith was a coin purse relying on both deposits and withdrawals. He came now to them with a substantial withdrawal but only modest deposits.

"I would hope that they take me in as someone in debt. I'd move them to pity."

He was uneasy about that decision, principally the part where he said it aloud.

"Do you suppose that planning on their pity would count against me?"

That idea was a failure, and his entire life was just as bad. He had led a life devoid of purpose. He would die in this hole and beg to the gods, relying solely on their forgiveness and nothing else. They had no reason to forgive him. Rather, in knowing that he was planning on their pity, he had given them reason not to forgive.

"If I survive this night, this will be my turning point, Becca." This would change everything. His vow to change would be the deposit. He pushed his nefarious intentions to game the system deep into a cellar within his own mind and then threw a blanket over the door to give a reason for his conscious mind to ignore.

"Tomorrow, I will lead a better life. It will have purposes that will align with those of the gods. You believe it, too. I can see the excitement in you, Becca. No, don't bark. Our return to life hinges on us surviving the night."

Becca ceased her bark, and he lost himself in thought. His mind had a few twists and even more turns in it still, and he was heading down a passage he would rather not.

"She," he said over a quivering lip. "She would have already figured this out. I would have gotten us to this cellar. I would have led us to survive the night. But she would have done the heavy lifting, guiding us through a better life together in partnership."

Tears puddled near the lids of his eyes until they flowed over.

"Everything good I've ever done was hers. She did it through me. I do not deserve a better life."

Becca inched forward to him and laid her head on his lap. Silence came in waves. First was the lack of sound. Then came the acknowledgment of it and the unwanted tension it placed on him. If a weight on his chest would prevent him from breathing, this weight would lie on his mind and kill him just the same.

Footsteps above broke the silence. They were coming for him. Now he would greet them. He was ready. Death was a contract he had signed long ago. She had died. He had borrowed his remaining years, but they belonged to her. He spent all this time running from the finality of it, and now he would accept it.

The door above him swung open, and he barely raised his eyes to catch it.

"There you are," Letty said. She pushed her head through the opening with a smile that, to Crisp, was upside down. "We've been looking everywhere for you. The gang's all gone. Stellamaris fixed it."

He took in all the breath he could and expelled it back out.

"Where'd you get all this wine?"

"Hi, Letty."

THIRTEEN

Another dream. They came in heavier in this place, more real than anything back home.

This dream was of his father. A cool-tempered man, Edgar's father wore a smile just enough never to be serious and also never angry. At least not overly so.

"I need to go away for a bit," his father said. "Not too long. Do you understand, Edgar?"

Edgar didn't respond, of course. He remembered this day, every speck of dried dirt on his father's hands as he cupped theirs. His skin was dry, like fresh construction paper. This was the day his father left.

"Why are you leaving?" Simon asked, his words rhythmically interrupted by reflexive sniffles through his tears. "You don't need to. There's work here."

"Sure, there's work here, but none that pays what I need to make." He turned to Edgar. "You understand, right? It's like this rock." He reached down and picked up a small stone, just larger than his palm. "If I tossed it to you…" He tossed it to Edgar, who instinctively caught it. His father smiled. "You'd catch it. More than that, you'd be able to bear the weight. But if I threw you a larger rock, like that one at the top of the Marimound Hill where we chased the lizards, that'd be too big. You wouldn't be able to catch it. It would be too big, too massive, and you wouldn't have the strength to hold it. Now, let's say no one threw it at you. It just fell your way, and you *had* to catch it. You still wouldn't be able to support it, except now it's no one's fault. It's just the way of things."

Edgar stood frozen, an unmovable slab of granite in black sneakers.

"I don't understand," said Simon. "What does that have to do with work?"

"Well, I need to make more money than I have. I can't make enough money to support the burdens I have. It's no one's fault. It's just the way of things. There's a job in Japan waiting for me. I can make more money there than I can here."

He turned his head back to Edgar. "You understand." It wasn't a question, but it also wasn't a statement. It was a hope.

The two Brave boys went inside after the car disappeared down the winding road. Their mother sat still as a lake on a windless day, staring out the back window.

The shutting door broke her trance, and she turned to them both.

"Boys, boys, come here." Her voice shook and, though the light was dim, Edgar could see her cheeks stained from the trail of tears washing down her face.

She approached the cluttered bookshelf and reached for a tin box covered in dust. She opened it and poured its contents into the drawer of the table near her.

As she approached them, they could see the faded design of stars and galaxies painted ages before.

She caught Simon's watery eyes first and handed it to him, though she addressed them both. "This is a time capsule. I want you to have it."

"What's a time capsule?" his brother asked.

"You take everything that's important to you and put it in this box. You do that and you hide it away, somewhere no one will find it. But you'll know where it is. You'll know it's there. And some day, many years from now, you'll find it. You'll open the time capsule and examine everything you cared so deeply about. You'll say to yourself, 'How silly of me to care so profoundly about something so little. Something that I've since forgotten about.' You'll say that and you'll laugh. Yes, it'll be fun."

The boys looked at each other, confused by the gift but not enough to say much of anything about it.

Their mother chuckled in an empty way and resumed her stare out the window. It was odd how simple the rest of the evening was, or perhaps that was just his memory of it. There was no fanfare. No question about their father or the gift. Simon said, "Thank you, Mom," nodding at the gift, though she had already turned her back.

And they walked down the hall to their room, not speaking about much beyond idle topics for the rest of the evening.

The sun rose, but Edgar did not. He had seen the lives of several men taken and questioned the safety of his own. Life had always been a constant where consistency was hard to find. He had always been alive and healthy, and that was what he could count on. One day, he would die, that much he knew. Yet enough mornings left him healthy and ready for breakfast that death seemed like a distant relative he wasn't confident existed. He had heard stories of this relative. Even the better part of his brain knew that no one would ever lie about such a thing. It wouldn't be until that person came rapping at the door that he would ever consider them anything worth thinking about. After last night, the world had changed. He had changed.

Edgar recalled his mantra from home: *The only way out is through.*

The safety of this village would have guaranteed his survival if it hadn't been for the raid. The party had made him comfortable. It was a warm blanket on a frosty night. Now he felt foolish. Duped by hope. He didn't want to admit to Jude that he had found comfort in this place.

He didn't know what the Laniakea had involved themselves in, and he didn't care to become involved himself. His sole purpose would be to get home with Simon and the rest of his friends.

His mind snapped to Elena. How selfish was he to find so much joy in this place while she was also missing? He was so determined to find Simon and so grateful to find Jude that he had forgotten there was another person for whom he was responsible. Where was Elena? He and Jude both had found a town to give them shelter. Did Elena enjoy such luck?

A commotion outside the hut broke his concentration. As he stood, he saw Jude climbing out of bed.

"Did you sleep?" Edgar asked.

"No, of course not. Not after all that."

Edgar was awake the entire night but hadn't engaged with his roommate. When he returned to the hut, Jude was lying in bed, seemingly asleep. If they both couldn't fall completely asleep, then they had apparently alternated twilights.

"So you saw it? You were awake for part of it?"

"How could I not be? The fire was so stinking loud. It woke me, and I watched everything from the door." Jude arose. "You don't think they have coffee here, do you?"

"I was just about to check. It sounds like people are up and awake. I'd bet they don't have coffee. They might have something that does the same thing, though."

Edgar walked outside to find bright green grass littered with people. Laniakean warriors swung blades and sticks, rehearsing movements repeatedly in what seemed to Edgar like a medieval form of track and field. The older warriors were the only ones trusted to train with metal blades. The younger students wielded long wooden rods and fought opponents equipped to match.

"Ah, it appears the young lad has awoken from his sweet slumber." Edgar looked up at Mahla, blocking the light of the sun. Dawn had gifted Mahla with a distinct sense of formality compared with the other times he had spoken with the giant. The Mahla that Edgar had come to know, albeit briefly, was a bumbling behemoth. The man before him carried a grace that was misplaced but also not forced. Perhaps there actually was coffee here, and that was all the man needed.

"Hi, Mahla."

"Surely someone has given you a proper tour. I'll offer it just the same, but I'm embarrassed on behalf of the Laniakea that you have not yet received one."

Edgar shook his head. "It's fine. But yes, I'd love one."

"I'm certain you saw the lake during the festivities, but there's a worn trail that leads behind it up to the king's crowning achievement along the stone wall."

"That would be awesome, but first I need to grab something to wake me up. Something warm. Do you have coffee here? It's a hot drink that makes you more alert."

"There are many such drinks here, most of which you are too young to drink. I believe there is a less potent version that the nah'airs drink when they need a jolt. Come, and I'll show you."

Before they could leave the door to Edgar's hut, a wooden stick, the kind the young warriors used for practicing, landed directly on Edgar's feet.

The young woman, Ahletta, stood before him. Edgar glanced down at the rod at his feet and then back up again at the woman. She settled into a defensive stance and, acknowledging the playful challenge presented to him, he picked it up.

This appeared to be a game, a sport mixed in with their training. Surely no one expected him to fight alongside the others training that day. Yes, he was certain her challenge was an invitation to a game and nothing more. He hoped they wouldn't ask him to fight in a war he knew nothing about.

"I'll leave you to this, my boy," said Mahla. "Come find me if you'd like that coffee."

Slowly and with false confidence, he walked toward the girl as her rod extended outward. He swatted it out of the way, and immediately she advanced the attack. In one fluid motion, she guided his staff up into the air, exposing his belly for a second attack, which she followed through. She swiftly sliced her staff along his gut. Had this been a real blade or an actual fight, she would have displayed his insides along the grass for all to see.

He looked down, confused. She appeared to be having fun, laughing and smiling as though they were children splashing among the waves. Meanwhile, attack after attack, she destroyed every fiber of security he had through her simulated battles, leaving him defeated each time.

He shook his head, frustrated. "You sad-sack," he said to himself.

"What is that?" Ahletta asked.

"What? This? This is the stick you gave me."

"No. What is a sad-sack? And where is it? You're looking at the ground. There is nothing there."

"Oh no, I was calling myself a sad-sack."

She laughed at him like he was a dog chasing its tail. "You look at the ground and call yourself a depressed bag? People across the sea are such strange ones."

"No, it's a saying."

"I know what you are saying. You told me."

"No, I'm saying that I'm clumsy."

In a blur, she lunged forward, sweeping his legs out from beneath him with her staff.

"Do not admit you're clumsy to your enemy." This was the first piece of advice she had offered during their encounter. "Or at least be direct about it. You call yourself an unhappy sack when you are clumsy? Just call yourself clumsy. I don't understand you people from across the sea."

He released a groan as he climbed back to his feet. "I'm understanding less and less myself, actually."

Ahletta swung her rod, beginning another duel. Stellamaris came to observe, finding a large stone to rest on. Edgar became visibly flushed at her presence. If he had any idea how to fight with a mock blade, he would have exaggerated his movements in a method he assumed was correct. As it was, he was now fully confident he knew nothing of battle, and any attempt at showing off in front of the King-Daughter was bound to fail.

What was perhaps more obvious was the way his partner reacted. Ahletta had talent. She had made that quite obvious after her countless victories. Still, at the presence of the King-Daughter, she straightened her back and hesitated with each swing of her faux blade. There was doubt built into every movement she took, enabling Edgar to mimic the first attack that Ahletta had taught him. He guided her staff up into the air, exposing her belly, and went in for the kill.

Stellamaris erupted in a cheer. "Great job, Edgar."

Ahletta threw down her staff and stormed into her hut. Without a partner, Edgar dropped his staff, panting, and joined Stellamaris near the rock. "I came out here looking for coffee and found your people fighting. Is this a normal activity, or is this because of last night?"

She paused, and he could sense some unease.

"We are a warrior tribe, so part of this is normal. Many of the neighboring towns have their strengths. In the north, they have wealth and organized forms of trade. They collect goods from parts of the world that are difficult for us to travel to. They then sell it to the rest of us. To the east they create goods, like weapons and tools for building. Kalagora is our closest neighbor, also due east, and they produce marvelous food and drink. In this town, we fight. We are allies with all the neighboring kingdoms, and so when one of them has a dispute that they cannot resolve peacefully, we come in to defend them. Never as an aggressor, always in defense. Last night was different. We have had aggressors in the past, but they've always had the respect to meet us in battle and never attack us while we rest, like cowards."

Stellamaris had tightened her jaw when speaking of the Drominion attack but swiftly shook off her anger. She straightened her back and turned back to Edgar, smiling.

"To answer your question, it is not uncommon to wake up and see a field full of the Laniakea wielding weapons, but in this case they are preparing for the king to announce what his reaction to last night's raid will be. The king is too smart and forward-thinking to do anything rash, but one does not attack the warrior tribe without response."

"Lady Stellamaris," Edgar said. His awkward formality caused him to stammer, and the King-Daughter smiled. She didn't seem to be the type of royalty that would insist on formalities. Although she also didn't seem ready to stop Edgar, if that was what he felt like he needed to do. "Thank you for saving me last night."

Her smile brightened, as if it were possible to shine brighter than it already did.

"Of course, Edgar. Actually, you and your friend remind me of our nah'airs. I'm growing rather fond of having you here, and I want you to feel safe."

Her eyes glowed, and she seemed genuine. Despite the impending doom that last night's threat had brought, he felt as though the safest place he could be was near this woman.

The events of the previous night forced their way to the front of his mind. The attempted abduction, the altercation between the abductor and Stellamaris. Her sword had flashed in the moonlight as the man vanished and his necklace fell to the dirt. It must still be there.

Edgar leapt from his seat and raced to the spot of the altercation with Alister. If he could locate the necklace, it might produce a clue on how he could find Simon. Alister was his only lead to locating his brother.

In a panic, he dashed from tree to tree, moving dirt and leaves aside in a frenzy. He was certain it was by one of these trees, but it was dark during the attack, and each tree looked the same. Finally, a glimmering reflection caught his attention. He slowed his movement and brushed aside clustered leaves to reveal the necklace. It was a thin leather rope holding a small, rugged stone, smooth enough to be metal and polished enough to reflect the sun.

He walked back into town and saw Stellamaris standing looking at him, confused. As he held the necklace high to show her, the king emerged from his hut and walked in their direction.

Nerves struck Edgar like lightning. He hadn't had many interactions with King Semian and realized that, out of the two royals, he felt more comfortable around the King-Daughter. While Stellamaris was approachable, like a mother, the king was a celebrity, more a statue than a person.

"My boy," the king said. He picked up the necklace, examining it. "Where did you find this?"

"It belonged to a fighter from last night. He was in the trees over there. I was trying to get to my friend, and he came at me. I recognized him from back home...across the sea. He kidnapped my brother." It all came spilling out of him. He wasn't sure why he had kept it in before, but in that moment he let the king know everything, only leaving out his trip through the wormhole. He told him about Elena and why they all were there.

Semian absorbed it all easier than Edgar would have expected. He smiled plainly. "Well then, it appears we have a common enemy. Perhaps we can help each other."

He stood tall and called out. "Mr. Crisp."

Mr. Crisp emerged from his hut. It looked as though he was just now waking.

"Yes, My King."

"Come examine this. Do you recognize it?"

The old man hobbled over with his dog in tow. He took the necklace and held it up in the light, squinting.

"It appears to be a particular metal. I believe this is the same metal mined at the base of the Evajocalyn centuries ago. There isn't much of it in the world. And frankly, this looks rather fresh. Normally, when I see jewelry like this, it has age markings on the side. This looks like someone mined it within the last few years."

"How far is the Evajocalyn?" Edgar asked.

"Oh, not far at all. We could travel there in several days' time. Less so if we packed light."

"What did this man...your brother's abductor...what did he look like?" asked King Semian. "Did he look like the men that attacked the town, or could he have been here by coincidence?"

"I saw him, Pietro," Stellamaris said. "He looked strange. He did not dress the same as Aiken's men. If you believe he was here by coincidence, then that doesn't sound too far-fetched."

"I ask because the Evajocalyn is a mystical place," said the king. "There aren't too many people that would go down there, let alone mine for metal. I wouldn't suspect even Aiken could convince his men to descend the Evajocalyn. And as for the mercenaries, if he paid them to go to a place they thought was haunted, then he'd need to pay them a considerable amount. Either that man had other reasons for being here last night, or Aiken has a plan that involves mystical metals."

Edgar's chest filled with excitement at the thought of finding his brother. Surely, with these primitive people, stories of haunted and mystical caverns were bound to be exaggerated. "I'd like to go to this place." Heads turned in his direction. Looks of confusion spread across the group. "If this helps find my brother, then I need to go. I've traveled a long way to get here. I will probably never get home. My only priority is finding my brother."

The king thought for a moment. "If we believe Aiken's army is at the base of the Evajocalyn, then it would be irresponsible to send you alone."

"I wouldn't suspect the army is there," said Mr. Crisp. "I've been there once before, and it is not ideal as a refuge."

"Then I will allow you to go if you can find a guide," said the king. Stellamaris appeared as though she would interject and then restrained herself. "You'll need someone that knows the area and has a reasonable chance of getting you home safely." As Semian spoke, he turned his head toward Mr. Crisp, who was oblivious to the insinuation.

"Oh, you mean me?"

The king nodded.

"Oh…I…well I could, but…I would do anything for you, My King."

"Think it over, Crisp. This is not something I'd send you or my guest to their death over. I wouldn't allow it. Take the night to think about your decision. If you feel as though you could take our guest there and safely return him here, then you can leave tomorrow.

"As for the rest of you," the king addressed the townsfolk who had gathered, "it is good you are preparing for battle. After the events from last night, I cannot sit idly by without meeting Aiken with our primary force of arms. Lane, prepare your battalion. We will march in three days. Aiken must not think he can shake us so easily. We are the mighty Laniakea, and he will hear the yawps of our battle cries. Think not only of the safety of our homestead, but of the north and east, the less capable whom we have sworn to protect. Do they have such might? Could they protect themselves when the raiders come with clenched fists and raised swords? We march, not for ourselves, but for the whole of the Coastal Cliffs."

The assembled crowd nodded at his words. Edgar noticed the honor held by each warrior, whether they were holding a blade or a practice staff. These were professionals embarrassed by the previous night's events. The king's words were precisely what they wanted to hear.

FOURTEEN

"I CANNOT GO, BECCA," said Mr. Crisp. The dog whimpered, but his word was final. Complete.

He arranged the books on his side table with fidgeting hands until he realized he liked them better the way they were before and then swiftly nudged them back.

"I cannot lead the boy down the Evajocalyn. It's just too dangerous. You already know this, and frankly, you bringing it up has pulled the end of my thread."

The old man avoided eye contact with the pup. Perhaps he didn't want to talk about it. Perhaps the decision embarrassed him. The notion that his companion had called him out added insult to injury. Some friend.

Against his better judgment, he stole a glance.

Whimper.

Damn you.

"Oh, don't look at me that way, Becca. You know I do this for the both of us. Your age is showing in the way you move. How do you expect to go on any more adventures?"

The dog, as cruel as ever, maintained her relentless glare.

"I know, I know. Believe me, I know. But lack of adventures is beside the point."

She grumbled under her breath as she trotted over to her bed to lie down. Such language. This was a side of his friend that he did not prefer.

"It was a slip of the tongue. I know you haven't been on any real adventures. Be off with it. Or at least stop complaining to me, if you wish to spare me even but a little of your tirade. The truth is...well...I'm too old myself. I've gotten up in age and can't afford to go on any more adventures."

The beast lay still in her bed, watching the dust fall from the air. Now she hadn't anything to say.

"Fine. Is it the word you don't like? *Adventures?* I'll stop using it. Would that please you, my master?"

Silence hung between them like a fog he could brush away with a swipe of the hand. After a moment, he felt as though he could hear the silence itself. His enemy that he kept inviting home.

"Yes. I understand. I suppose I have been on little adventures. Perhaps that's a point I should award you."

"I wish—" he said, stopping himself. A deep breath ballooned his lungs, preventing tears from leaking out, though he had enough saved. It wasn't a gush, but rather a slow leak that he didn't know was there until it had already made its damage permanent. "I wish you and I would have had more adventures."

He was no longer looking at Becca. Instead, it was an old wooden rocking chair that sat opposite him.

"It's a delicate thing, I suppose. Adventures. I've been practically a hermit all my life due in part to the labors of traveling and the dangers out there. It's like a paper doll. A doll that could break if you play with it. And there in lies the riddle, my sweet Becca. If you do not play with it, it will remain only paper. I could hardly call it a doll at that point. If instead you play with it and risk destroying it, well, I suppose that's what makes it a doll. A memory. Timeless. How do you make paper a doll, Becca, if not by using it?"

The next silence differed from the one that preceded it. A void that held him. Locked him in. Ten minutes or ten hours, it would be the same. If the earlier silence was a fog, this was the water itself. A feeling of drowning, broken only by a best friend that knew to bark.

"Oh yes, I suppose I haven't fed you yet."

Mr. Crisp fumbled with the dog food he had prepared the night before. He kept it in a small container in the back of the pantry. It was this same pantry he had grown up with. It belonged to this home, which belonged to him. But not only him. He shared it the same way he shared all his things.

"Perhaps that's why I don't want to leave."

It wasn't entirely his to leave unguarded. But how does paper become a doll, if not for risk of breaking?

"I'll do it."

Becca raised her eyes, but not her head.

"Oh, don't look at me that way, Becca. I've made my decision, and I'm rightfully confident it's the correct one. I'll take the boy to the base of the Evajocalyn, to the very place that brave men dare not go. Stop barking. Yes, you can come with me. I should hope you would, in fact."

He let out a sigh of resignation. "I shall tell him tonight."

He threw on his cloak and marched out the front door. As quickly as he had exited, he returned. He strode past Becca and walked to a small chest full of dry ice. From it he pulled a small bottle and dispensed the liquid into a glass. Swallowing the liquid, he proceeded back to the door.

"I've had enough judgment from you, my dear pup. Enough of it. Come along."

FIFTEEN

"YOU NEVER SHOULD HAVE rattled the people."

Dahl'Turan, the all-too-cool-headed lead council of the Laniakea, sat upon his stone chair next to his sister Laykia. She all too often agreed with her brother, something Stellamaris had warned her father would happen when she was first elected.

Her father sat opposite Dahl'Turan in his dark stone chair, his opinion as unchanging as his face. "We will respond, Dahl'Turan. The council may decide what we call it, but we will engage them in battle all the same."

Council meetings were all held in the same place and as formal as they could keep them. An inset stage carved into the side of a mountain perfectly matched the granite seats, formed in a circle. There were twelve seats, but Stellamaris didn't hold one of them. That day, she came to observe. Her father often encouraged it, since she might one day sit upon the dark stone. Her good friend Ilgene kept her company.

"But what is this council for if not to maintain peace and protection from the rule of a dictator?" Laykia said. "My apologies that I too boldly overspeak. Your people love you, My King. That much is certain. We must not think of our law as a ritual under the leader we favor, but a wall before the future leader we despise. If you can excite our warriors to march off without the support of the council, then a dictator will surely do the same, but quicker."

Semian turned to the woman. "Right you are, Laykia, but these raiders cut into us like a warm knife through butter. They shook the confidence of warriors that stake their lives on confidence. That is what Aiken took from us. My men's focus is on revenge, not because they are vengeful, but because the raiders stole a piece of them last night, and the crumb of confidence they still have needs it back."

"Forgive me, My King," said Dahl'Turan. "I do not question the direction we must take. Certainly, we should respond, and of course you should encourage them to regain their confidence. But promising a particular course of action when the council must reach their conclusion first is reckless. Again, forgive me for misspeaking. I must impress the importance of order."

"This is war," Semian said, the first crack in his composure showing.

"If we cannot use order during our most troubling times, then why do we do this at all? Why do we meet? Forgive me, My King, but I do not attend these meetings as a game, twiddling my thumbs. If we cannot find order in the Laniakea during times of war, then it is of no use during times of peace. If that is what you think of the council, then do not call this order; call it manners and nothing more."

King Semian released a gust of tension from his lungs, holding back the coiled spring in his chest. "Then what do you suggest?"

Dahl'Turan mimicked Semian in his gathering of composure. "I agree with you on one of your points. We must meet Aiken in a response. Might I suggest taking the route through the Doldrums? We will approach a satellite town of the Drominion that we can settle in to send a message. I believe our partners in Kalagora are along the way, which will allow our men a chance to gather supply and rest."

Semian exhaled, visibly frustrated. "You wish me to invade a small Drominion town to send a message?"

Dahl'Turan took his turn to hold the stony glare. "It will produce the least amount of casualties and put a strain on the Drominion economy. It seems the most appropriate message to deliver during peacetime, does it not?"

"Peacetime? They almost killed me in front of my people. I seek to sack Drominion itself."

"But they did not kill you. Do you not stand before us now, healthy as a bucking althorse?"

Semian, who looked surprised that he stood, slowly descended into his chair. His face lost all color at the casual bluntness of his council's words. He would have lashed out if not for the hurt that settled into his heart.

Dahl'Turan continued. "To declare war because something *almost* happened would cause division. Travel east of Drominion and you find that little of those towns have heard of the mighty Laniakea. Those who have hear of our prosperity, not our charity. Invade Drominion without a just cause and we will be the tyrants, not Aiken. You wish for a swift resolution, but invading the Drominion capital, even if the battle is successful, will start a war across the Eastern Network."

Silence hung between them as thick as mist. Many of the council shifted in their seats, gazing down at their notes scrawled on scrolls. Still, Semian did not challenge Dahl'Turan's logic.

Stellamaris knew her father's face. The man before her did not disagree; he simply felt betrayed. The casual disregard for any life was tragic, but to disregard the life of their king left an unremovable stain.

Dahl'Turan broke the silence, speaking through Semian's icy gaze. "It shows our strength but also our honor. We will not kill their people, or enslave them. They will probably thank us for freeing them. In fact, it is the council's position that we are freeing this town from the Drominion tyranny. *That* will be the message that will flow through the Eastern Network. Other towns, yearning for the prosperity of the Coastal Cliffs, will invite us in without conflict."

"Splendid idea," said Laykia. "We will free the people of..."

"Val Rea," said a mousy assistant behind the councilwoman.

"Yes, yes. The people of Val Rea will finally be free of the rule of Drominion."

Dahl'Turan raised his gavel. "All those in favor?"

A flurry of ayes sounded off and immediately settled with little excitement, save for the scowl of the king.

"It's settled then. The Laniakea will free the people of Val Rea, sending a message to Drominion and entering the Val Reans into free trade with the Coastal Cliffs. Prosperity for all."

"Prosperity for all." Voices echoed throughout the council. The council members scurried off like mice, scrolls gathered in a frenzy.

Stellamaris looked up at Ilgene beside her, reading his expression but unable to determine which side he favored. Her father was less mysterious. He threw himself from his seat and stormed toward his hut, the busy crowd before him clearing his path as though he gave off a repelling force.

Stellamaris felt a mixture of emotions, but the strongest was the feeling that their safety had leaked away, first in slow drips, but now as a steady stream. How much more could seep out before she, her town, her people, were empty?

At the moment Stellamaris entered her father's hut, he was thoughtfully selecting a blade from the collection upon his wall. His eyes darted from weapon to weapon with pursed lips. She knew this side of her father. Determination, but also fear. A raging fire beneath a hard outer shell.

She had seen that same face long ago, when she was a child falling from a large stone as he taught her to hunt. Temporary injuries littered her body, but nothing to cause genuine concern. Still, she had seen the man's heart beat in his eyes.

She saw that same heart beat through those old eyes today as he selected his long sword from the wall.

"There is something bothering you, my child." Semian did not cease his task when he spoke to her.

"You cannot just march into battle with some random town without putting thought behind it," Stellamaris said.

"I *have* put thought behind it. We all have. Were you not in attendance just now? You do not hear me. We must hasten our actions. Aiken sent those men as a test. He could do it again in another town. We are a powerful force, but if we are to be divided into protecting multiple towns at once, then we risk growing weaker. We do not have time for perfection when complete is what's required."

"I know your eyes, My King." Stellamaris spoke the words with a steady tongue, hiding a shaking hand. "Do not mistake me for a councilman. I have seen you send giants to their knees. I have seen specters of the Rambling Forest tremble at your name. Yet the eyes I see today are the eyes I saw when I was a hurt child. Desperate and afraid."

At this, he stopped.

"We are the Laniakea. The warrior tribe. We are the protectors of Cassini."

"I know we must go to war, but—"

"They bested us. They deceived the mighty warrior tribe in our own home, at our own celebration. We risk more than what I said earlier. It is true we cannot divide our forces amongst all tribes at once, but there is a larger threat."

Stellamaris stared at her father's trembling face. There were no tears in his eyes, but there never would be. Not from him. He was a stone. And seeing a stone tremble was far worse than tears.

"Our way of life is at risk, my daughter. If we are not the mighty Laniakea, we have nothing to trade for food, goods, and weapons."

She believed his words but persisted. "If we lose their trust, then we can rewrite the contracts."

The king laughed at this and she felt herself decrease in stature. "Trust. Trust is what the contracts are. If you have no trust, you have no ink in writing the contracts."

Stellamaris straightened her back and made a direct stride to the wall of blades. She took her favorite off the wall and handed it to him.

She had used with this sword through her training, though it was never hers. It was light, with a white metal that gleamed in the sun. Often, her father would catch her admiring the elegant pattern of a flower stem, tracing the blade down past the guard until it led to the design of a red jewel imitating a blossom at the pommel.

The great king smiled at his daughter and winked. Without explanation, he shook his head and returned the sword to the wall.

"I do not oppose recourse, but you need a plan. And you cannot act in fear."

He rested his shoulders, and Stellamaris could see the warmth of his face as though it were a smile he donned. "There's that anxiety I warned you about. You will be a great queen, but you can only be a mother to some, not all. Besides, I have a plan. I'll show you." He pulled out a map of the Cassini coast and laid it out across the table. Pointing to their village, he marked an X along the Cliff Coasts to the west. "We are going to travel southeast beneath Kalagora through the Doldrums." His fingers modeled his words, tracing along the path. "Then up north so that we're set to come out to the west of Val Rea. Ilgene has been scouting and knows where they keep their weapons. We'll slip in at night, steal their weapons, and take the capitol building while they sleep. The people of Val Rea will wake to a new government with their old king alive in a prison cell. I do not expect many casualties."

She looked at the map with uncertainty. There were flaws, but none she could see. Still, her chest clenched.

"My wonderful daughter," he said. "I know you're worried, but if we wait for everything to be perfect, we'll put ourselves in a place where we must divide our forces. If that happens, you would be correct to worry."

Her head shook in disapproval, replacing the words she couldn't find.

"I do this for you," he said, calm and yet defensive. "It would be worse if I were reckless about our long-term strategy. You must see this. This will reduce casualties. We'll keep Mahla's battalion behind to protect our home and take Lane's troop to

Val Rea. On our way home, we'll stop by Kalagora and recruit the townspeople to form a great army for the Coastal Cliffs."

She shook her head. "Kalagora doesn't have any soldiers. Only we do."

"That is precisely my point. The Coastal Cliffs need a larger army than the one the Laniakea provides. We'll make soldiers out of their men. We'll train them and make them skilled fighters."

She paused, looking deep into the map. Surely it hadn't come to this. She knew that Aiken and the Drominion were a different type of enemy than they were used to fighting. They calculated their every move and those of their enemies. The Laniakea typically enforced the law in each town and protected them from the wandering thief guilds and gangs. She wasn't sure how to handle such organized forces. "I see it. I understand it, and I am no child. To speak plainly, I don't like it."

She could have stormed off. Her mother would have. Instead, she wrapped her arms around her father and cried. She muttered the comforting name she had given her father, Pietro. At that moment, the mighty king, the busiest and greatest of the Laniakea, simply held his daughter and stroked her hair as tears streamed down her face.

SIXTEEN

"YOU THERE," CALLED A VOICE.

Edgar looked across the emerald field, past the training soldiers at the woman, Elix, setting aside her lute, sprawling her hands out, waving.

"She's subtle," said Mahla as he deflected a practice blade. "Subtle as the Cliffs of Seri."

"Oh, I know a tune or two of the ancient cliffs," said Elix, completing her dash across the meadow with little breath left. "You'll have to give me a second…to catch…"

"We've heard the song, Bard. The only things I fancy too much of are booze and…" Mahla stopped himself after glancing at the boy. "Just booze. Quit staring at me, boy, it's not important."

Mahla's sparring partner landed a strike across his shoulder and followed it with a fit of laughter.

"Never you mind, Elix. Go sing across the yard."

The two wandered to a tree stump near two wooden pots strewn along the grass. Elix picked up a pot and turned it over, thumping it along its base. She experimented with the vibration of the sides, which were higher in pitch.

"Perfect," she said. "Now here." She handed the pot to Edgar, who accepted it, bewildered. "No, don't just hold it for me, boy. Straddle it between your knees. No, no, sit down first. You look like someone struck you in the golden fancifuls... Okay, good. Stay like that. Now take the base of your palm and use it to strike the center of the pot... Good, good. Last, I'd like you to take your fingers and drum along the sides... That was less good... That sounded like a mouse falling down tiny steps."

"What are we doing?" Edgar asked.

"Yes, yes, boy, yes, yes. We are creating music."

"Okay, but why?"

She raised a single puzzled eyebrow. "Why make music? You ask me why make music? I tell you this, lad. Is it not easier to answer 'why *do* we live' than to answer 'why *should* we live?' We can answer the first question, the other we cannot, and yet here we are, living each day as best we can. The same goes for the mystery of song."

"I don't understand any of that."

"Good. You're farther along than I'd hoped. Now tell me how you got here to the Laniakea. We're going to write a song."

Edgar felt awkward at this request. If this were his home town, he'd prefer to retreat to his room in the Friar Home during uneasy times, staying clear of social activity. However, his journey so far had led him down so many twists and turns that he felt compelled to silence the shrieking introvert. In a world with no right answers, this seemed the least incorrect.

He recounted landing on the beach but left out the trip through space and time. Instead, he picked up the lie just as he had left it, claiming that he traveled across the sea to the west.

"Ah, the Poor Man's Sea," Elix said.

"That's its name?"

"Why not? Seems good as any, I'd say. Now continue, please."

"Well, we arrived, but our boat crashed, which separated me from my crew. Jude came here, just as I did, but my friend Elena is still missing." He looked at Elix, who was still squinting, and decided he needed to give her more. "Let's see, what else? I had a book from back home given to me by my foster father." Elix tilted her head, confused. "Oh, a *foster* parent is someone who takes care of you when your actual parent cannot. I'm from a special home. It's hard to describe. But I enjoy the people there; it's just different. Anyway, Mahla found me on the beach when I arrived and brought me here. I guess it's simpler than I thought."

"We'll fix that." Elix pulled up her lute and struck a staccato *thump thump thump thump* along the body of the instrument.

There once was a boy
'Cross the Poor Man's Sea
From a merry old home
Says the refugee

Well, up from the ocean came to be
A clapping bully old man, says he

Elix, continuing her percussive rhythm, signaled for Edgar to mimic her. He stumbled at first, milliseconds behind, but eventually caught up to her until they held a two-part harmony of quarter notes. She then swiftly removed a pick from behind her lute's neck and strummed full-bodied chords from the strings in a complementary pattern.

Well, up from the ocean came to be
A clapping bully old man, says he

With seaweed draped
Across his crown
May he brave that bitter sea down
May he brave the bitter sea down

Now man or myth
The boy could be
I've seen no man
Could cross that sea
But the good King Semian proud and free...
May he brave that bitter sea down

"That was amazing." Edgar dropped the pot, a laugh bursting from his chest. "I've never been part of a song before."

"Aye, young one. It's a grand feeling, truly it is. And this tune is exceptional. I shall have to work on it if more time is gifted, but I'm certain I should have to thank you. We best not meet at the Harvest Festival, with all that I owe you. You'll be drunk, and I'll be broke. There's no good that can come of that for either of us."

Edgar felt a familiar smile drape over his face. He remembered that smile from long ago. Before the Friars. Before his mother's incident. He remembered being happy then. It was that feeling that he had now, upon a stump, striking an old wooden pot.

Though that feeling did not last long. As soon as the poorly used muscles along the sides of his mouth ached from laughing, the strain reminded him of the pain it covered. His brother was missing, and these tunes and laughter would only remind him of a time when he was happy. A time with his brother, his only constant, now gone across the universe. Why did any of this have to happen? He didn't deserve it, and neither did Simon. He promised himself that one day he would allow himself to laugh and not have it remind him of an easier time. But that day was not today.

He did not say this aloud. Instead, the smile remained, as did the burden, still hidden behind the shadow vale.

Cave paintings smeared the walls of Elena's colosseum after a month's worth of suns and moons raced across the sky. Amongst the paintings was a personal calendar, comprising dashes boxed in groups of seven rather than the traditional five. She had made paint from the clay that settled along the corridor, mixing it with ash from her campfires for dark colors and innards of fish for other varying shades. Light colors were out of her range, but she did what she could by contrasting the different shades of dark.

Planes. Skyscrapers. The home she grew up in. All those objects that brought her some recollection of her old home lay scattered across the new one.

"Productive" was an accurate way to describe the last thirty days. She used stones as tools, chiseling away areas in the corridor that made the passage the most difficult to maneuver, creating steps and ledges for her feet and hands to find purchase. With enough work, it became a trip she could complete frequently and with ease, often holding food.

Food and water were its own accomplishment. On her luckiest of days, early during her stay, she found a small crustacean. It reminded her of a crab, but instead of red, its shell was completely transparent. Even the inner meat and organs past the shell were visible as it crept along the sand. Elena would often wonder idly what a sunburn on an organ felt like. Perhaps that was the reason it buried itself in the sand and mud so often.

The transparency also served as camouflage. She would have missed it if it hadn't been for the cracking sensation vibrating up her leg as she stepped on it.

A fit of glee flooded her stomach as she ached for food and spotted this worthy candidate. After having gone days without food, she dived after the creature. It was an easy catch, although it should be. Its cracked shell impaired its movement, and killing it with a long stick was not difficult. Half of her mind warned her not to eat raw meat, but the other half told her she'd die without risks like these.

It's probably like sushi.

It was more flavorful and savory than any feast back home. The meat itself was revolting, and a less hungry belly would have rejected it, giving it back to the sea. Rather, her stomach screamed for food, and her eyes found only rocks and saltwater. The meat filled her belly just fine.

Yet that wasn't the accomplishment she would have awarded herself. The shell of the creature had more utility than the meat. She kept it, at first, as a trophy. But after finding more animals of its kind, she came to realize the shell had much more to offer.

The same half of her brain that told her to take risks urged her to drink the saltwater that threatened madness. One evening, she nearly did.

She scooped the ocean water into a crab shell and crept it to her mouth with the shaking hands of an addict. Inches from her lips, an idea bullied its way in, causing her to drop the shell.

Curious to explore this new idea, she picked up the shell and examined it. It was curved, much like a lens.

She gathered sticks washed up along the shore and hurried back to her colosseum. There was no shortage of rocks there, and she desperately examined them all. As she assembled them with sticks and some clay from the corridor, she created a device to suspend her transparent crab shell up against the sunlight piercing through the opening above.

She spent the next day collecting wood and kindling, drying it with her new magnifying glass. It was that same wood and kindling she would use to create her first fire.

And soon enough, there it was, the glorious red and golden dancers that were essential to life. She wanted to sing. She was both soldier and queen. She had created flames that danced to their own melody. Fire itself, in all its glory, belonged to her, the mistress of heat.

I own this, and this is mine.

She scurried about, collecting rocks. Some were flat, others curved. She collected them all and waited for the fire to die down, for she would not kill it on her own.

She brushed aside the charred wood and laid her flat rocks beneath her magnifying glass. After some time she had built herself a fireplace, a stone bowl suspended above it. This would cook her fish. The curvature of the rock would hold the water as it boiled, collecting moisture on another device that she suspended higher still. She had successfully created a repeatable method of creating fire, boiling water, and cooking meat.

The water she finally tasted was more wonderful than any she could have had at home. This water she had created, and she was desperate for it. It slid past her chapped lips, making her weep.

What next? She recalled the fish. She had noticed their fascinating glow when she first arrived. That glow had made them easy to catch at night. What a glorious use for her invention!

Elena waited until nightfall and used a spear she had fashioned from a sharpened stick to harpoon the oceanic fireflies that trusted her just a little too much.

After several days' worth of attempts, she learned to catch the fish in the early morning, while they still emitted their glow. This would yield a fresher feast by the time the sun rose high enough to cast its rays upon her new stove.

Some days she would not eat, and other days she would catch too much for her to use and curse herself for reducing the supply. Her stomach eventually settled into a rhythm, allowing her to gorge herself and then last for several days more.

Perhaps her favorite activity was eating along the shoreline just before the sun descended into the sea. She had learned from past errors with the untrustworthy tide and found a ridge high above the sand. It was there that she ate her dinner and casually watched the island cliffs dip into the water and flood her beach, only to reposition and ascend with the tide rescinding.

No longer a victim of the chaotic tide, she found it therapeutic. She made a game of guessing the next place it would emerge from the water.

Sometimes it would emerge so far up the coast, she wasn't sure if it had risen at all. She'd watch it roll up like ripples in a pond. Other times it would appear close to her shore, and when the thrashing of the waves ceased, she would stare at it, feeling it tempt her to swim out and climb its cliffs.

As difficult as it was, she resisted, knowing too well that if it descended while she was on it, the water would pull her under and she would die.

At the end of her first week, she had hit enough low points to welcome such an end. After several more, she enjoyed her new home. After she slashed the thirtieth tick on her cave calendar, she enjoyed her first calm smile in the same number of days.

Still, on evenings upon her ridge, as she looked at the rise and fall of the cliffs, eating her dinner, she would think of her mother.

She recalled when her mom had met Jude's father and the joy that spilled out through her fingertips when she spoke of him. Elena didn't see what her mother saw in him, but he made her happy.

And then *happy* turned to dependance. "I need him," she would say. "If he leaves me, I won't find anyone better."

"You don't need anyone else," Elena would respond. "You have me."

Elena remembered her mother's shaky smile. The woman that was so strong became so weak.

After her mother's death, she looked back at all the warning signs, all the opportunities Elena had to help her.

As she sat along the beach, she smiled at the thought of her mother at peace and herself somewhere across the stars, away from her cursed life back home.

SEVENTEEN

THE BREEZE WHISPERED INTO Edgar's ear as he trod along the path, trying to keep up with Mr. Crisp and Becca, who maintained a considerable lead.

To Edgar, this was common. The boy regularly trailed at the end of the pack on walks and hikes back home, struggling to keep up, often giving up in favor of keeping his own comfortable pace.

He blamed it on the length of his legs. Edgar was five feet ten inches, not short or tall, but his torso was long, resulting in legs shorter than most. This wasn't the sort of thing to catch someone's eye. Many wouldn't even notice. He could only convince friends of this oddity by demonstrating how much he needed to adjust his chair compared with his neighbors'.

Becca barked from ten paces ahead, signaling her owner to look back at Edgar.

"Oh, will you please hurry?" Mr. Crisp complained. "I do want to get there before nightfall. I only have so much supplies, and if we have to set up camp before we even get to the tree, then we'll never..."

Mr. Crisp stopped short, jowls clenching. "Just hurry."

The boy hoisted his pack tighter along his shoulder and set into a jog.

After several repetitions of Crisp's steady pace, followed by frustrated waiting, the group decided on a compromised march. Crisp and Becca walked at a normal pace, with Edgar using a speedy stride and cheeks flushed.

"Mr. Crisp?" Edgar asked. This elicited a sneer and a sigh from the old man, whose preferred state seemed to be silence.

"Yes."

"The Laniakea has a king, but they also have a council, which sounds to me like the senate we have back home."

"Okay."

"So you have both?"

"Yes."

"So who reports to whom? Or do you vote?"

Mr. Crisp halted. The eyes of the old man gazed out beyond the mist, shadowed by the setting sun as its beams cast a dim light through breaks in the trees. He extended his arm out to stop Edgar and whispered a word just above his breath.

"Run."

Edgar had barely a moment to see Alister emerging from the brush ahead. The three dashed through a cluster of trees, and Mr. Crisp grabbed hold of Edgar's arm as they descended a steep hill, Alister's rapid footsteps closing in behind them.

The hill proved steeper than expected as they lost their footing and stumbled, each collecting dead leaves along their clothes as they rolled.

Edgar was the last to stop as a stiff hand pulled him behind a tree.

"Stop," Mr. Crisp whispered into his ear. "You mustn't speak."

They each held their breath as Alister came into view, searching desperately from tree to tree. Edgar attempted to slow his breath, despite his lungs pleading.

Alister halted several feet from them, though Edgar did not think he saw them. Instead, Alister froze. His eyes darted about, scanning for the source of twigs snapping and bushes rustling. Edgar cursed every breath he took, as though it might give them away.

After a pause that seemed like an eternity, Alister grunted and marched away.

They held their position for several more minutes, not wanting to betray their luck.

Soon, Edgar felt they must be safe now, and he released his breath, just for Mr. Crisp to silence him again.

This time, the old man wasn't frantic. He patiently pulled a finger to his lips, motioning for silence once more, and crept off past several trees as though spying on a doe.

Edgar followed Crisp's line of sight and settled on the image of a young woman. Edgar restrained a gasp as he recognized the girl from his first night along the beach. The same nine-year-old, with light brown hair and a flowing summer dress, knelt down to smell a flower just yards from them.

She inhaled the perfume of the flower, and it appeared to please her as a smile brushed her cheeks. Content, she glanced up at the three hikers.

Though Crisp did not acknowledge her. Nor did he run in fear.

"The Wondress." Again, Crisp's utterance was barely above a whisper.

"Who's the Wondress?" Edgar asked. "I saw that girl along the beach. Is that the girl from the campfire stories back with the Laniakea?"

"They are the same. We are most fortunate, you and I, that we may see her this day. Lore holds that her original name, or perhaps her name still, is Ada. Though when tales are told, she goes by only the one. The Wondress."

The girl stopped smiling at them and whisked up the flowers, assembling them with grace in a basket, as though they might break.

"You don't seem scared," Edgar said. "Doesn't this mean the Demon in the Water is close by?"

"No, I do not think she will harm us, child, and we are far from water." He spoke without breaking his gaze, without moving his arm from holding back Edgar. There did not seem to be a spell cast upon the man, for Edgar felt the same sense of awe. It was a feeling he had when he saw a historical tree in Northern California. A feeling of ancient beings, and Edgar was blessed with the gift of witnessing it.

Crisp continued. "The Wondress does not wish ill on another person. Nor does she act with charity. She holds no opinion. It is told she sets the tide in motion, resulting in waves that cause both life and destruction."

The girl tipped her brow toward the three as she glided into the trees.

"Should we follow her?"

"No, I don't think we should. If she wanted us to follow her, well, then we'd know it."

"And if she wanted us to follow her, and we refused?"

"You'd eventually follow her. If you refused, no war, no curse on your home. You'd eventually follow her, even if you didn't know you were."

To the dismay of Mr. Crisp, the group did not make it to the Evajocalyn by sundown, forcing them to make camp amongst the trees. Through endless hours, Edgar lay awake, fearing the eerie sounds of nocturnal alien animals communicating through chirps and squeaks, accompanied by the duet of his snoring companions.

As the sun peeked over the horizon, a gentle wind carried in the familiar scent of mint and eucalyptus, the receding night giving way to a welcoming morning.

"My, it's a lovely day for a hike," said Crisp, giving voice to his night aches as he moaned through every movement he took to stand. "Wouldn't you agree?" Without haste, he rose and pulled bits of food from his pack, offering them first to the dog and then to Edgar.

Edgar assumed the old man directed the question toward Becca, and so he did not answer. Instead, he stared out at the thinning mist, brushed away by the heavenly hand of the wind.

After glancing over his shoulder at the old man, he could see his suspicions were correct, and Mr. Crisp had directed the question to his dog.

Neither Crisp nor Edgar delayed before continuing their hike. Mr. Crisp folded their blankets with a shocking quickness, leaving little time for Edgar to offer help.

It was in this early morning that Edgar could enjoy the silence without the stain of voices. The absence of distraction as they hiked magnified subtle harmonies echoing off of the rocky cliffs not far ahead. The animals that had kept him awake at night had all burrowed into their homes, and the morning birds were now waking.

If he stayed silent long enough, he could hear the trickling of a riverbed competing with the faint sound of the breeze.

"It certainly is peaceful here," Edgar said. Crisp turned away from Becca to address Edgar's insertion into their conversation. He swiftly glanced back at Becca, exchanging a confused he's-still-here eye roll.

"Yes, this is actually the best time of year for us to be hiking. Several months earlier and sheets of rain would cover us. Several months from now, the moisture in the trees would freeze over. This entire forest would be rather hostile. You'd be cold, certainly. But, more than that, the ice frozen into the ground and trees would make the entire trip extremely unpleasant, if not impossible."

Edgar examined the ground. Though his shoes collected little mud, he noticed that the ground was slightly damp. Moss had collected along the bark of the trees and simply by grabbing hold of a low branch, he could see the trees had sponged up much of the moisture in the air.

"How fortunate that you arrived when you did," said Mr. Crisp.

"I don't feel very fortunate."

Mr. Crisp peered knowingly down at Becca, trotting along his side, sneering at Edgar as though he were a fly that needed to be swatted from his shoulder. "Yes, well, this place isn't all bad. I'm sure it will grow on you."

"Oh, I'm not staying for long. I just need to find my way home."

Crisp continued his nonverbal and not at all subtle interchange with his dog. Even when he wasn't directly talking with the hound, the two seemed to hold an unspoken conversation. It was as though they were a married couple with a shared mind. If the dog could talk, Edgar could imagine them finishing each other's sentences. Or perhaps theirs was a language where a sentence didn't need to be finished.

"Ah, here we are," said Mr. Crisp as the two exited the canopy. The sun had climbed high enough for the light of day to make him squint as he exited the trees.

In front of them lay a small lake with a constant trickle of water. The old man extended his arm upward. "Look, there lies the magnificent beast we've been hunting."

A long, lonely branch extended through a light waterfall. The trunk of the tree must have lain hidden. A tree within a cave, extending that single branch through the timid water. The constant drips left the branch slightly discolored. It must have been a sturdy wood to withstand such a consistent flow.

This branch would be easy to miss. A quiet child in a busy classroom, he could easily overlook it. It would seem almost embarrassing to bring it up under normal circumstances. Edgar might as well mention a rock on the ground or the pile of leaves that he kicked to the side to make a straighter path. But no, this branch was not insignificant.

Edgar began his search for a pathway up. He wasn't a strong climber, and his party didn't seem the type to traverse steep slopes, so finding an appropriate pathway meant first looking for a paved walking path and then dramatically reducing his standards with each iteration. Finally, as though he was going through the five stages of grief, Edgar landed on acceptance and simply started climbing.

"Why don't you stay here with Becca?" Edgar said. "You can start a small fire, and I'll be back this way in no time. It shouldn't be long, I wouldn't think. Hopefully, you brought a book."

Edgar turned to see that his hiking partners were no longer behind him, and he was apparently talking to no one. As he looked up, he saw that both Mr. Crisp and Becca had already reached the top and were looking down impatiently, waiting for Edgar to catch up.

"How did you do that?"

"I am your guide, aren't I? There's a path around the back, around that corner." Mr. Crisp pointed back behind him, where Edgar could see portions of the path that the old man had described.

Frustration and relief made for an odd cocktail as Edgar brushed the dirt from his legs and ascended up the path.

He reached the top and joined his party. He realized that the thin air had left him short of breath, and so he rested, perching upon the ridge alongside his companions.

From his new vantage point, he could see more of this strange planet than he ever had. He could see the beach where he first landed, waves brushing along the shoreline and receding just as slowly back into the sea. He could see the tall cliffs off the shore begin their dramatic descent into the water, just as they had on his first night.

"Ah, the Cliffs of Seri," said the old man with a deep sigh of admiration. "I remember the first time I laid my eyes on them as a child when I first moved here from Inland Chiles."

"They are certainly beautiful. Why do they move the way they do?"

"That is an excellent question, and likely one you've been wondering for quite some time. The Cliffs of Seri move on their own. They're always in that general area, although frequently moving around like a pent-up hound eager to escape. Legend speaks of them traveling where they're needed. Some storytellers claim they act on their own like a living beast.

Others say that magical beings, like that of the Treos, call upon it as they wish, wielding it like a weapon of war."

"How could it be a weapon?"

"Anything big can be a weapon, Edgar. It is the truly horrid among us that transform a peaceful giant into a thrashing beast."

"So it's alive or controlled by a magical being? Both possibilities seem hard to believe."

Just as he completed his sentence, the Cliffs ascended, causing the water surrounding them to thrash about.

The old man leaned forward and lowered his voice as the distant rumble of the Cliffs quieted to nothing.

"And yet there it is," he said. "You will find there are many things in the endless heavens and the great depths of the sea that are only explained in ways that you cannot understand. It is unexplainable to you simply because the explanation is far too wonderful."

Edgar allowed the old man's words to settle upon him. An endless list of questions came to mind. Were there other civilizations far away, on the other end of the globe, or deep within its sea? Were there kings here hundreds or even thousands of years ago? How old was this place? With everything he'd seen so far, what sort of magic existed on this planet that would surprise even the locals?

He realized he couldn't ask these questions. He settled on one.

"Mr. Crisp?"

The old man was eating a sandwich from his pack. It differed from the bread back home, appearing harder and spongier and filled with various types of meat, most of which Edgar could not place.

"Yes, boy?" said the old man.

"What's Treos?" Edgar asked.

"What's that you say?"

"The Treos. You spoke of them a moment ago."

"Well, I guess I was speaking about Regaldo, the second brother. Although Treos refers to all three. Many believe they're the reason all these magical things happen here."

"Regaldo? Brothers?"

"So no one has told you? Well, I suppose while we're resting I'll tell you the tale, or at least what I recall."

Mr. Crisp plucked a thin branch from a tree and sat next to Edgar.

"This is the lore of Treos, as passed down from cave paintings long ago." With the branch, he drew a small oval in the dirt. "There were once three brothers. The oldest was the wisest, the second had a power beyond comprehension, and the third, while also powerful, was deeply impressionable and looked up to both brothers with admiration. They found themselves lost one day traveling down a winding road. The wise brother found a clear path and suggested they take it, since it appeared straight and allowed them to see all obstacles."

Mr. Crisp used the branch to trace the oval in the dirt as he spoke. "What they didn't know was that this road was not straight, but circular. It also had no exits, only entrances, which meant they could not leave.

"They saw other travelers along the way and begged them to enter and help. But once the other travelers entered, they were stuck as well. Moreover, if a helpful traveler were to die along the road, their reincarnation would reappear upon the next loop around. Every person who tried to help them doomed themselves to the same fate.

"The second brother suggested magic that could allow them to leave, though none worked. Meanwhile, the wise brother insisted on following an intricate plan that only he could understand. They fought over this. Soon, the wise brother convinced the impressionable one to use his power to kill the second brother, but he failed.

"Saddened by their betrayal, the second brother rebuked them both, but they could not part from one another. The path cursed them to continue their battle with every iteration of the road."

Mr. Crisp stopped tracing the oval and placed the stick down in front of him.

"Like many tales, there are bits based in reality. There are three brothers that inhabit this world, and this legend is based on those brothers. One of them hired the gang you saw attack the village just the other night. His name is Aiken. It's complicated, but it boils down to this: Aiken wants something, and Regaldo, the second brother, doesn't want him to have it. Regaldo is the more powerful in forms of the Gift, plainly put, the magical art, but Aiken is the smarter, more cunning planner. The two have been battling one another their whole lives. Once, long ago, Aiken lured Regaldo into a trap. Aiken didn't kill his brother, but legend says that he humiliated Regaldo. Pride is the folly of the gifted. Regaldo became a hermit, and no one has seen him in centuries."

"How was he humiliated?"

"Well, I'm not sure, to be frank. But I know, on that day, Aiken took something from his brother. Regaldo deeply mourns the loss he endured that day."

"What about the other brother?"

"Hmm?" Mr. Crisp inquired.

"You said Regaldo was the second brother, but there are three. You've only talked about Regaldo and Aiken. Who's the third?"

Mr. Crisp smiled with excitement, and his eyes deepened. He reminded Edgar of Ben Friar when he got to talking about a story of great interest. "I don't know."

"You don't?" Edgar asked, astonished, after the emotion on the old man's face.

"No one does. Or few people do, at least. Locals often tell stories around the fire about Treos. Regaldo always had the best handle on the Gift. Aiken is the most strategic thinker, but no one really knows how to place the third brother. They don't even know his name. Does he balance the two brothers? Does he take sides with one over the other? Why is he hidden?"

"Hasn't someone asked Aiken? I mean, sure, Regaldo is a hermit, but surely people have spoken with Aiken. Can't someone ask him?"

"Aiken is a very secretive man. Perhaps those in his inner circle know about the third brother, but they're not the type to contribute to local lore. We'll all just have to be comfortable not knowing."

The old man climbed to his feet, and Becca followed. He pulled his pack over his shoulders and extended his hand to Edgar. "Shall we continue onward?"

"Actually, I had one more question," said Edgar.

"And that would be?"

"If that story is only a legend, and it's actually about Aiken, Regaldo, and the third brother, then how did the story originate from cave paintings? How could they possibly be that old?"

A sly smile slid across Mr. Crisp's face. "That is an excellent question. And maybe one day you'll be the one to find the answer."

EIGHTEEN

WHEN THEY GOT TO the top, the tension in his shoulders loosened as he found a small cave exposing a cramped passageway behind the waterfall. Edgar had been eyeing the branch the entire climb, wondering what he was going to do when he got there. He needed to get to the tree behind the waterfall. The famed Evajocalyn.

Mr. Crisp and Becca led the way, following the cave wall through a winding corridor. Eventually, the corridor ended, opening to a circular room behind the waterfall. Sunlight shone through the trickling water, exposing an inner chamber. Above, branches crept like roots along the ceiling until a single one emerged as the lonely branch encroaching on the trickling falls. The room seemed too well structured to be called natural. This looked man-made and cylindrical.

In the center of the room was the majestic tree, the Evajocalyn. Yet this was only part of the tree, only the top. This room was too small to hold the greatness of this giant. The rest of the tree extended downward into the earth through a gaping pit, with spelunking the only method to reach its base through the endless cavern below their feet. The room surrounded only the tip of the tree, as though it were a tree house from a childhood story.

Edgar crept forward toward the center of the room. There was a sizable gap between the ground and the trunk. As he looked down into the gap, he observed a vague glow where a bottom ought to be. The amber hue flamed from the supposed base of the tree, though it did not feel hot, just radiant. It was sobering to think that this was where he needed to go.

The entire experience was not what he expected, although Edgar wasn't sure what he should expect. A winding pathway wrapped around the giant tree and descended into the deep hole.

Edgar released a sigh of relief at the sight of the path. He had no climbing experience and did not know how he would have climbed down otherwise. The only reason he had made the trek here was simply that it seemed to be the next logical step. He figured he'd know what to do when he got here, and his impulse did not disappoint.

The pathway before him was not steep and allowed him to walk down to the bottom as though it were a long hike.

Still, to think there'd be no danger would be foolish. First, the path had no railing. With nothing to hold on to, he'd surely lose balance and fall if he were too careless. Last, the pit looked too deep to travel in a single day. If he needed to set up camp for the night, he would need to do so along the path and hope he didn't roll off the edge.

But his brother was missing. Of his days along the alien coast, staying with the warrior tribe of the Laniakea, this was the sole lead he had to find his brother.

The only way out is through.

It was then that Edgar realized how truly large this tree was. The pit was wide, a hundred feet in diameter. Yet the tremendous tree occupied most of the space. The bark maintained a dark red and brown with a rough exterior. The branches were sparse when present at all.

"Well," said Crisp. "After you." A gulp flexed his Adam's apple.

"You look nervous," said Edgar.

"That's because I am, Edgar."

"I thought you said you've been here."

"I said I've been to the tree, meaning I've been to this room. I've never been beyond this point."

Edgar took a step and then looked back up at his guide.

"You know, you don't have to come with me. You agreed to take me to the Evajocalyn. You've done that. You've done what you've needed to do. You and Becca can go back to the village, and I'll return with all the clues I can find on locating my brother. I'll take them back to you, and you can help me in the safety of your home."

Edgar had always considered Mr. Crisp was defined by his grumpy demeanor. At this moment, Edgar saw a determination on his face. While there were only slight differences between his appearance from the time they entered the corridor and this moment, something about the way he held himself had changed. There was a reason Mr. Crisp had agreed to be his guide, even if Edgar didn't know it.

"I'm coming with you. And so is Becca. My king sent me to ensure your security. I shall return with a live child if I return at all."

Edgar respected Mr. Crisp's commitment, but he could not focus on it for long enough to distract from the fear. The three travelers stared down at the pit, filled mostly with the massive tree. With his confidence wavering, Edgar silenced his mind and began his hike down the ominous tree.

The only way out is through.

It wasn't the sun that woke Elena that morning, but an idea. A splendid idea. A glimpse of normalcy if she could only make it happen.

The system she had created for transforming water into something drinkable, combined with her homemade skillet, had allowed for more interesting food. But that wasn't what jolted her from slumber.

Sushi. Or something close to it. That was what she would dedicate the day to.

She had seaweed and a reliable way of catching fish. A variety of plant life from the ocean had swept up along the shore the day before, but she couldn't use that, since flies had already claimed it. She needed something fresh.

Elena waded in the water for an hour before she determined it an unsuitable approach for spotting underwater plant life. There was no good angle, no vantage point, for her to see what she needed.

Rather than tread back to the shore, she waited for the next gentle wave to brush by. As it did, she launched herself from her feet and rode the wave in as far as it would take her, feeling the salty air brush across her cheeks.

Suddenly, a dark figure slid past beneath her legs. She flailed her arms in a panic, losing the pull of the wave.

As she surveyed the water, there was no sign of the creature. She had swum by many animals in her days along the beach, growing more comfortable with them with each passing day. This was different. She had learned to recognize them all, and none had the jet-black tone of this figure.

She recalled a similar feeling on her first night there. Among the various sounds haunting the coast that night was a gurgling from the water. She could explain most of everything she heard at night, but she had found no solution for the gurgling water. Could this dark figure in the water be it?

She gathered her composure and left the water. No longer enthusiastic about swimming along the waves, she settled on a pile of seaweed that had recently collected along the rocks.

She pulled off leaves, washed them in clean water, and toasted them in her skillet.

They tasted glorious.

Three dozen leaves she toasted and collected into piles. Some she wrapped in fish, though they were too brittle to wrap completely, resulting more in a sandwich than a roll. The others she saved for a snack. They reminded her of kale chips, with an odd aftertaste. Alien kale chips.

She would still need to eat for fuel and not comfort, but this wonderful meal gave her a welcome break from the sickening repetition of the same food with each tick of her cave calendar.

That night, as she sat perched along her rock, enjoying the sunset in the distance, she felt her heart beat harder at the sight of a vague shadow wisp across the water, just below the surface, in the light of dusk.

The dim light above reduced, approaching the head of a pin with every step, though the amber base of the tree did not appear closer. He had no sense of progress.

Edgar guessed they had traveled a mile before they saw the third glow. This was not the amber base or the pinhead tip. Rather, this was an additional source of light that radiated from the side of the pit wall.

"What do you think that is?" Edgar asked.

Mr. Crisp squinted. "I suppose we'll have to see. As I've stated, I've never been down here, so I'm afraid we've already exhausted my knowledge. All that's left are local legends. None of which I can back with any certainty."

"What do people say that glow at the bottom is?"

"Well, as you've probably noticed, it looks to be an enormous, ever-glowing fire. Of course, that's impossible, since such a fire in this confined area would cause us three to boil in our skins. It's not—hot, that is—as you can undoubtedly tell. Therefore, Sir Brave, I'm betting it's not a fire."

Mr. Crisp looked back as if he had just told a joke. If it was a joke, it was the first he had heard the old man tell. Edgar didn't laugh, but the nonverbal exchange between Crisp and the dog made him wish he had.

"Good point. What is it people say, though? You're right, it's probably not a fire, but do people say it is? I know I probably would if I saw it from above but was too frightened to climb down."

"Yes, actually. They've named it Refiner's Fire." Again, the old man looked back at Edgar for some acknowledgement, something that confirmed he recognized the phrase. Edgar did not, so he gave no such acknowledgement. "A refiner's fire removes impurities from metal. It makes the metal better. Since this pit is neither hot nor cool, people assume the hike down won't kill you. Which we'll soon prove correct, hopefully." Crisp sounded giddy. "Still, the trek will make you a better person for having done it. They say, looking directly at the fire, once you've reached the bottom, will refine your soul. As I've said, it's the Refiner's Fire."

"Has anyone actually done it? That sort of legend sounds like the kind people have actually completed and come out better on the other end. Or at least perceived to be better."

"You'd think so, but not in quite some time. People used to try frequently. I'm not aware of anyone succeeding. Once the opening at the top disappears from view, it's difficult to tell if you've made any progress at all. Wise men have returned mad. That's hardly what I'd hope to get out of lore as famous as this.

There's at least one explorer that never came back up. With one man missing and nearly the rest insane, the popularity of this hike waned."

"Why did you decide to come, then?"

"Excuse me?"

"I mean, a man of your age going on such a dangerous hike seems...odd."

The low grumble would have left Mr. Crisp's lips unnoticed had it not been for the echoing pit.

"Look, I'm sorry. That was rude of me. I shouldn't have called you old."

"It was rude, but that's not—" Mr. Crisp stopped, struggling to find words. "I am old, that's a fact. I'm not hurt by someone bringing an obvious point to light." He looked down at Becca as though pleading with her to find the right words so he didn't have to. "Why don't I tell you when we get back? How's that?"

"That sounds perfect. I'd like that."

As the three progressed, the light along the pit wall materialized into a cave. The light danced with the cadence of a campfire, although Edgar was reluctant to call it one for fear of suggesting that another person lived down there.

"Oh, by rite of metanoia, would you look at that?" said Mr. Crisp. "It's a cave. How fun."

"It would be nice to go over there and explore," Edgar said. "Anything to get a break from this monotony."

He examined the winding path before him. The three were on the tree, and the cave was on the stone wall opposite them. The gap was much too large to jump and the fall much too far to gamble.

To Edgar's sudden amazement, a disembodied voice spoke into his ear. "You should really take the stairs."

Edgar gasped. His eyes darted about but saw no one. "Did you hear that?"

"The stairs. They're right there." The voice spoke once more.

"I heard nothing," said Mr. Crisp.

Edgar looked down and saw a staircase he didn't recall seeing earlier connecting to the base of the cave. Was it there before? Surely he would have seen it earlier, and his senses simply deceived him. After all, he was hearing a voice.

That led to another question. If his senses were lying to him, then were the stairs truly always there, or could his eyes be lying to him even now as he claimed to see it?

"Do you see those stairs?" Edgar asked. "You don't hear the voice, but please tell me you see those."

"Ah, yes, how perfect. We can use those stairs to get to the cave. I told you this place used to be popular. Someone must have built them as a resting stop for weary travelers. Surely, we need one down here."

The stairs appeared to be made of the same wood as the tree, but the bridge appeared newer. The Evajocalyn appeared ancient. Old enough to turn to stone. The stairs were an infant by contrast.

Edgar hesitated and took a deep breath. Though his partner saw the stairs, it gave him no comfort when confronted with the disembodied voice. Still, he sighed, resigned to the risks he must take to find his brother. Risks like stepping onto mysterious steps, as directed by a voice that wasn't there.

Edgar extended his foot and laid it on the solid stair. He hesitated a moment but ultimately shifted his weight onto his new surface. Relief filled him as he realized the risk he had just taken, stepping onto an unproven staircase.

As he walked across, he felt a newfound confidence. He had chanced fate and everything was fine. New courage filled his veins with adrenaline, mixed with a dash of fear.

When he reached the opening of the cave, he saw what lit the cave. Torches lined a stone hallway twenty feet wide and long enough for the ending to fade from view.

Once on firm ground, Edgar turned to see that Mr. Crisp hadn't followed him. Neither had Becca.

The old man called to him. "You go ahead. The walk has made my dear Becca frightened." His companion gave a questioning whimper, glancing at her owner. "Don't start with that. I can feel you shivering. You just won't admit it."

Edgar, now alone, felt a chill as he entered the corridor. The dirt along the path had a perceptible stillness. Every step appeared to release dirt left undisturbed for centuries. Ahead of him lay a fork in the path.

"Go right," said the voice.

The adrenaline betrayed him, receding as panic set the hairs along his arms to rise. He looked behind him but could no longer see the Evajocalyn and his hiking party. He had traveled too deep into the cave.

Why was he listening to this voice? He suddenly regretted even climbing on the stairs to begin with.

The only way out is through.

I have to do this.

I shall fear no evil.

I will do this.

As he turned, he saw a small room carved from the stone, where a man stood quietly, cooking something blue on a pan over a flame in a makeshift kitchen. He was tall, likely a foot taller than Edgar, and middle-aged. A tattered black suit with frayed cuffs was draped over his boney frame, as though he were attending a wedding on the day he became homeless. Although the strangest thing about the suit was not that it was over-worn. It was that the suit was a style he knew from Earth and was nothing like what the other Cassinians wore.

His home looked self-assembled. Set into the wall of the cave, it had stones for seats and a wooden box set as both the dining room table and the central point for the man's cave-home. In the back, a small fire hissed as the man held a cast-iron skillet just high enough to produce medium heat for his meal.

Edgar stood before the entrance to the man's cave-home, unsure how to proceed. He didn't feel it appropriate to leave but lacked the courage to enter.

"You're not all that friendly, are you?" said the man.

"I'm... Well, I'm a bit surprised," said Edgar.

"Would you like an oro fish?" The man lifted his head and extended the plate out. "Also, my name is Mr. Gracie."

"Mr. Gracie?" Edgar tilted his head at the man.

"Child," Mr. Gracie said curtly. "I go by many things. Most of which you can't pronounce. Partly because you lack the skill of tongue, but mostly because the words in my native dialect, when spoken by you, would cause a series of firings in your mind that would lead you to lose your eyesight and the ability to hear vowels. Also, is that a 'no?'"

"A no?"

"Child, do pay attention."

A pause hung between them for a brief beat.

"Oh, the fish."

"Yes, the fish!"

"I'm actually...well, sure," Edgar said. His fear had not subsided, yet somehow he felt it reasonable to enter the room and take the proffered meal from a mystical homeless man in a cave deep within the ground. Edgar wasn't sure if his confidence came from the fact that the man had not yet harmed him or that he didn't feel as though Edgar was worth being harmed.

And so he ate. The texture resembled scrambled eggs from back home.

A familiar look came into Mr. Gracie's eyes. It was that of an upset mother, perhaps Susan Friar, expecting very little from her child after tracking mud indoors.

"You sure are eager," said Mr. Gracie.

"I'm very sorry. I'm normally much more polite than this. My name is Edgar, by the way."

"Well, hello Mr. Edgar."

"Just Edgar is fine."

"I still go by Mr. Gracie. These fish glow at night. Well, when they're alive they do. They swim by the shore and are incredibly easy to catch. They reproduce every sixty days, so you'll end up eating loads of these creatures here."

"Do you know me?" Edgar asked through a full mouth.

"I do not. Why?"

"Well, you speak like you know I'm a visitor, and you know my native language fluently enough to speak it. Actually, I've been wondering about that since I first met the locals here. They all pick up my language quickly and give me only a partial reason to explain it. On top of all that, you also know that *Mr.* is a common title where I'm from. You say you go by other names, but I'm certain a formal title from Earth and a last name that doesn't sound like gibberish to a person like me isn't one of them. What makes matters even stranger is the fact that I just left Mr. Crisp on the stairs, and this entire time I still don't understand why he goes by *Mr.* as well."

"Mr. Crisp?"

"Oh yes, he's an old man that is acting as my guide. He's back on the stairs."

"You left an elderly man on the stairs?"

"Well, he's not alone. He has his dog."

"That hardly improves things, boy."

Shaking his head, Mr. Gracie placed another fish on a plate and handed it to Edgar. For the first time after their introduction, Mr. Gracie's shoulders relaxed, and his face was no longer hard. Rather, a brief glimpse of kindness flashed across it. It wasn't a smile that Edgar caught. It was the look of a lonely man who was finally asked for advice.

"Things are simpler than they seem, and things are more complex than they seem."

"What does that mean?" asked Edgar.

"*a'Fellen* senses."

"*a'Fellen?*"

"You mentioned others that speak your language here?"

"Yes. Like I said, I've been wondering that for a while."

Mr. Gracie sat and shoveled a scoop of fish into his mouth. "Our minds interact at some level. People on this planet usually can lean on their *a'Fellen* senses to communicate, though some are better than others. Not because it's a talent. It's more like how perceptive someone is."

"You can read my mind?"

"No, of course not," Mr. Gracie scoffed. Edgar suddenly felt like he had asked a scientist if he performed magic.

"Well then, what is it? How can you tell all these things about me but not read my mind? How do you know the words I'm saying and also know formal titles, like *Mr.*, that I haven't said yet?"

"Can you tell when someone is mad at you?" asked Mr. Gracie.

"Yes. Well, sure."

"Can you tell why they're mad at you?"

"Sometimes. Not always. If I know I did something wrong, then it's probably that."

"It's similar but much more advanced. You have a sense that they're mad at you, but you can't read their mind to find the reason why. You can deduce some things, like if you know you've done something wrong. Our brains do a sort of dance here that allows us to speak to each other and know some surface-level things about one another, but I can never read your mind."

Mr. Gracie took a bite of his fish, making no pretense at hurrying along his delectable meal while Edgar waited. At one moment, Edgar had thought Mr. Gracie's explanation was complete and opened his mouth to speak, only to be silenced by a solitary finger issuing Edgar to wait. "I think it's an evolutionary trait," Mr. Gracie said once he swallowed his last bite, as though there were no interruption. "That's my own personal hypothesis. This planet has 300,000 native languages, and none of them really have that much in common. If you ask me what I think, early Cassinians probably had a much easier time surviving if they could deduce a fair amount of communication through nonverbal methods and then translate them through verbal means. After millions of years, we have this 'mind-reading' thing, as you call it. It's part of our biology."

They sat in silence for a short while, Edgar trying to understand what he had just heard and Mr. Gracie eating.

Finally, Edgar looked up at Mr. Gracie and asked him the question he had been wondering since he arrived.

"Mr. Gracie, you seem intelligent. In fact, the magic trick you did with the stairs and speaking to me from the Evajocalyn, you seem like you might be even a more advanced species than the people I have interacted with so far. Can I trust you with a question I've been wondering since I arrived?"

Mr. Gracie did not look up but also did not stop Edgar from continuing.

"I came to this planet through a portal," Edgar said, "following the man that kidnapped my brother. Even if I find him, I'm still unable to return home. I'm probably on the opposite side of the universe. How did I get here? Do you know? How did I travel across the universe within a single minute?"

Mr. Gracie calmly put down his food. In no hurry, he used a cloth to wipe his hands clean. As he placed the cloth on the box-made-table, he said aloud, "You know not the questions you need to ask."

"What?"

"Your question. You're not asking it."

"I just did. How did I get here?"

Mr. Gracie shook his head.

"Okay, fine. How do I get back once I find my brother?"

"Make no mistake, boy. This isn't a riddle. I do not intend to tease you with a lesson. Frankly, I do not care. Within this boundless universe, you will ask many questions. You'll find the answers and then query again. Those will lead to other answers, which lead to new questions. Still, you couldn't have asked the second or third questions without arming yourself with the answers from the first. Sometimes you're incapable of even asking them. In other cases you ask them, but ignorant fallacies and circular reasonings infest your questions so much that it's as adorable as a child and prone to an answer that wets your tongue but does not satisfy your thirst."

Edgar simmered in Gracie's words. *How do I get back?* was a fairly simple question. An important one. Still, playing the peculiar man's game would likely be his best path forward.

"What's at the bottom of the Evajocalyn?"

Mr. Gracie smiled. It was the smile that a father might give an innocent child. "That will have to do. You took a right at the fork, and that brought you here. Go left."

"If I go left, I'll get to the base of the Evajocalyn?"

Mr. Gracie didn't answer. Instead, he maintained his smile as his eyes warmed.

Edgar put down his food, half eaten, and stepped tepidly into the torched lighting of the path.

Mr. Gracie continued eating, seeming to give the entire situation little more thought.

NINETEEN

Mr. Gracie finished his food, leaving no scraps un-eaten, and placed the plate on the table in front of him. No matter how frequently he had the oro fish, he never seemed to grow weary of it.

He placed the folded napkin next to his plate and dusted off his trousers as he stood and walked down the cavern toward his spectral stairs.

The elderly man stood before the stairs, his dog panting beside him. Neither was entirely sure what to make of a stranger emerging from the torchlit tunnel that had just taken in Edgar. Gracie waved them both an invitation and turned back to his cave. The last sight Gracie saw before he turned was an exchanged look between man and beast and a whimper of confusion, unclear if it came from the hound or the man.

Mr. Gracie had just completed preparing two drinks in his makeshift kitchen when the elderly man shuffled in.

"You must be Mr. Crisp. I am Mr. Gracie."

The old man and his dog crept in, exploring the walls of his home as they entered.

The two men contrasted each other almost perfectly. Gracie, while he didn't consider himself a young man, had a clear thirty years of youth on Crisp.

Second, while Gracie was unusually tall, the man before him was unusually short. Even as they stood a room apart, the difference in their heights was obvious.

As a last point, Gracie would never have traveled with a dog. They made dreadful roommates and worse traveling companions. As the old man was wandering down the Evajocalyn with his hound at his side, Gracie could only conclude that Crisp preferred the company of animals, while Gracie barely stood the company of people.

"I'm sorry," Crisp said. "I didn't know anyone lived down here."

"Yes, I've lived down here a while now." Gracie handed him the drink. "Almost twenty years, if I were to guess. I find my way in and out through my own means. May I ask the name of your hound?"

"Oh, dear. Yes. My apologies. This is Becca."

"What a wonderful name. *Becca.* Would either of you like something to eat? I have a calmory that I don't think would upset Becca's stomach. I've also prepared oro fish in seven different ways. Although only three of which would I give to dogs."

"That would be nice, thank you. The calmory, I mean."

Mr. Gracie prepared two meals, one for his guest and another for the guest's companion, while Crisp darted his eyes about the cave, less subtle than he likely intended.

"Where is the boy? Where is Edgar?"

"Oh, yes. Edgar. He is questing. At least that's what we'll call it. The dear boy ought to do some sort of work, shouldn't he?"

"Yes, yes," Crisp said. "Although the boy is in my care, you see."

"Dear Mr. Crisp, you three are my guests. I would hardly send the boy on an adventure that would cause him harm and then concern myself with the food ingested by your dog."

"Ah, yes. Of course. True."

"I have to ask. It is odd to see the three of you down here. I haven't had guests in quite a while. Neither of you seems like an adventurer."

Mr. Crisp took a deep breath and stared down at his dog before answering. He had a burden that Gracie couldn't see. "Well, to be honest, my wife passed away not too long ago. This is quite a new chapter for me."

Crisp released the tension in his shoulders. For the first time since entering the cave-home of Mr. Gracie, an invisible shield fell from the old man.

"I am sorry to hear that," said Gracie.

"Yes, yes. It's all right. Her name was Becca."

"Oh, I must apologize. I misunderstood. I thought your dog's name was Becca."

Mr. Crisp shifted in his chair. While his ears could hear and his mouth could speak, his eyes fogged as though unable to see as he stared off into nothing. "The dog spent most of her life without a name. We called her Dog most of her life. To be more accurate, we called her Dog Thing. Primarily because we found her as a wild stray and didn't precisely know what type of animal she was. We tried on a few names, me and my wife, but none of them stuck. When Becca, my wife, passed away, I just started calling the dog by my wife's name."

Crisp paused. He placed his hand along his brow as though hoping to wipe the grief away. "I've told no one that, and to be honest, I don't know why I tell you now. When I call her Becca, it allows me to talk conversationally to her like I'm talking to my wife."

Mr. Gracie smiled, causing the age lines around his eyes to fold. "I promise not to expose your secret to a single soul," he said, gesturing to the empty cavern.

They sat in silence for a moment, Mr. Gracie sipping his drink and his guests eating.

Gracie was the first to break. "Does anyone ask you why you named your dog after your wife?"

Mr. Crisp looked up, warmth returning to his cheeks. "Names are fascinating. Some people take pride in knowing everyone's name, while others often admit that they don't remember. I'm a lonely man and genuinely don't know many of my tribe members' names. Frankly, I'm certain they don't know mine. Some do. The older folk and the members of the council that remember me in my earlier phases of life, but they hardly have time to interact with the townsfolk. I can't say anyone that I see regularly has ever made the connection between my late wife and my dog, or at least expressed it. There have been fleeting expressions on the faces of neighbors. I'm sure some realized that a strange truth is there, just beyond the fog, but then shrugged it off, assuming the error was theirs. The correct ones always think they're wrong, and the wrong ones always think they're correct. Isn't that funny?"

"It is." Mr. Gracie ceased eating to watch his new friend, straining to see the soul within the shell before him.

Crisp fidgeted, unsure where to place his hands and oblivious to the meal before him that he had unknowingly ignored. The observable silence between them was no help in soothing him.

Mr. Gracie smiled once more. "I don't think yours, or Becca's," he said, raising his glass to the dog, "is a name I'll forget."

As Edgar advanced along the tunnel, the torches that had illuminated his path just moments earlier were becoming scarce, each one placed farther than the one preceding. As he approached the last one, it felt as though he were crossing beyond the event horizon of a black hole. Beyond that point, he would have no hope of returning. He investigated the torch, hoping to lessen its hold on the ground by pulling and shifting it along its base. Instead, it remained a single body with stone beneath.

He inched forward, reluctant to allow the shadow's embrace as the light behind him faded to black.

Was this way better than the well-lit tree? Gracie was confident, though doubt slithered in as he realized the man that he shared a meal with was but a stranger and gave him little reason to gamble away his safety.

Edgar crept past the potholes that littered the ground.

He panicked. Would he unknowingly take a turn, preventing him from finding his way back? Would he die down here?

He had felt this feeling before, on the beach. On the first day. Trapped. That day felt so long ago. He had lived through so much in such a short time.

He kept moving, each step measured.

He pulled up a hand, placing it inches from his face, seeming as good a test as any. There was nothing. No light. No hand. Void, but for the sound of dripping water somewhere and the uneven ground beneath his soles. The taste of salt leaked into his mouth and stained his tongue.

He felt for the cave wall, relying solely on touch to navigate.

There had to be an easier way.

A small creature clicked past his feet, and he swung his body away. That was the last step he gave to the cave, the last step he gifted to Gracie. No more would he gamble so much, investing entirely without knowing more than a direction.

He turned around to walk back, but after several steps, his head hit a stone drooping from the ceiling. Pain brought the only color he could see. If the pinprick of the last lit torch came into view, the purple and blue in his eyes fogged it. He extended his hands once more to get his bearings.

Wet stone left a residue lacing his tattered hands. This was a different wall.

Am I headed in the right direction?

Three more steps landed his foot against a bolder, and he fell to the ground.

Another shade of hazy blue conquered his eyesight, though, this time it did not fade.

But it was not his own. Edgar looked up and saw the room dimly lit in a veil of a blue hue. The cave walls showed their shape, and he could see everything.

What was the source of that light?

He peered down the passage and saw a small orb floating, guided by a dancing wind that wasn't there.

As it turned down the corridor, Edgar, desperate not to lose it, dashed after it.

The fear pulled at each step, but he swept it away. He had seen the orb before. This would lead to Simon. To home.

He followed the blue light, darting around corners until he halted at the sight of a young girl. The girl from the beach. The girl that Crisp had spoken of.

This was The Wondress.

Somehow, she suddenly appeared older. She aged before him until she appeared as a middle-aged woman. How could that be? A cloak was draped over her head and wrapped around her body as though to keep her warm. She wore a kind smile and had trusting eyes the color of chocolate.

She wept, though radiating a smile.

"Hold, Edgar. Remove the burden from your back." Warmth covered Edgar, coupled with her soothing words. He wanted to stay in this place forever.

"I brought nothing," Edgar said. "I have nothing to remove."

The woman was weeping now and tilted her face slightly, exposing a knowing glimmer. "I know you, Edgar. I know your soul and the yoke that need not be."

"Why did you call me here? Where's my brother?"

"That will come in due time." Her glow darkened in shade, and her smile drifted.

"I don't have time. I need to find my brother."

"Hold, Edgar. Remove the burden from your back."

"You're teaching me something," Edgar said. A flood of anger replaced the warmth. "I don't need to be taught. I need my brother. That's it. It's simple. How do I get my brother back?"

The woman grew to dwarf him, and suddenly it was Edgar's turn to weep. His mind went into a tailspin as the Wondress increased. The cave expanded to give her room, yielding to her will.

She bellowed, shaking the stone walls. "Who sent the twin to the Rambling Forest? Who took the bow from the Graved Hunter? Did not I? Is it not I that guided and you that followed?"

Edgar felt small in her presence. He was raw and exposed, a wound to salt water.

The woman saw this in him and sighed, returning to her original form. She carefully examined the frightened boy, allowing her soothing warmth to return.

"I'm here to help you, Edgar. It is not the greatest among you that will turn the tide. It is only the cracked who is molded anew."

As she completed her sentence, she diminished into the floating orb and raced down the cave. Edgar darted after her, not allowing her to leave. He did not want his only chance at finding his brother to slip away, but more than that, the warmth he felt in her presence was an addiction that he craved.

The orb was reduced to a small marble and slipped into the cracks of the cave wall.

Edgar continued his momentum but halted at the crack. He peered into it, straining to see her once again. He pounded on the wall and felt something new, a thinner wall than he had felt earlier. This wall was hollow and cracked to give way to something just beyond.

Edgar picked up a stone the size of his head and took several steps back, maintaining his focus on the crack. He sprinted at the cave wall with the stone fixed ahead of him, ready for impact.

The rock wall exploded into a wall of sand.

Light broke in. It was the sun, hanging far off in the sky. Somehow, Edgar found himself once more on a beach, much like the one he had landed on, though this was noticeably smaller.

"Edgar?" said a far and frantic voice. "Edgar!"

The voice was Elena's. She wore her same clothes from home, now tattered, faded, and worn. Knots littered her hair, and her skin was a crisp leather.

"You're here! I thought I was going to die, but you're here! How are you here?"

Edgar said nothing. He simply embraced his long-lost companion and wept.

TWENTY

T HIS BEACH COULD HAVE been an island. It was just as
challenging to reach, boxed in by sentinel cliffs scraping
the clouds.

Edgar's brother would swim to coves such as this one, the
adventurer that he was. It would seem to some that Simon did
these things to exhibit his bravery, but he didn't need to be
brave. He didn't desire it, just as a full stomach doesn't desire
food. It was a part of him, an inner magnet leading north.

To Edgar, descending the Evajocalyn was a burden that he
had not chosen. There was no joy in hiking the giant tree,
though if he left it be, he would be no closer to finding Simon or traveling home. If Simon had any such burden at the
thought of adventure back home, he never acknowledged it.

If the two brothers switched roles, if a strange man kidnapped Edgar and there was only Simon left to save him, Simon would descend the Evajocalyn with an eager grin, an ad-

dict to his vice. The dark cave would have piqued his curiosity, inviting him in: *"here, let me show you the next part."*

They both would have traveled down the Evajocalyn, but for different reasons. Edgar needed to climb down the giant tree because it was the next step. Simon would have needed to because it was there. The tree would have been a puzzle beckoning to be solved.

"I have so many questions," Elena said, galloping through her words. "Where are we? How did we get here? How are we going to get home?"

Edgar shook his head. "I can't even guess. With everything that's happened over the last month, the questions just stack up, with no answers. There's a lot to talk about, but we also have a long walk back and not enough food."

"I have food here."

"You found food? Here?"

"Yes. I've been collecting this plant and catching fish. They're safe to eat. At least they haven't killed me yet. I've been collecting this seaweed and leaving it out in the sun to dry." Elena pointed over to a massive stone with several green and brown sheets splayed out in the harsh sun. "It tastes like kale chips when toasted."

"How do you know it's okay to eat?"

"I mean, I don't. But then again, I'm probably going to die here. Or at least I was until you came. But look, I not only have kale chips, but I have cooked fish and crab too. We can eat here and pack the kale for the walk back."

"You can cook your fish?" This impressed him. Suddenly, he no longer felt like he was rescuing her. He'd never be able to cook fish on an empty beach.

"Yes, I'll show you. But I have more questions. What happened after we went through the wormhole? I remember a lot of flashing lights. It looked like we had flown through space. Are we on another planet? We must be. I see nebulas at night and clusters of stars unlike anything at home."

Edgar shook his head, unsure how to unpack the thoughts bunched in his head. "Yes, I believe we are. There are people here that don't look like people at home. I can't explain it. An alien planet makes as much sense as anything else."

"How are we going to get home?"

Edgar shook his head. "My plan so far has just been to take the next thing that lands on my lap and run with it. That's how I ended up here, so you might say it's been working. It hasn't gotten me home, so maybe it's not perfect. The only thing I know for sure is that if I do nothing, I'm going to go crazy."

"So we're a lot alike."

"What do you mean?"

"I ate the strange alien kale because otherwise I'd die without trying. You're doing your thing because you might otherwise go insane without trying. We're both just trying to make do with what we got."

Edgar shrugged. "Yeah, I guess you're—"

A large spout of water erupted just off the coast.

"What was that?" asked Edgar.

"I don't know, actually. It happens from time to time. There's some dark creature beneath the water that I haven't quite met yet. There are a lot of strange things along this cove."

"Well, we need to go."

"Yes, but don't you want to take some food—"

The water off the beach erupted once more.

"Well, that's weird," Elena said. "It usually only does that every few hours. Not back to back. Whatever it is, it's usually kind of shy."

Two eyes emerged from the water, followed by a black, leathery face. Its ears drooped down like a hound's, only to flex up at the sight of Elena and Edgar.

The duo did not need to communicate. Both sprinted, trudging through deep sand, the sound of splashing water growing louder behind them as they struggled. They reached the large rocks leading up to the cave entrance Edgar had just come from. Paws padded along the sand as they climbed.

Edgar looked back. The creature had the body of a large hound with a sloped back, inclined toward larger hind legs. Small wings decorated its sides, but these wings would not aid in flight. They were as leathery as the rest of the creature's body and tilted enough to make them more appropriate for swimming through water than soaring through air. Its face sneered with jagged teeth randomly scattered across its jaw. It released a thunderous growl, cut short by the clamping of its jaw into a bite. As the beast gained its footing on the sand, it charged at its prey.

Edgar and Elena leaped over each rock, making their way up to the cave. The sun illuminated the darkness, exposing a pocked, uneven ground and jagged walls. The two ran through with little thought to tripping over potholes or rocks.

As they passed Mr. Gracie's home, Edgar quickly glanced to see if he was there, eager to warn him. The man's absence was a slight relief, but not enough to calm his pounding chest. He was unsure if Gracie could outrun the enormous beast. This poor person would have lived a long, happy life if Edgar hadn't invited in the stalking predator. But there was no Mr. Gracie. The cave home, with all its clutter tossed about, was now vacant.

His concern quickly moved to Crisp. He was older than Gracie. Edgar hoped that wherever Gracie was, he was safe and that Crisp was with him.

The chase continued to the staircase, pausing briefly as Elena gulped at the depth and grandeur of the Evajocalyn. When she looked down at the deep pit, her face went white with fear.

She's never seen this.

Edgar ushered her forward. "We don't have time."

The howling of the beast echoed through the chambers behind them.

Elena would not budge, and Edgar panicked. She must fear heights.

"Elena, you cooked fish on an empty beach. You can do this."

She did not respond.

The echo of the howling beast grew louder.

"We need to go, now."

He could now see a shadow of a galloping hound running desperately toward its next meal.

"You ruined my home," said the voice of Mr. Gracie, as calm as he was when they were eating fish in his kitchen. He stood in a small inset within the cave wall. He emerged with Crisp beside him, looking annoyed, as though he was inconvenienced with taking out the trash during a rainstorm.

"Mr. Gracie..."

"I really liked this place. It was quiet. No neighbors."

"There's a giant dog thing—"

"The ragaborean. I know." Mr. Gracie waited as though expecting Edgar to understand. "Fine, hold still."

Mr. Gracie strolled forward, pulling the group together.

The surrounding area faded, like being shaken from a dream. Edgar's eyes lost focus, and his sight faded into complete darkness. A scattering of small orbs emerged, surrounding him in a sphere. Edgar realized he had been in this place before. This was how he got here. This was the blue light he had flown through when he first went through the portal and landed on this planet. He looked over and saw Elena presumably making the same discovery as both awe and understanding painted her face.

The crew flew toward one particular light, and it absorbed them.

The darkness faded to light as gravity dragged them down the side of a cliff wall. Shades of amber and red raced past their flailing arms. They tumbled, Edgar only seeing the others in brief and frequent frames as he tumbled.

After an eternity, they landed on level ground. Edgar and the others regained their orientation.

Suddenly, there before them was the base of the Evajocalyn and the source of the amber glow.

A massive glowing ball hovered several meters above the ground. The surrounding space was an enormous circular cavern, likely a mile in diameter. The base of the giant tree lay centered in the cave, its roots disappearing into a moat of water surrounding the tree like potted soil to a houseplant.

Edgar and Elena stood mesmerized by the grandeur of the majestic scene. The tree from this viewpoint was an ageless being, as though the tree and the amber globe were twin souls, one never existing without the other. Even the globe, unlike anything Edgar's earthly eyes had gazed upon, submitted to the glory of the tree. The longer he stared at the pair, the more he could feel their bond. The sensation enveloped him. There was a love between these two, as though they lived and breathed only for each other. The tree had a hold on the amber globe and the globe a desire never to leave the tree.

The longer he stared, the more he felt his mind slip. He could feel the light pulling at him, tugging at his mind.

He could see the globe moving. Revolving. It wasn't fast enough to see without concentrating. Maybe he was losing his mind. Maybe it was too late.

"Sorry about that," Mr. Gracie said, snapping him out of his hypnosis. "I meant to get us to the top. I've never really been good at that trick."

TWENTY-ONE

E DGAR EXAMINED HIS MOTLEY crew of explorers. All but Gracie appeared afflicted, awe and dizzying confusion painted across their faces as they gasped at the redwood titan before them.

Gracie was different. This cavern being his home, the Evajocalyn was something he likely looked at often, and so as the others were experiencing a profound moment, he appeared preoccupied by other things. He seemed to be searching for something amongst the gravel, occasionally stopping to peer into the moat, shaking his head and resuming his hunt along dry land.

"How do we get back?" Elena asked. He did not respond. "You got us here, right? You have some sort of magic?" Her questions sounded more like statements, and she vigorously used those statements to usher Gracie forward toward some mode of rescue plan.

No nod of acknowledgment came from Gracie. His apparent mission pressed him forward like a train.

Edgar turned his attention to the tree. The moat surrounding it left them on the shore, backed against the wall of the cave. The glow of the amber orb fully lit the room and exposed the dizzying depth of the moat. He peered down, observing occasional ridges in the water, appearing close enough to reach but likely farther than they appeared.

The full depth was impossible to see, disappearing into shadow. The shallow ridges were small and disparate, the edges sloping drastically into an abyss, holding more mysteries than it willed to expose.

Examining more closely, Edgar could see no form of life in the glassy water. If there were any, they didn't live shallow enough to see or stir enough to cause ripples. No fish. No moss along the rocks near the shore. The cave appeared void of discernible life.

Mr. Gracie continued his clumsy hike around the cave, peering under rocks and within crevices of the wall.

"What are you looking for?" Elena asked. "You can get us out, right? You can..." She completed her sentence by waving her hands, mimicking what she had likely envisioned was an incantation.

For the first time since Edgar met the man, Mr. Gracie seemed curious. He studied her, furrowing his brow as though discovering a new species he didn't particularly like. He shook his head, took a deep breath to absorb the frustration, and continued his search.

"Who are these people?" Elena asked, now whispering to Edgar. "You brought two old men to rescue me?"

"I've only known him a little longer than you have. He was up there." Edgar subtly signaled up the tree, trying not to let Gracie notice. "And the other one is from a town I found. A town with food and shelter for us to live in until we find our way back home."

"You found a town? With people and food and shelter?" Elena lit up with excitement. As Edgar reexamined her tattered clothes and mud-smeared cheeks, he guessed she was looking forward to eating food that she hadn't caught and prepared herself.

"Yes, but we need to get out of here somehow."

"Where up there did you find him?"

"Which one?"

"The one that did the magic thing. The tall, *less old* one."

"I met him while I was on my way down to get you. He fed me strange blue fish. It looked like I was eating blue scrambled eggs."

"Well, I wouldn't mind food right now. Do you think he lives in this place?"

Mr. Gracie stopped and turned to face them. "You are maddeningly loud, the both of you."

"I was whispering," Elena said.

"We need to get to the top," said Mr. Gracie.

"Yes," said Mr. Crisp.

Elena flung her arms about. "Yeah, that's probably a good idea," she said mockingly.

"I can use *magic*, as you've put it, but I need an object to magnify it. Frankly, I'm not that good."

"Okay, what object?" Edgar asked. "Will this do?" He picked up a stone at random.

Mr. Gracie huffed his irritation through his nose. "No, not a rock. Do you think I'd be searching so thoroughly if the rock you just picked up would do the trick? It's a particular object. Something that belongs to me. I had it with me up there. When we leapt...when we *transported* down here, it should have come with me. It must have. We wouldn't have completed the journey without it. It's a coat, with ancient runes stitched along the inner lining. It's long and drapes down to about..." Mr. Gracie signaled down to below his knees but stopped himself. "On second thought, if you find any coat down here, that's probably the one I'm talking about."

Elena, who had been resting on a large stone, slapped her knees, standing up. "Let's spread out. I'll take this end." She turned and walked toward the cave wall directly behind her.

They each chose sections of the cave containing piles of rocks along the slope of the wall.

The group continued without speaking for a long while. Elena was now Edgar's closest ally and friend simply because they grew up in the same familiar town back on the same familiar Earth. Still, he didn't truly know her. He had never had a long conversation with her without mutual friends nearby, and being stranded together didn't entirely make them close. Maybe one day they would be close, having survived something as grave as this, but that was as much of a grasp at hope as the idea of them surviving at all.

While the others searched for the coat, Edgar searched for clues that would lead him to Simon. He was now at the base of the Evajocalyn and thus the location of the stone that Alister wore around his neck. Edgar had little to go by, but if he were to discover anything at all about his brother's disappearance, now would be the time.

He surveyed the cavern wall. Small tunnels lay scattered along the perimeter, revealing a gray stone contrasting the amber glow of the cave. As he approached each one, he noticed they only extended ten feet into the wall, each with their own mound of small stones resting along the floor. He disrupted several mounds, hoping to find some distinction that he could reasonably call a clue. There was none. Each tunnel was identical to the others, and each mound only varied in size.

Edgar expelled a huff of frustration as he sat down near one mound and sulked. This was his only chance to find out more about his brother's disappearance. The Wondress had given him little more than confusion and fear.

As he stood back up to join the others, he caught a glimmer of light coming from one tunnel. Edgar looked more closely, noticing one stone was more polished than the others, reflecting the light of the amber ball in the center of the cavern.

He plucked it from the tunnel and pulled Alister's necklace out of his pocket to compare. While these stones, whether piled into a mound or made into a necklace, were identical in type, the stone from Alister's necklace matched the polished finish of the one Edgar had just recovered. It was as though an alien jeweler had created the two but sacrificed this new one to the Evajocalyn.

He stuffed both stones back into his pocket and continued his hunt, but he found no other lead to go on.

Edgar returned to Mr. Gracie, compelled to fill his busy mind with the distraction of conversation. "So, what is this *magic?*"

Mr. Gracie paused but then continued to turn over stone after stone. Edgar rolled his eyes, assuming that Gracie had once again ignored him. But then he spoke.

"Well, it's not really magic. You call it magic because you don't understand it. It's like the *a'Fellen* senses that we talked about earlier. There's a reason for it. There's a pattern behind it. You would only call it magic if you didn't have any grasp on the pattern. You might call creating a fire from a spark *magic* if you had never seen someone create their own fire before."

"Then what do you call it?"

"We call that specific act leaping, but the art itself is Gifting."

"Okay, how do you leap?"

He stopped turning over rocks and instead stroked his chin as though deciding which road to take home. "I can't show you."

"Why not?"

"You'll kill yourself. In fact, I could have killed us all just then. I'm not a real Gifter, at least not anymore. If I had made a larger mistake than the one I did, we could have ended up within this wall. We'd still be alive, which would make it worse. Each one of us, frozen in stone with no way of getting out, with no way of even moving a finger. We'd stare at the darkness that fossilized us, alive, until we ran out of breath and died, strangled by the stone."

"Oh. Oh God. Why did you take that chance?"

"Eh, it's fine, really. You needn't overreact."

Edgar slowed his work without realization. He was thinking about what Mr. Gracie was telling him but also about home. "Would it be too dangerous to leap across the universe or leap to find someone who's lost, like my brother?"

"It would be dangerous if I knew how, but I don't. I knew how to leap here because I knew where I was going. It doesn't need to be a familiar spot, but, like traversing a map, I need to understand how I'm going to get there in order to arrive. I couldn't take you to your brother because I don't know where he is, or a pattern of who he is. As for your planet, even if I knew where it was, I'm not nearly talented enough. If I need my coat to get us to the top of the Evajocalyn, then, sadly, I'm not the one to take you across the universe."

Edgar's shoulders drooped at Gracie's words, and for a moment Mr. Gracie appeared to pity him.

"All right, fine. Gather near, younglings, and I'll explain this to you. Only once. If you ask again, I will use my coat to leave without you, once I find it. Really, this would have been much simpler had you asked me up in my home. The same home that beast is likely sniffing through as we speak. That being said, this will have to do."

Gracie took a long stone and used it to draw a large rectangle in the dirt with several stick figures contained inside the rectangle. He decorated his drawing, adding a sun, tree, and a line for the ground. It resembled a child's drawing, and Edgar found himself embarrassed at how this must have looked to Elena. He fought off his temptation to lean over to his fellow Earthling and remind her how little he knew about this man in front of them.

"Well, see, this is all wrong," Gracie said. "It's supposed to be flat. Completely so."

"Is it also supposed to be a child's drawing?" Elena asked. Apparently, she had noticed it too. Crisp raised his eyebrows in agreement, but not with the same embarrassment as Elena and Edgar. He seemed to regard it as a fact that he could verify and nodded at Elena as Becca whimpered curiously.

Gracie ignored all of them, extending out his hands with his palms facing outward toward the ground, as though he were going to push an invisible object into the earth. With one swift nudge, he pushed the air away from him, causing the dirt within the picture to flatten. It was as though he were laying concrete and used a trowel to remove imperfections. The structure of the drawings remained unchanged, but now the portrait looked more like he had drawn it on paper and with proper crayons.

"Imagine this is a self contained, two-dimensional world," he said. As he said this, he nodded toward the picture, and the stick figures moved as though he willed them to live. Elena and Edgar jumped at the sudden animation, though Crisp seemed intrigued, as though he were attending a university lecture.

"In this world, these flat people only know two dimensions, side to side and sky to ground as one flat plane of existence. They do not know our third dimension, nor will they ever truly understand it. Which is why, if you'll notice, none of them have acknowledged us. But if I were to do this..."

Gracie reached into the air above him and pulled out a red cube from nothing, a magician pulling a rabbit out of a hat. He then placed the cube on the drawing. In horrid panic, the stick figures ran about, away from the cube.

"They see the cube," Edgar said.

"Well, they see something, but it's not the cube," said Gracie.

He pulled the cube back into the air, exposing the square imprint the cube had made in the dirt. The stick figures still trembled but made no reaction to Gracie removing the cube. It was instead the imprint of the cube that left them shuddering.

"They are still only two-dimensional creatures and thus only capable of seeing a single side of the cube, since one side on its own is two-dimensional." As Gracie said this, he nodded toward the square in the dirt. "Most of a Gifter's craft involves using higher dimensions to manipulate ours, much like we did with the cube. Remember earlier when I spoke to you while you were hiking down the Evajocalyn?"

"Yes," Edgar said.

"Watch this," Gracie said. He cupped his hands around his mouth and released a bellowing yawp. "Minions, I am thou whom you shall obey."

At this, the stick figures scattered around the drawing. Though, unlike earlier, they didn't all agree on where the source came from. Some seemed scared of the tree, while others ran from the sun. Others still jumped from the ground as though they felt that the very earth they stood on was speaking to them.

The group, save for Gracie, stood in wonderment at the scene unfolding in front of them. Edgar felt pity for the stick figures and their fear, while Elena displayed a completely different sort of amazement. She leaned in with the grin of a child on Christmas Day decorating her face.

"How do you leap?" Elena asked, transfixed on the image before them.

"I'm glad you asked." Gracie extended his hand and mimicked the folding of a page. At this, two corners of the drawing lifted off the dirt like it was paper, the stick figures traveling with the page. Suddenly, the drawing no longer appeared as though it were part of the ground, but rather a manifestation of Mr. Gracie's.

Just as they didn't react to the cube being lifted, the figures did not react to their world being folded in half like the closing of a book. They simply continued their trembling.

When Gracie completed the folding, he made a tapping motion with his finger and swiftly unfolded the drawing, returning it to being flat. As the page unfolded, all figures along the lifted half of the page had fallen through their three-dimensional air and onto the stationary side of the two-dimensional world.

The figures all wailed in horror, realizing that they had abruptly transitioned to the opposite side of the page. They held one another, left with little to do but cower.

"They fell from one end of the page to the other," Elena said.

"Precisely," Gracie said.

"They didn't fall along the page. They fell through our air from one end of the folded page to the other."

"You are much quicker than your friend, young lady. Yes, it is just as you said. If I had an insect on my finger and flicked it to the dirt, it wouldn't slide down my hand. No, the act of flicking it would guide it toward the earth."

As though deaf to the wailing figures on the page, Elena smiled with glee. She did not seem bothered by their torment. Rather, she didn't seem affected by them in the slightest. She had gained a bit of knowledge that invaded the crevices of her mind, making the screams of the figures seem like white noise, the chirps of insignificant crickets.

"Enough," Edgar said. "End their pain. Please."

Gracie waved his hand, and the drawing vanished. "That is leaping. Although you need more dimensions for us, I'm afraid. 7.13 to be exact."

"7.13?" Elena asked.

"Yes, you don't need that much of the eighth dimension."

Elena looked at him, confused.

Mr. Gracie studied her face, understanding a puzzle. "That was humor. Your kind doesn't like it?"

"No, we do, but... Never mind. I am curious, though. It sounds like you can do almost everything using Gifting."

Gracie showed no subtlety in rolling his eyes. "Small child, I'm sure that appears so to you. More accurately, most phenomena you can imagine in this world are possible to a truly powerful Gifter, but not every Gifter is truly powerful. Actually, most can do only a small amount. The limitation in that regard is on your own mind and your ability to stretch it, not a limitation of the Gifting itself. Of course, it's easier for beings of higher dimensions, just as it was for us to drop the cube."

Edgar fluttered with excitement as a new idea entered his mind. "Can you travel back in time? I mean, not you, but a truly powerful Gifter or a Gifter in a higher dimension? Can we go back in time and change what happened to us?"

Gracie shook his head in mock amusement. "No, you poor boy. Your timeline is always in motion, even if it twists and turns. Frankly, you *could* go back and create an alternate Edgar, and that alternate Edgar would live carefree with alternate Simon and never know of the terrible world you now live in, but your timeline is in motion and will stay that way, uninterrupted. You can go back but never undo. You are distinct and immutable."

Edgar's excitement dissipated as he rested his back against the wall. There had to be an answer here. Something that could fix their predicament. He just wasn't sure what.

"You just teleported us from up there to down here," Elena said. "That must be an example of something that's easy."

Gracie gave a sneer at that remark but then shrugged.

Elena continued to question. "Can you give an example of something that's very difficult, even for a truly powerful Gifter?"

Gracie thought for a moment. Then his face lost all color, suddenly looking as though he'd prefer any other conversation to this one.

"There is something," he said. "It's called Mimicry. To project an image from another dimension is easy. To project a voice is as well. But Mimicry changes the appearance of something that already exists in your world by vibrating the particles through the dimensions just so. You're not projecting anything and you're not leaping from one end of the page to the other. You're changing millions of small particles to make the entity itself appear different. Some consider it a violation."

"Are you one of those people?" Elena asked. She appeared too eager, an addict approaching her vice. "Do you consider it a violation?"

"It depends, child. To use it on a willing participant for reasons that are honest is perfectly fine, although quite challenging. To use it on yourself for honest reasons is just the same. But too often it's used for dishonesty and just as often on the unwilling."

The room became silent, reflecting Gracie's discomfort. Edgar frantically tried to think of something else to discuss.

"I gotta say, I don't really understand," Elena said. "With all this talk of using higher dimensions, I want to understand more, but I can't wrap my brain around it."

Gracie chuckled softly to himself. "My dear one, the thought cannot fit inside your head. Not yours and not Edgar's."

Edgar scoffed.

"My dear boy, for once I do not mean to insult. It can no easier fit it in my own head. Not as a three-dimensional being. If you wish to understand in part, you must proceed forward knowing that you will never truly grip the ground on which you stand. When you find comfort in that, only then will you learn to be a Gifter."

The moment turned to a lull. Neither Edgar nor Elena wanted to speak next. With feet firm on the ground, they did not know how to step forward.

"But leaping? You're fine to use leaping to get us out of here?" Edgar asked.

"I can, but I need my coat, as I've stated."

"Yes, but you just did all that," Edgar said, waving his hands at the dirt where the drawing had been.

"Actually, that wasn't me. That was a projection from my old master. That entire experience that you just witnessed was like a recording he had made. I simply played it for you. As I'll remind you once more, I'm not actually very good. I left the order of the Nilleli when I was much younger. I use the coat to magnify my Gifting to help me get by."

"Could you scratch runes onto something else?" Elena asked.

Gracie's irritation reached a pinnacle as he slid his back down the wall and sat.

"You must stop asking these questions. I need my coat for all but the most basic. The creation of runes is far from basic Gifting. If it were as simple as you describe, a child's scribbles could harness the powers of the universe. Is that what you think of me? You think I wield a child's scribbles?"

"Fine," Elena said. "I understand. We'll look."

The group continued their search, spreading out evenly across the cave. As they did, Edgar watched Elena walk away, noticing how easily she climbed on the uneven terrain. He suspected she must have climbed a lot of rocks being stuck on the beach as long as she was.

"Does your kind always stare this much?" inquired Mr. Gracie.

"What? No, I mean. I wasn't staring. Well, I guess I was."

"And you're nervous. Oh goodness me, you like that poor girl."

"No. I mean, she's great, but that's not what I—"

"I can sense something through the pores of your skin. You're nervous. No, not nervous. Awkward. That's a better word, isn't it? You're very awkward."

"Can we just start looking?"

TWENTY-TWO

"DON'T YOU WORRY, MY dear girl," Crisp said. "We'll be out of here soon. You needn't worry in the slightest."

"I'm fine, really," said Elena.

Edgar nudged Elena. "He's talking to his dog."

"You'll be eating the juiciest of meats before sundown," continued Crisp. "Of that, I can assure you."

"What's with these people?" Elena said. "The tall one is rude and arrogant and the short one is off in his own little world, and somehow they're our rescue crew."

Crisp jolted with excitement, beckoning everyone over. "There it is. I found it. I did. It's right down there. See, Becca? We're saved. You wasted too much energy worrying."

The old man pointed deep into the moat. The pool was too deep to see the bottom, but a coat sat calmly upon a ledge, rippling in the still water. "Edgar, be a lad and go down there and fetch it for us."

"Me? I'm a horrible swimmer." He was a fine swimmer, but the indiscernible depth made him uneasy.

"Well, I certainly can't do it. I'm a frail man. Becca, tell them." The dog released a sharp bark before Mr. Crisp slyly dropped a treat from his pocket onto the rocks beneath Becca's paws.

"Really, my dear boy," said Gracie. "Between two older, refined gentlemen, a young lady, and a strapping lad, you're going to suggest anyone but you fetch the coat?"

Edgar stared down at the pool that seemed to expand at his gaze.

"Oh, give me a break," said Elena. "I'll do it."

"Well, I saved you back there," said Edgar in a timid decrescendo.

Elena removed her shoes. "So you expected to see me there on that beach? Please, you looked just as surprised to see me as I did you."

Without pausing for a response, she leapt into the water toward the coat. The remaining crew gathered to watch as she swam downward, struggling to reach it. Nearly there, she turned back, returning to the surface. "I can't make it that deep. I can barely hold my breath to the depth that I went."

The three men looked at one another, searching for an answer. Elena scoffed and dove back down. Several more attempts came and went, with little more progress than the first.

"I don't know what to do," Elena said, gasping for breath.

"I suppose there is one incantation I can produce on my own," said Gracie, walking to the edge of the water where Elena waded.

She hoisted herself upon a nearby stone and sat. Gracie, extending his hands, cupped the her face, gazing into her, attempting to reach the soul on the other end. Elena, an eager student, allowed the trance to embrace her as a pale sheet covered her face, her eyes glazing. "You'll find that space and time move differently for you now."

She nodded, signaling understanding, or at least trust.

Once more, she dove into the water.

"That one wasn't Gifting," Gracie said. "Just an old trick my grandmother tried on me when I complained about it being too cold out to collect firewood."

This time was different, more elegant, more efficient. She darted along a straight path through the water. The depth of her personal record disappeared, and she pushed deeper than ever before, deeper than Edgar thought a human could press. Crisp and Edgar contained their excitement, a cheer beneath their breath. She continued deeper. Even Becca barked with anticipation.

Conversely, Gracie seemed bored. He trotted over to the wall of the cave and tidied a broad stone before turning and resting upon it. Edgar huffed at him, though his actions weren't entirely surprising.

As Edgar returned his attention to the moat, a vague, dark fog formed beneath Elena. He strained his eyes to draw it into focus. Like a snake emerging from the sand, hidden until provoked, a dark creature ascended from the shadowy depths. An immense fish dwarfed Elena.

Cheers turned to cries of horror from all but Gracie.

"Oh, what is it now?" he asked.

"There's a creature down there," said Edgar. "A shark or something. It's huge."

"Ragmore? I didn't expect him to make a show today. Perhaps today isn't a complete waste."

"You knew about that thing and you didn't tell us?"

"Child, you really must stop overreacting."

"You mean it's not dangerous?"

"No, well, not to me. Although I've never been one to go for a swim."

"Elena's down there."

"Ragmore is a very docile animal. You needn't concern yourself. If she eats your friend, I'm sure it's unintended."

Edgar, in a panic, dove head-first into the water. Vague tones of gray clouded his sight, save for the blur he knew to be Elena.

She must have been on her way back up. Her trajectory had changed, leaving the blur of the beast behind her.

It was then that a faint blue glow caught Edgar's eye from the wall of the moat. He commanded his eyes to focus, noting similarities between this blue glow and the deep-sea cave he saw when he first arrived. There was something to this. Was this a twin of the original sea cave, or were his eyes betraying him?

The moment didn't last long as Elena swam past him, pulling him to the surface by the arm. As they broke the surface, Edgar screamed to Elena to get out. Once upon dry land, she looked frantically from face to face.

"What? What's wrong?"

"That thing down there," Edgar said. "You didn't see it?"

As he completed his sentence, the animal broke through the surface, launching into the air like a whale in a show. Water flooded the cave and knocked those standing off their feet.

As the water settled back into the moat, the beast calmly released a moan, shaking the walls of the cave, rattling rocks that had held their position for millennia. The creature did not thrash, hiss, or bite, despite its jagged teeth protruding from its closed jaw. The length of ten men, it waded as a giant in the water.

"I hate this place," said Edgar.

"This is my home, sir," said Mr. Gracie.

"You have your coat," Elena said, pushing it toward Gracie.

"Well, as they say, 'Let's not wait until the big fish eats us.'"

Crisp, Edgar, and Elena looked questioningly at Gracie's choice of words as they all vanished into a bright blue flash of light.

They landed in water. A desperate plea for air gurgled through cold liquid rushing along Edgar's mouth. Each fleeting bob to the surface met an equal and opposite tug downward.

A rushing current dragged him forward. His team floated by, each in a similar state as he, all struggling, but none beating the force.

He peered ahead and spotted a waterfall just ahead. With flailing arms, he hunted for a branch or large rock. Anything would do. At last, his hands found purchase on the thick root of a tree along the shore.

Strength draining, he grabbed hold of it, clutching through weakened hands, knowing that if he let go, he would die. If he had any luck, it would be that the root was strong enough to hold him. Years of collected moisture had made it rubbery and able to withstand the bending pull from his arms.

Mr. Gracie floated by and grabbed Edgar's shoulders. The root now held two lives.

He scanned for Elena and Crisp but spotted neither. Not a blurred color amongst the water matching Elena, or Crisp, or Becca. With as little control as he had in finding her, he had lost her again.

He redirected his attention once more to the root and pulled himself up. But no. The root slipped between his fingers, with Gracie unaware and gasping for air with every ebb of the water.

The root, his lifeline, slithered out from his hands as the two floated toward the deafening sound of a waterfall.

The rest happened too quickly to comprehend. The stones along the riverbed dissolved as water plunged him downward.

He was falling. The rushing water lay muted to the pounding of his heart and the upward thrust of his gut. The last thought before darkness was that he would die.

Edgar awoke on the shore, sprawled along the smooth but unforgiving stones. Trees surrounded him as water rushed past his feet, this time leaving him alone, lapping his feet like a once-fierce dog made friendly.

"Get up," said a whisper. Edgar glanced, eyes darting from tree to tree. He found no one. No source to the voice.

"You're vile!" Another disembodied cry, distinct from the first.

"Not welcome!" More whispers. "You're not welcome here. Leave. You must leave now."

The separate voices joined, overlapping one another in a wretched chorus of clashing notes. An invisible crowd surrounded him, though Edgar saw no one. There were only trees. Mammoth redwood trees.

"Edgar!"

The last voice sounded real, cutting through the specters.

"Edgar! You're alive!" He saw Elena in a staggered sprint, grabbing him, hauling him upward to his feet. "We need to get dry."

As the group lumbered into the township of the Laniakea, the sun had crossed mostly through the clear sky. Though they no longer felt the threat of death, to say they were in good spirits would be untrue.

Each had exhausted most of their energy to get home, and all but Elena and Gracie collapsed onto the grass as they wandered into town.

Other things occupied Elena. The thought of sleeping in a proper bed and eating food prepared by someone else particularly excited her. Though she longed for a cheeseburger, she could hardly expect one, and she wouldn't turn down much of anything at this point.

She observed the townspeople scurrying about. After meeting Crisp and Gracie, she was now acquainted enough with the appearance of the locals for them not to surprise her with their varying colors, oscillating between tones of yellow with red and green with blue. Though it shocked her how frequently they changed their shades. As she surveyed the townspeople, it was not uncommon for an individual to wear their green-blue tone and then immediately shift to yellow-red as easily as they would laugh at a joke.

The idle discussions during their hike home had also apprised her of the impending war. Still, witnessing their preparation first-hand, it had amazed her how everyone, young and old, had taken on a job to prepare for battle.

Under a large open hut, she saw two burly figures laugh, each taking large hammers, clanging them against long swords as they smiled at children clacking wooden rods in mock battle.

The figures appeared to be a man and woman of equal size and build. Elena assembled a story in her head that the two had married long ago, now owning and operating their own family smithy.

After examining this couple and the remaining townspeople, she glanced back at the two locals that had been her guides on the hike back. Crisp was an old man. Youthful energy still pulsed through his blood, but as she surveyed those preparing to fight and those preparing to support and govern, she guessed Crisp belonged in the latter. He would never see battle. He reminded her more of a spry grandfather, though grumpier.

Gracie was lean but still did not belong in this town. If these villagers were Olympians, Gracie was the man scheduling the Olympics in the back office. She knew from their conversations that he was bright and capable, but if there was a warrior in him, he kept it buried deep.

"Edgar!" A girl, slightly younger than Elena, scurried toward the group.

"Ahletta, it's great to see you."

Another woman joined Ahletta, likely twenty years her senior, introduced by Edgar as the Lady Stellamaris. "I'm glad to see you made it back in one piece." The woman maintained an elegant stride, contrasting with Ahletta's scamper. It clearly elated both women to see Edgar's return, but the older woman was better composed. Ahletta stumbled through her sentences, not giving herself room enough to blush.

Despite Stellamaris's serenity, there was a brightness to her eyes as she spoke, notably as they pointed at Edgar. Elena could see the complexity of the sea in her eyes. There was a motherly worry, keeping grief at an arm's length, swiftly washed away by relief at Edgar's return, with giddy laughter as the two bantered. She looked as though she would swipe him up to hug him, if only her noble status would permit it.

The proceeding introductions dulled Elena, though she smiled the entire time, eager to find a bed and food. They exchanged pleasantries, and Stellamaris guided them to their dining area.

Elena could not hide her excitement as she saw cooked meats brought out on platters. The bread was spherical, like a sponge ball. Although when she grabbed a hold of the loaf, the similarities stopped. Soft and warm, it allowed her to pluck out gobs with her fingers and stuff them in her mouth, barely allowing time to chew before she flooded her mouth with a cool drink to thrust it down.

"Letty," said Edgar to the young girl, leaning in like a schoolgirl spreading gossip. "I saw that demon you were talking about. The demon in the water."

"Did you? You mean it's real? I mean, of course it's real. I'm just glad you got to see it. But wait, I thought you already saw it. The cave. You said you saw a glowing cave when you first arrived here."

"This time I saw the real thing. It was an enormous beast that darted out of the water." Edgar threw up his hands to mime the creature. "It chased after us. Gracie here saved us."

"That wasn't the Demon in the Water," said Mr. Crisp with a grave shake of his head. The rest of the crew maintained their excitement, but Crisp looked as though he had descended into a place in his mind that he'd rather not be.

"But you said they take many forms. Wasn't that beast one form Mahla described?"

"Edgar, it wasn't the demon. It certainly almost killed us all. But believe me when I tell you that if you come across the demon, you will not survive. You cannot leap, as Gracie did. He will chase you across the universe."

Edgar hesitated for a moment on the edge of something he was about to say and then, looking as though he was taking a risk, he said it. "But you survived. You said you and Becca saw it, and here you are."

It was then that Crisp delivered a glare to Edgar, leaving Elena stunned and causing Edgar to recede into his shell. The man's glare was not that of insult but rather restrained contempt. The entire exchange made Elena glad they had the witnesses of the village to prevent the moment from escalating.

"Enough of this," Stellamaris said, cutting in to change the subject. "I enjoy a good ghost story, but seeing as Lane isn't here to rope you all in, I suppose it should have to be me."

"Where's Lane?" Edgar asked.

"Lane is leading the battalion against Aiken," Ahletta said. "They left shortly after you did. They're incredible fighters. The rest of us are here preparing for more battles, but I'd expect Lane's battalion will send such a powerful message, they won't retaliate. I'd even wager they'll sack Drominion in full."

"One would hope it was possible to accomplish an invasion so swiftly," said Stellamaris. "Since they are the aggressors, you could assume them well prepared, certainly before tempting the mighty Laniakea. King Semian and Lane are quite convincing. That is certainly true. Though let us not speak too quickly about their success. We'd all be wise to have quiet confidence and humbly welcome their success, if we are so blessed, lest we tempt their fate with our tongues."

Ahletta nodded a confirmation to Stellamaris but then winked at Edgar, drawing out a silent laugh.

Elena suddenly felt out of place, but not enough to hold herself back from another slab of meat.

Edgar took a moment to himself under the shade of a large tree. He pulled the two stones from his pocket and examined them, hoping to find something to lead him to Simon.

The original stone, owned by Alister, looked similar to a sword, though not a precise cut. If it were on display in a museum, it would resemble a Mayan stone carving more than something from Michelangelo.

He looked at the new stone that he had recovered from the Evajocalyn. It was identical in all but shape. While Alister's stone was a sword, this stone was more circular and flat, like a shield. As he examined it closer, he saw detailed designs carved along one side, while the other was plain.

He brushed off the dirt that had collected to see if he could spot more details, though he couldn't clean it fully. There was one small collection of dust that was stuck in a circular inset along the top. He grabbed a small stick from the ground and scratched away to reveal more. Eventually, it cleared away altogether, revealing a small hole.

This, too, was a necklace piece. The hole had proven it. A sword and shield. Perhaps they were twins, intended never to part.

He took the necklace, slid on the shield, and tied it along his neck.

While he wasn't sure how he felt wearing the jewelry of Simon's abductor, it gave him an odd sense of control. No one had forced him to wear it. He chose it instead. It was his.

He decided it would serve as a reminder to keep going, to push forward. It would be the momentum to his step. It was the control in the chaotic sea.

TWENTY-THREE

I T CALMED LANE TO see his king so happy on the eve of battle. He smiled often, drifting into thought like a rowboat with no oars.

The lines along Semian's eyes drew attention to his age. This man had fought many battles with Lane alongside him, though he wasn't always as happy as he appeared now. That confidence could spread throughout his men, winning them a victory, weaving the threads of a great tale he could tell his son when they returned.

"Do you see those clouds, Lane?" the old king asked.

"I do. They'll put the winds at our backs as we exit the Doldrums. That's a promising sign if I've ever seen one. On the other side of those hills lies fine grained dirt, almost sand."

The king laughed, amused. "The wind will push the dirt right in their faces. I know my kingdom well. Much more than that oaf, Aiken, if I were the type to boast. And I know my enemies just the same. Aiken will cut through the Rambling Forest and risk the specters in order to surprise us before we are ready. That is the way he thinks, the proud man. Proud men don't win battles, Lane."

"Yes, My King."

"You must never be so confident in your plan that you soar past its details. Pity the man who thinks of everything but never puts everything into a single thought, never studies the mustard seed despite its size. It is in the details that we live or die."

"He's grown too proud, Highness. You are correct."

"That he has. He hasn't been on this side of the Waste. He hasn't seen the coastal wind whirl around these hills before they drop off to a low void in the Doldrums' eye. Even if he has, he would not predict that the unfortunate weather would cause his plan to backfire when he's blinded by the sand while we lie in its windless center."

Lane smiled to himself. He surveyed his men. Most of them would make it home to see their families, bringing with them tales of valor and pride well earned.

"You'll see Karian before she has time to miss you, Lane."

"Thank you, Highness. I do not doubt it."

It had been a week's span since Lane had seen his wife and son. His child, Laneson, had been having trouble keeping a dry bed. Most of the children in the town had gained the sense of control while asleep by his age. Karian and Lane attempted various strategies to teach the boy. Karian would get up with him throughout the night, being the more proactive of the two parents.

In his younger years, Lane would train every day in the field for the chance at joining the King's Army. In the time since he enlisted, he might have fought over a hundred battles and slain more men than a respectable man would ever dare to say aloud. At that moment, he could think of nothing better than to be done with war altogether and resume his peacetime work as a farmer in Kalagora. A preparer of food and administer of trade. That wouldn't happen, of course. They would win this battle, but the conflict would continue. Lane had thought of leaning on his age as a crutch to let the younger, more passionate men fight his battles. He couldn't escape the war clouds in the distance, but he could work more tactically from a position within the council while staying close to his wife and child.

Distant screaming interrupted his thoughts.

"Did you hear that, Lane?" asked the king.

"I did, Highness."

The troops had stopped. There was a shrillness to the scream that put Lane on edge, and, looking around at the others, he could see it had done the same to his soldiers. Each person was now looking around frantically to find its source. With just the one scream to go by, each soldier had a different opinion as to the direction it came from. When it came a second time, everyone snapped to attention, gazing to their left. The sound was repeated a third time, and Lane forced himself to settle the dense sense of impending doom now lying as a stone in his chest.

"Stay here, Highness. The scout and I will see what's happened."

Lane had sent his best scout, Ilgene, ahead to hills surrounding the Doldrums to report on whether Aiken's troops had assembled. He peered over to his left, observing the second scout. The boy was small, a good decade younger than Lane.

"You will stand strong, boy," said Lane. The instruction came without a nod, knowing the boy had heard him. "Have you seen a battle?"

Silence.

"Answer me, boy. Laniakea do not repeat questions."

"I have not."

"You will stay tight. If we meet conflict, your sole task is to alert the greater battalion. You will fight only to enable the swift fulfillment of your only duty. Is that clear?"

"Yes. Yes, General."

The two rode up to the crest of a large hill, knowing that a low valley lay on the other side. Lane instructed the boy to walk stealthily for several more spans until he could see the source of the sound.

Lane glanced back and could see the impatient king galloping closer.

The boy did not need to travel far, as it seemed, for he was back much quicker than Lane had expected.

"It's just a small girl," said the scout.

A smile crept across Lane's face. The scout laughed, releasing the tension between the two.

"Well then, let's go see if she's all right. Shall we?"

As the two got closer to the child, details of her appearance became clearer. She was in a long, tattered dress with blackened edges, sobbing uncontrollably. The child's hair was tangled, resembling a bird's nest.

Lane reached for a blanket from his pack to wrap around her. He didn't know whether she was cold, but a clean blanket should comfort her and make her feel better.

He held her close, and as he did so, he noticed that the entire troop had traveled over to see what was happening. King Semian descended from his horse and walked over to the child.

"What's wrong, young one?"

The child stopped crying abruptly, and sullen silence thickened the surrounding air.

Her eyes dilated. No, it wasn't dilation. Her eyes blackened, turning to coals set in the sockets of a cold vessel. Despite Lane's disbelief, the child's sockets grew as the coals within them expanded until no face remained, only black pits.

Lane stumbled for his sword, as the Drominion soldiers assembled around them. He heard the faint words from the king identifying the creature that he now knew had lured them in.

"The Songbird."

It began with a gentle kiss to Karian before leaving for battle, as he had done so many times before. She helped load his horse with the packs they had assembled the night before. This time, though, he added something new to his routine. Altering the procedure was less of an instinct and more of a decision, made with confidence without a second thought.

He called Laneson over. His son toddled over to the doorway, where Lane crouched down to meet him at eye level.

He took a handmade necklace from his neck and placed it over the small boy. It was an amulet made from a metallic ring wrapped in leather, with a pattern of thread webbing at the center. It wasn't a valuable or ornate piece of jewelry. If he needed to sell his belongings for any reason, this necklace would undoubtedly never find a buyer. A moderately skilled jeweler could easily replicate it, creating a replica worth more than the original, if they ever bothered to waste their time. Still, it meant the world to Lane, since Karian made it with love solely for him. For that reason, there was none like it. Even if Karian were to make another, it would be the second of its kind, and this would be the first, the original.

The boy looked down at the necklace hanging on his chest.

"I need you to hold on to this while I'm away," Lane said, voice steady and just above a whisper. "You need to take care of your mother."

This was the decision he had made, to raise his child to know the happiness of willing servitude to his family. He would start simple with this minor act, a duty to protect his mother. His son was clearly not old enough to understand the full magnitude of this task. Even if he did, he wouldn't be able to carry it out in any tangible way. At Laneson's age, the lesson itself was where it began and ended. A lesson in parts, to be completed over a lifetime of small threads sewn into a flowing tapestry. He told himself he would return and give his son more threads as the years went by.

It was his duty to live in service to his family. His back would break and hands would bleed so that he might spare his wife and child that burden. Karian felt a similar sense of duty with equal, or at some times greater merit, but differently. If a year were to be stripped from Lane's life, he would plead to the gods that they add it to Karian's.

There was order to a happy death. Lane would prefer to go first, allowing Karian to live long enough to fight the subtle demons of life that Lane had not the mental prowess to defeat.

As he lay there, clothes caked in mud and with the dim light fading, Lane realized that while the timing was wrong, the order was right. He smiled and let himself diminish. The vale of life lifted to a smiling bridegroom. The warrior within him smiled back, knowing nothing of this new world yet recognizing everything.

TWENTY-FOUR

EDGAR WAS SIPPING AT warm tea when he heard the screaming. An elderly woman rushed the small children indoors, leaving their playthings scattered amongst the grass. Soldiers abandoned their training weapons to gaze upon the horrific image of Ilgene riding horseback into town, caked in dried blood. Streaks of dried tears, long ignored, stained his face in lines.

"Ilgene," Stellamaris said, just below her breath but still loud enough for Edgar to hear. She repeated his name as she sprinted toward him.

Edgar didn't realize he was running until he was halfway there, approaching the rider amongst the gathering crowd.

"The king," said Ilgene, voice shaking as he dismounted.

Stellamaris's eyes grew desperate. "What happened to King Semian? Where's the battalion? Why are you covered in blood?"

Stellamaris was always so formal, even when showing motherly affection. This was a side of her that Edgar hadn't seen. Through her voice came a frantic eagerness for news, desperate for him to say the words and still a subtle resistance to hearing them.

"The king. The men, all of them."

"Ilgene, I need you to tell me what happened to my father."

"He's dead." There was no light behind Ilgene's eyes as the crowd recoiled at his words. "All of them. The entire battalion is dead." Edgar wasn't sure if he'd expected the man to pour out tears, though from his face it appeared he had shed them all. What he saw instead was a shell who had seen more than his mind would accept.

He saw a variety of reactions from the assembled crowd. The soldiers were now split between emotions. Some had chosen rage, shattering barrels with their swords. Others remained still with clenched fists for a moment before reining in their emotional comrades.

Perhaps it was Mahla that confused Edgar the most. He knew little of restraint, and so Edgar expected him to thrash about like a bucking stag. Instead, he was one of the cooler heads, pivoting to walk away with head lowered and breathing slowed.

Edgar looked closest at the King-Daughter. She paused, though briefly, and collected a deep breath. She looked back at Ilgene and stared through glassy eyes. "Tell me everything."

"I had scouted ahead several spans." Ilgene's eyes were ghosts, hollow and fading. "It had been a while since I reported back to Lane, and he hadn't sent a runner, so I went back myself. They must have come in quick and silent, surprising them. I would have heard a blitz. This had to be a stealth attack. I didn't even hear the screams of my own men. I checked my king first." He glanced down at the blood on his clothing. "Then I checked for survivors."

With a hurricane of regret and doom deep in his sunken eyes, he shook his head. "There was no life in that field. All those bodies—only death."

Edgar looked back at Mahla, recalling the arguments between him and Lane before his departure, unsure if he meant them in jest or rage. The once jovial giant stood as still as a stone, deflated like a clown no longer laughing. Mahla shambled across the yard to the far end of the town and delivered the news to Karian, her child tumbling between her legs.

She fell into tears, draping her arms around Mahla, attempting to grab hold of his broad shoulders, though failing. Mahla fumbled as he sought to keep her from the ground, her weak grip doing little to help her legs that no longer supported her.

The child did not appear to comprehend what was happening. With Karian collapsed to the ground, the small boy hugged her head.

Elix stood back with Edgar. They glanced at one another, unsure what to do. It was then that Edgar realized how alike they were. Both were only guests for a short while until they discovered what came next. He guessed she felt the same awkwardness as he did. Two strangers at a wake, unsure how to console, or if they should even try.

While Edgar sat in unsettled silence, Elix chose her nervous twitch, strumming her lute, emoting through her instrument. Each string quivered with delicate notes of a minor key. Her words were sung more from feeling than tangible substance. The tune passed through Edgar, as thick as fog, leaving him still and uneasy.

He stepped forward, wishing to feel something different. Sadness lay like a blanket over the town, wrapping around everyone, young and old, elder and guest, exempting only Jude, who sipped his tea, showing little concern. Edgar couldn't understand Jude, not fully. He could not describe the boy by adding detail, only by describing what he lacked. He was a shell, a void. Even when he was angry, it wasn't genuine anger, but the lack of joy. It would not be accurate to say he produced either love or hatred. He produced a vacuum and then let it be.

Edgar shook Jude from his mind and glanced at the other soldiers as they gathered around Stellamaris, hungry for something, but they knew not what. There was a void, new and growing, within each of them. Why wouldn't they just let her mourn? They needed direction, even when it came from the one person who needed silence the most.

Recognizing them, the King-Daughter turned and addressed them.

"My Laniakea," said Stellamaris, her voice cold as stone. Another woman, anyone else, would have spoken through a wall of tears or would not speak at all. Edgar observed the same grief in her, though shelved somewhere deep within for now. "Many of you must feel anger, as I do. Many of you must feel cheated and robbed, as I do. But I must ask of you the impossible. I must ask you to hold your grief and name it. Transform it and use it as fodder for focus and for valor. Though I do not deny the loss, and I do not deny that there will be more. Hold, hold, Laniakea. For we are few, but we are mighty. And as long as there is a single breath in a single member of the valiant, they shall stand tall and say, 'I am the brave Laniakea, and I will not die this day.'"

Stellamaris could hear nothing but the beat of her heart against her eardrums, the air in her stomach knocked out with a wooden rod.

She escaped to her father's hut for a moment to herself. His old swords were scattered along the wall, displayed as tools transformed into trophies.

She must not show weakness to her people as they tried to fill the void of their fallen leader. Still, she allowed herself this moment.

Stellamaris fell to her knees, letting the flood wash over her. She grabbed a cushion from his old chair, breathing in his scent, allowing it to fill her lungs, and squeezed it to the point of tearing it.

She didn't know what she'd do now. She had looked upon her parents as gods her entire life. They would take in only things that made them strong, shedding defeat and weakness with ease.

When her mother died, she discovered that wasn't true. The strong die too. Now, with the death of her father, she found the loss to be inevitable.

Slowly, she rose. Before her stood her father's collection of swords. He had taken his favorite but left hers. She recalled handing it to him, though he put it back. Perhaps he was saving it to pass on to her.

This was no simple sword to Stellamaris. It was a work of art. The blade was strong but light. The elegant stem of a rose weaved through the blade and past the hilt, extending through the guard until it displayed the blossoming flower as a jewel at the pommel.

She swung it several times, slicing the air, just as her father had taught her.

"I will call you Pietro."

It was perhaps because Stellamaris stayed a little too long in her father's hut that Ilgene felt the need to search for her. As he delicately creaked the door, Stellamaris beckoned him in.

"Oh, my dear King-Daughter," Ilgene said. "How are you holding up?"

Though she appreciated Ilgene's concern, the answer to his question was too obvious and resulted only in a chuckle.

"I can't imagine what you're going through," he said. "You are a bold and worthy leader, but I dare say this is a lot for anyone to handle."

"Thank you, Ilgene." She could have said more. She wanted to say more. But her mind was an empty well, and what she gave was all she had. Silence built up between them, needing to be filled. Under normal circumstances, she'd feel the urge to do so. But these were not normal circumstances, so she allowed the silence to linger.

Ilgene lifted an apple to his mouth, removing a chunk from its side with one swift bite. He offered her the clean end. She politely declined.

"There are many choices ahead for all of us. I've often thought of leaving the Coastal Cliffs, roaming the countryside, as I did in my youth. It's remarkable how a man can claim to call himself wise without observing the sun rise and set along more than a single horizon. I have learned a lot in my youth by riding horseback down a long and dark road, not knowing where it would lead. Perhaps it's in me again to do just the same. These old bones still contain young marrow. These veins pulse the blood of a vibrant heart. After seeing my battalion murdered so coldly, perhaps a roam of the country is in my future."

"And I would not hold you back," Stellamaris said. "The Laniakea serve by choice, and you deserve some time to decide what your choice is from here forward."

He gave her a slight laugh with little more than a smile.

"Thank you, Stellamaris. I appreciate that. Though I know the way your father ruled and can assume the same will hold firm during this awkward time, I do not come to ask for such permission, but to invite you to join me."

"Me? Oh, no. I couldn't. I have the Laniakea. Rather, not just them, but all the partnering kingdoms we protect. I couldn't abandon them now."

"Now would be the most opportune time. You may be the assumed leader, but no one has elected you. There has been no formal transition. You could just as easily slip off to the side and allow the next leader to step forward. There is no obligation until you, or someone, fill the seat. Review, briefly, the members of the council. Are not all of them suitable leaders? Are not all of them just and honest men and women that loved your father deeply and would continue his will forward?"

She gave him a knowing smirk, and they both allowed themselves a laugh for that sliver of time.

"Okay, maybe not all of them are so great. Still, do you want this life, Stellamaris?"

She thought over his words, the empty well returning. Did she desire the life of a queen? Leadership was always her plan, but did it need to be? Did she want it, or did she want her father to smile upon her and be proud?

"Here," said Ilgene, lifting the apple once more, offering her a second chance. "Take a bite and follow me. I will show you a world with rolling hills and land as endless as the sea. I will show you caverns deep within the earth and spires that pierce the heavens. All this and more I can deliver to you. You needn't do more than follow me."

She extended her hand toward the apple but refused it, pushing it away with a polite smile.

"Thank you, Ilgene. I appreciate you thinking of me. Perhaps when we defeat Aiken, you can show me those spires. But I will always return to my people."

Ilgene smiled, though a sad regret filled his eyes. His teeth clamped down on the apple once more. "Perhaps."

TWENTY-FIVE

To say that Mr. Gracie felt uneasy about being caught in this conflict with the Laniakea and their war would be an understatement.

"That's the last time I leave my cave," he said, his whisper muted by the crowd.

Ever since he entered this town, the decision to speak with the King-Daughter had rattled around in his head. He knew her by reputation, but he had been a recluse for long enough, too long for anyone to know him. He had certainly never met the King-Daughter, or her father before his passing.

He knew the polite thing to do. The proper path of a gentleman entering a new land, under normal circumstances, would be to introduce himself to the King-Daughter after his step onto Laniakean soil. Surely he could request an arrangement to stay here for a couple of days in trade for his talents. He wasn't sure what the alternative would be. Certainly, he couldn't just find an unclaimed bed and sneak loafs of bread, could he? His stay would need to be legitimate, or he might as well leave right at that moment.

Yes, he needed to introduce himself to the King-Daughter. Though there was hesitation. The reasons for stopping him were two-fold.

First, they were obviously in the middle of a conflict that required her attention. He'd hardly consider it polite to burden her with his stay and cursed himself for giving it more than a moment's thought.

Second was the talent he could trade for a bed and food, which limited him. Whatever bit he had would be of little use to a kingdom at war. These people knew how to swing a hammer and sharpen a blade, which was precisely what they needed in times of war. If he didn't know how to do either of those, they'd use him as a rock to hide behind as arrows flew. They wouldn't describe it that way, but they would need him to fight, and he didn't know how. He'd do better if he were a mindless stone rather than a cowering pincushion for enemy weaponry. He'd stand next to them, a child surrounded by giants. Still, this was a warrior tribe matched against a foe they didn't entirely understand, and he could hardly advertise his talent for leaping between dimensions as a fair trade when he didn't get it right most of the time.

He decided he'd be better off traveling back home and restoring the cave the hound had likely destroyed. It had taken them most of the day to travel this far, but perhaps after he found some food, he could leave and return home shortly after nightfall. If activities escalated, he could use the Gift to travel the remaining way. That would be a last resort, however. The risks involved in Gifting from one location to the other were incredible, but he was fairly certain he could do it if the distance were small enough.

As he turned, he saw the old man, Mr. Crisp, standing with his arm and index finger slightly extended, about to tap Gracie on the shoulder.

"Oh, hello there," Crisp said, fidgeting.

"Oh, hello." Gracie mirrored his unease.

"Yes, Gracie, I was wondering if you're planning on staying for a bit. I mean, I'm not sure if you had considered it."

"The thought had crossed my mind, but there were a few factors I needed to figure out."

"Oh yes, of course. Well, if you consider those factors and decide you'd like to stay, my home has more than enough space for me and Becca. We'd gladly take you in."

Gracie hadn't expected this, and he felt his shoulders relax as he let the words settle. The kindness of others wasn't something he had prepared himself for. Frankly, he hadn't considered it at all. He had been alone in his cave for so long, relying on another human never entered his calculus. "Are you sure? I mean, that's awfully nice of you. I wouldn't want to put you out."

"It wouldn't be any trouble at all. You were very kind to me in that cave, offering me and Becca food, even though we were complete strangers."

"The cave? You mean my home?" Gracie said with a light mix of offense and amusement over the old man's bumblings.

"I don't mean to offend. It was a lovely home, and I appreciate all you did for us by giving us that stop along our journey. To top that, you've even made sure we made it back to our own home. The least I can do is offer you a stay in my extra bedroom."

He felt a smile creep in along his cheeks and a warmth that he didn't know what to do with. "That would be lovely."

The two spoke for a short while longer before the King-Daughter approached them in swift step.

"Hello," she said, addressing Gracie, eyes soft though focused. "My name is Stellamaris. I am the King-Daughter of this township. I've heard that you were remarkably useful in escaping the Evajocalyn."

"Oh, yes, well, I'm glad to be of service. The Evajocalyn is my home, actually—"

"Edgar tells me you could travel using some sort of magic. Do you use the Gift?"

"I do, well, I know how. I did back then."

"I can use you. As you can see, we are at war. You may have heard of the Laniakea. While we are very capable warriors, we are facing a new sort of enemy. A man named Aiken of the Drominion. While I've heard he does not possess knowledge or use of the Gift, he employs all the tools at his disposal to accomplish what he craves. If I can count on your Gifting, then I can expand our toolset beyond simple force of arms."

"I'd be more than happy to help my King-Daughter," Gracie said, assembling all formality and composure. "All that I have is yours, but you should know that I am no master. I'm actually not very talented at all."

"I can use a candle to ignite a forest fire. All I need from you is to know that you are willing and that you trust me for the rest. In return, everything I have here is yours to share with my people."

As she said this, she motioned to the township. All the shops, homesteads, and busily working people were part of her family. She offered this all to him, with no exception, for trust.

He delivered a nod.

She gripped his shoulder as a comrade, looked into his eyes, and said, "Welcome to the Laniakea, Mr. Gracie."

Stellamaris marched swiftly from the center of town where she had left Mr. Gracie. She had too much to do to prepare for what was to come. Next on her schedule was the council meeting. Butterflies fluttered through her stomach as she realized this was her first time speaking. That was always her father's job, but now that her father had passed, the duty fell to her.

She took her position, opting to stand rather than rest upon the cold stone that had once been her father's. The circle seemed more intimidating now that she was in it. A simple clearing of her throat drew more attention than she preferred.

She had known this time would eventually come. Though she didn't yet have the right of leadership, she had the right of lineage and therefore held an interim seat in her father's stead.

Dahl'Turan was the last to the circle as he swept in and took his seat. "Laykia, let's shelve the carryover items for next time. We have far too much to discuss." The man rummaged through the scrolls before him, handing most off to his assistant and issuing several commands beneath his breath before steadily drawing in a full chest of air and addressing Stellamaris with a full scowl. "Let's get started, shall we?"

"Yes, I believe we should," said Stellamaris.

She paused, prepared to rattle off her points, before Dahl'Turan cut her short. "My dear King-Daughter, if you are here to deny igniting our people into chaos after the most horrid news of our king's untimely demise, then I assure you we don't have the time for it. Now, Laykia, if you wouldn't mind beginning the minutes, we must begin with the first item at hand—"

"The *murder* of the king," said Stellamaris, her words cutting briskly into the Lead Council.

Stunned silence blanketed the council at Stellamaris's words.

"With all due respect, King-Daughter—"

"I do not believe you mean the slightest bit of respect, Lead Council, but I agree that our time is short and we must act. I have prepared—"

"You assume too much, King-Daughter. If you believe you are to come in here, without a proper election, in an interim seat, and take command of a council that has led our people for hundreds of years, then I suggest you take note. I realize the people respect you, but as it stands our primary force of arms was just eliminated. We are now stuck with..." he paused as though hunting for the right word, but then shrugged, "... the B team. That is who you lead, if you lead anyone at all."

Dahl'Turan's speech diminished to a stammer as the awkward steps and sighs of Mr. Crisp fumbled toward the only remaining empty seat. "Forgive my lateness, Lead Council," said Crisp, sucking in his belly to inch by court patrons, pausing occasionally to deliver a biscuit to his hound. "I was growing weary of voting by proxy. Laykia, you may tally one more on your roster, if you would be so kind."

Dahl'Turan fumed but shelved his anger before returning to his scolding.

"As I was saying, King-Daughter—"

"Actually," said Crisp, in no particular hurry, "if you wouldn't mind, Dahl'Turan, I would like to hear the plan Stellamaris has prepared. As I just heard you state so eloquently, she leads the B team, and, seeing as they are now our primary force, I would love to hear what she has planned."

"Mr. Crisp. You are a highly respected council member and have been for decades. Though, in these peculiar circumstances—"

"Yes, these circumstances are peculiar, and it is for that reason that I do not think we should waste any more time with these sorts of..." he paused in a subtle imitation of Dahl'Turan, "...*power struggles*." Crisp coolly brushed his hand over the phrase as though it were too insignificant to keep. "Now, Stellamaris, please continue."

Dahl'Turan had flames in his eyes but kept his words locked behind his lips.

Stellamaris inched into the conversation. "We are short on warriors, and I believe Aiken plans to invade other towns that are lesser equipped. As my father warned, we would need to divide to protect our partners. Aiken's plan to diminish our numbers has succeeded, but I believe there is a way we can still defeat him."

Dahl'Turan held back the fire on his tongue but ushered Stellamaris to continue.

"We must enlist citizens of Kalagora as soldiers."

"That cannot happen," Laykia interjected. "The Laniakea swore to protect the partnering kingdoms in our trade agreement. We cannot ask them to enlist. We would weaken our value in trade as the Warrior Tribe. Do the Kalagora ask us for aid in food and wine in dry summers?"

"We risk weakening our value even more if we allow a single kingdom to be sacked. If the Kalagora would like to use our land in the next drought, so be it. We need soldiers, and every kingdom needs protection. We wrote our trade agreements during peace times, and the Laniakea represented keepers of that peace. Now, we are at the cusp of war, and new agreements need to be made."

Laykia looked as though she had more to say but held back, curious to hear more.

"I can train them. We will elect three commanders, and Mahla and I will teach them to lead using our strategies."

Dahl'Turan raised a brow. "We risk too much with this plan."

"We risk more by doing nothing. Surely you're not suggesting we rush back into battle with the numbers we have."

"She has a point," Mr. Crisp said. "And, Dahl'Turan, if I might be so bold, I'm certain that scroll you've been glancing at can't suggest that we rush back into battle. After all, they are...what did you call them...ah yes, the B team, correct?"

Dahl'Turan boiled in silence, but Stellamaris could see he was not so bold as to speak ill of Crisp to his face.

"Shall we vote, Laykia?" Mr. Crisp smiled at her as she scratched down words.

Laykia issued the cadence in a deep sigh. "All in favor?"

A majority of hands sprang into the air, leaving deflated looks across the sibling council members.

"All opposed?" Three hands were raised, including Dahl'Turan and Laykia's. "That settles it." Laykia's gavel struck stone. "We will enlist the help of our Kalagora allies."

Stellamaris held back a wide smile as she left with Crisp, the sibling council members staying behind, gathering their scrolls with their timid assistant.

TWENTY-SIX

I T WAS PERHAPS THE dull glint of the sun as it settled in below the waves that gave Edgar his melancholy stare and Elix a sullen strum to her strings.

Edgar knew what depressed him, but Elix was a riddle. The two had exchanged enough dancing glances to warrant Edgar's question.

"Your songs have turned, Elix. Why are you so down?"

It was true. Her songs had been so jovial before. Now Edgar suddenly felt as though he had stepped into a puddle wearing only socks.

She slowed her strum to an idle pluck as she looked off at the mist crawling in. "It's you folk. You and the locals. You're all so depressed, and the moods of others have a tendency of staining me. They linger like a wafting scent. But it's you I don't understand. These people just lost half their town and their king. Why are you so glum? Or do beautiful sunsets often drain your spirits?"

Edgar was suddenly sheepish. He wasn't the type to shed his feelings, and somehow he told Gracie, and found himself about to tell Elix, about his brother and his yearning for home. It all mixed in his chest, threatening an influx of pain but only delivering consistent micro doses.

He drew back from his original temptation to tell her everything and settled on a smaller truth. "It's my brother. He's missing, and I have no way of finding him."

Edgar hadn't realized how much he enjoyed the music until she stopped playing. It was a subtle chirp that put his mind to sleep, now painfully waking him with its absence.

He glanced at her, too abashed to do so directly. For a moment, she appeared to feel deep empathy, only to break the awkwardness with a single percussive strum.

"All right, all right. Let's try this one out, shall we?" said Elix, strumming a chord as though she were stretching before a race.

"What are you doing?" Edgar asked.

"You've only just met me, but surely you know by now we're about to write another song. 'Tis only appropriate after you depress me so. Let me see, wee lad, you traveled across the Poor Man's Sea. That much is clear. But how shall we trudge forward?"

In a vessel made of...

"What boat did you ride in on?" Elix asked.

Edgar laughed and thought for a moment. "Light itself."

"Fine, fine. Be coy with your metaphors. Just remember, I'm the creative one in this relationship, here, darling."

In a vessel of light
I travel 'cross the sea
Just my luck I discover
The dreary lost was me

Edgar sat up with a puzzled brow. "Well, that's all fine, but my brother really is the one missing."

"Yes, yes, but that's verse two. Honestly, are you always this impatient? Shall I skip to the end as well? I suppose not. Now where was I? Tell me about your brother."

With a roll of his eyes, he released a slight chuckle. "First off, he's certainly annoying."

Elix ignited into frolicking notes.

If e'er there was a donkey hide
As a person, that'd be Simon

Edgar extended his palm to stop her. "No! He's not a donkey hide."

"Well, fine then, wee one, but with all this help you're giving me, I dare say we won't be playing this for actual people. It's the swine that'll hear this tune, if I'm forward enough to be helpful."

Edgar was happy to see Stellamaris break the tension as she marched past them, arms full of supplies.

"Ah, there, my lady," said Elix, standing to attention and then bending in a bow that was more awkward to watch than perform.

"My dear boy," said Stellamaris. "I'm glad to have run into you."

"Yes, yes, my lady, yes, yes." Elix resumed her playing once more. "I shall play you a light tune while you two speak. It'll be a half step above the singing birds and a fair amount more beautiful, if I may be so bold."

Elix slipped off into a light plucking of her strings as Stellamaris sat next to Edgar.

Stellamaris lowered her voice so that only Edgar could hear. "Young one, I'm going to go away for a short while."

Edgar was uncertain why this news bothered him. If she had simply left, he would not be concerned. After all, why shouldn't she leave? She had a town to lead and an assembly of soldiers to command. It was perhaps the familiarity of this conversation. It reminded him of one just like it, so many years ago.

Still, he felt a new sort of bond with this woman. A motherly bond that he hadn't felt for a long time. There were moments over the last few days when she'd checked on his wellbeing with a genuine kindness in her eyes that disarmed him. It filled a hole deep within his heart that he didn't know needed to be filled.

"I have enjoyed our time together since you arrived," Stellamaris said with a tender smile. "I have had little time with you. Not nearly as much as I would prefer. I wonder if you might stay a while longer after I return. You are, of course, welcome here as long as you need. But more than that, I enjoy you being here, and I would prefer more time with you."

Her words warmed him, as a thick blanket on a winter's day. This was a feeling he was less familiar with but liked very much. Ben and Susan Friar had shared similar feelings in the past. Yet the Friar house felt more temporary, despite his tenure. He knew he'd one day leave that home for something more permanent. He wasn't sure when he'd first started feeling it, but lately Stellamaris felt like a mother to him. How could that be? Why would he feel a sense of permanence with a woman so new to his life?

He wasn't certain how to respond, so he simply said, "I'd like that."

Stellamaris smiled as Edgar allowed the elegant song of Elix's lute to embrace him.

The kind words from Stellamaris were unearned. This guilt that he felt, the feeling of *less than*. It had held more of his soul than he'd thought. His brother. The responsibility. His own weakness. It all rushed in with Elix in harmony.

The sweet smells of honey and spice floated along the breeze as Stellamaris and Mahla approached the eastern town of Kalagora.

Her horse was doing rather well for needing food and drink, save for the lazy drag of its hooves along the loose dirt.

As a small child, Stellamaris would always look forward to these expeditions, visiting such a glorious town as this. Each time she traveled to this township, she felt more than tempted to indulge in the sweets that they generously offered. It would be rude to turn them down, and so she never did. But when she had one bite of the honey loaf, she often would have several more, followed swiftly by wine or aged cider.

Since there were only two of them, she and Mahla traveled the thin road to the north, rather than through the Doldrums. It was a more pleasurable passage, winding up along the mountains, lending an elegant bird's-eye view of the Coastal

Cliffs, emerald and granite, as they turned into the desert spires and rolling dunes of the Doldrums, eventually yielding to the farmland of Kalagora.

The transition was best observed from on high, but she could never take her battalion along such a thin road. An attack would leave them defenseless, whereas traversing directly through the desert waste gave them plenty of options.

"Honey loaf," Mahla said, half to himself. "Can you smell it, Stell?"

She laughed. If it was difficult for her to resist the temptations of this town, it was impossible for him. He could eat an entire vernagrande and possessed the build to hide it well.

"Not all of us can recover so quickly from honey loaf and sweet wine, Mahla. I do not doubt that you will make the ride home better than I. Still, this is a brief trip. We must be on our way soon."

"Soon? I can eat quite a bit in *soon*. My Queen Mother has just given me my first quest." Mahla eyed Stellamaris with a playful grin.

A smirk pushed its way out. "I am not the Queen Mother yet. The Laniakea will need to accept me."

He scoffed. "Frankly, I'm surprised they didn't accept you directly after that speech of yours."

She smiled as though talking to an innocent child, although she did not demean him. She adored children, and for the same reason, she adored Mahla's spirit. In small kingdoms such as theirs, friendships like the ones she had with Mahla, Ilgene, and Lane allowed her to know her limits with each.

Ilgene was fun to laugh with, but he needed to be involved in the joke. She could snicker at Lane, before his passing, but not in front of his men. He required a clear distinction between jovial fun and respect. Mahla had no such requirements and wasn't nearly as sensitive. In the rare case when he appeared insulted, he'd forget the offense when the first butterfly stole his attention.

"Thankfully, for all our sakes, that's not how it works. I have the right of lineage, but we are in no state to determine the right of leadership directly after the death of our king."

He batted his hand in dismissal and sneered. "Silly law."

"You'll appreciate that law a lot more when I die and someone you *don't* like tries for the right of leadership."

He suddenly grew quiet and stared ahead, as though he were a small boy appraising the sunset. The two rode in silence for a moment before Stellamaris broke it.

"Did I offend you, Mahla?"

"Never, Queen Mother," he said, holding his gaze on the town ahead. "It's that talk of you dying that makes me feel so, particularly after losing Lane and the king. By my sword and good fortune, I will die before ever seeing your death."

She blushed in waves, first at the sweetness of the man and then at the number of times he had made her smile.

"So that sounds like someone else's problem," he said, reminding her of what they were talking about. "Besides, the only person I wouldn't ever want to see take the throne would be that bastard Dahl'Turan. Maybe his sister, but I'd doubt she would make a play considering how tightly she holds to Dahl'Turan's heels."

The familiar face of young Rellie, first servant to the Kalagoran queen, welcomed them with a bright smile just outside the massive stone doors of the town. Her robe was light of fabric and rich with bright shades of pink and green. Aside from accenting her elegant face, the expensive dyes showed her elevated status when roaming through the kingdom, seeing to the queen's personal tasks. She could ask a shopkeeper for samples of dew cider, and she would leave with too many bottles to carry.

Rellie didn't need to speak a word as she motioned them past the front guards, so she didn't. Stellamaris gave the guards a subtle bow, recognizing them both from previous trips out east. They nodded back respectfully.

Mahla gave both guards a knowing smile, showing Stellamaris that the three had a shared experience that embarrassed the guards and left Mahla entertained. She knew not to ask Mahla about the incident, since such a story would come out too easily and cause her to blush more than she'd prefer before her visit with Kalagoran leadership.

A familiar cadence took hold as they entered and descended from their horses. Stable masters led the horses off, feeding them carrots of a richer shade of orange than she could recall herself ever eating.

Servants swiftly removed their packs and draped them in robes to match Rellie's, though darker in shade. They promptly found a golden goblet of sweet wine in their right hand, although, through the commotion, neither could say when the cup entered their grasp.

Shopkeepers lined the street leading to the king and queen's stone hut, each one offering samples of delicate pastries and rich fruits, each larger than any they had in Laniakea. Stellamaris refused all, leaving room for what the king and queen would offer, though Mahla made a sport of trying every sample without slowing their pace.

The king and queen's hut was large enough to house ten families. Massive blocks of brown stone, shaped in the eastern river, were stacked up to build a long palace, traced in gold trimmings.

As they entered, a huge table filled the center, set with large plates and an array of massive meats and colorful sweets.

At the head of the table sat the queen herself, with the king's seat empty.

The queen wore a robe similar to Rellie's, with bright shades of pink and green. However, the queen's robe was noticeably more intricate in its patterns. Through Stellamaris's childhood, she had come to find that the brightness of the colors of one's clothing showed the class of wealth, and the more dynamic designs within the cloth would determine the rank within one's class. This custom became more pronounced within the upper classes, since the lower classes concerned themselves less with formality the lower their station.

Curiously, she halted before the queen, who coolly sipped her wine and delivered an icy glare at her plate, not gifting the guests with a direct glance.

"I'm glad to see the Laniakea graced us with their council," said the queen with a hint of bitterness on her tongue.

"Are you displeased by something?" Stellamaris asked. Despite her many visits to Kalagora as a child, she had yet to meet the royal family. Typically, her father would lead the procession down the middle of town, and the servants would usher her elsewhere to enjoy dining with the townsfolk while leadership met privately.

"This quarrel with Aiken has gone on long enough." The words bolted out as though from a loaded spring. The queen paused as Stellamaris stood with her mouth dangling open.

Stellamaris had not expected this. She had assumed the looming threat would be reason enough to ask the queen to enlist her citizens as Laniakean soldiers. Suddenly, she felt herself needing to take a more defensive stance.

The queen nodded to Stellamaris's seat, held out by one of the servants. Stellamaris's cheeks flushed as she sat. Mahla was already deep into the thigh of an enormous bird. "We are partners in trade, are we not?"

"We are, Your Highness."

"We have provided your people with enough food to keep your army strong, have we not?"

"That you have, of course."

"We need to see that strength. The only service you have to trade are your skills of protection and order. We have provided our goods to you, and you have provided nothing in return as of late. If you cannot provide us with safety at these most troubling of times, then you are but a leach on the skin of a dying man."

"My apologies. Aiken's army and gangs have caused us many losses, but we were unaware of any losses that you had taken."

The queen collected herself before sipping her drink. "You'll forgive me, King-Daughter. I just heard word this morning."

"Word of what?" Stellamaris asked.

"We had heard of the attacks on your village. We know that you have a lot to deal with. Still, we have no army here of our own. If you are busy protecting your own kingdom, then you'll lose your focus in lending protection to those you swore to protect in our trade agreements. I need to ensure coverage in case Aiken sacks the Laniakea, if I may be so blunt. We sent a man of our own to spy on Aiken. He returned just this morning to tell us we are to be invaded. They spoke about a recent battle between the two of you and that you'd respond soon. Our man says that they intend to invade Kalagora while you respond."

It was as if the wind had died away. All that had happened, the raid, her father's death. It was all planned in precise order. At some level, she already knew. Aiken's strength lay not with the might of his soldiers, as it did with the Laniakea, but through the forethought of Aiken himself. It furthered the case that they must think before rushing into battle. She now had half the warriors, twice the towns to protect, and there was a grander trap that they were clearly falling into.

She doubted herself. Did Aiken expect even this? She had come here for more soldiers. Had Aiken expected this move and crafted it into his plan?

"So tell me, King-Daughter, assumed interim ruler of the Laniakea," said the queen. "With all the swords of the coastal cliffs and the Drominion at our doorstep, what do you plan to do with this position entrusted to you?"

Elena drifted into a deeper slumber in the Laniakean town than she had along the beach. Her dreams were more real here and presented memories she'd rather not recall.

She dreamed of flashing lights at night and police tape littering her once perfect home.

An officer wrapped her in a blanket and handed her a Styrofoam cup of coffee while she watched two stretchers wheeled away, each with a blanket draped fully over the body.

She looked away for fear she might vomit again from the sight.

Along the shadows between homes, she saw Jude. Somehow, he was smiling through all this. He didn't stay long. He simply tipped his head knowingly and drifted away.

TWENTY-SEVEN

ANGIBLE SILENCE CREPT THROUGH the chilled morning dew as Edgar observed the warrior tribe preparing for battle. It was a sensation he never would have experienced had he not leapt through the glowing blue light.

Back home, he had no intention of joining the armed forces and felt fairly comfortable with the fact that while wars happened, they happened somewhere else.

Here, not only was war at his doorstep, but it also held a presence that he hadn't expected. There were no drums beating or raging soldiers clanging their shields. Only focus. Only discipline.

He had played out battle scenes as a child. He and his friends would gather large sticks from the field behind his house. If they were thick enough to clang together without immediately breaking, then they would make a suitable tool for their fictional war.

He had played many games that way. Now that he was playing some part in a war himself, however small, he wasn't sure that he liked it. Rather, he was confident that he didn't.

He knew Stellamaris did not intend for him to fight. Still, he knew that didn't make him safe. If he stayed in their village, Aiken could still raid it. If he fled into the forest, he would die from starvation or become a feast for the unfamiliar animals. Edgar did not know how to survive on his own. It was an eerie feeling to know that his best bet at staying alive was to remain with a village engaged in active war.

He peered inside his hut, observing Jude was still asleep. His roommate had been mostly silent since their arrival. A simple acquaintance from his high school, he didn't know the teen much at all, and somehow the trip to Cassini did not strengthen their bond.

Edgar had instead grown a deeper friendship with Ahletta and Stellamaris, members of a completely separate species.

Elena was a different puzzle.

He thought of her as he tiptoed around the hut and opened the small door to the cast iron oven that warmed his room. He stoked the embers as he recalled his female companion.

Elena was a curious one.

He had always assumed that she and Jude were dating, yet she wanted nothing to do with the boy now that they were a universe away from their friends.

Now, in the early hour of daybreak, Edgar teased the idea of climbing back into bed and catching more sleep, but the tension of everything made him fidget, unable to sleep for longer than an hour at a time.

Instead, he threw on a warm cloak gifted to him by Ahletta and went to observe the soldiers prepare outside.

The brisk air over the mountain cliffs contrasted with the heated hut. He peered out at the soldiers. He could see there was a routine in their movement, a learned motion. He noticed repetitive swings and blocks. The opponent would stop at a point in which both fighters agreed that one of them had either won or produced an error that needed correction. They would then retake their stance and start over.

The town had an energy to it, even at this early hour. He was not used to this. These warriors trained knowing they might die. Those young trainees who erred on a grassy field would find themselves slain if the same error were to happen in battle. Their lives, their lineage, their names, would only continue on if they were flawless or fortunate enough not to make a mistake at an inopportune time.

He found his mind wandering to the idea of disappearing into the woods. The idea pulled at him, though he knew that if he needed to find his own food, he would surely die.

Still, he felt the eerie desire to wander over behind his hut, unsure of what he was looking for.

The woods beckoned to him. He had daydreamed about a life in the wild, finding his own food. He imagined stumbling across a doe when he needed food.

What would he do?

He would need a spear.

How would he make one?

This series of thoughts led his tired mind down an avenue of twists and turns until he discovered an unfamiliar hand cover his mouth.

He tried to scream and wriggle his torso. An arm restrained his movement, a chokehold practiced many times. Only a few seconds had passed before he realized his captor knew more about holding him than he knew about escaping. Desperation led to one last fleeting fit before his sight dimmed and faded to darkness.

Stellamaris had returned from Kalagora at dusk. As tired as she was, she didn't rest the full night, instead tossing in her bed and waking up to a cool sweat.

She had led battles before, but she could always fall back on her father. If there was a detail unaccounted for, a weakness that would leave her warriors exposed, he always had a backup plan. That security had drifted away, a leaf in the wind.

She had generals, certainly. Mahla had taken over after Lane's death, and there were plenty of counselors to assist her. With the leadership team she had assembled, they could cover a fair amount of ground.

Still, if she overlooked a speck of detail, the fault would fall to her. If it led to the death of a single soul, the weight of that death would be hers alone to bear.

A fog glided into her mind and rested. Did she want this responsibility? Should she have left when Ilgene extended the offer? Perhaps he was right. There were plenty of council members, some more experienced than her, that would leap at the opportunity to lead their people to victory.

They knew they could die, and they had prepared for it. That was the way of the Laniakea. Not to die without thought, but to sacrifice that which they valued most for a cause that was greater than themselves. The cause of safety. The cause of freedom for young children to sleep warm in their beds, safe from persecution. They would grow old, and the frailty of age would be a gift that these warriors would grant them with their sacrifice.

If their battalion had been fully prepared, she'd still shudder at the loss of a single one of them, but she'd know they died in honor. If she had missed a detail that had gotten them killed, that would be something else entirely. Not only would they have died in vain, but they would also have died for her vanity.

"King-Daughter," said a voice. A young woman soldier was entering her hut, her sword already mounted along her side.

"Yes, Reeves."

"We have received word from the Kalagorans. We must ride now."

She hesitated a moment but persisted despite it. The fog of doubt still hung, but she whisked it away.

Was that vanity or confidence that pushed the doubt aside?

"Prepare the soldiers. Command that they form ranks and wait for my lead."

Reeves nodded and darted off.

Stellamaris stepped out from her hut. She had intended so much for this morning. A full belly and a complete bath while she still could. Instead, she would ride as she was and rely on the community for food along the way.

In the distance, near Edgar's hut, a piece of metal reflected the light of the young sun. At first she ignored it, but her interest persisted.

She approached it and pulled the object from the dirt. She observed the necklace that Edgar had worn after the encounter with the man that was bent on kidnapping him. The metal that decorated the necklace was the same that had led the child to base of the Evajocalyn.

Without announcing herself, she poked her head through the entrance of the boy's hut. Jude lay in bed, just waking up.

"Do you know where Edgar is?" she asked, eschewing her usual pleasantries.

"No, I haven't seen him yet. He seemed restless last night, though. I don't think he could sleep. I'd bet he got up to stretch his legs, maybe went out to drink some of that stuff you have. The coffee-tea drink you have here."

She closed the door to the hut and glanced around. Her soldiers were responding to her earlier commands. For now, she'd have to continue forward, assuming that Edgar was completely fine and simply stretching his legs. She had a battalion to lead, and that took priority.

Before dismissing it completely, she saw Ahletta across the field and beckoned her.

"Letty, would you go fetch Edgar? He should be somewhere close by."

"Yes, Queen Mother," Ahletta said. She hadn't earned that title yet, but she wouldn't stop a child from using a respectful phrase.

As Ahletta disappeared around the huts, Stellamaris's stomach began turning.

"This is one of those details I wish I knew," she whispered before venturing off to the head of the formation.

Edgar dreamt of a locked door and a key no longer beneath their ceramic frog statue. A rattle of the doorknob and the pounding of fists against the window received no response.

Edgar and Simon squinted through the fogged window.

A silhouette lay just beyond, their mother sitting upright and motionless in an armchair, transfixed on a wall of photographs, all framed neatly, but none matching the others.

"Mom," they both said, but the silhouette stayed still.

They continued to plead as cars drove by, heads magnetically turning as they passed.

The rest was sand down an hourglass. Concerned neighbors, police officers, women hiding the two boys as adult men rammed the door in.

She was fine, or rather, she was alive. Though her eyes were glass and her soul elsewhere.

A woman arrived. She had deep eyes and a bright smile. She gave off the feeling of comfort, as though it was a superpower that none possessed but her. "I have a family for you two to stay with, but only for a short while."

"No," said Simon, his head shaking. "We have a father. Mom, tell her where our father is."

But their mother didn't respond past an empty look, as the police officers gingerly ushered her into their car.

"Can you tell me your father's name?" asked the woman, now with a pad of paper and pencil.

Aggression spread across Simon's face. "Mom, talk to them. Say something. Say anything."

Their mother said nothing. She simply watched, as much a spectator as those who collected along the sidewalk.

Hostility built up in Simon, reddening his face. He rushed their mother, and an officer intercepted him. They rattled the world when they fell, and a crack echoed against the trees. They pulled Simon up, though he could not stand.

"Tell them where our father is," said Simon to their mother, grabbing hold of his broken leg.

Still, there was nothing. Their mother was gone, though she stood just before them.

And then there was Edgar, unable to move. Once a coiled spring of reaction, now drifting to a fragile filament as he stood bankrupted, a shell just like their mother.

He visited this memory often, though only as a spectator.

Edgar awoke to the smell of smoke and the crackling of embers. As he first opened his eyes, he squinted at the sun, which was a fair bit brighter than when he had left his hut that morning.

His head pounded, but he felt no bump along the back of his head.

Where was he? How far had they traveled?

The campfire before him had almost died down to nothing. What would once have been a bustle of wood sticks and logs was now collected into a heap, a slight orange glow from the aged flame disrupting the ash.

He saw the familiar silhouette of the man he had feared since Simon disappeared. This was the man that had been hunting him. This was Alister.

Alister sat before the campfire with his back to Edgar. His shirt hung from a post, which doubled as the support for a small tent.

Edgar looked down at his hands and feet, both unbound. He could flee while Alister stayed transfixed by the dying fire.

Edgar pushed himself up but discovered an extraordinary weight pushing him back down. He looked around, trying to be discreet, but found no source. No object forced him down. After more movement, he noticed his own muscles fought back.

His arms seemed to have a will of their own. No chains bound him, but the effect was the same. He couldn't move, despite the danger before him. He commanded his limbs, "move," and they refused.

"Lethargy," Alister said. "*A'tolora pacasimo.*"

Edgar looked around for who he might have been talking to but saw no one.

"Edgar," Alister said in his thick accent. "You have lethargy. I give it. You need to stay."

Whatever color he had in his face drained. Alister was talking to him.

"You speak English?" Edgar asked.

"Little. *Ma' lahraya.*"

"Do you understand me?"

He turned to Edgar, but only nodded silently. With Alister's shirt removed, Edgar could see a small tattoo over the man's heart. A rose. The pedals had small stitching, giving the appearance of leather or cloth pedals sewn together into a makeshift flower.

"Where is my brother? Where is Simon?"

Alister shook his head.

"He's dead?" Edgar's anger ignited, though he still couldn't stand. "You killed my brother? He was just a boy."

Alister shook his head once more. "I look." He pointed at his eyes and then at Edgar, and then gestured to the surrounding cliffs.

Edgar didn't understand but also knew that it would be pointless trying to get a detailed answer out of the man. He found an odd comfort in that last shake of his head. Edgar interpreted that to mean either that Simon wasn't dead or that Alister had lost Simon and was now unsure of his brother's whereabouts. Either way, the news gave him hope.

"Who are you?"

"Nilleli. I am Alister. I am Nilleli."

The man turned back around to face the fire.

Edgar's muscles pleaded for sleep in his unyielding, curious mind. He returned his head to where he had originally lain and rolled over onto his side, barely accomplishing that simple motion through the relentless weight pulling him to the earth.

Alister stood with an iron tray filled neatly with food in his hand. He didn't say a word or look Edgar in the eyes when he walked over and placed the tray in front of him.

Edgar looked down and saw an array of what looked like chicken wings of various sizes. Beside them was a toasted plant that Edgar couldn't place. At first, he didn't think he should eat it. Then his stomach growled, and the hunger convinced him that if Alister was going to kill him, it likely wouldn't be through poison.

He could move his hands enough to feed himself. The meat was sweet, with a crisp, burnt outer layer. It was good. Under different circumstances, he might even have paid the man a compliment.

"You like?" Alister asked without looking up.

Edgar didn't respond. While he was grateful that this man had fed him, there was no place in his heart for anything resembling forgiveness. He certainly didn't feel like indulging in idle chatter.

Still, he had questions, and this man was the only one who could answer.

"Why did my teeth hurt when I saw you on Earth, but they don't hurt here?"

It was as though a mousetrap had snapped shut. Alister darted a look at Edgar, distressed and pleading. He almost dropped his food to the floor as he bolted to his feet.

"*Tre al'tre bohem*," he yelled. "Second brother. Not me. Second brother is Mimic."

The outburst caused Edgar to pull back. His extreme lethargy prevented him from standing and running, but he feared if he stayed, he would not live for long.

Alister appeared to reign in his temper. Still, there was a fire to his glare, but now under control and no longer directed toward Edgar.

He collected himself and sat back down. He buried his head in his hands and repeated in a hushed tone, "Mimic. Mimic."

TWENTY-EIGHT

ELENA LEFT THE CONFINES of her hut, finding a stillness in the air, a stale quiet marking the lack of familiar chatter. There were scatterings of townspeople, too young or old for battle, remaining behind without much more than a nod to one another.

She scanned the grassy field. Several children, young enough for Elena to babysit, held wooden rods, cracking them together in mock battle. A large log assumed the role of a bench along the side of the grass. It was unused, so she sat.

She recollected all that had happened as she rubbed her fingers along the smooth stone in her pocket. The same stone given to her by the frogling when she first arrived.

All of this had started with her jumping through the portal.

No, it started before that. The portal wasn't the beginning. She was the first to jump through the bright light, and she had assumed, or hoped, she'd be the only one of the three. She was glad to see that Edgar had survived the trip and admired his courage to rescue Simon, no matter how idiotic.

But her reasons for jumping through were more complex than Edgar's. Perhaps it was easier for her. Perhaps that's why she went first. Edgar was running *toward*, but Elena was running *from*.

To run *toward* required a choice, which came with hesitation, inward thought.

To run *from* was an instinct. Animals did it. Even an insect would run from its attacker. She'd leapt through the blue orb with little more thought than a spider scurrying from an angry child.

She ran from Jude. She ran from the life that had formed around her back home. That was no life, and she knew as soon as she saw the portal that whatever lay beyond it would be better than the life she left behind.

Why would Jude run after her? She would have had a fulfilling life here if he hadn't ruined it by following her. There would be no reminders of her mother's death or of the man that killed her. She'd be free.

Relief had blanketed Elena when Edgar brought her back to this town. She assumed she would die along the beach, baked in the alien sun. Learning about the town meant that she would have the support it provided. She could pick up a trade and be part of a community. When she saw Jude emerge from his hut, the idea of dying along the beach felt less cruel.

Her hatred materialized as Jude opened the door of his tent and sauntered over to Elena's log. A smirk, one she wished she didn't recognize, crept along his face. She could have left and continued to avoid him, but she wouldn't give him that gift.

"You still can't seem to get rid of me," he said.

She didn't answer. She didn't coldly ignore his presence, either. He had provided a statement rather than a question, and she would not banter.

"Our deal's not off," he continued.

"You and I feel differently," she said. "We're no longer on Earth. We get a fresh new start. Both of us, actually. You could choose to be a new person here."

"You killed a man, Elena." The words stung, though she held her face firm.

"And we're here, guests of the Warrior Tribe. They kill every day. Do you really think they'll see it the same way?"

"Oh, I do. You killed a poor, defenseless father."

She shook her head. "I don't understand you. What did your father do to you to make you this way?"

"Ha! You're just as bad as me; you're just not honest with yourself. Or maybe you just hide it better."

"I would never blackmail someone that just lost their mother."

He leaned in. "That's just because you're not very creative."

She leaned in as well, no longer afraid. "There's no more deal. I'm not going to get arrested here. You have no leverage."

"You and I think differently. Are you confident you can talk your way out of it? They've grown fond of our Edgar. When they see the look on his face when he hears the news, they'll know not to trust you. Who knows how they treat people of your kind here? I see no judge, no jury. I doubt they have the concept of 'cruel and unusual punishment' here. The most you could hope for is to be thrown out of town. Have you enjoyed sleeping in a nice, warm bed, Elena? Have you enjoyed the food they've given you?"

She tried not to react until she had something well thought-out to say. Since nothing came to mind, she remained silent.

"You're risking a lot," he said. "Like I said, being banished from town is probably the best-case scenario. Are you confident you'll find another town that will take you? If you find one, are you confident it won't be partners with the Laniakea? You'll just receive a punishment from them instead? How are the winters here, Elena? If you survive without food or shelter, if you survive the next storm, what will you do when it becomes winter here? Your last breath would slip through chattering teeth as you freeze."

Her blood warmed to boiling, but she said nothing. Several young trainees noticed them talking. Jude slid closer.

"Now snuggle up close," he said. "Just like back home. You wouldn't want people to think we were conspiring anything."

"I can't get you drugs anymore," she said. "I have no dealer here. Honestly, I don't know what you could want from me."

"I guess you're not as creative as me." Thousands of tiny pins poked in a wave up her spine. He leaned until his mouth was an inch from her ear. "I'll find a use for you. Likely more than back home."

He nibbled the lobe of her ear. Shame overwhelmed her. Not from anything she'd done back home. No, this shame was from not attacking him there on that log. The moment he bit her ear, her soul left, vacuumed from her body. The moment came to pass, and she remained still. Provoked, but unmoving. She could still feel the imprint of his teeth against her ear after he stood up. It felt like a stain she needed to scrub away.

She wanted to do so much and felt like she could do so little. At home, she might cry. Here she had no tears to give.

TWENTY-NINE

EDGAR AND ALISTER MARCHED through the tall grass within view of the coast. Alister had released the mystical weight on him that kept him from running away, but Edgar still could not escape.

Several times, he tried to sprint off into the trees while Alister started a fire or prepared camp. His legs grew heavy in an instant, as though running through waist-high water. Alister would see this, walk up to him, and pull him to the ground by the shoulder, muttering angry words in his own language as he did so.

It was this way their entire trek. When they slept, Alister tied Edgar's arms and legs. Perhaps sleep prevented Alister from using the Gift. Maybe concentration had a role to play. In either case, the weight of Alister's spell only pressed on him when Alister had Edgar in view.

"Are you from Cassini?" Edgar asked during a long stretch of hiking. He had wondered about this for a while. Like King Semian, Alister looked human but was not from Earth.

Alister marched without giving a response. He heard Edgar, but with lack of English, perhaps he didn't understand.

Edgar repeated. "This planet. Are you from here?"

Alister slowly turned his head toward the boy, presented a darkened scowl, and shook his head. He looked back upon the trail and continued hiking.

Edgar pressed on. "Everyone else here is amazing at picking up English within a single conversation. You seem to know very little."

Under normal circumstances, Edgar would have worried about being too forward with his questioning. But these were hardly normal circumstances.

Alister proceeded without responding.

"English. How did you learn English?" Edgar asked, attempting to simplify his question.

Alister halted and turned. At first he seemed agitated, but he swiftly released any tension in his shoulders and took a deep, calming breath before responding. "I from..." He pointed at the sky, moving his hand around to many locations. To Edgar, this suggested he was from everywhere but Cassini.

Edgar thought about his gesture for a moment. It was far from a sufficient answer. "You're from space?"

Alister shrugged and gave a half-nod as though the answer was only partly correct, though a roll of the man's eyes hinted Edgar was mostly wrong.

"Why are you here?" Edgar asked.

"I am Nilleli." Alister trudged forward through the grass without looking back at Edgar.

"Is Nilleli a planet you're from?"

Alister shook his head without looking back. "Nilleli here. And…" He gestured to sky once more.

"I see," Edgar said. "The Nilleli is like a club."

Alister cringed, and Edgar felt the Gift push his jaw shut. He tried to yell through his teeth, but his tongue was unwilling to move.

Alister looked back once more, and for the first time since he met the strange man, Edgar saw him laugh.

"You look nervous, Gracie," Stellamaris said, staring down at the man from her saddle, the sun just beginning its slow descent from after mid-day.

He glanced down at the mud on his boots, a sneer of revulsion spreading across his face. "I'm having a less than ordinary day, my lady."

"I am honored to have you on our side," she said, chuckling to herself as she watched the dignified man experience minor discomforts.

"I still am eager to lend a hand." A glop of muck flung from his boot as he treaded along the trail. "Although after today, I suspect I will do better to assist with strategy off the battlefield somehow. Is there any room on the council? Yes, I do believe that will suit me more."

"You're welcome to tag along the back of my horse if you'd prefer to be out of the mud. Once we reach the crest, the ground hardens. You'll get out of the mud for the trip and then find a good vantage point to *advise* once we're on more solid ground."

She smirked as she said this but reined it in once she saw how serious he was taking himself. She feared the man truly felt he could race to an advisor's position after knowing them so little. Still, she'd never stifle a rising star, though a simple tease wouldn't hurt.

He appeared to consider her offer, though still not preferring it.

He batted his hand at the wind. "My lady deserves her own horse."

"Suit yourself." She instinctively winked at him as she nodded, a smile slipping out.

The battalion of Laniakean warriors marched in a formation suitable for long trips, allowing for some groups to rest while others remained ready for a surprise attack. It would take over a day to reach their destination. Still, after her father's ambush, she wouldn't take anything for granted. They'd know what was coming without wasting too much time and resources slowing down their pace.

The sun had passed its midpoint. The Doldrums were mostly flat, save for a few jagged cliffs that jutted out from the ground. Compared to their fertile town, this was a barren wasteland where an ill-prepared traveler might get lost with every horizon looking the same and no river or plant life from which to draw sustenance.

The dreary colors dragged on the spirits of her warriors. The soldiers trudged through the mud without speaking a word. No complaint or idle conversation, not even as a passing whisper. The silence hung in the air for several hours. The shaking of armor and slopping of mud turned to white noise.

It was then that the harsh call of a young child cut through the static.

"Help! My lady!"

She glanced toward the source, barely able to make it out.

There, just beyond the mist, lay a teen boy. His identity and form were indiscernible from a distance, but she could make out enough detail to determine that he was too young to be a warrior. A strong pull tugged at her, steering her horse in its direction.

Her horse galloped forward, with a dozen of her men following close behind. She abruptly stopped and signaled for the others to do the same.

A small voice, an instinct, drew her focus, not toward the boy, but toward the unnatural pull that this boy had on her. It wasn't simply that someone was calling for help and she wanted to help him. There was an unnerving strangeness to this call. The voice was real. This much was clear by the expressions on the men in her battalion. Rather, her temptation was more pleading, more anxious than she might expect. It was as though an invisible chain wrapped around her waist, tugging her forward.

"Mahla," she said. "Have the scouts returned with an update?"

"No, Queen Mother," he replied. "But the boy, what shall we do?"

She ignored him. She turned instead to Gracie and delivered a command just above a whisper.

"Gracie, I feel something abnormal with this plea for help."

Stress lines formed across Gracie's face as he struggled to concentrate through the screams of the boy. "I don't know what you could mean, my lady. It's a child calling for help."

She hesitated, doubting her instincts at first, but then doubling down.

"I need you to trust me," she said.

Mr. Gracie stopped and listened. He glanced around and then spotted something opposite of the source of the screaming. His movement halted, his eyes avoiding a particular spot along the horizon.

"Help me, My Queen!" said the boy once more. Stellamaris's eyes focused on the child, and she could make out the form of Edgar trapped in the mud. Her hands gripped the reins. Her body wanted to race forward, though it would need to disobey the caution in her mind.

Paranoia settling in, she noticed how peculiar the situation was.

Gracie's words were just above a whisper. "My lady, there is a scout that I do not recognize atop that cliff." Instead of pointing, he inched his shoulder in the direction he was showing. "I now believe this is a trap."

She did not glance at the scout lest she give away that they had seen him. Instead, she would return Gracie's trust with her own.

"Mahla," she said. "I need one of your warriors, a rogue, swift and silent. Have that scout brought to me. If he can bring him alive, then do so. But we must not reveal ourselves. That is our priority. As for us, stay back but begin a wide formation. Make it look like we are falling for this trap, but do not approach. We need the scout to doubt their timing."

Commands scattered throughout the battalion through an array of murmurs. Moments passed that felt like hours. With each heartbeat, doubt burrowed deeper. What would come of the child if it really was Edgar? What would happen to her men if she pursued the boy, and it was a trap? If she allowed too much time to pass, would the enemy swarm her battalion?

Soon, Stellamaris looked up and saw that scout was no longer there. Moments later, Mahla's warrior returned with only a blade in his hand.

"My lady, I attempted to apprehend the scout, but he called for help, and so I had no choice. I hid the body so no one would find him."

"Did you see anything else? Did you spot the enemy battalion?"

"Yes, my lady. There is a small camp of soldiers on the other side of that cliff. The campsite was massive and well equipped, but I only saw a few men. I do not believe their entire battalion is there. If you give the command, we could defeat them here."

She mulled it over but dismissed it. "No, we need to stick to the plan. Attacking too early would be shortsighted."

She needed her warriors to remain calm and silent. A chill rippled down her spine as she imagined her father facing a similar situation.

She knew something would happen soon, but she must do nothing to alert the enemy.

A howl filled the air. The warrior tribe folded over, hunching down and covering their ears.

She looked. The false Edgar had mutated into a stark white creature. Fangs dripped with saliva. Long, gangly arms and legs extended from a slim, oblong form. It ignited into a gallop toward the battalion.

Mahla lifted his bow immediately and buried an arrow through the creature's chest.

"A Songbird," Gracie said, stumbling back and gasping for air.

"What was that thing?" asked Mahla.

Gracie caught his breath. "In single combat, a Songbird will eat a man whole. But in battle they are meant to lure you in while the enemy battalion surrounds you."

Stellamaris darted her gaze along the horizon, worried she might find the enemy soldiers emerge from behind the cliffs. Had they heard the creature?

It was then that she recognized how vulnerable they were. While they were reacting to the Songbird, they had positioned themselves in the Doldrums' heart. If Aiken's soldiers were to hear the cry and attack, they would be on familiar terrain and could swarm in on them.

"Run toward the mountains. Run toward higher ground. Do it quick and silent. Do not give us away."

Her soldiers followed her lead. Each clop of a hoof or neigh of a horse felt far too loud for her comfort.

They arrived at the base of the mountain opposite the enemy battalion. They listened through the silent wind. Had they been seen?

With no movement, it appeared they had gone unnoticed.

"We can take them, Queen Mother," said Mahla. "They are few and are not aware we know about them. We could surprise them."

Doubt crept in. His soldier had suggested the same thing. Was she making the right decision?

"No, we have a sound plan as it is. This would be a surprise attack indeed, but your man said that not every soldier is at the camp. We risk being pulled into another trap. Aiken's men could hide in the hills along the border of the valley. They could lure us in the same way they tried to lure us in with that creature. That *Songbird*." She nearly spat when she said its name. "We will change our route to avoid being noticed, but we will not cancel the greater plan in place of a minor victory. Send word to our scouts."

Mahla nodded and instructed the rest of the men. They marched off along a winding road leading up through the mountain caps far outside the Doldrums. It was difficult terrain and added time, but a stark alternative awaited them if they stayed on their original path.

"A Songbird." She committed the word to memory as they continued onward. "Horrid creature."

THIRTY

STELLAMARIS HAD HER DESTINATION in view when she heard the hoofbeats against the dry, cold dirt. They came from behind, but a quick glance at the reaction from her soldiers showed that there was no threat. The gallop slowed as the horse approached. Warriors parted as little Ahletta came through the crowd on her modest horse and up to Stellamaris.

"Letty?" Stellamaris said, shock and worry across her face. "Why are you here? You're not prepared to fight." Suddenly, the worry turned to desperation as she became pale. "What happened back home?"

"It's Edgar. You told me to find him." Color was restored to Stellamaris's cheeks, knowing that the town was okay. Still, a knot formed in her stomach.

"It's fine, Letty. This is no place for a child. You can deliver your news when we return. For now, you need to return home."

"If I may, my lady," she said with forced formality. The child seemed aware of all the eyes on her as she delivered her report. "When I couldn't find Edgar, I investigated further. I asked around, and no one has seen him all day."

As much as this unnerved her, she needed to focus on the task at hand. They were at war, and as troubled as she was for the boy, this was something she would need to postpone until she returned home. She dismissed Ahletta, but the young girl persisted.

"Finally, I interviewed the other boy, Jude. At first he had little to say, but soon he recalled a memory like a dream. In the haze of his sleep, he forgot an important detail. He recalled seeing a bright flash of light seep through the cracks of their hut shortly after Edgar rose in the early morning."

The sky fell apart, and clouds rushed into her eyes as she heard the words. She suddenly felt her heart pulsating through the veins in her neck.

"A flash of light? Are you sure?"

"That's what the boy said, my lady. I was worried about Edgar, so I rushed here as fast as I could."

Stellamaris recalled the night the would-be captor attempted to kidnap Edgar. He disappeared in a wisp of light. The boy, *her* boy, was in grave danger.

"Mahla," she called.

"Yes, Queen Mother."

"How well do you know the plan?"

"I can execute it drunk, my lady."

She glared at him with stony eyes.

"I know it well, Queen Mother," he said determinedly. "I'm not drunk, I promise."

Warriors muttered frantically around her. Stellamaris heard someone whisper, "Is she leaving?" followed by "She can't do that on the eve of battle."

She looked at Mahla and for a moment let doubt seep out of her eyes before she pulled it back in. She let the moment pass and turned to address the assembled soldiers.

"Laniakea, I place my trust in Mahla and know that he will lead you well. I will fight beside you when I return. For now, the weakest of our tribe is in danger. I could stay and be a symbol or leave and save a life. I tell you this now so that you know truly if your life were in danger, I would do the same."

Should I be doing this? I could leave my throne behind. But he's my boy. He's a stranger from far off, but he's mine to care for and protect.

Stellamaris could feel the sense of betrayal spread through her soldiers. She made one last plea to her people. "Laniakea, hear me! There is no crown for one that leads the strong in sacrifice of the weak."

Her soldiers stood silent for a moment. It was a moment that she didn't have. She swiftly turned and found Gracie. "I need use of the Gift." His deep exhale pulled out the light from his eyes as fear rushed in to replace it. "Can you take me to where Edgar is?"

"Oh, my King-Daughter. I...I can't... Normally I envision a place, my lady. I cannot find a person when I do not know where they are." Her restlessness at his words caused her horse to jostle. Gracie observed it and combed his mind. "There is a way for me to envision a person whom I have met. I might try..." He stopped himself from rambling, fumbling as though he were a child, cold in heavy rain. He stopped himself short of a full explanation and collected himself. "It will be a risk, but I can try."

She accepted whatever he offered. It had to work.

"Mahla," Stellamaris redirected toward her general, "I need you to take over lead of the battalion. Do everything exactly as instructed."

"I shall, Queen Mother." A warrior's grin spread across his face.

"Mahla..." She reined in his focus. "Follow the plan, precisely as I've instructed. Not too early, and certainly not too late."

As Mahla straightened his back, looking unduly professional, Stellamaris held back the smirk that wrestled onto her lips.

She ignored the sneers from her soldiers as she dismounted. This would not win her the crown. A good queen would lead their warriors to battle from the front. Still, she could not live while she knew with certainty that the weakest of her clan had died and she could have prevented it. She told herself that she could still rescue him and be back in time to lead the warriors, but the more reasonable part of her mind dismissed the idea.

She turned to Gracie. He looked stricken. "I must stress that this is a critical risk."

"You're my best Gifter and today a Laniakean Warrior. I have full faith in your abilities. Now make haste."

And in a wisp of blue light, the two disappeared into the ether.

The ghostly blue light dissipated as Gracie and Stellamaris stumbled out.

Stellamaris needed to catch her bearings. Where was she? It all seemed so unrecognizable.

They stood in a meadow bordered by all, ancient trees. The sun had barely set, leaving streaks of orange and purple through the ancient sky. To her left she heard a man's gasp as he threw water, dousing a campfire, and grabbed Edgar by the arm.

That's them. That's my boy and that horrid man.

She dashed at them, unwilling to spare the distance as they leapt into the forest. If they went too far in without her keen eyes following, she'd lose them forever.

Their silhouettes danced amongst the trees, barely visible in the shadows.

Behind her, Gracie pleaded. His faint voice echoed around her as he shouted he could try again, that he could get them closer. She did not slow her step. Not now. With no time for doubt, no time for second guesses, she relied on sheer will and trust in her legs to propel her forward.

That man had taken her boy.

She pushed forward with a new purpose, a new thirst.

Who is this man? Who dares to take the one I protect?

She didn't know when she started calling him that. *My boy.* He had an endearing, kind-hearted nature that he hadn't yet truly come to understand. He had pushed forward to find his brother, despite his shortcomings. Despite the obstacles.

This was not the life he deserved. She knew little about him except that he was not an immigrant from a far-off land over the sea, as her father had guessed. He was more than that, a young man with a purpose he was too young to understand. It was not a life he wanted, yet he took his yoke upon his shoulders and carried it. Scared and unprepared, he continued on. That was her boy. He had to live past this, and she had to live long enough to ensure his safety.

She reached the trees and saw the boy and the man exit the forest on the far side. It was now obvious where they were going. This forest was actually only a patch of trees that bordered the beach, leaving a half span of sand between the trees and the water. They headed toward the ocean, though she didn't know why.

At that moment, she realized how disoriented she was. She assumed she ran east, but the ocean in front of her told her otherwise. This place was unfamiliar, even to her. Perhaps she was farther north and simply turned around.

The Coastal Cliffs looked different from this. This beach was accessible from the forest, whereas her beach lay framed by tall cliffs that kissed the clouds. Trees only grew at the peak.

This place was different. The redwoods encroached on the sandy shore. Patches of tall grass littered the otherwise white mounds.

Her legs screamed as she trudged through the loose sand. Her body begged her to stop, but she didn't. She couldn't. She never would.

Where's the boy?

She spotted him. He climbed a sharp incline along the coast, in tow with that man. The trail led up to the top of a tall cliff near the water. The stranger, the intruder, had her boy gripped by the arm as they climbed.

Anger lashed out as she pressed her legs past the exhaustion.

A distant part of her mind broke in, as though to slow her down long enough to think. She needed a plan, though her rage muted any clear thinking.

She was still a long way off, still a quarter span behind the boy. Even with the weight of Edgar slowing him down, she would never catch up to him.

But where is he going?

It came to her like a wave, knocking her off her feet. She knew that hill. She knew where they were.

The hill they were climbing was steep and rigid, but it wasn't the first time someone had climbed it. Small nah'airs would climb it frequently to prove that they were mature enough to progress into adulthood. Its steep incline was frightening, but no one ever died in the attempt. Now she knew where she was. She was forty spans north of the Laniakean beach, still part of the network of the Coastal Cliffs. At the top of the hill, a small valley would overlook the Poor Man's Sea. The valley met its end at a sharp drop-off into the sea.

She stopped, her legs failing after running from mound to mound. She closed her eyes and tried to focus on that distant part of her mind that she had muted earlier.

What do I need to do?

The ground trembled. She opened her eyes to see the sand rattle near her feet as tiny animals scurried into their homes or hid in the closest available space. As she looked on to the shore, the waves broke like wild beasts eager for the last slab of meat.

It's the Cliffs of Seri. He's taking him to the mystical rising Cliffs of Seri.

She knew what she would do. Without hesitation, she darted toward the edge of the beach near the water. The same legs that refused to listen were now in harmony with her body. She leapt through the soft sand. It was still difficult to run in, but she kept her knees high and persisted.

The waves would have been too difficult to fight against, so she turned up toward the side of the hill where a large rock allowed her to climb far enough past the chaos of the shoreline to get farther out into the water.

Upon the large stone, she could peer down, a far drop into the sea.

The ground shook once more, and the tide blitzed the sand. She reached the end of the rock, trying to gain whatever balance she could, but the ground shook with such force that any effort to fight it was useless.

There was nothing to hold on to, and so she fell. Her skull cracked against the stone, and a rush of purple and blue flooded her sight. As she looked up, she could see nothing through her blurred vision and the spiraling colors. Barely making out the direction of the sun, she attempted to push herself up to her feet.

Dizziness broke her movement, causing her to lose balance once more. She stumbled and fell, but this time she did not hit the rock. She hit nothing. Gravity took her through the air, down toward the unforgiving sea. There was time for only a single deep breath before she hit the water and sank.

THIRTY-ONE

"It's simple, really," Captain Rel said as he raised the glass of his favorite red wine and sipped. "I do not want a single drop of blood needlessly lost from our men."

Rel's first lieutenant, Simbi, nodded in agreement, though he knew he would. Not that Simbi was overly agreeable, but the plan was sound.

"The Kalagora are not well armed," said Simbi. "I suspect sheer intimidation will cause a swift surrender. You are truly a good leader to care so much for your soldiers."

"We'll save them for the Laniakean invasion."

"Oh, I see."

"I need the numbers for when we sack the Coastal Cliffs. But I agree with your point; intimidation will do nicely. Are the men ready?"

"Yes, Captain. They're waiting for you now once you are ready."

He took his time and savored his drink. This was always his favorite part, the moment before battle. The hairs along his arms would all rise in chorus. It was the flawless execution of a well-laid plan that thrilled him the most.

If he were younger, he would abandon his drink as it was and march out the door in haste. Now that he was a seasoned captain, he had learned to savor the moment, as fleeting as it was.

As the last drop dripped onto his tongue, he set the glass on the tablecloth and tidied the sides of his mouth with his napkin. He pulled out his chair, stood, and strolled out the door of the tent.

Torches illuminated the rich farmland surrounding the Kalagoran walls. Each of Aiken's soldiers held a sword, javelin, or hand axe. Many of them held a torch in their nondominant hand, filling the night air with dancing light.

It was not ideal for the men to hold the torches, and the captain knew this. He planned on there being no actual attack. The torches paired with the armed men presented the perfect intimidation.

If he could force the Kalagoran king to flee into the desert, the supplies of the town would provide his men with the food and shelter he needed to maintain a long-term presence near the Laniakea.

Kalagora was not a well-armed town, as Simbi had mentioned. The Laniakea were their only protection. Meanwhile, the Laniakea were without an experienced leader. Their own protection preoccupied them. Simply intimidating Kalagora would be enough. To kill them risked the lives of his own men as the stronger Kalagoran citizenry attempted to protect themselves.

His men would sleep well this night with full bellies and enormous grins. Most would survive this entire conflict. They'd be able to give their families a better life with all the wealth that the coastal and inland tribes possessed. There would be casualties, but all generations had casualties. At least now they were being proactive about it. It was the proactive ones that controlled fate's hand.

He looked ahead of him as he walked in no particular hurry toward a tall man and his wife, the presumed king and queen, as they stood in front of the gates.

The fiery brigade marched in step behind him, each with their standard brass armor and tattoos climbing up their arms to their faces.

The king and queen held no weapons and wore no armor, despite the blade the captain and his lieutenant displayed at their side. This was good. There would be a surrender if all went well.

"Greetings," the tall king said. He wore thin but well-appointed clothes, brightly colored, as did his wife. He looked beyond nervous as he attempted, and failed, to suppress his shaking voice. "I am King Roland of Kalagora, and this is my queen. I see your men are well armed, but I assure you we do not wish to engage you in battle."

He paused, and Rel knew the king was waiting for him to speak. But this was the part Rel enjoyed the most, and he would not give it up. Not now. He allowed the moment to hang for a moment longer.

Rel examined the king more closely as he paced around him and the queen. He looked closely at the thickness of King Roland's beard. There was no hesitation when he felt the fabric of his expensive shirt and made a nod of approval.

"You'll find that we have cakes, wine, and enough food to feed your entire battalion for several months. It will be entirely yours at no cost. We simply ask that you give us the night to prepare our people to leave their homes and enough of our own food and supplies to complete the journey."

"Give me this," Rel said, finally, reaching out and feeling the fabric of the king's clothes with his fingers. "I would like your shirt."

The old king inhaled, visibly insulted. Still, he pushed down his pride and removed his shirt. Rel casually took it from the king and stuffed it into the space between his scabbard and his waist.

He enjoyed this part, making his enemy feel weak, mocked. He stretched the time out, using it as a tool for further intimidation. Though he knew he didn't need it. He had already won. This part was for him. It was pure enjoyment.

Rel paused and let the moment hang between them until the king looked even more uneasy. When Rel was ready, he said, "Now get on your knees and lower your head."

Horror spread across the faces of the monarchs. The queen interjected first. "No," she said in a breathy plea.

"That wasn't part of the deal," the king said. "I have been more than fair to you. I have men here willing to fight for me."

"No, you don't," Rel scoffed. "What sort of king's man would let their king reduce himself the way you just did? I could kill you right now and invade your town with force if you resist, or you could get on your knees now, and I'll let your woman and subjects live."

"No," the queen said in desperation.

"Marian, I have to do this. You need to collect our family and prepare to leave."

"No, no."

The old king lowered himself to his knees and bowed his head to expose his neck.

The captain sent a brutal kick to King Roland's nose, propelling him backward and onto the ground, where he held his face, sobbing in pain. The queen rushed to him as Rel spat on them both.

"You will leave now," Rel said. "I will not give you the night to wait for the Laniakea to rescue you."

"But we need to gather food and supplies for travel," said the queen.

"I think it's obvious you have a better deal now than you could ever bargain for. Now go, before I remove the limbs from your feeble husband."

The queen picked up her husband and guided him back to the gate, occasionally glaring back at the captain.

It took an hour to collect the town, but Rel was impatient. He knew well that assembling an entire town in an hour was actually fairly impressive. They must have seen him coming and known they'd need to leave.

His brigade did not wait until everyone left to loot the town. They forced their way into homes and shops. They casually pulled blankets off of food carts closed for the night and helped themselves to the fruits and breads abandoned by their owners.

The treasures were greater than he could have hoped for. Mounds of gold and brightly colored jewelry filled the center of town, spilling out of pockets as the soldiers collected their prize.

"Oi, look what I found," a man said as spittle sprayed through his lips. He rolled a barrel of ale out from a dispensary. Men dropped what they held, some allowing ripe melons to fall and splatter upon the dirt street, to rush at the newly discovered treasure.

Rel snapped at his men. "Not yet. Wait until the last of them leave before you get drunk. You still have a job to do."

An echo of whispered complaints rumbled through his men, but they obeyed.

The Kalagorans filed out the gate with drooped shoulders, the honorable king taking the rear as he scanned for stragglers.

The soldiers taunted him and occasionally whipped his feet with short ropes. He was nearly out of the gate when the men discovered they could strike the pommel of their swords against the back side of his knee to get him to fall.

"Leave him be," Rel said. "You'd think you'd be more eager to celebrate."

As the king stumbled through the gate, the men shut it and cheered.

They rummaged for glasses to hand out and crowded around the ale. They had collected five barrels. The first soldier to partake lay flat on the dirt and allowed the drink to pour directly down his throat.

"Come on, come on," another man said, kicking him in the side.

Within seconds, every soldier had a glass to his mouth, ale dripping down his beard.

A young soldier, not much older than the Rel's son, laughed with giddy excitement. He peered through jet-black, shabby hair. He was far too thin for battle. A sudden fall from a horse would break every bone in his body. Yet perhaps the most profound feature was his eerie smile, paired with a knowing look. Rel perceived it as arrogance, but more than that, it seemed like the boy knew a practical joke was about to happen, and he sat there observing from the shadows with anticipation.

"That went rather well, I'd say," said the boy, nudging Rel in the side.

"Hold your tongue, child," said Rel. "Who are you to speak so casually to your captain?"

The boy straightened his back, but the smirk remained stained across his face.

"My name is Dorian," the boy said.

"That's *sir*," Rel corrected.

Dorian laughed. "Oh, I'm no sir yet. Give it time, though. I joined the forces last fall. My apologies, o Captain. I've mopped up after these brutes for the last year, and the smell of aged wine and vomit has seeped a little too deep into their skin."

Dorian's smug smile left Rel unsettled.

"You have experience with a mop, then? Looks like we've found someone to clean up after us over our stay here."

The smile remained. Further still, his eyes focused on the captain as though memorizing his soul. "Yes, sir," Dorian said, adding a wink.

The captain left Dorian, but not before he yanked the drink from the boy's hand just to pour it down his own throat.

"You will drink when all our men have had their fill."

The boy nodded, maintaining his stare.

"That's 'yes, sir,' not a simple nod, boy."

"Yes, sir."

The boy's voice was calm and all too casual. Rel would wipe that arrogance from his mouth before they left.

Dorian exaggerated a bow. Rel had had enough of the boy's mocking nature. He balled his fist and struck Dorian on the back of the head. The boy fell to the ground, only to climb to his feet with the smile still on his face.

Before Rel could strike him again, the boy took hold of the broom and began sweeping. Rel let it go. There was too much to do that night.

The captain watched as several men poured the ale down their gullets and chomped through cakes and meats. After a dozen men had had their fun, the captain felt the temptation to partake of several more pints.

Rel laughed as he shoved Dorian aside. "Come on, come on. Be useful and grab me a leg of vernagrande."

They cheered and sang as the dusk turned to night. Then, like an unseen wave, the captain became suddenly and deeply ill.

This was not that familiar feeling of drunkenness. The towers of the town appeared to tilt, and he fell over in agony. He looked up at the other men to help him, but they all were just as debilitated as he. Some to a lesser extent, and others completely passed out.

"Don't feel too well, do you?" a voice said. This voice did not sound sick. "It's called Revenge Ale. On a normal day, you'd be fine if you slept it off. This isn't a normal day, though. Not for you."

"Let me at this one, Mahla," said the familiar voice of the king of Kalagora. "I'm owed it after you let me get that close to death."

"Ah yes," said the grizzled man they called Mahla. "Sorry about that. It was all part of the plan."

"To let me die? Goodness, man, I'm a king."

"Oh, no, well, I'm a 'see how it goes' sort of planner. It worked out, though, didn't it? Would you like to use my sword for this next part?"

Rel pulled himself partially up from his prone position and rested on his hands and knees.

As he peered out across his men, he saw a disarray of soldiers in various states. Some pulled the blades from their scabbards, swiftly defeated by Laniakea warriors. The larger and stronger-willed men pressed through their drunkenness, but the Laniakea quickly swarmed them, taking them to the ground in a cloud of dirt.

Amazed, his eyes focused in disbelief as the ground lay stained by the corpses of his once strong battalion.

He looked up to see the owners of the two voices. One was a bearded giant in Laniakean armor. The other, the familiar voice, was the crooked-nosed king.

Soon, more Laniakea warriors came into view, though still blurry.

"Are you going to kill me?" Rel asked.

"We'd prefer to take prisoners, but we certainly don't have enough room for all of you," said Mahla.

A slow clap came from the shadows and revealed the smirk of the young boy, Dorian.

"Oh, I like this one," Dorian said as he appraised Mahla. "I do enjoy a cocktail of sin and ale. But please, you cannot supply such wonderful food and drink and protest when your patrons enjoy themselves…" he paused and kicked the side of a soldier that had vomited, barely missing his foot, "…a little too much. You are simply better hosts than this."

"This one's not sick," said the king. "Grab him before he attacks or escapes."

"Oh, I didn't drink any of your ale, though I enjoyed the treasures your town provided."

Mahla's men surrounded him, though being apprehended did not affect the boy's mood. Instead, he seemed proud.

"You think of yourselves as the heroes, I suspect. You live in comfort along the ocean cliffs with full bellies every night, ignorant of the past that got you here."

"And you know the past better than us?" Mahla asked. "You're a child. You're barely old enough to hold a blade."

"The hungry know why they're hungry. The full often don't even know they're full. But please do not be shy. You wish to kill me, so get on with it."

Mahla strolled over to Dorian. "We can afford three prisoners. Let's have you be one, eh?"

He picked up his sword and extended the pommel above his head before Dorian spoke once more, interrupting Mahla's stride.

"If I may, good sir, and I do believe you are good, allow me to give you one piece of advice before you do what you must. I believe you'll need it, and I'm just kind enough to lend my wisdom."

Mahla hesitated with his sword still in the air. "You sure talk a lot." He lowered his sword to his side. "Fine, you may deliver your advice."

"Do not fear the wicked who speak the truth. Fear the good that lie, and lie well."

"That's the advice? You could have told me to hold my elbows higher when I swing a blade. Why are you telling me this?"

"Because I believe you are a good man. I said as much earlier, if you were paying attention. You must know that a man who lies well is like a slow drip on rotted wood, and I truly believe you can do nothing to save yourself from the rot. So, my new friend, I risk little by telling it and you gain all too much by listening."

Mahla hesitated long enough to consider what the boy said but continued with his planned blow to Dorian's head. The boy fell limp to the ground as the soldiers tied his hands.

"I don't like it when children are smarter than me. It makes me nervous."

The king approached Rel, who was still trying to keep the vomit in.

"I don't think you'll be a prisoner, do you?" asked the king. "Now give me my shirt."

THIRTY-TWO

STELLAMARIS DRIFTED ALONG THE ebb and flow of sea waves as clusters of stars striped the night sky overhead. In her foggy mind, a distant voice, one that she had brushed off earlier, now begged to make some attempt, any at all, to save her own life.

Her vision came into focus before her mind could take it all in. The water was clear. Though it was dark, the two moons illuminated the water, exposing the bottom of the sea through clear water as though it were just out of grasp. The glow of blue oro fish swarmed around her and tickled her skin as they nibbled.

There, deep beneath the surface, her oro fish congregated near a small cave. The distant glow shined like a flame along the sea floor.

Is that where they call home?

More questions came. Why was her mind foggy? Had she hit her head? Yes, she must have. Where was her boy?

My boy. I need to find my boy.

The world around her shook once more, the same tremble that had shaken her loose from the stone and caused her to fall. This time, she noticed something new, something she hadn't before. The source of the shaken earth was the bottom of the ocean itself. The magnitude had grown since she landed in the water.

Her mind gradually sharpened. This was where the Cliffs of Seri would rise.

The cliffs were always a far-off echo she would fall asleep to. Now she was there, where the ground trembled, where the cliffs would soar to the clouds.

Several contrasting currents of water pushed past her as she twirled. How could she survive? Her fate was in a tidal lock with the boy. She must endure if she was going to save Edgar.

Frantically, she surveyed the water. The cliffs would rise soon.

She peeked back below the water and searched for the first spire to protrude through the ocean floor. Changes had taken shape. The sand sifted between rocks as sea life fled.

As sudden as a bolt of lightning, the crags expanded with a force that knocked the wind from her chest. The spires tossed aside all plant life to make room for the emergence of the island.

The ground absorbed her as she held on with sheer will. It pulled her up into the air as though she herself were a part of it. As she glanced down, plants and animals shrank to the size of insects. Her white knuckles clung on to any safe hold she could find as the wind rushed against her body, pressing sharp chills along her spine.

The cliffs slowed as they settled into place. She could now see the valley where the stranger had ascended.

No, that wasn't all.

She could see *them both*, her boy and that demon of a man. A ten-foot gap separated the Cliffs of Seri from the top of the hill where they were, but that was no longer an obstacle. Not for her.

Adrenaline gave new strength to her legs. She stood, pulled the sword from her scabbard, and let the war cry of her ances-tors loose from her lungs as she jumped the gap.

The shrill song of Stellamaris's war cry vibrated through Edgar's spine and echoed across the valley. Her blade hung high above her head, ready for a downward thrust as she rushed at Alister.

He threw Edgar back, and the two warriors clashed, igniting into a hurricane of motion. Despite Stellamaris's advancement, Alister did not waver. Instead, he deflected each swing and marched backward in a defensive step.

The battle was elegant. Efficient. An ancient dance they both knew well. Their swords clanged together, leaving no room for wasted movement.

With Stellamaris taking the offense, Alister flung up his blade in small but vigorous counter motions as he deflected her blade in incremental blocks. As much as Edgar admired the King-Daughter, the two seemed equal, despite the continuous offense that Stellamaris pursued.

Edgar stumbled toward the trees. This was his only moment to find safety. There was no sign of when the duel would end.

The red trees lay at the edge of the valley at the top of the hill. He dashed to the closest one with low branches and climbed. The harsh bark scraped his arms and legs as he reached out and climbed to the fourth branch. He felt hidden and secure, though he shook with fright.

He stared out through the pine needles and continued to watch the fight before him. Stellamaris drove Alister back, not allowing him to do more than block. The King-Daughter would leave no room for him to counter.

Then, with an elegant rotation of his body, Alister disappeared into a wisp of blue light and left Stellamaris alone in the valley.

Was he gone?

Was it safe?

The cool wind was now the only disruption to the stillness of the valley. Stellamaris's eyes darted from edge to edge, scanning for Alister.

After some time, Edgar mustered the courage to descend from the tree.

The only way out is through.

Stellamaris stopped to regain her composure. Where did that demon go? He'd return, she knew he would. For a fleeting moment, she felt hopeful that he had left, though she knew better.

And where was Edgar? Had he found safety?

Though she hoped to hold him tight, providing safe refuge, she knew that if she didn't know where he was, neither did his abductor.

There, off along the edge of the valley, in and amongst the trees, Edgar descended from a large sequoia.

Her stomach dropped as a faint blue light materialized in the space between them. He was back.

She didn't hesitate. Her legs ignited into a sprint that closed the distance and abruptly clashed with her enemy as he stepped out from the glowing flame.

Not expecting this, he stumbled back, though he deflected her blow to save his life. As he fell to the ground, he disappeared once more.

Stellamaris darted her eyes at Edgar. "Run! Hide!"

With wide eyes and pale skin, her boy darted off and disappeared into the woods.

She did not follow him. This needed to end.

Stellamaris focused her senses, drawing in deep breaths and noting the chirping of birds and scent of pine along the wind. She readied her blade and settled back, prepared to spring when she saw the man.

She waited.

Nothing happened.

It was then that the air along her back felt warm, toasting her shoulders. In a burst of blue light, the man appeared and caused her to stumble. She did not hesitate as she turned and swung her blade with an upward thrust, clashing against his own. He would not gain the offensive. She pushed forward as he rapidly blocked and disappeared once more.

But now she knew how to sense it. The air would be warm. She ran sporadically and eventually found a hot pocket of air. Her blade swung before he could materialize, and still he was there to deflect it.

He lunged, but she countered with a whirl of her blade as she deflected his.

He vanished once more, though this time it was longer. Her heart thumped. She wasn't sure where he would return and felt no warm air nearby.

The realization came to her all too suddenly. She knew what his next move would be, and the blood drained from her face.

He'd go for her boy. Could he tell where he had gone?

As she scanned the horizon, she saw no one in the light of the moons, no dancing shadows. She was alone, hearing only the chirps of nocturnal insects.

She wanted to be near Edgar but would not risk calling to him lest she betray his position.

A rustle along the bordering trees snatched her attention. It was Edgar. He had hidden in the trees and now descended.

"Get back."

She ran toward him as he dropped to the ground, the demon appearing beside him. At the sight of Edgar's abductor, she corrected her path and tackled him, grabbing hold of his sides.

Another blue light ignited before they hit the ground. This time, the light took them both.

The world disappeared, and she was unaware of the new one that replaced it. This was not the same Gift that Gracie had used. This was far more profound.

Scattered pinpricks of light blanketed the dark abyss as the ground beneath her feet vanished. There were no walls, no cliffs. There was no place for her feet to find purchase, yet she did not fall. Gravity taunted her, but she did not give in.

She felt a longing to stay there. It was so beautiful. She wouldn't need anything else. At that moment, she was no longer Laniakea, no longer Cassinian. She was simply an entity, nothing and everything.

She saw her father. Her sweet father. Why was he crying?

"Go," he said. She tried not to listen. This place would protect her from her fears. This place was what she needed. "Go now." Why would he say that? If she could have her father back, why would anything else at all matter? There was nothing in the world that meant more than this man. She had him there at that moment. How dare he push her away?

"You are Laniakea. Even here, where Laniakea cannot be."

She had no words, no voice to make them. She beckoned with her eyes, pleaded with her soul.

"Go now, Queen Mother. Go."

The last word from her father was a fleeting whisper as it pulled her from that heaven. She glided from euphoria until she found physical form.

She was suddenly aware of who she was again and what she must do.

Instinct extended her blade and found its purchase in something solid and now wet. Her eyes dilated and retracted as they focused. She met the gaze of the man, the demon, inches from her face. With his warm breath against her cheek, she saw the life drain from his eyes as he took his last breath. His face now pale and vacant, she watched him drop.

She looked down at the torn cloth left in his shirt by her blade.

Beside the wound, she saw a tattoo and recognized it. In her days as King-Daughter, she had seen many tattoos amongst her tribesmen. Many had meaning, but only to the owner. She knew immediately that this was different.

Before her, on the chest of her enemy, was the tattoo of the Leather Rose.

She stopped as numbness replaced victory. That tattoo changed everything.

Edgar ran up and hugged her as she pulled back from this new hold.

"You're safe, my boy," she said, the tattoo still calling to her. "You're safe."

THIRTY-THREE

WEIGHT COVERED STELLAMARIS IN layers.

The first weight was exhaustion. As much as she'd like to give the appearance of being a tireless leader, unmovable against the tides that threatened, that was simply not true.

The road into battle, the chase and clash against Alister, and her stagger back to the battalion that she left behind now left her drained.

The second weight was a realization, one she refused to look directly at. Her mind awakened to regret at what she had done during the fight. There upon the dead man's chest was the tattoo of the Leather Rose. It would haunt her until her last day.

That weight she placed aside, pocketed it, deciding to deal with it another time. She felt the pestering threat of it returning even as she set it aside.

The final weight was regret. She'd left her men after being their sole leader for less than a week. She'd placed confidence in Mahla and knew he could handle the battle. But how did her men see her? What about the morale of her people? She had fled. Would they see her as an unfit ruler, fearful and riddled with doubt? Were they more correct than she would admit?

She reminded herself that she was not yet queen. The Laniakea assumed her role as leader, but only for wartime and only temporarily. It was not her earned position in any legitimate sense. They would need to recognize her, an act she grew less confident of with every passing moment. Would they recognize her now that she had abandoned them before the battle that would avenge their fallen king, her father? Would they doubt her love for him, for them, after her actions?

She had abandoned her chance to fill her father's shoes when she abandoned her people.

The doubt that she had shelved now rushed in. She wanted to cry.

It was then that she saw the boy next to her, and she exhaled in calm comfort. Edgar was now free, though still weak. She was still a leader to him and would need to stay strong. She drew air into her lungs and continued to march forward, her face as placid as a stone.

Mahla was the first to see her approach. As he ran out the open gates of Kalagora, others followed. The blood that stained their clothes was proof of the battle now complete, and their gleeful smiles made their victory clear. At least that comfort settled her heart. If her people did not accept her, at least they were alive to do so.

As Mahla picked up his pace, she thought through what she would say to him. She'd defend her actions and plead for forgiveness.

But he did not allow that.

His arms lunged up and around her before she could speak, not allowing for an explanation. Not now. To this man, forgiveness came first.

The giant released his hold on her, turning to face the crowd.

"My brothers. My sisters. We were victorious on this day because of the well-laid plans of this woman. She placed the pieces together personally in such a way that even a fool like me could carry them out. But the weakest among us needed her bravery. I have heard your grumblings and know many of you did not approve of her leaving. I ask you this: if there is one among you who would sacrifice the weak to build up the strong, step forward now. If there is one among you who would allow your own child to be the one sacrificed, step forward now."

There was silence as an anxious mist crept in, invisible but all too real. No man or woman moved at Mahla's words, though their faces were mixed. After a moment of inaction from the crowd, Mahla withdrew his sword from its scabbard and placed it at the feet of Stellamaris.

"Hail, Stellamaris, Queen Warrior of the Laniakea," he said, and then bowed.

The ceremony had started.

The next moment would define it all. Would they follow his lead?

The air was still as Mahla waited. His unease betrayed him as he shifted his stance.

Soon, a small woman pushed through the crowd and continued the ceremony, placing her sword at Stellamaris's feet. "Hail, Stellamaris, Queen Warrior of the Laniakea."

A large man and his son followed suit. Gradually, more warriors came forward, pledging their swords. She felt the grace of the moment flood her heart. She looked down. A pile of swords, axes, and shields lay at her feet.

If Elix were there, a song would ring from her lungs to herald in the new queen. But no, the silence of the wind blowing the scent of pine was the melody that lifted her soul.

As she looked at the crowd of warriors with heads bowed, she noticed that one of them, though he had no weapon to give, was Edgar, her boy.

Stellamaris reclined upon a large boulder as the Kalagoran king approached.

It was odd. King Roland's features did not match the stories she had heard. This was the king who had stayed true to their plan, even as the Drominion battalion spat on him and threatened death. It appeared to be more than threatening, from what she had heard. It sounded as though the captain had raised his sword to strike. Still, the king did not appear to her as beaten down. He seemed a cross between a pleasant old man who would invite her in for warm bread and a crotchety old kook that would throw her off his doorstep the second she entered. She didn't know which one he'd be, because he hadn't spoken yet.

He hoisted himself upon the rock, taking longer than expected to find a place beside her. The stone was uneven, and he carefully examined the placement of his rear against the rock before he reluctantly committed. Finally settled, he removed a handkerchief from his pocket and covered the favored spot before he sat.

As he did so, a gust of wind released from his lungs, which seemed to communicate several messages. He was old, didn't like where he was sitting, and Stellamaris should be grateful for him stooping to this level.

She gave him a sideways glance as he spoke his first words. "Now tell me, new queen and leader of the Laniakea, what do you plan to do next?"

"What do you mean? Are you not content with the result of last night's work?"

"Well, yes, yes, of course. Last night was a victory. But if you expect that the Battle of Kalagora is the only battle you'll need to lead, then you're not nearly as well prepared as I had hoped."

She paused a moment and pushed down her puzzlement at his words. Instead, as the new queen of Laniakea, she kept her shoulders high and chest puffed out. She made her best attempt to exude confidence, no matter how false, and treated King Roland as though he were an adversary in mental warfare, even though he was clearly her greatest ally.

"I do know there will be more," she said. "And I have a plan."

"Perhaps you do. And perhaps with my experience, I can aid you in that plan."

"Now, Highness, take this respectfully, but..."

"My Queen, forgive me for interrupting, but I sensed hostility where there needn't be any. I intend to see you as empress of the coastal kingdoms. I assure you, I will be the first to bow to you when that day comes."

"Empress?"

"Surely you've thought about how Aiken slaughtered...my apologies...defeated your strongest battalion and half your warriors in the Battle of Songbird. You have taken over as leader of the warrior tribe. Meanwhile, you have half the warriors and many more kingdoms than Kalagora to protect."

Stellamaris had thought of this, but she hadn't had the time to come up with a solution yet. Vengeance for the Battle of Songbird had been her sole concern as of late.

"What are you suggesting?"

"Well, My Queen and future empress, I have skills in trade bargaining. I have relationships with the partnering kingdoms and can convince them to enlist in the Laniakean army. You can train their recruits and better equip the future empire to handle the impending war. It is truly our best chance at winning."

"I will not profit from war, Highness."

"You will not be profiting. It's the only way. You don't have your warriors. And even if you did, Aiken wants to invade all the coastal kingdoms. He will divide your battalions until he can tactically defeat them each on his terms. Your army must grow. Partnerships are fine during peacetime, but that is not where we are. If you maintain simple partnerships with independent but small kingdoms, you will maintain low numbers, and the only thing that will grow will be the hostility of your partners as they die while you divide your troops to protect them."

Stellamaris considered this. He was certainly seeking some sort of profit, yet all his points were correct. She was also in no state to refuse help.

"Tell the coastal kings to meet in one month in Laniakea," she said. "We will decide together. If they decide, just as you, that I should lead them, then I will clarify that I do not intend to continue my rule past when it is necessary."

"Of course, My Empress."

"Do not call me that. The people must select a ruler, and we will bind agreements that ensure our long-lasting independence from a sole authority after this war is behind us."

"Naturally." He bowed his head.

"Highness?" she asked. "What is it you wish to gain by electing me as empress?" She surprised herself with the directness of the question. He had played a mental game with her, and she brazenly acknowledged it, risking giving offence.

He smiled and addressed her with the confidence of a true king. "It is solely peace that I wish to gain. Peace within the coastal kingdoms. I saw a glorious future in your father. I'm glad to see that same promise in you."

She took a deep breath and thought for a moment. She knew there was something more he wished to accomplish, but that didn't mean he was wrong about the need for more warriors.

"We'll start with the meeting of the coastal kingdoms," she said. "We'll discuss what happens next as a group."

"A wise choice," King Roland said. "You have echoes of your father."

She prayed his words would prove true.

THIRTY-FOUR

The Laniakean troops drifted home with blistered feet and mouths thirsting for a cold drink as the town was ablaze with streamers sailing in the gentle wind. Stringed lanterns connected the huts and illuminated the dusk. Spirits were high, though their energy waned.

Edgar watched as those who had stayed behind skipped with singsong giddiness to the celebratory plucking of Elix's lute. The town had decorated the central yard with bright colors.

"Queen Mother?" Edgar asked, bashful. "How did they know to prepare when they didn't know if we'd be alive now?"

"Why, this is the Harvest Festival. We've been planning this for weeks, those not entangled in war, that is. As for whether they'd be in a state to celebrate or mourn, I sent a scout ahead to tell them of our victory. I'm certain they needed little news more than that. You'll find that the Laniakea will take any excuse to celebrate." She smirked at Edgar. "Do you grow tired of our parties?"

"Oh no, that's not it at all. I'm just impressed they pulled it together so quickly."

She laughed, and he felt more like a boy than he had since he arrived along the beach, what now seemed like so long ago. In his younger years, he would never have welcomed the sensation of being looked at as a child, younger than he wanted to be. Now, since his parents left, and now his trip across the universe, he'd had enough of adulthood.

Now, between the songs of the townspeople and the blood-stained faces of the warriors, he adored how Stellamaris looked at him as though he were too young. It was the truth. He was a child creeping down a dark road, pushed along by others. This place had become a pocket he wished he could stay in, a warm blanket he could burrow under, hoping never to leave.

He looked back up at Stellamaris, who was blanketed in an explosion of flower petals catching the fabric of her garments. "My dear Edgar, when you hold as many gatherings as we do, the challenge is not in setting them up; it's in keeping them fresh. But this is our annual Harvest Festival, and the comfort of an old shoe is finer than anything new could ever be. For this, we gladly choose the familiar. You'll see our people decorate as easily as they would dress themselves in the morning."

As they marched along, Edgar noticed the familiar faces of the townspeople who had stayed behind. Some were too young for battle, others were far too old.

Ahletta dropped a brightly colored cloth as she darted toward Edgar. Beside her was Ilgene, though he seemed preoccupied by the prisoners in tow. It was the bound boy prisoner that captured his attention the most, the one just slightly older than Edgar. Dorian was an oddity to Edgar as well, often spooking the horses as they marched home. Perhaps Ilgene sensed a similar discomfort from him.

As Ahletta dashed across the field, Edgar dodged to his right to avoid being tackled by the young lady. "You're home and safe. Thank goodness. Oh, tell me about the battle. Did you fight? Who'd you kill?"

"Letty!" Stellamaris said forcefully.

"What's wrong? Am I asking too many questions again?"

"It is not right to ask anyone whom they killed during battle."

"I didn't kill anyone," Edgar said. "But I have a crazy story for you. Is it too early for food and drinks? You're going to have to show me what I can have, though. Someone snuck me ale that made me sick last time."

"Oh, that was me," Ahletta said, her face now a pale shade of her blue skin tone. "I've been told that was the wrong thing to do, no matter how funny it was." She paused as she guided Edgar away from Stellamaris's ear. "It was hilarious."

This discovery could have flushed him with annoyance at the girl's flippant actions. Even a month ago it would have had him scolding Letty until she either ran away in tears or knew to leave him be. Instead, Edgar laughed as an unfamiliar feeling of belonging replaced his frustration. Perhaps it was the daring trip down the great trunk of the Evajocalyn, led by a village elder, or the selfless rescue by his new Queen Mother, but he felt an unusual form of affection for this village and its citizenry, not least of which was his new friend Letty. "It's fine. At home, people pull pranks on new friends all the time. It's called hazing."

"Does that mean I can do it again? If I haze this time?"

"No, not to me. Maybe to Jude, though."

The iron gate creaked open as Ilgene slipped in with barely a nod of acknowledgment to the guard.

"Which one you here to see, sir?" the guard asked, squinting to see the man as he settled back in the shadows.

"That's my business, not yours. Now, if you'd be so kind as to show me to the roster so that I may navigate…"

The guard extended a hand as though to ward off excitement. "Sir, it is your business, but I need to know which cell you are visiting so that I can check in on you. It's for your protection that I know where visitors are, you understand."

Ilgene stood tall and straightened his spine to assume the superior position. "I do understand, but now you must as well. I am a warrior of the Laniakea, battle-worn and fully capable of protecting myself against bound men in cages."

"It's protocol, a particular command from the Queen Mother. The prisoner could disable you and escape."

Ilgene scoffed. "He won't, believe me. But if you must know, I am visiting the boy. I believe they identified him as Dorian. Now lead me to him immediately."

"Fine, fine, sir. He's just this way." The guard's tone was submissive, though clearly perturbed.

Their shoes clopped against the bricks of the stone cave. Typically, the Laniakea preferred wooden huts to stone, since proper stone structures required material and talent they could only trade for. This was the sole solid structure, built underground, using clay reinforced by imported black bricks, each the size of Ilgene's chest. Lining the hallway were small openings in the ceiling that would normally let in the light of day. Now, as the sun began its descent, lit torches filled the prison with dancing light.

They arrived at Dorian's cell. The guard gave Ilgene a subtle nod with a less-than-subtle gust of breath through his nostrils as he turned and marched off to his post.

Ilgene waited until the guard had cleared the corner before he approached the prisoner, speaking just above a whisper. "What are you doing here?"

Dorian released the giddy smile of a hyena approaching a wounded gazelle. "Well, hello there. What a wonderful day we are having! I hear there's a festival aboveground. Are you coming to deliver an invitation, or have you smuggled me a brandy to enjoy from my cage?"

Ilgene remained curt, with no desire to follow the boy down this dark road he loved so much. "You're not supposed to be here."

"Now, Ilgene, my dear, I've waited far too long to have my fun. To be blunt, I'm here to play my part in all of this, and I will insist that you play yours. Frankly, I'm surprised you haven't already."

Ilgene lunged forward, stopping just shy of rattling the cage doors as spittle dripped from his lips. He glanced down the dim hallway, hoping not to attract too much unwanted attention from the guard.

He calmed his breath and regained composure. "They trust me here, and I've spent years gaining it. If I act in haste, I will give myself away. I planned on taking the boy when they marched off to Kalagora, but that Alister fellow rescued him." As he said this, he spidered his fingers through the air as though they were climbing the wind. "By Kyel, I would have nabbed him back on Earth if it weren't for that man. Do not come here and lecture me as you gaze on from the comfort of the Drominion towers. Alister has been a thorn in my side for far too long."

Dorian let nothing that Ilgene said bother him. He sat in his cell as though he were soaking in a steaming bath and sipping aged wine. "Well, he's gone now, from what I hear. Lucky you, you have nothing to hold you back."

Offended by his brazen response, Ilgene lashed back. "What? Now? Not tonight. He's surrounded by Stellamaris's soldiers. It wouldn't surprise me in the slightest if he were sitting on her lap as we speak, eating cakes and plucking grapes as she held up the vine. If I take him now, they'll know for certain who I am."

Ilgene observed a smirk slither across the face of the boy, as though he were holding back a laugh. "You, with all your glory, fear the Warrior Queen?"

"What is it you think of me, Dorian? You think me a thug, good for a swift job and an easy payout? I've invested my time and trust over the years. I've given my life to a long game. How dare you suggest that I simply expose myself now, after all these years? I am no pawn, dealt out and disposed."

Dorian cocked his head back in joyous laughter. "Oh, dear child..."

"Don't call me a child."

For the first time that night, Dorian rose to his feet and presented his first peek of irritation. "Do not worry about what I call you. And do not concern yourself with the pride that you've earned." Dorian regained his smirk and slowly appraised the man before him, starting from his feet before he met his eyes. "Your cover here has served its purpose, and we need you back home."

Dorian completed his statement with a nod to Ilgene, almost in dismissal, as he returned to his comfortable position along the floor.

Ilgene realized at that moment that he had subconsciously taken several steps back, despite the bars that separated the two men. Now, when he spoke, the confidence that had once been there seemed stolen away by a rogue sprite. His resistance remained, but now hanging back in the shadows of his false confidence. "And what of you? You've gotten yourself captured. Shall I break you out then?"

"Oh no, of course not. As I've stated, I've just started having my fun, and I do believe this next part will be very fun. Or perhaps that isn't the right word. Joyful is better. This brings me such joy."

Elena used the festival as a tool. She hoped it would distract them, the warriors, elders and general merrymakers alike as they clanked together their wine glasses and spilled gobs of food on the ground for the dogs to eat. They were all too kind taking her in, but this was no home of hers. Until now, she wasn't sure she knew what a home was. At least not in the full meaning of the word.

She smuggled plates of food into sacks that she had stolen from the supply area. It wasn't difficult to get away with thieving party supplies during a party. If someone had stopped her, she'd simply tell them she was getting things in order, grateful guest that she was. No one stopped her, though. Not a soul grabbed her arm to keep it from an apple. No one yelled "thief" at the sight of a young woman as she filled sacks with meats, water, wine, and bread. Either these people were too trusting, or she, the young woman with no shortage of friends back home, was truly and awfully alone. Too alone to stand out in a field full of people preoccupied by life.

She had found a long rope and thought, *This will do just nicely.* She tied knots around bags to daisy chain the sacks together and flung the arrangement over her shoulder. It was heavy, but she'd make the trip. She had organized the loot into the bags based on priority. That way, if she needed to let one loose because of the burden, she could start with the least important.

This was the most opportune time to flee. She needed to reassure herself of that truth. Everyone, the locals and her earthly kin alike, was busy celebrating their Harvest Festival and the new season that came with it. And why shouldn't they? They had their recent victory and the crowning of their new queen. Surely they should enjoy themselves. She could carry the food and supplies she had stolen directly through the middle of town, and no one would think anything of it. Though she wouldn't take the chance. Instead, she'd creep out and around her hut and into the trees to be gobbled up by the forest.

Her hatred for Jude seeped through the pores in her brow and boiled the blood in her veins. There were moments late at night when she'd catch herself clenching her teeth while in idle thought of the man.

He had assumed too much when he said she couldn't survive on her own. She had proven to herself that she could live on that beach for quite some time. Starvation wouldn't take her. Storms and winter were unknown factors, but she had something now that gave her confidence. The beach was not new. She had conquered it once and did it well. Elena would do it again, though now willingly. It would be hers to command. The wind could blow like a cold Medusa, but if she died, she'd die on her terms.

He won't hold anything over me.

She ventured out of her hut, thumbing the smooth rock given to her by the frogling so long ago. It seemed like ages had come and gone since that day. At least one age had: the age of victimhood.

She ducked out of view and pushed forward into the dark forest. The shadows wrapped around her, delivering the embrace of an old friend. She'd be the night. She'd be her own soul.

Elena would head back to the beach, back to the Colosseum.

She liked that name and had always described her home, her cavern behind the beach, as *a* colosseum, likening it to the one in Rome. Now that was its name, one that suited it. The Colosseum.

"I've named it, and it is mine."

Ilgene slithered through the tall grass behind the old king's hut. He glanced around and, confident that he was alone, whistled his slow, mellow tune in harmony with the wind chimes at the late Semian's doorway.

Fire felt right. A simple distraction, appropriate for what he needed to do. A cruel symbol. It could either destroy or make pure.

And that was what he would do, make pure through destruction.

For the Laniakea to have hold of the boy was an outrage, a perversion of something beautiful, a beauty that the boy would help the Drominions achieve. Perhaps Simon was a mistake, a wasted effort toward a greater cause, but surely Edgar would make all things whole again. Aiken would be proud once more of his brother. Proud if he brought home the boy after the catastrophe on Earth, the catastrophe with Alister. Ilgene would restore the position he once held at the right hand of the Drominion throne and the future empire of all Cassini.

He gazed upon the glory of King Semian's wall of swords. It was a masterpiece, simply put. It was certainly possible to forge each weapon here along the Coastal Cliffs, but if the old king had stayed local, no one would ever consider the wall in front of him a work of art. As it stood, the Laniakea could not traverse time and space as easily as the few Gifters still alive, and so to gather such weaponry from across Cassini was quite a feat. A masterpiece through blistered fingers and bloodied feet.

Such a shame to burn it down.

Ilgene, unable to see the masterpiece in its full glory amongst the shadows of the hut, extended his hand and ignited a flame in his palm.

How did the king do it? How did the old man travel to those places without the Gift?

"Is that you, Ilgene?"

The door to the hut flung open to reveal Mahla. Poor, simple Mahla. Why did he have to be the one to discover him? It would be a shame to lose such a good man, like spilling wine on an exquisite rug and allowing the droplets to settle among the fibers, knowing full well that the damage had already happened.

"How are you holding that flame?" asked Mahla, with pupils shrunk to dots and the color drained from his face, swift and silent. "How does it not burn your skin? Ilgene, tell me what's going on."

"You ask, but I suspect you already know." Ilgene smirked and slowly stepped forward. He gazed into the brute's pupils as though he could see the truth materialize just beyond the void of Mahla's eyes. "You should not have come here. I liked you."

"You will not destroy my king's hut." Mahla straightened and removed the sword from its scabbard, positioning himself for attack. Ilgene laughed as though he observed a child who held a paper doll and called it precious. So too was the innocent, naïve Mahla.

Part of Ilgene, deep in the recesses of his mind, did not know why he laughed. To kill a beautiful thing was grotesque. This, he believed, was true in his heart. And yet still he laughed. Oh, how conflicted a frayed life could be.

THIRTY-FIVE

I T ALWAYS AMAZED STELLAMARIS to observe the sun settle in below the horizon just as the night came alive.

Paper lanterns littered the air, dangling from wires strung hut to hut. The bonfire had been lit.

Elix sang a mesmerizing chorus as musicians thumped large drum heads tilted on their sides, the mallets rattling against vibrating metallic bowls to make a backing harmony.

The food was just now being served, but the townspeople had already leapt ahead to get a few songs' worth of dance in before the feast.

Stellamaris saw Edgar sitting along a log beside the fire. The glow from the flames illuminated his face as he stared into the embers, transfixed.

She sat next to him, smiling. "You're not dancing?" she asked, knowing the answer.

He took a deep breath and pulled himself away from his trance. "Thank you for saving me from that man."

There was more to what he said, something just below the surface that would bubble up if she let it. And so she let him simmer, acknowledging his thanks but saying nothing. The boy needed the space she gave, room for him to think, reflect, and remain on the mental path before him.

"I hated that man," he said, fists balled. "He stalked us back home, and I know he kidnapped Simon. He must have. Alister was the only one there before Simon went missing, and he could produce...that *thing*. Whatever it was, that portal. Now he's gone, and I still don't know where my brother is."

She wasn't sure how to respond, or even if she should. The weight she had set aside before had returned, a knot that had settled into her chest.

"What was that tattoo?" he asked as he turned his gaze to the fire.

Her eyes widened as the color drained from her face, leaving behind a quivering jaw. "You saw his tattoo?"

"Yes, and as strange as it sounds, it looked intriguing. Many people have tattoos, even here. I think you know what I'm talking about. It looked *off*."

Now it was her turn to stare into the flame. She collected her thoughts and spoke slowly, treading carefully down a fire walk as though hot stones lay just below her feet. "It's called the

Leather Rose." The hairs on her arm stood on edge as though warning her not to go on. Speaking the words aloud brought more dread than she had expected. "The Nilleli get it tattooed on them."

Edgar looked up at Stellamaris, innocence joined with determination in his eyes. "Oh yes, I remember. Alister said he was a Nilleli. Who are they?"

"You may have heard the lore about the Three Brothers called Treos?"

"Yes, Mr. Crisp told me the story on the way to the Evajocalyn. Something about them being stuck on a circular path. It's confusing, though. I don't understand how that relates to anything."

"Some of it is just a legend, just made-up or exaggerated stories meant for children to keep them from wondering too far from town. Scholars refer to the circular path as a parable or a metaphor for something much more complex. Pieces of it are true, though, and honestly, I don't know which stories to believe anymore. Anyway, two of the brothers have been at war with each other for as far back as stories go. They didn't seek the Coastal Cliffs until recently, but they've been in conflict for millennia."

"How long could they possibly live?" His voice had softened to a whisper, and it was then that she noticed he was mimicking her. Her voice had recoiled, reduced into fear.

"Like I said, some of it is false, but the stories say they've been alive for a very long time. Some claim to have seen them depicted in cave paintings. By all historical accounts I've heard, they are possibly older than the formation of modern Cassini itself. The eldest is Aiken, the one we're presently at war with. The youngest has hidden himself, but we don't know his name or who he aligns with." She threw up her hands to shrug him off. "A man named Regaldo is the middle brother and most powerful of the Three Brothers. He is a brilliant, kind, and powerful man, or so I've heard. I've never actually met him, you understand. Still, I've never heard a negative tale about him. There are tales that vibrant flowers grow along the trails he walks. His followers have deemed him a demigod among mortals. The Nilleli is a group of loyal followers of Regaldo. They hail from distant lands, many so different in appearance that some question if they're from Cassini at all. The Nilleli are well versed in the Gift. We are extraordinarily fortunate not to call them an enemy."

She watched the boy as he absorbed what she had told him. There was more to the story, too much to tell there by the fire as the song of the drums echoed through the trees. Still, he seemed to understand enough.

"You said the youngest brother has hidden himself and no one knows where he is. When I was being held by that man, Alister, he said that one brother is Mimic. Who's Mimic? Maybe he knows where my brother is."

That's it!

Tears pushed through and slid down her cheeks as the realization flooded her mind. She turned to look directly at the boy. "What did you say?"

"Mimic, the missing brother's name is Mimic. At least according to Alister."

She panicked. "When did he tell you that word? Tell me the context."

"When I saw Alister back home, my teeth hurt whenever he was near. I've never felt that from him here all the times he tried to abduct me, so I asked him why. He got really upset and told me that the brother is Mimic. I didn't understand it back then, and I still don't now."

"Mimic is not the name of a person. Oh, child, it's worse than I thought."

"What? What's worse? How can it be worse? My brother's missing. We've killed the man that kidnapped him, but we still don't know where Simon is. How can this possibly get worse?"

Her thoughts came in random flashes. She had to collect herself in order to explain. She owed him that. The poor boy had been through so much, and she feared he'd be in store for so much more.

"There are people here that hold the Gift, similar to the Nilleli," she said as she forced herself to calm down. "You know one. Mr. Gracie."

"Yes."

"Others include Regaldo and Alister. We don't know who the missing brother is or who he aligns with, but some have suspected that he is also a Gifter, and he used his Gift to avoid being seen." She collected her thoughts, unsure if she should proceed. The boy deserved to know everything, but she wasn't sure how safe he would feel if she revealed too much. "My boy, 'Mimic' isn't a name. Mimicry is a type of Gifting in which the Gifter can take the form of other people. Honorable Gifters will interact with the wide space around them, but they will not violate the fabric itself. Mimicry changes particles in a harsh sin against the object they make up. They can take on the look and behavior of the person they mimic. Mimic isn't the name of a person; it refers to their type of Gifting."

She looked into Edgar's eyes as they stared back at her. He listened to every syllable she spoke. Would he trust her if she revealed to him the thoughts that rattled through her mind? "Alister had the tattoo of the Leather Rose, which showed that he was a member of the Nilleli and a follower of Regaldo, an ally. I didn't know this until after I killed him, I swear to you." Sweat beaded on her brow and joined the tears along her face as she slowed her pace to control her panic. "When you asked Alister about your teeth back home, he told you that the missing brother was a Mimic, likely imitating *him*."

She gazed at the fire as she forced herself forward. "My boy, I fear that the Alister you know from this world actually tried to protect you. I fear I may have killed the wrong man."

What have I done?

In her new role as queen, she felt like an imposter. She was like a mother to her people, but half of her still felt like a child. It was the child in her she tried to push down and prevent from seeing the light of day. Her people would regard a mistake from their new queen as the actions of that child. The child within her, the inexperienced, reckless child, had killed Alister, an ally and the only person who could give Edgar any hope of finding his brother.

"Edgar," she said. "I fear the missing brother, not Alister, kidnapped Simon."

A moment hung between them, and she realized she had not taken a breath since she last spoke. Edgar stared off into the fire, his mind racing through his eyes.

He spoke gently, almost to himself. "I think about that night a lot. Alister at first seemed to taunt us. He whistled and smiled at us as though we were playthings. Then, suddenly, once Simon was gone from the world, Alister seemed so much different. There was a panic in his eyes. Do you think the real Alister was trying to help me?"

Stellamaris, with pain in her eyes, nodded slowly.

Edgar stood, though more calmly than she expected. She looked up at him, curious about what he would say, what he would think of her. To her wonderment, he extended his hand for her to take. Unsure, she accepted it, and he helped her stand.

He took his next few breaths with difficulty, as though pleading for the tears to be pulled back from his cheeks. This boy before her had all the innocence of a child thrust into the role of an adult and somehow accepting it with all the strength of the mighty Laniakea.

"You protected me," he said. "I need to thank you for that. I grew up without a mother. Well, I had one, but she didn't fill the role. The only people that really tried to protect me were the Friars, and they had lots of people to protect. You have a ton too, more, actually, and you left them to save me when I was the one that needed it more." He took a deep breath through a trembling mouth. "No one's ever done anything like that for me before. Thank you. Thank you so much."

A cocktail of love, relief, and honor mixed and flooded her cheeks as the tears trickled down her face. She nodded subtly as a smile burrowed out. "You're welcome."

Stellamaris held her boy tight. His words, like his embrace, warmed her heart. A large part of her still felt remorse. She wanted to deny his words in favor of her own self-pity. And yet it was the pity that was addictive. Food for the weak. She was a queen this day. She was Stellamaris, the Queen Warrior of the Laniakea and a mother to this child-made-man. Self-pity would not take her.

And yet an unfamiliar voice took occupancy in her mind.

You killed him, Stellamaris. What did you do?

She had felt regret before, but this was new. Who was this demon?

You killed him, Stellamaris. Why? Did you rush in too quickly?

"We will find your brother," she told Edgar as she silenced her demon, allowing room for her new sense of honor.

"We will," he said. "In fact, you've helped me more than you know."

"How's that?"

"If the Mimic took Simon, and the Nilleli sent Alister to help, then I need to find our ally. I need to find Regaldo."

Their moment was interrupted as the sudden crackling of a new, distant fire disrupted their conversation. Frantic eyes looked about for the source and settled on the hut of the old king.

Stellamaris's skin swiftly shifted red in a flash of panic.

"Stay here," she said, pushing Edgar down.

Stellamaris held her sword ready as she rushed through the door of her father's hut, still aflame. Warriors, eager to protect their queen, positioned themselves in front of her, rushing the intruder.

Suddenly, a flash of light forced her free hand over her face as she stumbled back.

As she surveyed the ground before her, several of her men lay bloodied along the floor, their swords and axes nowhere to be seen.

Mahla lay prone but hurried to his feet. His eyes and hands scattered about, looking for a sword that wasn't there. He settled in, ready with his hands as his only weapon.

She ordered her men back as black smoke filled the room. Too many heroes rushing toward unknown obstacles would lead to too many unnecessary deaths. "Stop now. There will be no more bloodshed." She looked at Ilgene, centered within the hut, as shadows danced along his face to the music of the flames. "Ilgene, what is this? Are you doing all this?"

A smile burst onto Ilgene's face, and he spoke without urgency despite the roaring fire. "My apologies, dear queen. It is quite difficult to hear you, and I fear this fire is preventing our pleasant conversation."

His fingers spidered along the air in a motion that appeared all too comfortable to her lifelong friend. Immediately, the walls of the hut turned to ash, and the weaponry along the wall disintegrated with them as they all fell to the ground like blackened powder.

Without her instruction, the Laniakea charged. Like the hut, the swords and shields in their hands all fell to ash upon the dirt as each warrior stumbled to the ground as though they raced over an invisible trip wire.

A plague of fear drifted in through a ghostly cloud, causing each soldier to tremble and recoil. The same fear infected the queen, despite her resilience. Stellamaris was afraid, though unnaturally so. This fear forced its way in against her will, an unwanted invasion of her soul.

Her soldiers pulled back, eyes dilated in horror.

She stood tall as she fought off an inner voice warning her not to proceed.

"Do not use that here," she said as she pushed forward. "You dare invade the Laniakea?"

Ilgene looked insulted as a new arrogance stained his face. "And yet you dare speak such words to me? Do you know who I am?"

"I do."

"Say it then, Warrior Queen. Do not mince words. If we are to speak to each other civilly, you must know with whom you speak."

"You are the Mimic. You pretended to be a member of the Nilleli to abduct a child. Is that what you wanted me to say? That you attack children?"

He smiled, not giving much more. "You have your father's eyes. And his spirit, I'm afraid."

She forced her legs to move forward as though she were trudging through thick, thigh-deep mud. Ilgene made a swift gesture with his fingers, and exhaustion pushed her to the floor. That too she resisted as she inched forward with each step she could muster.

"That is impressive," he said as he crept over to where she struggled and peered into her eyes. "You're still trying. You must know that you do this to yourself."

Ilgene straightened his spine and ballooned his lungs. He made a vague gesture to the night sky, and Stellamaris felt the air thicken around her. Suddenly there was wind, though not the sort with which she was familiar. A forceful, hyperdimensional gust pulled her up and through the world, defying the limitations of her three-dimensional home. She peered down at the world beneath her and saw it all through a fisheye lens.

This wind was otherworldly, knocking her from plane to plane as though it caught her between two conflicting tides.

For that time, she did not know what was real and what was sorcery. It was as though an ominous force had violently dragged her from a dream to reality and then back into a dream, leaving her dizzy and pleading for rest.

The fisheye lens flattened, and she was once more lying at the feet of Ilgene.

He leaned down and extended his index finger to lift Stella-maris's face by her chin. "Lead me to the boy."

Edgar's teeth were flooded with pain, just as they had back home, so many worlds ago.

He looked on, beyond the bonfire at the scene before him, off in the distant shadows, knowing all too well what he needed to do.

He recalled a memory from the day his mother left in a police car. His father was long gone, and Simon was in a weak state. He approached the only counsel he had, a priest and family friend who had arrived with the police to lend an ear to the boy, if that was what he needed.

Edgar unloaded his problems, exposing the sores on his soul. It poured out like the blood of a wounded soldier.

The priest took a deep breath and gestured to the crowd. "Look out at all these people. I've heard all their confessions and forgotten just as many. All are frayed. All are flawed. Your past is your past, distinct and immutable. Do not hold on to a stained past. Only judge whether the path you're taking is the one you ought to be on."

But as he stood there, hidden behind the Laniakean bonfire, watching his friends suffer, he knew of only one path: the path before him. To press on and not to cower.

The only way out is through.

Edgar Brave took a gradual step out from behind the bonfire.

The only way out is through.

He drew air into his lungs and balled his fists.

The only way out is through.

Stellamaris was suffering for him, but that was not her role. It was only his.

The only way out is through.

Ilgene looked down at her, sneering as though she were dirt.

Stellamaris pushed herself up, despite the pain. She must push through this.

Ilgene seemed to allow her resistance as she straightened her legs and back, fully standing in defiance.

He looked her up and down as though trying to see how far she would take this. Patiently, he delivered another gesture with a nod of his head. "Now fall."

Her legs gave way, and she collapsed to the earth. Why couldn't she stand? Why couldn't she rise? He forced his will into every limb, whispering insults that accused her of being weak and unworthy until every muscle believed it. Her legs obeyed the disgraced commands but ignored her own. It pained her to feel her body betray her so willingly.

Still, the pain, that horrid pain, was just a pinprick compared to the sight of Edgar as he stepped forward from the crowd.

Ilgene removed his focus from Stellamaris and peered off at her boy.

Edgar crept into the center of the circle and spoke with his face as placid as a lake with no wind, his voice as steady as a stone settled in the earth. "Take me to Simon."

Ilgene smirked, a new fire in his eyes, greedy as a pig to its slop. "To that, I'll humbly oblige."

"But you need to let her go," Edgar said.

Once again, he smiled but offered little else. He looked down at the fallen queen as she ignored the collected mud along her cheeks, the anger of a raging sun deep in her heart.

Ilgene stood before them all in the dim light of the distant bonfire. "You have little room to make demands, young one. Still, I tire of this place." He surveyed the surrounding land, the warriors in pain, convulsing along the dirt, and the children rushing off to their mothers. At this, his former home, he sneered in disgust. "Oh, you pitiful few, the great Laniakea, unable to see your own betrayer. Look amongst you, fear armored in false bravery. Just moments ago, you celebrated here as though you had won. Still, you'll eat, though you do not know that you are full." He looked down at the queen, bathed in ash, and shook his head with a pity that gave sustenance to the demon that had burrowed its home in her soul. "You should have eaten the apple, Stellamaris."

In a swift flash of light, Ilgene darted at the boy, grabbed him, and vanished into an orb of blue.

The warriors all shook loose of their curse, and Stellamaris suddenly regained the ability to stand once more.

She looked around.

"Where is he?" she asked, knowing all too well the answer.

No one spoke. The air felt thick like muck, no one wishing to trudge forward.

She continued in desperation. "He's here somewhere. He must be."

Again, no one dared move, save for Mahla, who picked his queen up off the dirt. He shook his head, acknowledging the truth that she already knew.

"My boy. He's my boy. Find Edgar."

Elix stood motionless, transfixed by the panicking queen. Her lute lay before her, unplayed and sorrowful, abandoned among the rocks.

She saw Jude watch from a distant hut as he sipped a small glass of ale. Calm indifference blanketed his face, as though he were observing a caged animal from his safety beyond the bars.

"Come, Queen Mother," Mahla said. "We will find him." Though she did not believe him.

THIRTY-SIX

The Friar home was quiet enough to hear the struggling breath of Susan's half snore. The disk of the moon bathed the kitchen window in white light as Ben washed one of many bowls strewn along the counter.

He sang a tune through stale air, half in his head and half aloud as he placed the clean dish upon the stack, just tall enough to be an accomplishment but not tall enough to fall.

It was common for him to be the sole creature awake at that hour, save for the mice that scurried in the walls.

Each child was asleep, a monumental accomplishment for his wife, which was why she had no hesitation when she fell into bed ahead of her husband. Sleep was the trophy she gave herself for a crowd mostly managed.

It was at that sink in the Friar kitchen that lay within the antique home, on his comfortable planet, that Ben hummed the same familiar tune he had so many nights before.

Occasionally, his foster children would join him, though that would only happen with the newly acquainted members of the home.

His song cut through the silence with little concern for the children asleep in their peaceful beds. Not that he disregarded their sleep; he just had confidence that these children would not wake. And if they did, they'd fall swiftly back to sleep or eventually learn to, as motley Friars.

The song he sang was his favorite. If a child were awake, he'd certainly discuss the tune, invariably causing them to rush back to their beds.

When he reached his favorite lyric, he transitioned from a gentle half hum to the memorized lyrics that wormed his ears.

The path that you walk now
The past of the true
The beaten, forgotten
The meek and the few

The twin tides, they're locked
The footsteps, the lore
All that's forgotten
Forgotten no more

Ben flashed the grin that, try as he might, he could not contain within those old, age-beaten cheeks.

All that's forgotten
Forgotten no more

"Be strong, dear Edgar. Be strong, my brave giant. My tamer of beasts. My leader of worlds."

BEFORE YOU GO

Curious what happens next? Join my mailing list to receive updates on the timeline for the second installment of The Archives of Edgar Brave series:

adamwschmitz.com/mailing-list

While you have your phone out, please consider helping others find this book by reviewing it on Amazon.

https://www.amazon.com/dp/B0BJ7WYVYD

AFTERWORD

What just happened to Edgar? What's the deal with Elena and Jude? And what about the Nilleli, the Leather Rose and the Three Brothers? Well, I promise all roads lead somewhere, and if you're reading this far and wondering if a particular plot point will get the attention it deserves, you can rest assured that it will. The story of Edgar Brave has been marinating in my head since I was a child. It has many twists and turns, and requires more than one book to fully tell the complete tale.

The spark that led to Edgar Brave started when I was a young boy. I believe I was twelve, but I might be misremembering since most of my personal history starts when I was twelve and I doubt that year was so exciting. Either way, I started playing a video game called *The Dig*. You don't need to know the details of this particular video game except that it was in the Fantasy/Science Fiction genre, and was the first game I had played that involved an actual plot.

I loved it. I played it for hours, and would pull in friends and family members to help me figure out any puzzles that were particularly difficult. When I eventually beat the game, I was faced with a troubling question: what do I do now?

I wanted another game like it, but there were few plot-based games to choose from at the time.

"Why don't you create your own game?" my parents suggested.

I was taken aback by that question. It had never occurred to me that I could simply make my own game. Other people created video games, were they smarter than me? If they had knowledge that I didn't, could I obtain that same knowledge? Of course, I was only twelve, and I now realize my parents were simply putting forth the challenge to test how far I'd be able to run with it. But at the time, I had no concept of it being an impossible task for a child.

I sat with that question for quite some time before I settled on three things I would need to learn.

First, I would need to learn computer animation. I had been saving up for a drum set by mowing lawns, eventually raising $500. When my sister's friend said that he thought AutoCAD was what I needed in order to create 3D drawings, I got incredibly excited and blew my drum set money on AutoCAD. The tragedy was that AutoCAD was *not* what I needed. But I spent enough time creating spheres and cubes to realize that

3D graphics was not where my passion was. Perhaps things would have been different if I had a mentor to help me pick the right program and teach me how to make more interesting things, but at the time all I had were spheres and cubes and that didn't hold my attention.

The second topic I needed to learn was programming. I bought books on C++, Python and HTML. I made calculators, websites and all sorts of exciting things. But the app itself was not what was exciting. It was that I could create something powerful out of nothing but the code that I wrote out on the screen. I now had a super power. I could bend bits to my will.

The third thing I needed to learn was writing. This was perhaps the most important part of the plot-based video game, and equally as wonderful as learning how to move bits where I wanted them. Just as before, I could make things out of nothing, except this time it was an entire world that would not have existed unless I released it from my mind.

There was a sorcery to moving a character from my brain to the paper and then into the mind of another person. What would happen if the character lived in that other person's brain past when I forgot about them? Would they have a life of their own at that point?

Time went by, and I pursued a career in software development, taking creative writing classes and joining writers groups on the side. I wrote various version of Edgar Brave, and had notes scattered across journals and computer files (the scene where Stellamaris fights Alister was originally one of the many scenes that I emailed myself, nested in the folder titled *When I Write Edgar Brave*).

Then one day in 2019 I decided to assemble all my notes together and just do it. I wrote out a writing schedule, with a weekly goal. I used project management practices that I learned from a career in software development and created charts to illustrate my productivity. I allowed myself breaks, celebrated my wins, and used my losses as fodder to improve my process.

And an amazing thing happened once I started writing consistently. I felt the characters and the message behind them. They felt real. They felt like they need to be. Edgar needed a home that wasn't a folder in my email app. And the message between the pages, laced in the ink, needed to be read. Maybe they'd be interpreted in a way I didn't expect, but that made it better. Because Edgar no longer felt like he belonged to me.

The boy that was pushed into adulthood didn't need to be perfect. He needed to exist.

About the Author

Adam lives in San Marcos, California with his wife and kids. He has three daughters with one child on the way, at the time of this writing. They are waiting to be surprised on whether the baby is a boy or a girl, but at this point, a fourth girl is just as shocking as a first boy.

Aside from writing, Adam spends his spare time with his family, and enjoys playing music. He has played drum set since he was a young teen, and recently revived an interest in piano during the COVID lockdowns. Here's hoping it sticks.

Acknowledgments

Creative writing is an art form of many layers. The first is personal enjoyment. Most of us start with a story idea that doesn't exist yet, and we think it ought to. We assemble words in such a way that makes us smile as a song would. This layer is just for us.

It is in this first layer that I would like to thank my wife for her support and love, and my children for their inspiration. They know not how much they give, and that is perhaps the most precious part.

The second layer involves others. Writers solicit feedback in place of a coach or mentor. After months of rattling ideas around in our heads, jotting them down, rearranging the words just so, this feedback tells us if it's any good and if there are spots we should fix. A teacher can correct mistakes in realtime, whereas a writer often only receives feedback when he is ready for others to see it. If we have a lot invested in that first layer I spoke of, then it can often take many iterations before we're ready for other eyes to see it.

I have many to thank in this second layer. My beta readers and critique partners invested their personal time in 36 chapters that they had no idea whether or not they'd enjoy. And they did it to be helpful. You truly were.

I have a new respect for beta readers. I read slowly, enjoying every word as though it were a sip of fine wine. Because of that, every book I read is an investment of my personal time. I know many of my beta readers read the same way, and so I am increasingly grateful when they invest their time in my book and helping me grow as a writer.

And then there's the last layer. It's the layer us writers don't talk about nearly as much as we should. It's the part where we see others enjoy our work.

I think we don't talk about it, because the drive to write should really come from within. It needs to be something that we do for ourselves, and not because we're turning out a product. But if we stumble across a reader that genuinely enjoyed the story and wants to know what will happen to Edgar and Simon, or what the heck is going on with Jude and Elena, that's a gift that hugs the soul.

Among my beta readers, I had some that I could tell were truly intrigued to find out what will happen next and wanted to be part of the writing process for Book Two. Thank you. You are the fuel that keeps me motivated.

Lastly, thank you to the professionals. Tim Barber at Dissect Designs created a beautiful cover that I stare at daily. Allister Thompson did a wonderful job editing and pointing out things that only a trained eye could catch. And Ellen Walters as a Developmental Editor gave the story just what it needed, helping me mold it into what it is. If anyone reading this has an opportunity to work with these wonderful people, consider yourselves fortunate.